Phantom

Jo Nesbo

PHANTOM

Translated from the Norwegian by Don Bartlett

Harvill Secker
LONDON

Published by Harvill Secker 2012

2 4 6 8 10 9 7 5 3 1

First published with the title *Gjenferd* in 2011
by H. Aschehoug & Co. (W. Nygaard), Oslo

First published in Great Britain in 2012 by
HARVILL SECKER
Random House
20 Vauxhall Bridge Road
London SW1V 2SA

www.rbooks.co.uk

Addresses for companies within The Random House Group Limited
can be found at: www.randomhouse.co.uk/offices.htm

The Random House Group Limited Reg. No. 954009

A CIP catalogue record for this book is available from the British Library

ISBN 9781846555213 (hardback)
ISBN 9781846555220 (export trade paperback)
ISBN 9781846556418 (UK trade paperback)

The Random House Group Limited supports The Forest Stewardship Council
(FSC®), the leading international forest certification organisation. Our books carrying
the FSC label are printed on FSC® certified paper. FSC is the only forest certification
scheme endorsed by the leading environmental organisations, including Greenpeace.
Our paper procurement policy can be found at
www.randomhouse.co.uk/environment

Text designed by Jim Smith

Maps by Darren Bennett

Typeset in Scala by Palimpsest Book Production Limited, Falkirk, Stirlingshire

Printed and bound in Great Britain by Clays Ltd, St Ives plc

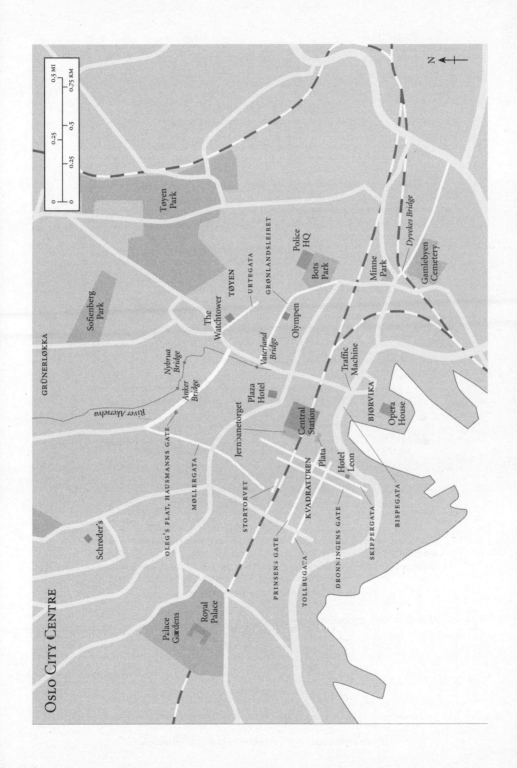

OSLO CITY CENTRE

GRÜNERLØKKA

Schroder's

Sofienberg Park

Tøyen Park

Royal Palace

Palace Gardens

OLEG'S FLAT, HAUSMANNS GATE

MØLLERGATA

STORTORVET

River Akerselva

Anker Bridge

Nybrua Bridge

Jernbanetorget

Plaza Hotel

Vaterland Bridge

The Watchtower

TØYEN

URTEGATA

GRØNLANDSLEIRET

Olympen

Police HQ

Bots Park

Minne Park

Dyvekes Bridge

Gamlebyen Cemetery

Central Station

Plata

Hotel Leon

Traffic Machine

KVADRATUREN

PRINSENS GATE

TOLLBUGATA

DRONNINGENS GATE

SKIPPERGATA

BISPEGATA

BJØRVIKA

Opera House

N

0   0.25   0.5   0.75 KM
0   0.25   0.5   0.5 MI

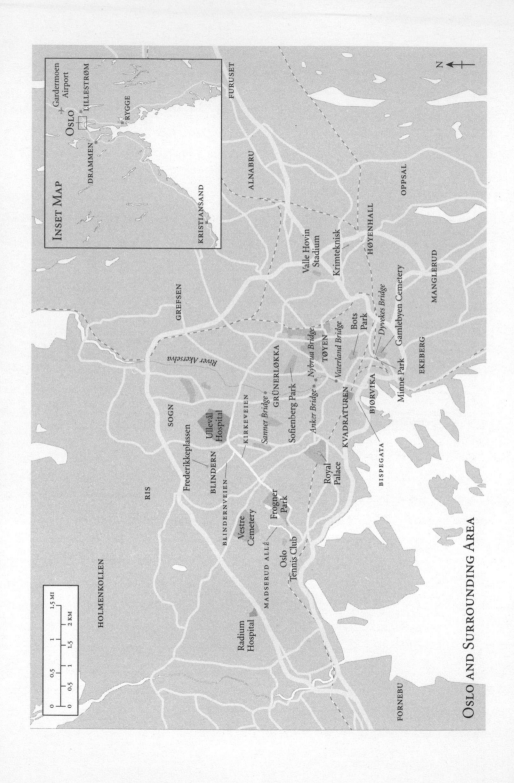

OSLO AND SURROUNDING AREA

PART ONE

1

THE SQUEALS WERE CALLING HER. Like acoustic spears they pierced all the other noises of the night in Oslo city centre: the regular drone of cars outside the window, the distant siren that rose and fell, and the church bells that had begun to chime nearby. She went on the hunt for food. She ran her nose over the filthy linoleum on the kitchen floor. Registering and sorting the sounds as quick as lightning into three categories: edible, threatening or irrelevant for survival. The pungent smell of grey cigarette ash. The sugary sweet aroma of blood on a piece of cotton wool. The bitter odour of beer on the inside of a bottle cap, Ringnes lager. The gas molecules of sulphur, saltpetre and carbon dioxide filtered up from an empty metal cartridge case designed for a lead bullet of nine by eighteen millimetres, also called a Makarov after the gun to which the calibre was originally adapted. Smoke from a still-smouldering cigarette with a yellow filter and black paper, bearing the Russian imperial eagle. The tobacco was edible. And there: a stench of alcohol, leather, grease and tarmac. A shoe. She sniffed it. And decided it was not as easy to eat as the jacket in the wardrobe, the one that smelt of petrol and the rotten animal from which it was made. Then the rat brain concentrated on how to force its way through what lay in front of her. She had tried from both sides, tried to squeeze past, but, despite the fact that she was

3

only twenty-five centimetres long and weighed well under half a kilo, she couldn't. The obstacle lay on its side with its back to the wall blocking the entrance to the nest, and her eight newly born, blind, hairless babies were screaming ever louder for her milk. The mountain of flesh smelt of salt, sweat and blood. It was a human body. A living human being; her sensitive ears could detect the faint heartbeats between her babies' hungry squeals.

She was frightened, but she had no choice. Feeding her young took precedence over all dangers, all exertions, all her other instincts. Then she stood with her nose in the air waiting for the solution to come to her.

The church bells were ringing in time with the human heart now. One beat, two. Three, four . . .

She bared her rat teeth.

July. Shit. You should not die in July. Is that really church bells I can hear, or were there hallucinogens in the bloody bullets? OK, so it stops here. And what sodding difference does it make? Here or there. Now or later. But did I really deserve to die in July? With the birds singing, bottles clinking, laughter from down by the Akerselva and fricking summer merriment right outside your window? Did I deserve to be lying on the floor of an infected junkie pit with an extra orifice in my body, from which it all runs out: life, seconds and flashbacks of everything that led me here? Everything, big and small, the whole bundle of fortuitous and semi-determined events; is that me, is that everything, is that my life? I had plans, didn't I? And now it is no more than a bag of dust, a joke without a punchline, so short that I could have told it before that insane bell stopped ringing. Fires of hell! No one told me it would hurt so much to die. Are you there now, Dad? Don't go, not now. Listen, the joke goes like this: my name's Gusto. I lived to the age of nineteen. You were a bad guy who porked a bad woman and nine months later I popped out and was shipped to a foster family before I could say 'Dad'! And there I caused as much trouble as I could. They just wrapped the suffocating care blanket around even tighter and asked me what I wanted

4

to calm me down. A fricking ice cream? They had no bloody idea that people like you and me would end up shot at some point, eradicated like a pest, that we spread contagion and decay and would multiply like rats if we got the chance. They have only themselves to blame. But they also want things. Everyone wants something. I was thirteen the first time I saw in my foster-mother's eyes what she wanted.

'You're so handsome, Gusto,' she said. She had entered the bathroom – I had left the door open, and refrained from turning on the shower so that the sound wouldn't warn her. She stood there for exactly a second too long before going out. And I laughed, because now I knew. That is my talent, Dad: I can see what people want. Have I taken after you? Were you like that as well? After she had gone out I looked at myself in the large mirror. She wasn't the first to say it: that I was handsome. I had developed earlier than the other boys. Tall, slim, already broad-shouldered and muscular. Hair so black it gleamed, as if all light bounced off it. High cheekbones. Square chin. A big, greedy mouth, but with lips as full as a girl's. Smooth, tanned skin. Brown, almost black eyes. 'The brown rat', one of the boys in the class had called me. Didrik, think that was his name. He was going to be a concert pianist. I had turned fifteen, and he said it out loud in the classroom. 'That brown rat can't even read properly.'

I just laughed and, of course, I knew why he had said it. Knew what he wanted. Kamilla. He was secretly in love with her; she was not quite so secretly in love with me. At the class party I had had a grope to feel what she had under her jumper. Which was not a great deal. I had mentioned it to a couple of the boys and I suppose Didrik must have picked up on it, and decided to shut me out. Not that I was so bloody concerned about being 'in', but bullying is bullying. So I went to Tutu at the MC club, the bikers. I had already done a bit of hash dealing for them at school, and said that I needed some respect if I was going to do a decent job. Tutu said he would take care of Didrik. Later Didrik refused to explain to anyone how he had got two fingers caught under the top hinge of the boys' toilet door, but he never called me 'brown rat' again. And – right – he never

5

became a concert pianist, either. Shit, this hurts so much! No, I don't need any consoling, Dad, I need a fix. One last shot and then I'll leave this world without any bother, I promise. There, the church bell has rung again. Dad?

2

IT WAS ALMOST MIDNIGHT AT Gardermoen, Oslo's principal airport, as SK-459 from Bangkok taxied into its allocated spot by Gate 46. Captain Tord Schultz braked and brought the Airbus 340 to a complete halt; then he quickly switched off the fuel supply. The metallic whine from the jet engines sank through the frequencies to a good-natured growl before dying. Tord Schultz automatically noted the time, three minutes and forty seconds since touchdown, twelve minutes before the scheduled time. He and the first officer started the checklist for shutdown and parking as the plane was to remain there overnight. With the goods. He flicked through the briefcase containing the log. September 2011. In Bangkok it was still the rainy season and had been steaming hot as usual, and he had longed for home and the first cool autumn evenings. Oslo in September. There was no better place on earth. He filled in the form for the remaining fuel. The fuel bill. He had had to find a way of accounting for it. After flights from Amsterdam or Madrid he had flown faster than was economically reasonable, burning off thousands of kroner worth of fuel to make it. In the end, his boss had carpeted him.

'To make what?' he had yelled. 'You didn't have any passengers with connecting flights!'

'The world's most punctual airline,' Tord Schultz had mumbled, quoting the advertising slogan.

'The world's most economically fucked-up airline! Is that the best explanation you can come up with?'

Tord Schultz had shrugged. After all, he couldn't say the reason, that he had opened the fuel nozzles because there was something he himself had to make. The flight he had been put on, the one to Bergen, Trondheim or Stavanger. It was extremely important that *he* did the trip and not one of the other pilots.

He was too old for them to do anything else to him but rant and rave. He had avoided making serious errors, the organisation took care of him, and there were only a few years left before he reached the two fives, fifty-five, and would be retired whatever happened. Tord Schultz sighed. A few years to fix things, to avert ending up as the world's most economically fucked-up pilot.

He signed the log, got up and left the cockpit to flash his row of pearly-white pilot teeth set in his tanned pilot face to the passengers. The smile that would tell them that he was Mr Confidence in person. Pilot. The professional title that had once made him something in other people's eyes. He had seen it, how people, men and women, young and old, once the magic word 'pilot' had been enunciated, had looked at him and discovered not only the charisma, the nonchalance, the boyish charm, but also the captain's dynamism and cold precision, the superior intellect and the courage of a man who defied physical laws and the innate fears of mere mortals. But that was a long time ago. Now they regarded him as the bus driver he was and asked him what the cheapest tickets to Las Palmas were, and why there was more leg room on Lufthansa.

To hell with them. To hell with them all.

Tord Schultz stood at the exit next to the flight attendants, straightened up and smiled, said 'Welcome back, Miss' in broad Texan, the way they had learned at flying school in Sheppard. Received a smile of acknowledgement. There had been a time when he could have arranged a meeting in the arrivals hall with such a smile. And indeed had done. From Cape Town to Alta. Women. Many women. That had been the problem. And the solution. Women. Many women. New women. And

8

now? His hairline was receding beneath the pilot's cap, but the tailor-made uniform emphasised his tall, broad-shouldered physique. That was what he had blamed for not getting into fighter jets at flying school, and ending up as a cargo pilot on the Hercules, the workhorse of the sky. He had told them at home he had been a couple of centimetres too long in the spine, that the cockpits of Starfighters, F-5s and F-16s, disqualified all but dwarfs. The truth was he hadn't measured up to the competition. His body was all he had managed to maintain from those times, the only thing which hadn't fallen apart, which hadn't crumbled. Like his marriages. His family. Friends. How had it happened? Where had he been when it happened? Presumably in a hotel room in Cape Town or Alta, with cocaine up his nose to compensate for the potency-killing drinks at the bar, and his dick in not such a Welcome-Back-Miss to compensate for everything he was not and never would be.

Tord Schultz's gaze fell on a man coming towards him down the aisle. He walked with his head bent, yet still he towered over the other passengers. He was slim and broad-shouldered like himself. Younger though. Cropped blond hair stood up like a brush. Looked Norwegian, but was hardly a tourist on his way home, more likely to be an expat with the subdued, almost grey tan typical of whites who had spent a long time in South-East Asia. The indisputably tailor-made brown linen suit gave an impression of quality, seriousness. Maybe a businessman. Thanks to a not altogether thriving concern, he travelled economy class. But it was neither the suit nor his height that had caused Tord Schultz's gaze to fix on this person. It was the scar. It went from the left corner of his mouth and almost reached his ear, like a smile-shaped sickle. Grotesque and wonderfully dramatic.

'See you.'

Tord Schultz was startled, but did not manage to respond before the man had passed and was out of the plane. The voice had been rough and hoarse, which together with the bloodshot eyes suggested he had just woken up.

The plane was empty. The minibus with the cleaning staff stood parked on the runway as the crew left in a herd. Tord Schultz noticed that the small, thickset Russian was the first off the bus, watched him dash up the steps in his yellow high-visibility vest with the company logo, Solox.

See you.

Tord Schultz's brain repeated the words as he strode down the corridor to the flight crew centre.

'Didn't you have a boarding bag on top?' asked one of the flight attendants, pointing to Tord's Samsonite trolley. He couldn't remember what her name was. Mia? Maja? At any rate he had fucked her during a stopover once last century. Or had he?

'No,' Tord Schultz said.

See you. As in 'see you again'? Or as in 'I can see you're looking at me'?

They walked past the partition by the entrance to the flight crew centre, where in theory there was room for a jack-in-the-box customs officer. Ninety-nine per cent of the time the seat behind the partition was empty, and he had never – not once in the thirty years he had worked for the airline – been stopped and searched.

See you.

As in 'I can see you, alright'. And 'I can see who you are'.

Tord Schultz hurried through the door to the centre.

Sergey Ivanov ensured, as usual, he was the first off the minibus when it stopped on the tarmac beside the Airbus, and sprinted up the steps to the empty plane. He took the vacuum cleaner into the cockpit and locked the door behind him. He slipped on latex gloves and pulled them up to where the tattoos started, flipped the front lid off the vac and opened the captain's locker. Lifted out the small Samsonite boarding bag, unzipped it, removed the metal plate at the bottom and checked the four brick-like one-kilo packages. Then he put them into the vac, pressed them into position between the tube and the large dust bag he had made sure to empty beforehand. Clicked the front lid back, unlocked the cockpit door and activated the vacuum cleaner. It was all done in seconds.

After tidying and cleaning the cabin they ambled off the plane, stowed the light blue bin bags in the back of the Daihatsu and went back to the lounge. There was only a handful of planes landing and taking off before the airport closed for the night. Ivanov glanced over his shoulder at Jenny, the shift manager. He gazed at the computer screen showing arrival and departure times. No delays.

'I'll take Bergen,' Sergey said in his harsh accent. At least he spoke the language; he knew Russians who had lived in Norway for ten years and were still forced to resort to English. But when Sergey had been brought in, almost two years ago, his uncle had made it clear he was to learn Norwegian, and had consoled him by saying that he might have some of his own talent for picking up languages.

'I've got Bergen covered,' Jenny said. 'You can wait for Trondheim.'

'I'll do Bergen,' Sergey said. 'Nick can do Trondheim.'

Jenny looked at him. 'As you like. Don't work yourself to death, Sergey.'

Sergey went to a chair by the wall and sat down. Leaned back carefully. The skin round his shoulders was still sore from where the Norwegian tattooist had been plying his trade. He was working from drawings Sergey had been sent by Imre, the tattooist in Nizhny Tagil prison, and there was still quite a bit left to do. Sergey thought of the tattoos his uncle's lieutenants, Andrey and Peter, had. The pale blue strokes on the skin of the two Cossacks from Altai told of their dramatic lives and great deeds. But Sergey had a feat to his name as well. A murder. It was a little murder, but it had already been tattooed in the form of an angel. And perhaps there would be another murder. A big one. If *the necessary* became necessary, his uncle had said, and warned him to be ready, mentally prepared, and to keep up his knife practice. A man was coming, he had said. It wasn't absolutely certain, but it was probable.

Probable.

Sergey Ivanov regarded his hands. He had kept the latex gloves on. Of course it was a coincidence that their standard work gear also ensured that he would not leave any fingerprints on the packages if things should go wrong one day. There wasn't a hint of a tremble. His hands had been doing this for so long that he had to remind himself of the risk now and then to stay alert. He hoped they would be as calm when *the necessary – chto nuzhno*

– had to be performed. When he had to earn the tattoo for which he had already ordered the design. He conjured up the image again: him unbuttoning his shirt in the sitting room at home in Tagil, with all his urka brothers present, and showing them his new tattoos. Which would need no comment, no words. So he wouldn't say anything. Just see it in their eyes: he was no longer Little Sergey. For weeks he had been praying at night that the man would come. And that *the necessary* would become necessary.

The message to clean the Bergen plane crackled over the walkie-talkie.

Sergey got up. Yawned.

The procedure in the second cockpit was even simpler.

Open the vacuum cleaner, put the contents in the boarding bag in the first officer's locker.

On their way out they met the crew on their way in. Sergey Ivanov avoided the first officer's eyes, looked down and noted that he had the same kind of trolley as Schultz. Samsonite Aspire GRT. Same red. Without the little red boarding bag that can be fastened to it on top. They knew nothing of each other, nothing of motivations, nothing of the background or the family. All that linked Sergey, Schultz and the young first officer were the numbers of their unregistered mobile phones, purchased in Thailand, so they could send a text in case there were changes to the schedule. Sergey doubted Schultz and the first officer knew of each other. Andrey limited all information to a strictly need-to-know basis. For that reason, Sergey hadn't a clue what happened to the packages. He could guess though. For when the first officer, on an internal flight between Oslo and Bergen, passed from airside to landside there was no customs check, no security check. The officer took the boarding bag to the hotel in Bergen where the crew was staying. A discreet knock on the hotel door in the middle of the night and four kilos of heroin exchanged hands. Even though the new drug, violin, had pushed down heroin prices, the going rate on the street for a quarter was still at least 250 kroner. A thousand a gram. Given that the drug – which had already been diluted – was diluted once more, that would amount to eight million kroner in total. He could do the maths. Enough to know he was underpaid. But he also knew he would have done enough to merit a bigger slice when he had done *the necessary*. And after a couple of years on that salary he could buy a house in Tagil, find himself a good-looking Siberian girl, and perhaps let his mother and father move in when they got old.

Sergey Ivanov felt the tattoo itch between his shoulder blades.

It was as though the skin was looking forward to the next instalment.

3

THE MAN IN THE LINEN suit alighted from the airport express at Oslo Central Station. He established it must have been a warm, sunny day in his old home town, for the air was still gentle and embracing. He was carrying an almost comical little canvas suitcase and exited the station on the southern side with quick, supple strides. From the outside, Oslo's heart – which some maintained the town did not have – beat with a restful pulse. Night rhythm. The few cars there were swirled around the circular Traffic Machine, were ejected, one by one, eastwards to Stockholm and Trondheim, northwards to other parts of town or westwards to Drammen and Kristiansand. Both in size and shape the Traffic Machine resembled a brontosaurus, a dying giant that was soon to disappear, to be replaced by homes and businesses in Oslo's splendid new quarter with its splendid new construction, the Opera House. The man stopped and looked at the white iceberg situated between the Traffic Machine and the fjord. It had already won architectural prizes from all over the world; people came from far and wide to walk on the Italian marble roof that sloped right down into the sea. The light inside the building's large windows was as strong as the moonlight falling on it.

Christ, what an improvement, the man thought.

It was not the future promises of a new urban development he saw, but the past. For this had been Oslo's shooting gallery, its dopehead territory, where they had injected themselves and ridden their highs behind the barracks which partially hid them, the city's lost children. A flimsy partition between them and their unknowing, well-meaning social democratic parents. What an improvement, he thought. They were on a trip to hell in more beautiful surroundings.

It was three years since he had last stood here. Everything was new. Everything was the same.

They had ensconced themselves on a strip of grass between the station and the motorway, much like the verge of a road. As doped up now as then. Lying on their backs, eyes closed, as though the sun was too strong, huddled over, trying to find a vein that could still be used, or standing bent with bowed junkie-knees and rucksacks, unsure whether they were coming or going. Same faces. Not the same living dead when he used to walk here, they had died long ago, once and for all. But the same faces.

On the road up to Tollbugata there were more of them. Since they had a connection with the reason for his return he tried to glean an impression. Tried to decide if there were more or fewer of them. Noted that they were trading in Plata again. The little square of asphalt to the west of Jernbanetorget, which had been painted white, had been Oslo's Taiwan, a free trade area for drugs, established so that the authorities could keep a wary eye on what was happening and perhaps intercept young first-time buyers. But as business grew in size and Plata showed Oslo's true face as one of Europe's worst heroin spots, the place became a pure tourist attraction. The turnover for heroin and the OD statistics had long been a source of shame for the capital, but nonetheless not such a visible stain as Plata. Newspapers and TV fed the rest of the country with images of stoned youths, zombies wandering the city centre in broad daylight. The politicians were blamed. When right-wingers were in power the left were in an uproar. 'Not enough treatment centres.' 'Prison sentences create users.' 'The new class society creates gangs and drug trafficking in immigrant areas.' When the left was in power, the right were in an uproar. 'Not enough police.' 'Access for asylum seekers too easy.' 'Six out of seven prisoners are foreigners.'

So, after being hounded from pillar to post, Oslo City Council came to the inevitable decision: to save itself. To shovel the shit under the carpet. To close Plata.

The man in the linen suit saw a youth in a red-and-white Arsenal shirt standing on some steps with four people shuffling their feet in front of him. The Arsenal player's head was jerking left and right, like a chicken's. The other four heads were motionless, staring only at the dealer in the Arsenal colours, who was waiting until there were enough of them, a full cohort, maybe that was five, maybe six. Then he would accept payment for the orders and take them to where the dope was. Round the corner or inside a backyard where his partner was waiting. It was a simple principle; the guy with the dope never had any contact with money and the guy with the money never had any contact with dope. That made it harder for the police to acquire solid evidence of drug-dealing against either of them. Nonetheless, the man in the linen suit was surprised, for what he saw was the old method used in the 1980s and 90s. As the police gave up trying to catch pushers on the streets, sellers had dropped their elaborate routines and the assembly of a cohort and had started dealing directly as punters turned up; money in one hand, drugs in the other. Had the police started arresting street dealers again?

A man in cycling gear pedalled past, helmet, orange goggles and heaving, brightly coloured jersey. His thigh muscles bulged under the tight shorts, and the bike looked expensive. That must have been why he took it with him when he and the rest of the cohort followed the Arsenal player round the corner to the other side of the building. Everything was new. Everything was the same. But there were fewer of them, weren't there?

The prostitutes on the corner of Skippergata spoke to him in pidgin English – Hey, baby! Wait a minute, handsome! – but he just shook his head. And it seemed as if the rumour of his chasteness, or possible pecuniary difficulties, spread faster than he could walk because the girls further up showed no interest in him. In his day, Oslo's prostitutes had dressed in practical clothing, jeans and thick jackets. There hadn't been many of them; it had been a seller's market. But now the competition was fiercer, and there were short skirts, high heels and fishnet stockings. The African women seemed to be cold already. Wait until December, he thought.

He advanced deeper into Kvadraturen, which had been Oslo's first town centre, but now it was an asphalt-and-brick desert with administrative buildings and offices for 250,000 worker ants, who scuttled home at four or five o'clock and ceded the quarter to nocturnal rodents. When King Christian IV built the town in square blocks, according to Renaissance ideals of geometrical order, the population was kept in check by fire. Popular myth had it that down here every leap year's night you could see people in flames running between houses, hear their screams, watch them burn and dissolve, but there would be a layer of ash left on the tarmac, and if you managed to grab it before the wind blew it away the house you occupied would never burn down. Because of the fire risk Christian IV built broad roads, by the standards of Oslo's poor. Houses were erected in the un-Norwegian building material of brick. And along one of these brick walls he passed the open door of a bar. A new violation of Guns N' Roses' 'Welcome to the Jungle', dance-produced reggae pissing on Marley and Rose, Slash and Stradlin, belted out to the smokers standing around outside. He stopped at an outstretched arm.

'Gotta light?'

A plump, top-heavy lady somewhere in her late thirties looked up at him. Her cigarette bounced provocatively up and down between her red lips.

He raised an eyebrow and looked at her laughing girlfriend, who was standing behind her with a glowing cigarette. The top-heavy one noticed and then laughed as well, taking a step aside to regain her balance.

'Don't be so slow,' she said in the same Sørland accent as the Crown princess. He had heard there was a prostitute in the covered market who got rich by looking like her, talking like her and dressing like her. And that the 5,000-kroner-an-hour fee included a plastic sceptre which the customer was allowed to put to relatively free use.

The woman's hand rested on his arm as he made to move on. She leaned towards him and breathed red wine into his face.

'You're a good-looking guy. How about giving me . . . a light?'

He turned the other side of his face to her. The bad side. The not-such-a-good-looking-guy side. Felt her flinch and slip as she saw the path left by the nail from his time in the Congo. It stretched from mouth to ear like a badly sewn-up tear.

He walked on as the music changed to Nirvana. 'Come As You Are.' Original version.

'Hash?'

The voice came from a gateway, but he neither stopped nor turned.

'Speed?'

He had been clean for three years and had no intention of starting again.

'Violin?'

Least of all now.

In front of him on the pavement a young man had stopped by two dealers; he was showing them something as he spoke. The youngster looked up as he approached, fixing two searching grey eyes on him. Policeman's eyes, the man thought, lowered his head and crossed the street. It was perhaps a little paranoid; after all, it was unlikely such a young police officer would recognise him.

There was the hotel. The dosshouse. Leon.

It was almost deserted in this part of the street. On the other side, under a lamp, he saw the dope seller astride the bike, with another cyclist, also wearing professional cycling gear. The dope seller was helping the other guy to inject himself in the neck.

The man in the linen suit shook his head and gazed up at the facade of the building before him.

There was the same banner, grey with dirt, hanging below the third- and top-floor windows. 'Four hundred kroner a night!' Everything was new. Everything was the same.

The receptionist at Hotel Leon was new. A young lad, who greeted the man in the linen suit with an astonishingly polite smile and an amazing – for Leon – lack of mistrust. He wished him a hearty 'Welcome' without a tinge of irony in his voice and asked to see his passport. The man assumed he was often taken for a foreigner because of the tanned complexion and the linen suit, and passed the receptionist his red Norwegian passport. It was worn and full of stamps. Too many for it to be called a good life.

'Oh, yes,' the receptionist said, returning it. Placed a form on the counter and handed him a pen.

'The marked sections are enough.'

A checking-in form at Leon? the man thought with surprise. Perhaps some things had changed after all. He took the pen and saw the receptionist staring at his hand, his middle finger. The one that had been his longest finger before it was cut off in a house on Holmenkollen Ridge. Now the first joint had been replaced with a matt, greyish-blue, titanium prosthesis. It wasn't a lot of use, but it did provide balance for his adjacent fingers when he had to grip, and it was not in the way as it was so short. The only disadvantage was the endless explanations when he had to go through security at airports.

He filled in *First name* and *Last name*.

Date of birth.

He wrote knowing he looked more like a man in his mid-forties now than the damaged geriatric who had left Norway three years ago. He had subjected himself to a strict regime of exercise, healthy food, plentiful sleep and – of course – absolutely no addictive substances. The aim of the regime had not been to look younger, but to avoid death. Besides, he liked it. In fact he had always like fixed routines, discipline, order. So why had his life been chaos instead, such self-destruction and a series of broken relationships between dark periods of intoxication? The blank boxes looked up at him, questioningly. But they were too small for the answers they required.

Permanent address.

Well, the flat in Sofies gate was sold right after he left three years ago, the same applied to his parents' house in Oppsal. In his present occupation an official address would have carried a certain inherent risk. So he wrote what he usually wrote when he checked in at other hotels: Chungking Mansion, Hong Kong. Which was no further from the truth than anything else.

Occupation.

Murder. He didn't write that. This section hadn't been marked.

Telephone number.

He put a fictitious one. Mobile phones can be traced, the conversations and where you make them.

Next of kin's telephone number.

Next of kin? What husband would voluntarily give his wife's number when he checked in at Hotel Leon? The place was the closest Oslo had to a public brothel, after all.

The receptionist could evidently read his mind. 'In case you should feel indisposed and we have to call someone.'

Harry nodded. In case of a heart attack during the act.

'You don't need to write anything if you don't . . .'

'No,' the man said, looking at the words. *Next of kin.* He had Sis. A sister with what she herself called 'a touch of Down's syndrome', but who had always tackled life a great deal better than her elder brother. Apart from Sis there was no one else. Absolutely no one. All the same, next of kin.

He ticked 'Cash' for mode of payment, signed and passed the form to the receptionist. Who skimmed through it. And then at last Harry saw it shine through. The mistrust.

'Are you . . . are you Harry Hole?'

Harry Hole nodded. 'Is that a problem?'

The boy shook his head. Gulped.

'Fine,' said Harry. 'Have you got a key for me?'

'Oh, sorry! Here. 301.'

Harry took it and noticed that the boy's pupils had widened and his voice constricted.

'It . . . it's my uncle,' the boy said. 'He runs the hotel. Used to sit here before me. He's told me about you.'

'Only nice things, I trust,' Harry said, grabbing his canvas suitcase and heading for the stairs.

'The lift . . .'

'Don't like lifts,' Harry said without turning.

The room was the same as before. Tatty, small and more or less clean. No, in fact, the curtains were new. Green. Stiff. Probably drip-dry. Which reminded him. He hung his suit in the bathroom and turned on the shower so the steam would remove the creases. The suit had cost him eight hundred Hong Kong dollars at Punjab House on Nathan Road, but in his job it was an essential investment; no one respected a man dressed in rags. He stood under the shower. The hot water made his skin tingle. Afterwards he walked naked through the room to the window and opened it. Second floor. Backyard. Through an open window came the groans of simulated enthusiasm. He grasped the curtain pole and leaned out. Looked straight down onto an open skip and recognised the sweet smell of rubbish rising forth. He spat and heard it hit the paper in the bin. But the rustling that followed was not of paper. There was a crack, and the stiff green curtains landed on the floor on either side of him. Shit! He pulled the thin pole out of the curtain hem. It was the old kind with two bulbous pointed ends; it had broken before and someone had tried to stick it together with brown tape. Harry sat down on the bed and opened the drawer in the bedside table. A Bible with a light blue synthetic leather cover and a sewing kit comprising black thread wound round card with a needle stuck through. On mature reflection, Harry realised they might not be such a bad idea after all. Afterwards guests could sew back torn fly buttons and read about forgiveness of sins. He lay down on the bed and stared at the ceiling. Everything was new. Everything . . . He closed his eyes. On the flight he hadn't slept a wink, and with or without jet lag, with or without curtains, he was going to have to sleep. And he began to dream the same dream he had had every night for the last three years: he was running down a corridor, fleeing from a roaring avalanche that sucked out all the air, leaving him unable to breathe.

It was just a question of keeping going and keeping his eyes closed for a bit longer.

He lost a grip on his thoughts; they were drifting away from him.

Next of kin.

Kin. Kith.

Next of kin.

That's what he was. That's why he was back.

Sergey was driving on the E6 towards Oslo. Longing for the bed in his Furuset flat. Keeping under 120, even though the motorway was virtually empty so late at night. His mobile phone rang. The mobile. The conversation with Andrey was concise. He had spoken to his uncle, or *ataman* – the leader – as Andrey called Uncle. After they had rung off Sergey could not restrain himself any longer. He put his foot down. Shrieked with delight. The man had arrived. Now, this evening. He was here! Sergey was not to do anything for the moment, the situation might resolve itself, Andrey had said. But he had to be even more prepared now, mentally and physically. Had to practise with the knife, sleep, be on his toes. If the necessary should become necessary.

4

TORD SCHULTZ BARELY HEARD THE plane thundering overhead as he sat on the sofa breathing heavily. Perspiration lay in a thin layer on his naked upper body, and the echoes of iron on iron still hung between the bare sitting-room walls. Behind him were his weights and the mock-leather upholstered bench glistening with his sweat. From the TV screen Donald Draper peered through his own cigarette smoke, sipping whiskey from a glass. Another plane roared over the rooftops. *Mad Men*. The sixties. USA. Women wearing decent clothes. Decent drinks in decent glasses. Decent cigarettes without menthol and filters. The days when what didn't kill you made you stronger. He had bought only the first season. Watched it again and again. He wasn't sure he would like the next series.

Tord Schultz looked at the white line on the glass coffee table and dried the edge of his ID card. He had used his card to chop it up, as usual. The card that he attached to the pocket of his captain's uniform, the card that gave him access to airside, the cockpit, the sky, the salary. The card that made him what he was. The card that – with everything else – would be taken from him if he was found out. That was why it felt right to use the ID card. There was – in all the dishonesty – something honest about it.

They were going back to Bangkok early tomorrow morning. Two rest days at Sukhumvit Residence. Good. It would be good now. Better than

23

before. He hadn't liked the arrangement when he flew from Amsterdam. Too much risk. After it had been discovered how deeply involved the South American crews were in cocaine smuggling to Schiphol, all crews, regardless of airline, risked having their hand luggage checked and being subjected to a body search. Furthermore, the arrangement had been that, on landing, he would carry the packages and keep them in his bag until later in the day when he flew an internal flight to Bergen, Trondheim or Stavanger. Internal flights that he *had to* make, even if it meant he was forced to absorb delays from Amsterdam by burning up extra fuel. At Gardermoen he was airside all the time of course, so there was no customs check, but occasionally he had to store the drugs in his bag for sixteen hours before he could deliver them. And deliveries had not always been without risk, either. Public car parks. Restaurants with far too few customers. Hotels with observant receptionists.

He rolled up a thousand-krone note he'd taken from an envelope he'd been given the last time he was here. There were especially designed plastic tubes for the purpose, but he was not that kind: he was not the heavy user she had told her divorce lawyer he was. The sly bitch maintained she wanted a divorce because she did not wish to see her children growing up with a drug-addict father and she had no interest in watching him sniff away their house and home. And it had nothing to do with air stewardesses, she couldn't give a damn, she had stopped worrying about that years ago, his age would take care of that. She and the lawyer had given him an ultimatum. She would take over the house, the children and the remnants of the inheritance he hadn't squandered. Or they would report him for possession and use of cocaine. She had gathered together enough evidence for even his own lawyer to say that he would be sentenced and dumped by his airline.

It had been a simple choice. All she had allowed him to retain were the debts.

He got to his feet and went to the window and stared out. Surely they would be here soon, wouldn't they?

This was quite a new arrangement. He was to take a package on an outward flight, to Bangkok. God knows why. Fish to Lofoten, as they said in Norwegian, and so on. Anyway, this was the sixth trip, and so far everything had gone without a hitch.

There was light in the neighbouring houses, but they were so far apart. Lonely habitations, he thought. They had been officers' quarters when Gardermoen had been a military base. Identical single-storey boxes with large, bare lawns between the houses. Least possible height so that a low-flying machine wouldn't collide. Greatest possible distance between the houses so that a fire following a crash wouldn't spread.

They had lived here during his compulsory national service when he had been flying Hercules transport planes. The kids had run between houses, visiting other children. Saturday, summer. Men round the barbecues wearing aprons and holding aperitifs. Chatter coming from the open windows where the women were preparing salads and drinking Campari. Like a scene from *The Right Stuff*, his favourite film, the one with the first astronauts and the test pilot, Chuck Yeager. Damned attractive, these pilots' wives. Even though they were only Hercules pilots. They had been happy then, hadn't they? Was that why he had returned? An unconscious urge to go back in time? Or to find out where it all went wrong, and make amends?

He saw the car coming and automatically checked his watch. Logged that they were eighteen minutes late.

He went to the coffee table. Breathed in twice. Then placed the rolled-up note against the lowest end of the line, bent down and sniffed the powder up his nose. It stung the mucous membrane. He licked his fingertip, ran it over the remaining powder and rubbed it into his gums. It had a bitter taste. The doorbell rang.

It was the same two Mormon guys as always. One small, one tall, both wearing their Sunday best. But tattoos protruded from under their sleeves. It was almost comic.

They handed him the package. Half a kilo in one long sausage that would just fit inside the metal plate around the telescopic handle of the cabin bag. He was to remove the package after they had landed in Suvarnabhumi and put it under the loose rug at the back of the pilots' locker in the cockpit. And that was the last he would see of it; the rest would probably be sorted out by the ground crew.

When Mr Big and Mr Small had presented the opportunity to take packages to Bangkok, it had sounded like lunacy. After all, there was not a country in the world where the street price of dope was higher than in Oslo, so why export? He hadn't probed, he knew he wouldn't get an answer, and that was fine. But he had pointed out that smuggling heroin to Thailand carried a sentence of death if caught, so he wanted better payment.

They had laughed. First the little one. Then the big one. And Tord had wondered if maybe shorter nerve channels produced quicker reactions. Maybe that was why they made fighter-jet cockpits so low, to exclude tall, slow pilots.

The little one explained to Tord in his harsh, Russian-sounding English that it was not heroin, it was something quite new, so new that there wasn't even a law banning it yet. But when Tord asked why they had to smuggle a legal substance they had laughed even louder and told him to shut up and answer yes or no.

Tord Schultz had answered yes as another thought announced its presence. What would the consequences be if he said no?

That was six trips ago.

Tord Schultz studied the package. A couple of times he had considered smearing washing-up liquid over the condoms and freezer bags they used, but he had been told that sniffer dogs could distinguish smells and were not fooled so easily. The trick was to make sure the plastic bag was fully sealed.

He waited. Nothing happened. He cleared his throat.

'Oh, I almost forgot,' said Mr Small. 'Yesterday's delivery . . .'

He slipped his hand inside his jacket with an evil grin. Or perhaps it wasn't evil, perhaps it was Eastern bloc humour. Tord felt like punching him, blowing unfiltered cigarette smoke into his face, spitting twelve-year-old whiskey in his eye. Western bloc humour. Instead he mumbled a thank-you and took the envelope. It felt thin between his fingertips. They had to be big notes.

Afterwards he stood by the window again and watched the car disappear into the darkness, heard the sound being drowned by a Boeing 737. Maybe a 600. Next generation anyway. Throatier and higher pitched than the old classics. He saw his reflection in the window.

Yes, he had taken their coin. And he would continue to take it. Take everything life threw in his face. For he was not Donald Draper. He was not Chuck Yeager and not Neil Armstrong. He was Tord Schultz. A long-spined pilot with debts. And a cocaine problem. He ought to . . .

His thoughts were drowned by the next plane.

Bloody church bells! Can you see them, Dad, the so-called next of kin all standing over my coffin? Crying crocodile tears, their sombre mugs saying: 'Gusto, why couldn't you have just learned to be like us?' Well, you sodding self-righteous hypocrites, I couldn't! I couldn't be like my foster-mother, a daft, spoilt airhead, going on about how wonderful everything is, provided you read the right book, listen to the right guru, eat the right fricking herbs. And whenever anyone punctured that woolly wisdom she had bought into, she always played the same card: 'But look at the world we have created: war, injustice, people who don't live in harmony with themselves any longer.' Three things, baby. One: war, injustice and disharmony are natural. Two: you are the least harmonious of all in our disgusting little family. You wanted only the love you were denied, and you didn't give a shit about the love you were given. Sorry, Rolf, Stein and Irene, but she had room only for me. Which makes point three all the more amusing: I never loved you, baby, however much you considered you deserved it. I called you Mum because it made you happy, and life simpler for me. When I did what I did it was because you let me, because I couldn't stop myself. Because that's the way I am.

Rolf. At least you told me not to call you Dad. You really tried to love me. But you could not fool nature; you realised you loved your own flesh and blood more: Stein and Irene. When I told other people you were 'my foster-parents' I could see the wounded expression in Mum's eyes. And the hatred in yours. Not because 'foster-parents' shrank you to the only function you had in my life, but because I wounded the woman you, incomprehensibly, loved. I think you were honest enough to see yourself as I saw you: a person who at some point in your life, intoxicated on your own idealism, undertook to raise a changeling but soon understood that your account was in deficit. The monthly sum they paid you for care did not cover the real expense. Then you discovered that I was a cuckoo in the nest. That I ate everything. Everything you loved. Everyone you loved. You should have realised earlier and thrown me out, Rolf! You were the first to see that I stole. Initially it was only a hundred kroner. I denied it. Said I'd been given it by Mum. 'Isn't that right, Mum? You gave it to me.' And Mum nodded after some hesitation, with tears in her eyes, said she must have forgotten. The next time it was a thousand. From your desk drawer. Money that was meant for our holiday, you said. 'The only holiday I want is from you,' I answered. And then you slapped me for the first time. And it was as if it triggered something in you, because you went on hitting. I was already taller and broader than you, but I have never been able to fight. Not like that, not with fists and muscles. I fought in another way, one where you win. But you kept hitting me, with a clenched fist now. And I knew why. You wanted to destroy my face. Take my power away from me. But the woman I called Mum intervened. So you said it. The word. The Thief. True enough. But it also meant I would have to crush you, little man.

Stein. The silent elder brother. The first to recognise the cuckoo by the plumage, but smart enough to keep his distance. The clever, bright, smart lone wolf who upped and left for a student town as far away as possible and as soon as he could. Who tried to persuade Irene, his dear little sister, to join him. He thought that she could finish school in fricking Trondheim, that it would do her good to get away from Oslo. But Mum put a stop to Irene's evacuation. She knew nothing of course. Didn't want to know.

Irene. Attractive, lovely, freckled, fragile Irene. You were too good for this world. You were all I was not. And yet you loved me. Would you have loved me if you had known? Would you have loved me if you had known that I was shagging your mother from the age of fifteen? Shagging your red-wine-soaked, whimpering mother, taking her from behind against the toilet door or the cellar door or the kitchen door while whispering 'Mum' in her ear because it made both her and me hot. She gave me money, she covered my back if anything happened, she said she only wanted to borrow me until she was old and ugly and I met a nice, sweet girl. And when I answered, 'But, Mum, you *are* old and ugly,' she laughed it off and begged for more.

I still had the bruises after my foster-father's punches and kicks the day I rang him at work and told him to come home at three, there was something important I had to tell him. I left the front door ajar so that she wouldn't hear him come in. And I spoke into her ear to drown his footsteps, said the sweet nothings she liked to hear.

I saw the reflection in the kitchen window, of him standing in the kitchen doorway.

He moved out the next day. Irene and Stein were told that Mum and Dad had not been getting on well for a while and had decided to separate for a bit. Irene was broken-hearted. Stein was in his student town, and he answered with a text: 'Sad. Where would u like me to go 4 Xmas?'

Irene cried and cried. She loved me. Of course she searched for me. For the Thief.

The church bells rang for the fifth time. Crying and sniffling from the pews. Cocaine, incredible earnings. Rent a city-centre flat in the West End, register it in some junkie's name who you pay off with a shot, and start selling in small quantities by stairways or gates, ratchet up the price as they begin to feel secure; coke folk pay anything for security. Get on your feet, get out, cut down on dope, become somebody. Don't die in a squat like a bloody loser. The priest coughs. 'We are here to commemorate Gusto Hanssen.'

A voice from far back: 'Th th thief.'

Tutu's tribe sitting there in biker jackets and bandanas. And even further back: the whimpering of a dog. Rufus. Good, loyal Rufus. Have you come back here? Or is it me who has already gone there?

* * *

Tord Schultz placed his Samsonite bag on the conveyor belt winding its way into the X-ray machine beside the smiling security official.

'I don't understand why you let them give you such a schedule,' the flight attendant said. 'Bangkok twice a week.'

'I asked them to,' Tord said, passing through the metal detector. Someone in the trade union had proposed that the crews should go on strike against having to be exposed to radiation several times a day. American research had shown that proportionally more pilots and cabin crew died of cancer than the rest of the population. But the strike agitators had said nothing about the average life expectancy also being higher. Air crew died of cancer because there was very little else to die of. They lived the safest lives in the world. The most boring lives in the world.

'You want to fly that much?'

'I'm a pilot. I like flying,' Tord lied, taking down his bag, extending the handle and walking away.

She was alongside him in seconds, the clack of her heels on Gardermoen's grey antique foncé marble floor almost drowning the buzz of voices under the vaulted wooden beams and steel. However, unfortunately it did not drown her whispered question.

'Is that because she left you, Tord? Is it because you have too much time on your hands and nothing to fill it with? Is it because you don't want to sit at home—'

'It's because I need the overtime,' he interrupted. At least that was not an outright lie.

'Because I know exactly what it's like. I got divorced last winter, as you know.'

'Ah, yes,' said Tord, who didn't even know she had been married. He shot her a swift glance. Fifty? Wondered what she looked like in the morning without make-up and the fake tan. A faded flight attendant with a faded flight attendant dream. He was pretty sure he had never rogered her. Not face on, anyway. Whose stock joke had that been? One of the old pilots. One of the whiskey-on-the-rocks, blue-eyed fighter pilots. One of those who managed to retire before their status crashed. He accelerated as they turned into the corridor towards the flight crew centre. She was out of breath, but still kept up with him. But if he maintained this speed she might not have enough air to speak.

'Erm, Tord, since we've got a stay-over in Bangkok perhaps we could . . .'

He yawned aloud. And felt no more than that she had been offended. He was still a bit groggy after the night before – there had been some more vodka and powder after the Mormons had gone. Not that he had ingested so much he would have failed a breathalyser test, of course, but enough for him to dread the fight against sleep for the eleven hours in the air.

'Look!' she exclaimed in the idiotic glissando tone that women use when they want to say something is absolutely, inconceivably, heart-rendingly sweet.

And he did look. It was coming towards them. A small, light-haired, long-eared dog with sad eyes and an enthusiastically wagging tail. A springer spaniel. It was being led by a woman with matching blonde hair, big drop earrings, a universally apologetic half-smile and gentle, brown eyes.

'Isn't he a dear?' she purred beside him.

'Mm,' Tord said in a gravelly voice.

The dog stuck its snout into the groin of the pilot in front of them, and passed on. He turned round with a raised eyebrow and a crooked smile, as if to suggest a boyish, cheeky expression. But Tord was unable to continue that line of thought. He was unable to continue any line of thought except his own.

The dog was wearing a yellow vest. The same type of vest the woman with the drop earrings was wearing. On which was written CUSTOMS.

It came closer, and was only five metres from them now.

It shouldn't be a problem. Couldn't be a problem. The drugs were packed in condoms with a double layer of freezer bags on the outside. Not so much as a molecule of odour could escape. So just smile. Relax and smile. Not too much, not too little. Tord turned to the chattering voice beside him, as though the words that were issuing forth demanded deep concentration.

'Excuse me.'

They had passed the dog, and Tord kept walking.

'Excuse me!' The voice was sharper.

Tord looked ahead. The door to the flight crew centre was less than ten metres away. Safety. Ten paces. Home and dry.

'Excuse me, sir!'

Seven paces.

'I think she means you, Tord.'

'What?' Tord stopped. Had to stop. Looked back with what he hoped did not appear to be feigned surprise. The woman in the yellow vest was coming towards them.

'The dog picked you out.'

'Did it?' Tord looked down at the dog. How? he was thinking.

The dog looked back, wagging its tail wildly, as though Tord was its new play pal.

How? Double layer of freezer bags and condom. How?

'That means we have to check you. Could you come with us please.'

The gentleness was still there in her brown eyes, but there was no question mark behind her words. And at that moment he realised how. He almost fingered the ID card on his chest.

The cocaine.

He had forgotten to wipe down the card after chopping up the last line. That had to be it.

But it was only a few grains, which he could easily explain away by saying he had lent his ID card to someone at a party. That wasn't his biggest problem now. The bag. It would be searched. As a pilot he had trained and practised emergency procedures so often it was almost automatic. That was the intention, of course, even when panic seized you this was what you would do, this brain kicked in for lack of other orders: the emergency procedures. How many times had he visualised this situation: the customs officials asking him to go with them? Thinking what he would do? Practising it in his mind? He turned to the flight attendant with a resigned smile, caught sight of her name tag. 'I've been picked out, it seems, Kristin. Could you take my bag?'

'The bag comes with us,' the official said.

Tord Schultz turned back. 'I thought you said the dog picked me out, not the bag.'

'That's true, but—'

'There are flight documents inside which the crew needs to check. Unless you want to take responsibility for delaying a full Airbus 340 to Bangkok.' He noticed that he – quite literally – had puffed himself up, filled his lungs and expanded his chest muscles in his captain's jacket. 'If we miss our slot that could mean a delay of several hours and a loss of hundreds of thousands of kroner for the airline.'

'I'm afraid rules—'

'Three hundred and forty-two passengers,' Schultz interrupted. 'Many of them children.' He hoped she heard a captain's grave concern, not the incipient panic of a dope smuggler.

The official patted the dog on the head and looked at him.

She looks like a housewife, he thought. A woman with children and responsibility. A woman who should understand his predicament.

'The bag comes with us,' she said.

Another official appeared in the background. Stood there, legs apart, arms crossed.

'Let's get this over with,' Tord sighed.

The head of Oslo's Crime Squad, Gunnar Hagen, leaned back in his swivel chair and studied the man in the linen suit. It was three years since the sewn-up gash in his face had been blood red and he had looked like a man on his last legs. But now his ex-subordinate looked healthy, had put on a few sorely needed kilos, and his shoulders filled out the suit. Suit. Hagen remembered the murder investigator in jeans and boots, never anything else. The other difference was the sticker on his lapel saying he was not staff but a visitor: HARRY HOLE.

But the posture in the chair was the same, more horizontal than sitting.

'You look better,' Hagen said.

'Your town does too,' Harry said with an unlit cigarette bobbing between his teeth.

'You think so?'

'Wonderful opera house. Fewer junkies in the streets.'

Hagen got up and went to the window. From the sixth floor of Police HQ he could see Oslo's new district, Bjørvika, bathed in sunshine. The clean-up was in full flow. The demolition work over.

'There's been a marked fall in the number of fatal ODs in the last year.'

'Prices have gone up, consumption down. And the City Council got what it craved. Oslo no longer tops OD stats in Europe.'

'Happy days are here again.' Harry put his hands behind his head and looked as if he was going to slide out of the chair.

Hagen sighed. 'You didn't say what brings you to Oslo, Harry.'

'Didn't I?'

'No. Or, more specifically, to Crime Squad.'

'Isn't it normal to visit former colleagues?'

'Yes, for other, normal, sociable people, it is.'

'Well.' Harry bit into the filter of the Camel cigarette. 'My occupation is murder.'

'*Was* murder, don't you mean?'

'Let me reformulate that: my profession, my area of expertise, is murder. And it's still the only field I know something about.'

'So what do you want?'

'To practise my occupation. To investigate murders.'

Hagen arched an eyebrow. 'You'd like to work for me again?'

'Why not? Unless I'm very much mistaken I was one of the best.'

'Correction,' Hagen said, turning back to the window. 'You were *the* best.' And repeated in a lower tone: 'The best and the worst.'

'I fancy one of the narco murders.'

Hagen gave a dry smile. 'Which one? We've had four in the last six months. We haven't made an ounce of headway with any of them.'

'Gusto Hanssen.'

Hagen didn't answer, continued to study the people sprawled over the grass. And the thoughts came unforced. Benefit cheats. Thieves. Terrorists. Why did he see that instead of hard-working employees enjoying a few

34

well-earned hours in the September sunshine? The police look. The police blindness. He half listened to Harry's voice behind him.

'Gusto Hanssen, nineteen years old. Known to police, pushers and users. Found dead in a flat in Hausmanns gate on 12 July. Bled to death after a shot to the chest.'

Hagen burst out laughing. 'Why do you want the only one that's cleared up?'

'I think you know.'

'Yes, I do,' Hagen sighed. 'But if I were to employ you again I would put you on one of the others. On the undercover cop case.'

'I want this one.'

'There are, in round figures, about a hundred reasons why you will never be put on that case, Harry.'

'Which are?'

Hagen turned to Harry. 'Perhaps it's enough to mention the first. The case has already been solved.'

'And beyond that?'

'We don't have the case. Kripos does. I don't have any vacancies. Quite the opposite, I'm trying to make cuts. You're not eligible. Should I go on?'

'Mm. Where is he?'

Hagen pointed out of the window. Across the lawn to the grey-stone building behind the yellow leaves of the linden trees.

'Botsen,' Harry said. 'On remand.'

'For the moment.'

'Visits out of bounds?'

'Who traced you in Hong Kong and told you about the case? Was it—?'

'No,' Harry interrupted.

'So?'

'So.'

'Who?'

'I might have read about it on the Net.'

'Hardly,' Hagen said with a thin smile and lifeless eyes. 'The case was in the papers for one day before it was forgotten. And there were no names.

35

Only an article about a drugged-up junkie who had shot another junkie over dope. Nothing of any interest for anyone. Nothing to make the case stand out.'

'Apart from the fact that the two junkies were teenage boys,' Harry said. 'Nineteen years old. And eighteen.' His voice had changed timbre.

Hagen shrugged. 'Old enough to kill, old enough to die. In the new year they would have been called up for military service.'

'Could you fix up a chat for me?'

'Who told you, Harry?'

Harry rubbed his chin. 'Friend in Krimteknisk.'

Hagen smiled. And this time the smile reached his eyes. 'You're so damned kind, Harry. To my knowledge, you have three friends in the police force. Among them Bjørn Holm in Krimteknisk. And Beate Lønn in Krimteknisk. So which one was it?'

'Beate. Will you fix me up with a visit?'

Hagen sat on the edge of his desk and observed Harry. Looked down at the telephone.

'On one condition, Harry. You promise to keep miles away from this case. It's all sunshine and roses between us and Kripos now, and I could do without any more trouble with them.'

Harry grimaced. He had sunk so low in the chair now he could study his belt buckle. 'So you and the Kripos king have become bosom pals?'

'Mikael Bellman stopped working for Kripos,' Hagen said. 'Hence, sunshine and roses.'

'Got rid of the psychopath? Happy days . . .'

'On the contrary.' Hagen's laugh was hollow. 'Bellman is more present than ever. He's in this building.'

'Oh shit. Here in Crime Squad?'

'God forbid. He's been running Orgkrim for more than a year.'

'You've got new wombos, I can hear.'

'Organised crime. They merged a load of the old sections. Burglary, trafficking, narc. It's all Orgkrim now. More than two hundred employees, biggest unit in the Crime Department.'

'Mm. More than he had in Kripos.'

'Yet his salary went down. And you know what that means when people take lower paid jobs?'

'They're after more power,' Harry said.

'He was the one who got the drugs market under control, Harry. Good undercover work. Arrests and raids. There are fewer gangs and there's no in-fighting now. OD figures are, as I said, on the way down . . .' Hagen pointed a finger at the ceiling. 'And Bellman's on the way up. The boy's going places, Harry.'

'Me too,' Harry said, rising to his feet. 'To Botsen. I'm counting on there being a visitor's permit in reception by the time I arrive.'

'If we've got a deal?'

'Course we have,' Harry said, grabbing his ex-boss's outstretched hand. He pumped it twice and made for the door. Hong Kong had been a good school for lying. He heard Hagen lift the telephone receiver, but as he reached the threshold he turned nonetheless.

'Who's the third?'

'What?' Hagen was looking down at the keypad while tapping with a heavy finger.

'The third friend I have in the force?'

Unit Head Gunnar Hagen put the receiver to his ear, sent Harry a weary look and said with a sigh: 'Who do you think?' And: 'Hello? Hagen here. I'd like a visitor's permit . . . Yes?' Hagen laid a hand over the receiver. 'No problem. They're eating now, but get there for around twelve.'

Harry smiled, mouthed a thank-you and closed the door quietly after him.

Tord Schultz stood in the booth, buttoning up his trousers and putting on his jacket. They had stopped short of examining orifices. The customs official – the one who had stopped him – was waiting outside. Standing there like an external examiner after a viva.

'Thank you for being so cooperative,' she said, indicating the exit.

Tord guessed they'd had long discussions about whether they would say 'we're sorry' whenever a sniffer dog had identified someone, but no dope was found. The individual stopped, delayed, suspected and shamed would undoubtedly consider an apology appropriate. But should you complain about someone doing their job? Dogs identified innocent people all the time, and a complaint would be a partial admission that there was a flaw in the procedure, a failure in the system. On the other hand, they could see by his stripes that he was a captain. Not a three-striper, not one of the failed fifty-year-olds who had stayed in the right-hand seat as a first officer because they had messed up their career. No, he had four stripes, which showed that he had order, control; he was a man who was a master of the situation and his own life. Showed that he belonged to the airport's Brahmin caste. A captain was a person who ought to welcome a complaint from a customs official, whether it was appropriate or not.

'Not at all, it's good to know someone is on the mark,' Tord said, looking for his bag. In the worst-case scenario they had searched it; the dog hadn't detected anything there. And the metal plates around the space where the package was hidden were still impenetrable for existing X-rays.

'It'll be here soon,' she said.

There were a couple of seconds when they silently regarded each other.

Divorced, Tord thought.

At that moment another official appeared.

'Your bag . . .' he said.

Tord looked at him. Saw it in his eyes. Felt a lump grow in his stomach, rise, nudge his oesophagus. How? How?

'We took out everything and weighed it,' he said. 'An empty twenty-six-inch' Samsonite Aspire GRT weighs 5.8 kilos. Yours weighs 6.3. Would you mind explaining why?'

The official was too professional to smile overtly, but Tord Schultz still saw the triumph shining in his face. The official leaned forward a fraction, lowered his voice.

'. . . or shall we?'

*　*　*

Harry went into the street after eating at Olympen. The old, slightly dissipated hostelry he remembered had been renovated into an expensive Oslo West version of an Oslo East place, with large paintings of the town's old working-class district. It wasn't that it wasn't attractive, with the chandeliers and everything. Even the mackerel had been good. It just wasn't . . . Olympen.

He lit a cigarette and crossed Bots Park between Police HQ and the prison's old, grey walls. He passed a man putting a tatty red poster on a tree and banging a staple gun against the bark of the ancient, and protected, linden. He didn't seem to be aware of the fact that he was committing a serious offence in full view of all the windows at the front of the building which contained the biggest collection of police officers in Norway. Harry paused for a moment. Not to stop the crime, but to see the poster. It advertised a concert with Russian Amcar Club at Sardines. Harry could remember the long-dissolved band and the derelict club. Olympen. Harry Hole. This was clearly the year for the resurrection of the dead. He was about to move on when he heard a tremulous voice behind him.

'Got'ny violin?'

Harry turned. The man behind him was wearing a new, clean G-Star jacket. He stooped forward as though there were a strong wind at his back, and he had the unmistakable bowed heroin knees. Harry was going to reply when he realised G-Star was addressing the poster man. But he carried on walking without answering. New wombos for units, new terms for dope. Old bands, old clubs.

The facade of Oslo District Prison, Botsen in popular parlance, was built in the mid-1800s and consisted of an entrance squeezed between two larger wings, which always reminded Harry of a detainee between two policemen. He rang the bell, peered into the video camera, heard the low buzz and shoved the door open. Inside stood a uniformed prison officer, who escorted him up the stairs, through a door, past two other officers and into the rectangular, windowless Visitors' Room. Harry had been there before. This was where the inmates met their nearest and dearest. A half-hearted attempt had been made to create a homely atmosphere. He avoided the sofa, sat down on a chair, well aware of what went on during the few minutes the inmate was allowed to spend with a spouse or girlfriend.

He waited. Noticed he still had the Police HQ sticker on his lapel, pulled it off and put it in his pocket. The dream of the narrow corridor and the avalanche had been worse than usual last night, he had been buried and his mouth had been stuffed with snow. But that was not why his heart was beating now. Was it with expectation? Or terror?

The door opened before he had a chance to reach a conclusion.

'Twenty minutes,' the prison officer said, and left, slamming the door behind him.

The boy standing before him was so changed that for a second Harry had been on the point of shouting that this was the wrong person, this was not him. This boy was wearing Diesel jeans and a black hoodie advertising Machine Head, which Harry realised was not a reference to the old Deep Purple record but – having calculated the time difference – a new heavy metal band. Heavy metal was of course a clue, but the proof was the eyes and high cheekbones. To be precise: Rakel's brown eyes and high cheekbones. It was almost a shock to see the resemblance. Granted he had not inherited his mother's beauty – his forehead was too prominent for that, it lent the boy a bleak, almost aggressive appearance. Which was reinforced by the sleek fringe Harry had always assumed he had inherited from his father in Moscow. An alcoholic the boy had never really known properly – he was only a few years old when Rakel had brought him back to Oslo. Where later she was to meet Harry.

Rakel.

The great love of his life. As simple as that. And as complicated.

Oleg. Bright, serious Oleg. Oleg, who had been so introverted, who would not open up to anyone, apart from Harry. Harry had never told Rakel, but he knew more about what Oleg thought, felt and wanted than she did. Oleg and he playing Tetris on his Game Boy, both as keen as each other to smash the record. Oleg and he skating at Valle Hovin; the time Oleg wanted to become a long-distance runner and in fact had the talent for it. Oleg, who smiled, patient and indulgent, whenever Harry promised that in the autumn or spring they would go to London to see Tottenham playing at White Hart Lane. Oleg, who sometimes called him Dad when it was late, he was sleepy and had lost concentration. It was years since Harry had seen him, years since Rakel had taken him from Oslo, away from the grisly reminders of the Snowman, away from Harry's world of violence and murder.

And now he was standing there by the door, he was eighteen years old, half grown up and looking at Harry without an expression, or at least one Harry could interpret.

'Hi,' Harry said. Shit, he hadn't tested his voice; it came out as a hoarse rasp. The boy would think he was on the verge of tears or something. As if to distract himself, or Oleg, Harry pulled out a pack of Camel cigarettes and poked one between his lips.

He peered up and saw the flush that had spread across Oleg's face. And the anger. The explosive anger that appeared from nowhere, darkening his eyes and making the blood vessels on his neck and forehead bulge and quiver like guitar strings.

'Relax, I won't light it,' Harry said, nodding to the NO SMOKING sign on the wall.

'It's Mum, isn't it?' The voice was also older. And thick with fury.

'What is?'

'She's the one who sent for you.'

'No, she didn't, I—'

'Course she did.'

'No, Oleg, in fact she doesn't even know I'm in the country.'

'You're lying! You're lying as usual!'

Harry gaped at him. 'As usual?'

'The way you lie that you'll always be there for us and all that crap. But it's too late now. So you can just go back to . . . Timbuktu!'

'Oleg! Listen to me—'

'No! I won't listen to you. You've got no business here! You can't come and play dad now, do you understand?' Harry saw the boy swallow hard. Saw the fury ebb, only for a new wave of blackness to engulf him. 'You're no one to us any more. You were someone who drifted in, hung around for a few years and then . . .' Oleg made an attempt to snap his fingers, but they slipped off each other without a sound. 'Gone.'

'That's not true, Oleg. And you know it.' Harry heard his own voice, which was firm and sure now, telling him that he was as calm and secure as an aircraft carrier. But the lump in his stomach told him otherwise. He was used to being yelled at during interrogations, it made no difference to him, at best it made him even calmer and more analytical. But with this lad, with Oleg . . . against this he had no defence.

Oleg gave a bitter laugh. 'Shall we see if I can do it now?' He pressed his middle finger against his thumb. 'Gone . . . there we are!'

Harry held up his palms. 'Oleg . . .'

Oleg shook his head as he knocked on the door behind him, without taking his dark eyes off Harry. 'Guard! Visit's over. Lemme out!'

Harry remained in the chair for a few seconds after Oleg had gone.

Then he struggled to his feet and plodded out into a Bots Park bathed in sunshine.

Harry stood looking up at Police HQ. Pondering. Then he walked up to the custody block. But he stopped halfway, leaned back against a tree and pinched his eyes so hard he could feel he was squeezing out water. Bloody light. Bloody jet lag.

5

'I JUST WANT TO SEE them. I won't take anything,' Harry said.

The duty officer behind the counter at the custody block eyed Harry and wavered.

'Come on, Tore, you know me.'

Nilsen cleared his throat. 'Yeah, but are you working here again, Harry?'

Harry shrugged.

Nilsen tilted his head and lowered his eyelids until his pupils were only half visible. As though he were filtering the optical impression. Filtering out what was unimportant. And what was left evidently fell in Harry's favour.

Nilsen released a heavy sigh, disappeared and returned with a drawer. As Harry had assumed, the items found on Oleg when he was arrested were held there. Only when it was decided prisoners would be on remand for longer than a couple of days were they moved down to Botsen, but personal effects weren't always transferred.

Harry studied the contents. Coins. A ring with two keys, a skull and a Slayer badge. A Swiss army knife with one blade and the rest screwdrivers and Allen keys. A throwaway lighter. And one more object.

It shook Harry, even though he already knew. The newspapers had called it 'a drugs showdown'.

It was a disposable syringe, still in its plastic wrapper.

'Is that all?' Harry asked, taking the key ring. He held it under the counter as he scrutinised the keys. Nilsen clearly did not like Harry holding anything out of his sight and leaned over.

'No wallet?' Harry asked. 'No bank card or ID?'

'Doesn't seem so.'

'Could you check the contents list for me?'

Nilsen picked up the folded list at the bottom of the drawer, fiddled around with his glasses and looked at the sheet. 'There was a mobile phone, but they took it. Probably wanted to see if he had rung the victim.'

'Mm,' Harry said. 'Anything else?'

'What else should there be?' Nilsen said, skimming the sheet. And concluded he had checked everything. 'Nope.'

'Thanks, that was all. Thanks for your help, Nilsen.'

Nilsen nodded slowly. Still wearing his glasses. 'Keys.'

'Yes, right.' Harry put them back in the drawer. Watched Nilsen making sure there were still two.

Harry left, crossed the car park and went into Åkebergveien. Continued down to Tøyen and Urtegata. Little Karachi. Small greengrocers, hijabs and old men on plastic chairs outside their cafes. And to the Watchtower, the Salvation Army cafe for the town's down-and-outs. Harry knew that on days like today it would be quiet, but as soon as winter and the cold came they would be flocking round the tables. Coffee and freshly made sandwiches. A set of clean clothes, the previous year's fashion, blue trainers from the army surplus store. In the sickroom on the first floor: attend to the latest wounds from the narcotic battlefields or – if the situation was dire – a vitamin B injection. Harry considered for a moment whether to drop in on Martine. Perhaps she was still working there. A poet had once written that after the great love there were minor ones. She had been one of the minor ones. But that was not the reason. Oslo was not big, and the heavy users gathered either here or at the Mission Cafe in Skippergata. It was not improbable that she had known Gusto Hanssen. And Oleg.

However, Harry decided to take things in the right order, and started to walk again. Passed the Akerselva. He looked down from the bridge. The brown water Harry remembered from his childhood was as pure as a mountain stream. It was said you could catch trout in it now. There they were, on the paths either side of the river: the dope dealers. Everything was new. Everything was the same.

He went up Hausmanns gate. Passed Jakobskirke. Followed the house numbers. A sign for the Theatre of Cruelty. A graffiti-covered door with a smiley. A burnt-down house, open, cleared. And there it was. A typical Oslo tenement building, built in the 1800s, pale, sober, four storeys. Harry pushed the front door, which opened. Not locked. It led straight to the stairway. Which smelt of piss and refuse.

Harry noted the coded tagging on the way up the floors. Loose banisters. Doors bearing the scars of smashed locks with newer, stronger and additional ones in place. On the second floor he stopped and knew he had found the crime scene. Orange-and-white tape criss-crossing the door.

He put his hand into his pocket and took out the two keys he had removed from Oleg's key ring while Nilsen was reading the checklist. Harry wasn't sure which of his own keys he had used to replace them, but Hong Kong was not, after all, the hardest place to have new ones made.

One key was an Abus, which Harry knew was a padlock since he had once bought one himself. But the other was a Ving. He inserted it in the lock. It went half in, then stopped. He pushed harder. Tried twisting.

'Shit.'

He took out his mobile phone. Her number was listed in his contacts as B. As there were only eight names stored, one letter was enough.

'Lønn.'

What Harry liked best about Beate Lønn, apart from the fact that she was one of the two best forensics officers he had worked with, was that she always reduced information to the basics, and that – like Harry – she never weighed a case down with superfluous words.

'Hi, Beate. I'm in Hausmanns gate.'

'The crime scene? What are you doing . . .?'

'I can't get in. Have you got the key?'

'Have I got the key?'

'You're in charge of the whole shebang up there, aren't you?'

'Course I've got the key. But I've no intention of giving it to you.'

'Course not. But there are a couple of things you've got to double-check at the crime scene, aren't there? I remember something about a guru saying that in murder cases a forensics officer can never be thorough enough.'

'So you remember that, do you.'

'It was the first thing she said to all her trainees. I suppose I can join you and see how you work.'

'Harry . . .'

'I won't touch anything.'

Silence. Harry knew he was exploiting her. She was more than a colleague, she was a friend, but most important of all: she was herself a mother.

She sighed. 'Give me twenty.'

Saying 'minutes' for her was superfluous.

Saying thank you for him was superfluous. So Harry rang off.

Officer Truls Berntsen walked slowly through the corridors of Orgkrim. Because it was his experience that the slower his steps the faster time went. And if there was anything he had enough of it was time. Awaiting him in the office was a worn chair and a small desk with a pile of reports that were there mostly for appearances' sake. A computer he used mostly for surfing, but even that had become boring after there had been a crackdown on which websites they could visit. And since he worked with narc and not sexual offences he could soon find himself having to give an explanation. Officer Berntsen carried the brimful cup of coffee through the door to the desk. Paid attention not to spill it on the brochure for the new Audi Q5. 218 horsepower. SUV, but not a Paki car. Bandit car. Left the Volvo V70 patrol car standing. A car that showed you were someone. Showed her, she of the new house in Høyenhall, that you were someone. Not a nobody.

Keeping the status quo. That was the focus now. We've achieved definite gains, Mikael had said at the general meeting on Monday. Which meant: make sure no one new gets their oar in. 'We can always wish there were even fewer narcotics on the streets. But having achieved so much in such a short time there is always the danger of a relapse. Remember Hitler and Moscow. We shouldn't bite off more than we can chew.'

Officer Berntsen knew in rough terms what that meant. Long days with your feet on the desk.

Sometimes he longed to be back at Kripos. Murder was not like narc, it wasn't politics, it was just solving a case, period. But Mikael Bellman himself had insisted Truls should accompany him from Bryn to Police HQ, said he needed allies down there in enemy territory, someone he could trust, someone who could cover his flank if he was attacked. Said it without saying it: the way Mikael had covered Truls's flank. As in the recent case of the boy on remand with whom Truls had been a bit heavy-handed and who, so terribly unfortunate, had received an injury to the face. Mikael had given Truls a bollocking, of course, said he hated police violence, didn't want to see it in his department, said that now, alas, it was his responsibility as boss to report Truls to the police lawyer, then she would assess whether it should go further to the Special Unit. But the boy's eyesight had returned to almost normal, Mikael had dealt with the boy's solicitor, the charge of possessing drugs had been dropped, and nothing happened after that.

The same as nothing happened here.

Long days with feet on the desk.

And that was where Truls was about to put them – as he did at least ten times a day – when he looked out onto Bots Park and the old linden tree in the middle of the avenue leading up to the prison.

It had been put up.

The red poster.

He felt his skin tingle, his pulse rise. And his mood.

In a flash he was up, his jacket was on and his coffee abandoned.

Gamlebyen Church was a brisk eight-minute walk from Police HQ. Truls Berntsen walked down Oslo gate to Minne Park, left over Dyvekes Bridge and he was in the heart of Oslo, where the town had originated. The church was unadorned to the point of appearing poor, without any of the trite ornaments on the new Romantic church by Police HQ. But Gamlebyen Church had a more exciting history. At least if half of what his grandmother had told him during his childhood in Manglerud was true. The Berntsen family had moved from a dilapidated city-centre block to the satellite town of Manglerud when it was constructed at the end of the 1950s. But, strangely enough, it was them – the genuine Oslo family with Berntsen workers spanning three generations – who felt like immigrants. For most people in the satellite towns were farmers or people who came to town from far away to create a new life. And when Truls's father got drunk in the seventies and the eighties and sat in their flat shouting at everyone and everything, Truls fled to his best – and only – friend, Mikael. Or down to his grandmother in Gamlebyen. She had told him that Gamlebyen Church had been built on top of a monastery from the 1200s, in which the monks had locked themselves away from the Black Death to pray, though folk said it was to escape their Christian duty to tend the contagion carriers. When, after eight months without a sign of life, the Chancellor broke down the doors of the monastery, rats were feasting on the monks' rotting bodies.

His grandmother's favourite bedtime story was about when a lunatic asylum – known locally as 'The Madhouse' – was built on the same site, and some of the inmates complained that hooded men were walking the corridors at night. And that when one of the hoods was ripped off, a pale face was seen, with rat bites and empty eye sockets. But the story Truls liked best was the one about Askild Øregod, Askild Good Ears. He lived and died more than a hundred years ago, at the time Kristiania, as Oslo was known then, became a proper town, and a church had long existed on the site. It was said that his ghost walked the cemetery, adjacent streets, the harbour district and Kvadraturen. But never further because he had only one leg and needed to get back to his grave before light, his grandmother said. Askild Øregod had lost his leg under the wheel of a fire wagon when he was three, but Truls's grandmother said the fact that they gave him a nickname based on his large ears instead was an example of Oslo East humour. They were hard times, and for a child with one leg the choice of occupation was fairly obvious. So Askild Øregod begged and became a familiar sight hobbling through the burgeoning town, always friendly and always ready for a chat. And in particular with those sitting in pubs during the day. Without a job. Yet sometimes they suddenly had money in their hands. Then the odd coin often came Askild's way as well. But occasionally Askild needed a bit more, and then he would tell the police which of them had been extra generous of late. And who, well into the fourth glass, and – unsuspecting of the harmless beggar on the periphery – told others that they had been offered the chance to rob the goldsmith in Karl Johans gate, or a timber merchant in Drammen. Rumours began to spread that Askild's ears were indeed good, and after a gang of robbers in Kampen were arrested, Askild disappeared. He was never seen again, but one winter's morning, on the steps of Gamlebyen Church, a crutch and two severed ears appeared. Askild had been buried somewhere in the graveyard, but as no priest had pronounced his blessing, his spirit still walked abroad. And after the onset of night, in Kvadraturen or around the church, you could bump into a man, hobbling with his cap pulled well over his head, begging for two øre. And then it was bad luck not to give the beggar a coin.

That was what his grandmother had told him. Nevertheless, Truls Berntsen ignored the lean beggar with the foreign coat and tanned skin sitting by the cemetery gate, strode down the gravel between the gravestones as he counted, turned left when he got to seven, to the right when he got to three and stopped by the fourth gravestone.

The name carved into the gravestone meant nothing to him. A. C. Rud. He had died as Norway gained its independence in 1905, only twenty-nine years old, but apart from the name and the dates there was no text, no imperative to rest in peace, nor any other winged words. Perhaps because the coarse gravestone was so small. But the blank, rough surface of the stone meant it was perfect for chalking messages, which must have been why they chose it.

LTZHUSCRDTO RNBU

Truls deciphered the text, using the simple code they had developed so that casual passers-by wouldn't understand. He began at the end, and read the letters in pairs, moving backwards along the line until he reached the final three letters.

BURN TORD SCHULTZ

Truls Berntsen didn't write it down. Didn't need to. He had a good memory for names that brought him closer to the leather seats in an Audi Q5 2.0 6-speed manual. He used his jacket sleeve to erase the letters.

The beggar looked up as Truls passed on his way out. Brown doggy eyes. There was probably a band of beggars and a big, fat car waiting somewhere. Mercedes, wasn't that what they liked? The church bell rang. According to the price list, a Q5 cost 666,000 kroner. If there was a hidden message in those figures, it went way over Truls Berntsen's head.

'You look good,' Beate said as she inserted the key into the lock. 'Got a new finger, as well.'

'Made in Hong Kong,' Harry said, rubbing the short titanium stump.

He observed the small, pale woman as she unlocked the door. The short, thin, blonde hair held in a band. Her skin so fragile and transparent that he could see the fine network of veins in her temple. She reminded him of the hairless mice they used in experiments for cancer research.

'As you wrote that Oleg was living at the crime scene I thought his keys would give me access.'

'That lock was probably destroyed ages ago,' Beate said, pushing the door open. 'You just walked straight in. We had this lock fitted so that none of the addicts would come back and contaminate the scene.'

Harry nodded. It was typical of crack dens. No point having a lock, they were destroyed immediately. First of all, junkies broke into places where they knew the occupants might have drugs. Second, even those who lived there stole from each other.

Beate pulled the tape to the side, and Harry squeezed in. Clothes and plastic bags hung from hooks in the hall. Harry peered into one of the bags. Paper towel rolls, empty beer cans, a wet bloodstained T-shirt, bits of aluminium foil, a cigarette packet. Against one wall was a stack of Grandiosa boxes, a leaning tower of pizza that rose halfway to the ceiling. Four identical white coat stands. Harry was puzzled until he realised they were probably stolen goods they had been unable to convert into cash. He remembered that in junkie flats they were forever coming across things someone had thought they could sell at some point. In one place they had found sixty hopelessly out-of-date mobile phones in a bag, in another a partly dismantled moped parked in the kitchen.

Harry stepped into the sitting room. It smelt of a mixture of sweat, beer-soaked wood, wet ash and something sweet which Harry was unable to identify. The room had no furniture in any conventional sense. Four mattresses lay on the floor as if round a campfire. From one protruded a piece of wire bent at ninety degrees, shaped into a Y at the end. The square of wood floor between the mattresses was black with scorch marks around an empty ashtray. Harry assumed the SOC unit had emptied it.

'Gusto was by the kitchen wall, here,' Beate said. She had stopped in the doorway between the sitting room and kitchen, and was pointing.

Instead of going into the kitchen Harry stayed by the door and looked around. This was a habit. Not the habit of forensics officers, who worked the scene from the outside, started the fine-combing on the periphery and then made their way bit by bit towards the body. Nor was it the habit of a uniformed officer or a patrol car cop, the first police on the scene, who were aware they might contaminate the evidence with their own prints or, worse, destroy the ones there were. Beate's people had done what had to be done ages ago. This was the habit of the investigating detective. Who knows he has only one chance to let his sensory impressions, the almost imperceptible details, do their own talking, leave their prints before the cement sets. It had to happen now, before the analytical part of the brain resumed its functioning, the part that demanded fully formulated facts. Harry used to define intuition as simple, logical conclusions drawn from normal impressions that the brain was unable, or too slow, to convert into something comprehensible.

This crime scene, however, did not tell Harry much about the murder that had taken place.

All he saw, heard and smelt was a place with floating tenants who gathered, took drugs, slept, on the rare occasion ate and, after a while, drifted off. To another squat, to a room in a hostel, a park, a container, a cheap down sleeping bag under a bridge or a white wooden resting place beneath a gravestone.

'Of course we had to do a fair bit of clearing up here,' Beate said in answer to a question he had not needed to ask. 'There was rubbish everywhere.'

'Dope?'

'A plastic bag containing unboiled wads of cotton wool.'

Harry nodded. The most tortured or destitute junkies would save the cotton wool they used to cleanse the impurities from the dope as they drew it into the syringe. Then, on rainy days, the cotton wool could be boiled and the brew injected. 'Plus a condom filled with semen and heroin.'

'Oh?' Harry raised an eyebrow. 'Any good?'

Harry saw her blush, an echo of the shy policewoman fresh out of college he still remembered.

'Remains of heroin, to be precise. We assume the condom was used to store it, and then after it was consumed, the condom was used for its primary purpose.'

'Mm,' Harry said. 'Junkies who worry about contraception. Not bad. Did you find out who . . .?'

'The DNA from inside and outside the condom match two old acquaintances. A Swedish girl and Ivar Torsteinsen, better known to undercover men as Hivar.'

'Hivar?'

'Used to threaten police with infected needles, claimed he had HIV.'

'Mm, explains the condom. Any violence on his record?'

'No. Just hundreds of burglaries, possession and dealing. Plus a bit of smuggling.'

'But threatened murder with a syringe?'

Beate sighed and stepped into the sitting room, her back to him. 'Sorry, Harry, but there are no loose threads in this case.'

'Oleg has never hurt a fly, Beate. He simply doesn't have it in him. While this Hivar—'

'Hivar and the Swedish girl are . . . well, they have been eliminated from inquiries, you might say.'

Harry looked at her back. 'Dead?'

'OD'd. A week before the murder. Impure heroin mixed with fentanyl. I suppose they couldn't afford violin.'

Harry let his gaze run around the walls. Most serious addicts without a fixed abode had a stash or two, a secret place where they could hide or lock up a reserve supply of drugs. Sometimes money. Possibly other priceless possessions. Carrying these things around with you was out of the question, a homeless junkie had to shoot up in public places and the moment the dope kicked in, he was prey to vultures. For that reason stashes were sacred. An otherwise lifeless addict could invest so much energy and imagination in hiding his gear that even veteran searchers and sniffer dogs failed to find it. Addicts never revealed hiding places to anyone, not even to best friends. Because they knew, knew from experience, that no one could ever be closer than codeine, morphine or heroin.

'Have you looked for a stash here?'

Beate shook her head.

'Why not?' Harry asked, knowing it was a stupid question.

'Because I presume we would have had to rip the flat apart to find anything, and it wouldn't have been relevant to the investigation anyway,' Beate said patiently. 'Because we have to prioritise limited resources. And because we had the evidence we needed.'

Harry nodded. The answer he deserved.

'And the evidence?' he asked in a soft voice.

'We believe the killer fired from where I'm standing now.' It was a custom among forensics officers not to use names. She stretched out her arm in front of her. 'At close quarters. Less than a metre. Soot in and around the entry wounds.'

'Plural?'

'Two shots.'

She eyed him with a sympathetic expression that said she knew what he was thinking: there went the defence counsel's chance to maintain the gun had gone off by accident.

'Both shots entered his chest.' Beate spread the first and middle fingers of her right hand and placed them against the left side of her blouse, as though using sign language. 'Assuming that both victim and killer were standing and the killer fired the weapon on instinct, the first exit wound reveals that he was between one eighty and one eighty-five. The suspect is one eighty-three.'

Jesus. He thought of the boy he had seen by the Visitors' Room door. It seemed like only yesterday when they used to wrestle each other and Oleg had barely reached up to Harry's chest.

She walked back into the kitchen. Pointed to the wall beside a greasy stove.

'The bullets went in here and here, as you can see. Which is consistent with the second shot following the first quite quickly as the victim fell. The initial bullet punctured a lung, the second passed through the top of his chest nicking a shoulder blade. The victim—'

'Gusto Hanssen,' Harry said.

Beate stopped. Looked at him. Nodded. 'Gusto Hanssen did not die at once. His fingerprints were in the pool of blood and there was blood on his clothes, showing that he moved after he fell. But it can't have taken long.'

'I see. And what . . .?' Harry ran a hand over his face. He would have to try to get a few hours' sleep. 'What ties Oleg to the murder?'

'Two people rang the switchboard at three minutes to nine saying they had heard what might have been gunshots coming from the block. One lived in Møllergata, over the crossing, the other just opposite here.'

Harry squinted through the grimy window looking out onto Hausmanns gate. 'Not bad going, being able to hear from one block to another in the very centre of the city.'

'Don't forget it was July. Warm evening. All the windows are open, Summer holidays, barely any traffic. The neighbours had been trying to get the police to close this nest, so the threshold for reporting noise was low, one might say. The officer in the Ops Room told them to stay calm and asked them to keep an eye on the block until patrol cars arrived. The uniforms were alerted at once. Two cars arrived at twenty past nine and took up position while waiting for the cavalry.'

'Delta?'

'Always takes the boys a bit of time to don helmets and armour. Then the patrol cars were informed by Ops that the neighbours had seen a boy leaving by the front door and walking round the block, down towards the Akerselva. So two officers went down to the river, and there they found . . .'

She paused until she received an almost imperceptible nod from Harry.

'. . . Oleg. He didn't resist, he was so doped up he hardly knew what he was doing. We found gunshot residue on his right hand and arm.'

'Murder weapon?'

'Since it's an unusual calibre, a nine-by-eighteen-millimetre Makarov, there are not many alternatives.'

'Well, the Makarov is the favourite gun for organised crime in former Soviet countries. And the Fort 12, which is used by the police in Ukraine. Plus a couple more.'

'True. We found the empty cartridges on the floor with powder residue. The Makarov powder has a different mix of saltpetre and sulphur, and they also use a bit of spirit, like in sulphurless powder. The chemical compound of the powder on the empty cartridge and around the entry wound matches the residue on Oleg's hand.'

'Mm. And the weapon?'

'Hasn't been recovered. We had divers and teams searching in and around the river, with no success. That doesn't mean the gun isn't there, with all the mud and sludge . . . well, you know.'

'I know.'

'Two of the guys who lived here said that Oleg was flashing a pistol and boasting it was the type the Russian mafia used. Neither of them is gun-savvy, but after being shown pictures of about a hundred guns both are supposed to have picked out an Odessa. And it uses, as you probably know . . .'

Harry nodded. Makarov, nine by eighteen millimetre. It was unmistakable. The first time he had seen an Odessa, he had been reminded of the old futuristic-looking pistol on the cover of *Foo Fighters*, one of many CDs that had ended up with Rakel and Oleg.

'And I assume they're rock-solid witnesses with only a tiny little drug problem?'

Beate didn't answer. She didn't need to. Harry knew she knew what he was doing, grasping at straws.

'And Oleg's blood and urine samples,' Harry said, straightening his jacket sleeves, as if it were important, here and now, that they didn't ride up. 'What did they reveal?'

'Violin was an active ingredient. Being high might be seen as a mitigating circumstance of course.'

'Mm. That presupposes he was high before he shot Gusto Hanssen. But what about the motive then?'

Beate sent Harry a vacant stare. 'The motive?'

He knew what she was thinking: is it possible to imagine one addict killing another for anything other than dope? 'If Oleg was already high why would he kill anyone?' he asked. 'Drug-related murders like this one are as a rule a spontaneous, desperate act, motivated by a craving for drugs or the start of withdrawal symptoms.'

'Motive's your department,' Beate said. 'I'm in Forensics.'

Harry breathed in. 'OK. Anything else?'

'I imagined you would want to see the photos,' Beate said, opening a slim leather case.

Harry took the pile of photographs. The first thing to strike him was Gusto's beauty. There was no other expression for it. Handsome, attractive didn't cover it. Even dead, with closed eyes and his shirt soaked in blood, Gusto Hanssen still had the indefinable but evident beauty of a young Elvis Presley, the kind of looks that appeal to both men and women, like the androgynous beautification of idols you find in every religion. He thumbed through. After several full-length shots the photographer had taken close-ups of the face and the bullet wounds.

'What's that?' he asked, pointing to a picture of Gusto's right hand.

'He had blood under his fingernails. We took swabs, but I'm afraid they were destroyed.'

'Destroyed?'

'It can happen, Harry.'

'Not in your department.'

'The blood was destroyed on the way to DNA testing in the Pathology Unit. In fact, we weren't that upset. The blood was quite fresh, but still congealed enough for it not to be relevant to the time of the murder. And, inasmuch as the victim was a needle addict, it was highly probable it was his own. But . . .'

'. . . But if not, it's always interesting to know who he had been fighting with that day. Look at his shoes . . .' He showed Beate one of the full-length shots. 'Aren't they Alberto Fascianis?'

'Had no idea you knew so much about shoes, Harry.'

'One of my clients in Hong Kong manufactures them.'

'Client, eh? And to my knowledge original Fasciani shoes are manufactured only in Italy.'

Harry shrugged. 'Impossible to see the difference. But if they are Fascianis they don't exactly match the rest of his clothes. Looks like an outfit doled out by the Watchtower.'

'The shoes could be stolen,' Beate said. 'Gusto Hanssen's nickname was the Thief. He was famous for stealing anything he came across, not least dope. There's a story going round that he stole a retired sniffer dog in Sweden and used it to sniff out drug stashes.'

'Perhaps he found Oleg's,' Harry said. 'Has he said anything under questioning?'

'Still as silent as a clam. The only thing he says is it's all a black void. He doesn't even remember being in the flat.'

'Perhaps he wasn't.'

'We found his DNA, Harry. Hair, sweat.'

'He did live and sleep here.'

'On the body, Harry.'

Harry fell silent, stared into the distance.

Beate raised a hand, perhaps to put on his shoulder, but changed her mind and let it drop. 'Have you had a chat with him?'

Harry shook his head. 'He threw me out.'

'He's ashamed.'

'Guess so.'

'I mean it. You're his idol. It's humiliating for him to be seen in this state.'

'Humiliating? I've dried the boy's tears, I've blown on his grazes. Chased away trolls and left the light on.'

'That boy no longer exists, Harry. The present Oleg doesn't want to be helped by you now; he wants to live up to you.'

Harry stamped on the floorboards while looking at the wall. 'I'm not worth it, Beate. He knows that.'

'Harry . . .'

'Shall we go down to the river?'

Sergey stood in front of the mirror with both arms hanging down by his sides. Flicked the safety catch and pressed the button. The blade shot out and reflected the light. It was an attractive knife, a Siberian switchblade, or 'the iron' as the urkas – the criminal class in Siberia – called it. It was the world's best weapon to stab with. A long, slim shaft with a long, thin blade. The tradition was that you were given it from an older criminal in the family when you had done something to deserve it. However, traditions were receding; nowadays you bought, stole or pirated the knife. This knife, though, had been a present from his uncle. According to Andrey, *ataman* had kept the knife under his mattress before it was given to Sergey. He thought about the myth that if you put the iron under the mattress of a sick person it absorbed the pain and suffering and transferred them to the next person stabbed with it. This was one of the myths the urkas loved so much, like the one that claimed if anyone came into the possession of your knife he would soon meet with an accident and death. Old romanticism and superstition, which were on their way out. Nonetheless, he had received the gift with enormous, perhaps exaggerated, reverence. And why shouldn't he? He owed his uncle everything. He was the one who had got him out of the trouble he had landed in, organised his papers so that he could come to Norway; his uncle had even sorted out the cleaning job at Gardermoen for him. It was well paid, and easy to find, but apparently it was the type of work Norwegians declined; they preferred to draw social security. And the minor offences Sergey brought with him from Russia were no problem either; his uncle had had his criminal record doctored. So Sergey had kissed his benefactor's blue ring when he was given the present. And Sergey had to admit that the knife in his hand was very beautiful. A dark brown handle made from deer horn inlaid with an ivory-coloured Orthodox cross.

Sergey pushed from the hip the way he had been taught, could feel he was properly poised, and thrust upwards. In and out. In and out. Fast, but not so fast that the blade did not enter to the hilt, each and every time.

The reason it had to be with the knife was that the man he was going to kill was a policeman. And when policemen are killed the hunt afterwards was always more intensive, so it was vital to leave as few clues as possible. A bullet could always be traced back to places, weapons or people. A slash from a smooth, clean knife was anonymous. A stabbing wasn't quite as anonymous, it could reveal the length and shape of the blade, that was why Andrey had told him not to stab the policeman in the heart, but to cut his carotid artery. Sergey had never cut anyone's throat before, nor stabbed anyone in the heart, just knifed a Georgian in the thigh for no more than being a Georgian. So he had decided he needed something to train on, something living. His Pakistani neighbour had three cats, and every morning he walked into the entrance hall the smell of cat piss assailed his nostrils.

Sergey lowered his knife, stood with bowed head, rolled his eyeballs upwards so that he could see himself in the mirror. He looked good: fit, menacing, dangerous, ready. Like a film poster. His tattoo would reveal that he had killed a police officer.

He would stand behind the policeman. Step forward. With his left hand he would grab his hair, pull him backwards. Place the knife tip against his neck, to the left, penetrate the skin, arc the blade across the throat in a crescent shape. Like that.

The heart would pump out a cascade of blood; three heartbeats and the flow would diminish. The man would already be brain-dead.

Fold the knife, slip it into his pocket as he left, fast, but not too fast. Don't look anyone in the eye. Walk, and feel free.

He stepped back a pace. Stood up straight, inhaled. Visualised the scene. Released his breath. Stepped forward. Angled the blade so that it had a wonderful glint, like a precious jewel.

6

BEATE AND HARRY CAME OUT of Hausmanns gate, turned left, rounded the corner of the block and crossed the site of the burnt building, still with blackened glass shards and scorched bricks in the rubble. Behind it, an overgrown slope ran down to the river. Harry noted there were no doors at the back of Oleg's block and that, in the absence of any other way out, there was a narrow fire escape descending from the top floor.

'Who lives in the neighbouring flat?' Harry asked.

'No one,' Beate said. 'Empty offices. It's where *Anarkisten*, a little newspaper that—'

'I know it. It wasn't a bad fanzine. The writers of the culture section work on the big papers now. Were the rooms unlocked?'

'Broken into. Probably been open for a long time.'

Harry watched Beate, who with a resigned air nodded confirmation of what Harry didn't need to say: someone could have been in Oleg's flat and escaped unseen. Straws.

They walked down to the path along the Akerselva. Harry established that the river was narrow enough for a boy with a decent throwing arm to lob the gun over to the opposite bank.

'If you haven't found the gun yet—' Harry said.

'The prosecuting counsel doesn't need the gun, Harry.'

He nodded. Gunshot residue on his hands. Witnesses who had seen him showing off with the gun. His DNA on the dead boy.

Ahead of them, leaning against a green iron bench, two white boys in grey hoodies saw them, put their heads together and shuffled off down the path.

'Looks like pushers can still smell the cop in you, Harry.'

'Mm. Thought it was just Moroccans who sold hash here.'

'Competition has moved in. Kosovar Albanians, Somalis, Eastern Europeans. Asylum seekers selling the whole spectrum. Speed, methamphetamine, Ecstasy, morphine.'

'Heroin.'

'Doubtful. There's almost no standard heroin to be found in Oslo. Violin is what counts, and you can get that only round Plata. Unless you want to travel to Gothenburg or Copenhagen, where apparently violin has made a recent appearance.'

'I keep hearing about this violin stuff. What is it?'

'New synthetic dope. It doesn't hinder breathing as much as standard heroin, so even if it ruins lives there are fewer overdoses. Extremely addictive. Everyone who tries it wants more. But it's so expensive not many can afford it.'

'So they buy other dope instead?'

'There's a morphine bonanza.'

'One step forward, two steps back.'

Beate shook her head. 'It's the war on heroin that's important. And he's won that one.'

'Bellman?'

'So you've heard?'

'Hagen said he's busted most of the heroin gangs.'

'The Pakistani gangs. The Vietnamese. *Dagbladet* called him General Rommel after he smashed a major network of North Africans. The MC gang in Alnabru. They're all banged up.'

'The bikers? In my time biker boys sold speed and shot heroin like crazy.'

'Los Lobos. Hell's Angels wannabes. We reckon they were one of only two networks dealing in violin. But they were caught in a mass arrest with a subsequent raid in Alnabru. You should have seen the smirk on Bellman's chops in the papers. He was there when they carried out the operation.'

'Let's do some good?'

Beate laughed. Another feature he liked about her: she was enough of a film buff to be on the ball when he quoted semi-good lines from semi-bad films. Harry offered her a cigarette, which she declined. He lit up.

'Mm. How the hell did Bellman achieve what the Narc Unit wasn't even close to achieving in all the years I was at HQ?'

'I know you don't like him, but in fact he's a good leader. They loved him at Kripos, and they're pissed off with the Chief of Police for taking him to Police HQ.'

'Mm.' Harry inhaled. Felt it pacify his blood's hunger. Nicotine. A polysyllabic word, like heroin, like violin. 'So who's left?'

'That's the snag with exterminating pests. You upset a food chain and you don't know if all you've done is make way for something else. Something worse than what you removed . . .'

'Any evidence of that?'

Beate shrugged.

'All of a sudden we're not getting any info off the streets. Our informers don't know anything. Or they're keeping shtum. There are just whispers about the man from Dubai. No one has seen him, no one knows his name, he's a kind of invisible puppeteer. We can see violin is being sold, but we can't trace it back to its source. The pushers we nab say they've bought off other sellers at the same level. It's not normal for tracks to be covered so well. And that tells us this is a simple, very professional outfit controlling import and distribution.'

'The man from Dubai. The mysterious mastermind. Haven't we heard that story before? And then he turns out to be a run-of-the-mill crook.'

'This is different, Harry. There were a number of drugs-related murders over the new year. A type of brutality we haven't seen before. And no one says a word. Two Vietnamese dealers are found hanging upside down from a beam in the flat where they worked. Drowned. Each one had a plastic bag filled with water on his head.'

'That's not an Arab method, it's Russian.'

'Sorry?'

'They hang them upside down, put a plastic bag over their heads and tie it loosely, around the neck. Then they begin to pour water down their heels. It follows the body down to the bag and fills it up. The method's called the Man on the Moon.'

'How do you know that?'

Harry shrugged. 'There was a wealthy surgeon called Birayev. In the eighties he got his hands on one of the original astronaut suits from *Apollo* 11. Two million dollars on the black market. Anyone who tried to pull a fast one on Birayev or didn't pay a debt was put in the suit. They filmed the face of the poor guy as they poured in the water. Afterwards the film was sent round to other debtors.'

Harry blew smoke towards the ceiling.

Beate sent him a lingering look and slowly shook her head. 'What have you been doing in Hong Kong, Harry?'

'You asked me that on the phone.'

'And you didn't answer.'

'Exactly. Hagen said he could give me another case instead of this one. Mentioned something about an undercover guy who was killed.'

'Yes,' Beate said, sounding relieved that they were no longer talking about the Gusto case and Oleg.

'What was that about?'

'A young undercover Narc agent. He was washed ashore where the Opera House slopes into the water. Tourists, children, and so on. Big hullabaloo.'

'Shot?'

'Drowned.'

'And how do you know it was murder?'

'No external injuries; in fact, it looked as if he might have fallen into the sea by accident – his beat was the area around the Opera House. But then Bjørn Holm checked his lungs. Turned out it was fresh water. And Oslo fjord is salt water as you know. Looks like someone chucked him in the sea to make it look as if he had drowned there.'

'Well,' Harry said, 'as a Narc agent he must have wandered up and down the river. That's fresh water and it flows into the sea by the Opera House.'

Beate smiled. 'Good to have you back, Harry. But Bjørn thought about that, and compared the bacterial flora, the content of microorganisms, and so on. The water in his lungs was too clean to have come from the Akerselva. It had been through water filters. My guess is he drowned in a bath. Or in a pool below the water-purification plant. Or . . .'

Harry threw the butt down on the path in front of him. 'A plastic bag.'

'Yes.'

'The Man from Dubai. What do you know about him?'

'What I've just told you, Harry.'

'You didn't tell me anything.'

'Exactly.'

They stopped by Anker Bridge. Harry checked his watch.

'Going somewhere?' Beate asked.

'Nope,' Harry answered. 'I did it to give you a pretext to say you've got to be off, without feeling you were dumping me.'

Beate smiled. She was quite attractive when she smiled, Harry thought. Strange that she wasn't with someone. Or perhaps she was. One of the eight in his phone contacts list, and he didn't even know that.

B for Beate.

H was for Halvorsen, Harry's ex-colleague and the father of Beate's child. Killed on active duty. But his number still hadn't been deleted.

'Have you contacted Rakel?' Beate asked.

R. Harry wondered if her name had come up as a result of association with the word 'dump'. He shook his head. Beate waited. But he had nothing to add.

They both started to speak at the same time.

'I suppose you've—'

'In fact, I have—'

She smiled. '—got to be off.'

'Of course.'

He watched her walk up towards the road.

Then he sat on one of the benches and stared at the river, at the ducks paddling in a quiet backwater.

The two hoodies returned. Came over to him.

'Are you five-o?'

American slang for police, stolen from a supposedly authentic TV series. It was Beate they had smelt, not him.

Harry shook his head.

'After some . . .?'

'Some peace,' Harry completed. 'Peace and quiet.'

He took a pair of Prada sunglasses from his inside pocket. He had been given them by a shopowner on Canton Road who was a bit behind with payments, but who considered himself fairly treated. They were a ladies' model, but Harry didn't care, he liked them.

'By the way,' he called after them, 'got any violin?'

One snorted by way of response. 'Town centre,' the other said, pointing over his shoulder.

'Where precisely?'

'Look for Van Persie or Fàbregas.' Their laughter faded as they headed towards Blå, the jazz club.

Harry leaned back and studied the ducks' strangely efficient kick that allowed them to glide across the water like speed skaters on black ice.

Oleg was keeping his mouth shut. The way the guilty keep their mouths shut. That is their privilege and sole rational strategy. So where to go from here? How do you investigate something that is already solved, answer questions that have already found adequate answers? What did he think he could achieve? Defeat the truth by denying it? The way he, in his role as a Crime Squad detective, had seen relatives produce the pathetic refrain: 'My son? Not a chance!' He knew why he wanted to investigate crimes. Because it was the only thing he could do. The only thing he had to contribute. He was the housewife who insisted on cooking at her son's wake, the musician who took his instrument to his friend's funeral. The need to do something, as a distraction or a gesture of comfort.

One of the ducks glided towards him, hoping for a few crumbs of bread perhaps. Not because it was confident, but you never knew. It had calculated consumption of energy versus probability of reward. Hope. Black ice.

Harry sat up with a start. Took the keys from his jacket pocket. He had just remembered why he had bought the padlock that time. It hadn't been for himself. It had been for the speed skater. For Oleg.

7

OFFICER TRULS BERNTSEN HAD HAD a brief discussion with the duty inspector at the airport. Berntsen had said yes, he knew the airport was in the Romerike Police District, and he had nothing to do with the arrest, but as a Special Operations detective he had been keeping an eye on the arrested man for a while and had recently been warned by one of his sources that Tord Schultz had been caught with narcotics in his possession. He had held up his ID card showing he was a grade 3 police officer, employed in Oslo Police District by Special Operations and Orgkrim. The inspector had shrugged and without further ado taken him to one of the three remand cells.

After the cell door had slammed behind Truls he looked around to ensure the corridor and the other two cells were empty. Then he sat down on the toilet lid and looked at the slat bed and the man with his head buried in his hands.

'Tord Schultz?'

The man raised his head. He had removed his jacket, and had it not been for the flashes on his shirt Berntsen would not have recognised him as the chief pilot of an aircraft. Captains should not look like this. Not petrified, pale, with pupils that were large and black with shock. On the other hand, it was how most people looked after they had been apprehended for the first time. It had taken Berntsen a little while to locate Tord Schultz in the airport. But the rest was easy. According to STRASAK, the official criminal register, Schultz did not have a record, had never had any dealings with the police and was – according to their unofficial register – not someone with known links to the drugs community.

'Who are you?'

'I'm here on behalf of the people you work for, Schultz, and I don't mean the airline. Screw the rest. Alright?'

Schultz pointed to the ID card hanging from a string around Berntsen's neck. 'You're a policeman. You're trying to trick me.'

'It would be good news if I was, Schultz. It would be a breach of procedures and a chance for your solicitor to have you acquitted. But we'll manage this without solicitors. Alright?'

The airline captain continued to stare with dilated pupils absorbing all the light they could, the slightest glimpse of optimism. Truls Berntsen sighed. He could only hope that what he was going to say would sink in.

'Do you know what a burner is?' Berntsen asked, pausing only briefly for an answer. 'It's someone who destroys police cases. He makes sure that evidence becomes contaminated or goes missing, that mistakes are made in legal procedures, thus preventing a case from being brought to court, or that everyday blunders are made in the investigation, thus allowing the suspect to walk away free. Do you understand?'

Schultz blinked twice. And nodded slowly.

'Great,' Berntsen said. 'The situation is that we are two men in free fall with the one parachute between us. I've jumped out of the plane to rescue you, for the moment you can spare me the gratitude, but you must trust me one hundred per cent, otherwise we'll both hit the ground. *Capisce?*'

More blinking. Obviously not.

'There was once a German policeman, a burner. He worked for a gang of Kosovar Albanians importing heroin via the Balkan route. The drugs were driven in lorries from the opium fields in Afghanistan to Turkey, transported onwards through ex-Yugoslavia to Amsterdam where the Albanians channelled it on to Scandinavia. Loads of borders to cross, loads of people to be paid. Among them, this burner. And one day a young Kosovar Albanian is caught with a petrol tank full of raw opium, the clumps weren't wrapped up, just put straight into the petrol. He was held in custody, and the same day the Kosovar Albanians contacted their German burner. He went to the young man, explained that he was his burner and he could relax now, they would fix this. The burner said he would be back the next day and tell him what statement to make to the police. All he had to do was keep his mouth shut. But this guy who had been nabbed red-handed had never served time before. He had probably heard too many stories about bending over in the prison showers for the soap; at any rate he cracked like an egg in the microwave at the first interview and blew the whistle on the burner in the hope that he would receive favourable treatment from the judge. So. In order to get evidence against the burner the police put a hidden microphone in the cell. But the burner, the corrupt policeman, did not turn up as arranged. They found him six months later. Spread over a tulip field in bits. I'm a city boy myself, but I've heard bodies make good manure.'

Berntsen stopped and looked at the pilot while waiting for the usual question.

The pilot had sat up straight on the bed, recovered some colour in his face and at length cleared his throat. 'Why . . . erm, the burner? He wasn't the one who grassed.'

'Because there is no justice, Schultz. There are only necessary solutions to practical problems. The burner who was going to destroy the evidence had become evidence himself. He had been rumbled, and if the police caught him he could lead the detectives to the Kosovar Albanians. Since he wasn't one of their brothers, only a corrupt cop, it was logical to expedite him into the beyond. And they knew this was the murder of a policeman the police would not prioritise. Why should they? The burner had already received his punishment, and the police don't set up an investigation where the only goal they will achieve is to inform the public about police corruption. Agreed?'

Schultz didn't answer.

Berntsen leaned forward. The voice went down in volume and up in intensity. 'I do not want to be found in a tulip field, Schultz. Our only way out of this is to trust each other. One parachute. Got that?'

The pilot cleared his throat. 'What about the Kosovar Albanian? Did he have his sentence commuted?'

'Hard to say. He was found hanging from the cell wall before the case came to court. Someone had smashed his head against a clothes hook.'

The captain's face lost its colour again.

'Breathe, Schultz,' Truls Berntsen said. That was what he liked best about this job. The feeling that *he* was in charge for once.

Schultz leaned back and rested his head against the wall. Closed his eyes. 'And if I decline your help outright and we pretend you've never been here?'

'Won't do. Your employer and mine don't want you in the witness box.'

'So, what you're saying is I have no choice?'

Berntsen smiled. And uttered his favourite sentence: 'Schultz, it's a long time since you had any choice.'

Valle Hovin Stadium. A little oasis of concrete in the middle of a desert of green lawns, birch trees, gardens and flowerboxes on verandas. In the winter the track was used as a skating rink, in the summer as a concert venue, by and large for dinosaurs like the Rolling Stones, Prince and Bruce Springsteen. Rakel had even persuaded Harry to go along with her to see U2, although he had always been a club man and hated stadium concerts. Afterwards she had teased Harry that in his heart of hearts he was a closet music fundamentalist.

Most of the time, however, Valle Hovin was as now, deserted, run-down, like a disused factory which had manufactured a product that was no longer used. Harry's best memories from here were seeing Oleg training on the ice. Sitting and watching him try his hardest. Fighting. Failing. Failing. Then succeeding. Not great achievements: a new PB, second place in a club championship for his age group. But more than enough to make Harry's foolish heart swell to such an absurd size that he had to adopt an indifferent air so as not to embarrass both of them. 'Not bad that, Oleg.'

Harry looked around. Not a soul in sight. Then he inserted the Ving key in the lock of the dressing-room door beneath the stands. Inside, everything was unchanged, except more worn. There was refuse on the floor; it was clearly a long time since anyone had been here. It was a place you could be alone. Harry walked between the lockers. Most were not locked. But then he found what he was looking for, the Abus padlock.

He pushed the tip of the key into the jagged aperture. It wouldn't go in. Shit.

Harry turned. Let his eyes glide along the bulky iron cabinets. Stopped, went back one locker. That was another Abus padlock. And there was a circle etched into the green paint. An 'O'.

The first objects Harry saw when he opened up were Oleg's racing skates. The long, slim blades had a kind of red rash along the edge.

On the inside of the cabinet door, stuck to the ventilation grille, were two photographs. Two family photographs. One showed five faces. Two of the children and what he assumed were the parents were unfamiliar. But he recognised the third child. Because he had seen him in other photographs. Crime-scene photographs.

It was the good looks. Gusto Hanssen.

Harry wondered whether it was the good looks that did it, the immediate sensation that Gusto Hanssen did not belong in the photograph. Or, to be precise, that he didn't belong to the family.

The same, strangely enough, could be said about the tall, blond man sitting behind the dark-haired woman and her son in the second photograph. It had been taken one autumn day several years ago. They had gone for a walk in Holmenkollen, waded through the orange-coloured foliage, and Rakel had placed her camera on a rock and pressed the self-timer button.

Was that really him? Harry could not remember having such gentle features.

Rakel's eyes gleamed, and he imagined he could hear her laughter, the laughter he loved, of which he never tired, and always tried to recall.

She laughed with others too, but with him and Oleg it had a different tone, one reserved for them alone.

Harry searched the rest of the locker.

There was a white sweater with a light blue border. Not Oleg's style, he wore short jackets and black T-shirts emblazoned with Slayer and Slipknot. Harry smelt the sweater. Faint perfume, feminine. There was a plastic bag on the hat shelf. He opened it. Quick intake of breath. It was a junkie's kit: two syringes, a spoon, a rubber band, a lighter and some cotton wool. All that was missing was dope. Harry was about to replace the bag when he spotted something. A shirt at the very back. It was red and white. He took it. It was a football shirt with an imperative on the chest: Fly Emirates. Arsenal.

He looked up at the photograph, at Oleg. Even he was smiling. Smiling as though he believes, at least then, that there are three people sitting here who agree that this is wonderful, everything will be fine, this is how we want things to be. So why would it go off course? Why would the man with his hands round the wheel drive off course?

'The way you lied you would always be there for us.'

Harry removed the photos from the locker door and slipped them into his inside pocket.

When he emerged the sun was on its way down behind Ullern Ridge.

8

CAN YOU SEE I'M BLEEDING, Dad? I'm bleeding your bad blood. And your blood, Oleg. It's you the church bells should be tolling for. I curse you, curse the day I met you. You'd been to a gig at Spectrum, Judas Priest. I had been hanging around and joined the crowd of people coming out of the venue.

'Wow, cool T-shirt,' I said. 'Where did you get it?'

You gave me a strange look. 'Amsterdam.'

'Did you see Judas Priest in Amsterdam?'

'Why not?'

I knew nothing about Judas Priest, but at least I had done some swotting and found out it was a band, not a guy, and that the lead singer's name was Rob something or other.

'Great. Priest rules.'

You stiffened for a second and looked at me. Concentrated, like an animal that had caught a scent. A danger, or prey, a sparring partner. Or – in your case – a possible soulmate. For you carried your loneliness like a wet, heavy raincoat, Oleg, you walked with a bent back and shuffled your feet. I had picked you out precisely because of your loneliness. I said I'd buy you a Coke if you told me about the Amsterdam gig.

So you talked about Judas Priest, the concert at Heineken Music Hall two years ago, about the two friends of eighteen and nineteen who shot themselves after listening to a Priest record with a hidden message that said 'Do it'. Except that one of them survived. Priest were heavy metal, had been into speed metal. And twenty minutes later you had spoken so much about goths and death that it was time to introduce meth into the conversation.

'Let's hit the high spots, Oleg. Celebrate this meeting of like minds. What do you say?'

'What do you mean?'

'I know some fun people who are going to do a bit of smoking in the park.'

'Really?' Sceptical.

'No heavy stuff, just ice.'

'I don't do that, sorry.'

'Hell, I don't do it either. We can smoke a bit of pipe. You and me. Real ice, not the powder shit. Like Rob.'

Oleg stopped in mid-gulp. 'Rob?'

'Yes.'

'Rob Halford?'

'Sure. His roadie bought from the same guy I'm going to buy from now. Got any money?'

I said it in such a casual way, such a casual and matter-of-fact way that there was not a shadow of suspicion in the serious eyes he fixed on me. 'Rob Halford smokes ice?'

He forked up the five hundred kroner I asked him for. I told him to wait, got up and left. Down the road to Vaterland Bridge. So, when I was out of range, to the right, I was over the road and down the three hundred metres to Oslo Central Station in minutes. Thinking that would be the last I saw of Oleg fricking Fauke.

It was only when I was sitting in the tunnel under the platforms with a pipe in my mouth that I realised he and I were not finished with each other yet. Nowhere near. He stood above me without saying a word. He leaned against the wall and slid down beside me. Stuck out his hand. I gave him the pipe. He inhaled. Coughed. And stuck out his other hand. 'The change.'

With that, the team of Gusto and Oleg became a fact. Every day, after he had finished at Clas Ohlson, where he had a summer job in the warehouse, we went down to the city centre, the parks, bathed in the filthy water in Middelalder Park, and watched them building a new part of town around the Opera House.

We told each other about all the things we were going to do and become, about the places we would go, smoking and sniffing everything we could buy with his summer job money.

I told him about my foster-father, how he had thrown me out because my foster-mother had made advances on me. And you, Oleg, talked about a guy your mother had been with, a cop called Harry you claimed was 'top notch'. Someone you could trust. But something had gone sour. First of all, between him and your mother. And then you had been dragged into a murder case he was working on. And that was when you and your mother had moved to Amsterdam. I said the guy probably was 'top notch', but it was a pretty corny expression. And you said 'fricking' was even cornier. Had anyone told me the word was 'frigging'? Even that was childish. And why did I speak such exaggerated cockney Norwegian? I wasn't even from the East End of Oslo. I said exaggerating was a principle I had, it emphasised a point and 'fricking' was so wrong it was right. And the sun shone, and I thought that was the best thing anyone had said about me.

We begged for money on Karl Johans gate for fun. I nicked a skateboard from Rådhusplassen and swapped it for speed on Jernbanetorget half an hour later. We took the boat to Hovedøya, swam and bummed beers. Some girls wanted me to join them in Daddy's yacht and you dived from the mast, only just clearing the deck. We caught the tram to Ekeberg to see the sunset and there was the Norway Cup, and a sad football coach from Trøndelag was looking at me, and I said I would give him a blow job for a thousand kroner. He stumped up and I waited until his trousers were round his ankles before I scarpered. And you told me afterwards he had looked 'totally lost' and turned to you, as if asking you to take over the job. Jeez, how we laughed!

That summer never ended. Then it did after all. We spent your last pay packet on spliffs, which we blew into the pale, empty night sky. You said you were going to return to school, get top grades and study law, like your mother. And that afterwards you would do fricking Police College! We laughed so much we had tears in our eyes.

But when school began I saw less of you. Then even less. You lived up on Holmenkollen Ridge with your mother while I crashed on a mattress in the rehearsal room of a band who said I was fine there so long as I kept an eye on their gear and stayed away when they were practising. So I gave up on you, thinking you were comfortable back in your conventional little life. And that was about the time I started dealing.

It happened quite by chance. I had milked a woman I was staying with, then I went to Oslo Central and asked Tutu if he had any ice. Tutu had a bit of a stammer and was slave to Odin, the boss of Los Lobos in Alnabru. He had got his name from the time Odin, needing to launder a suitcase of drugs money, had sent Tutu to a state bookies' in Italy to put a bet on a match that Odin knew was fixed. The home team was supposed to win 2–0. Odin had instructed Tutu how to say 'two–nil', but then came the turning point. Tutu was so nervous and stammered so much as he tried to place the bet that the bookie only heard tu-tu and wrote it on the coupon. Ten minutes before the end the home side was of course leading 2–0, and everything was peace and light. Except for Tutu, who had just seen on the betting slip that he had put the money on tu-tu: 2–2. He knew that Odin would kneecap him. He has a thing about kneecapping people. But then came turning-point number two. On the away bench was a new forward from Poland whose Italian was as bad as Tutu's English, so he hadn't picked up that the game was a fix. When the manager sent him onto the field, he played as well as he thought they had paid him to do: he scored. Twice. Tutu was saved. But when Tutu landed in Oslo that night and went straight to Odin to tell him about his stroke of good fortune, his luck evened out. He started by giving the news that he had blundered and put the cash on the wrong result. And he was so worked up and stammered so much that Odin lost patience, grabbed a revolver from a drawer and – turning-point number three – shot Tutu in the knee long before he came to the bit about the Pole.

Anyway, that day at Oslo Central Tutu told me there was no more ice to be h-h-had, I would have to make do with p-p-powder. It was cheaper and both parts are methamphetamine, but I can't stand it. Ice is lovely white bits of crystal that blow your head off whereas the stinking yellow shit you get in Oslo is mixed with baking powder, refined sugar, aspirin, vitamin B12 and the devil and his mother. Or, for connoisseurs, chopped-up painkillers that taste of speed. But I bought what he had with a tiny bulk discount and had enough money left for some A. And since amphetamines are an unadulterated health food compared with meth, just a bit slower to work, I sniffed some speed, diluted the meth with more baking powder and sold it at Plata with a fantastic mark-up.

The next day I went back to Tutu and repeated the biz, plus a bit more. Sniffed some, diluted it and sold the rest. Ditto the day after. I said I could take more if he put it on the tab, but he laughed. When I returned on the fourth day Tutu said his boss thought we should do this on a more est-st-stablished basis. They had seen me selling, and liked what they saw. If I sold two batches a day that meant five thousand straight, no questions asked. And so I became a street pusher for Odin and Los Lobos. I got the goods from Tutu in the morning and delivered the day's takings with any leftovers to him by five. Day shift. There were never any leftovers.

All went well for about three weeks. One Wednesday on Vippetangen quay, I had sold two batches, my pockets were full of cash, my nose was full of speed, when I suddenly saw no reason to meet Tutu at the station. Instead I texted him to say I was going on holiday and jumped on the ferry to Denmark. That's the type of blackout you have to reckon with when you take bumblebees for too long and too often.

On my return I heard a rumour that Odin was on the lookout for me. And it freaked me out a bit, especially as I knew how Tutu got his nickname. So I kept my head down, hung out round Grünerløkka. And waited for Judgement Day. But Odin had bigger things on his mind than a pusher who owed him a few thousand. Competition had come to town. 'The Man from Dubai'. Not in the bumblebee market, but in heroin, which was more important than anything else for Los Lobos. Some said they were White Russians, some said they were Lithuanians, and others a Norwegian

Pakistani. All agreed, however, it was a professional organisation, they feared no one and it was better to know too much rather than too little.

It was a crap autumn.

I had gone broke long ago, I no longer had a job and was forced to keep a low profile. I had found a buyer for the band's equipment in Bispegata, he had been to see it, I'd convinced him it was mine, after all I did live there! It was just a question of agreeing a time to collect it. Then – like a rescuing angel – Irene appeared. Nice, freckled Irene. It was an October morning, and I was busy with some guys in Sofienberg Park when there she was, almost in tears with happiness. I asked if she had any money, and she waved a Visa card. Her father's, Rolf's. We went to the nearest cashpoint and emptied his account. At first, Irene didn't want to, but when I explained my life depended on it, she knew it had to be done. We went to Olympen and ate and drank, bought a few grams of speed and returned home to Bispegata. She said she'd had a row with her mum. She stayed the night. The next day I took her with me to the station. Tutu was sitting on his motorbike wearing a leather jacket with a wolf's head on the back. Tutu with a goatee, pirate's scarf round his head and tattoos protruding from his collar, but still looking like a fricking lackey. He was about to jump off and run after me when he realised I was heading towards him. I gave him the twenty thousand I owed plus five in interest. Thank you for lending me the holiday money. Hope we can turn over a new leaf. Tutu rang Odin while looking at Irene. I could see what he wanted. And looked at Irene again. Poor, beautiful, pale Irene.

'Odin says he wants f-f-five more,' Tutu said. 'If not I've got orders to give you a b-b-b-bea-bea-bea . . .' He took a deep breath.

'Beating,' I said.

'Right now,' Tutu said.

'Fine, I'll sell two batches for you today.'

'You'll have to p-p-pay for them.'

'Come on, I can sell them in two hours.'

Tutu eyed me. Nodded to Irene, who was standing at the bottom of Jernbanetorget steps, waiting. 'What about h-h-her?'

'She'll help me.'

'Girls are good at s-s-selling. Is she on drugs?'

'Not yet,' I said.

'Th-thief,' Tutu said, grinning his toothless grin.

I counted my money. My last. It was always my last. My blood's flowing out of me.

A week later, by Elm Street Rock Cafe, a boy stopped in front of Irene and me.

'Say hello to Oleg,' I said and jumped down from the wall. 'Say hello to my sister, Oleg.'

Then I hugged him. I could feel he hadn't lowered his head; he was looking over my shoulder. At Irene. And through his denim jacket I could feel his heart accelerating.

Officer Berntsen sat with his feet on the desk and the telephone receiver to his ear. He had rung the police station in Lillestrøm, Romerike Police District, and introduced himself as Thomas Lunder, a laboratory assistant for Kripos. The officer he was speaking to had just confirmed they had received the bag of what they assumed was heroin from Gardermoen. The standard procedure was that all confiscated drugs in the country were sent for testing to the Kripos laboratory in Bryn, Oslo. Once a week a Kripos vehicle went round collecting from all the police districts in Østland. Other districts sent the material via their own couriers.

'Good,' Berntsen said, fidgeting with the false ID card displaying a photo and the signature of Thomas Lunder, Kripos, underneath. 'I'll be in Lillestrøm anyway, so I'll pick up the bag for Bryn. We'd like such a large seizure to be tested at once. OK, see you early tomorrow.'

He rang off and looked out of the window. Looked at the new area around Bjørvika rising towards the sky. Thought of all the small details: the sizes of screws, the thread on nuts, the quality of mortar, the flexibility of glass, everything that had to be right for the whole to function. And felt a profound satisfaction. Because it did. This town did function.

9

THE LONG, SLIM FEMININE LEGS of the pine trees rose into the skirt of green that cast hazy afternoon shadows across the gravel in front of the house. Harry stood at the top of the drive, drying his sweat after mounting the steep hills from Holmendammen and observing the dark house. The black-stained, heavy timber expressed solidity, security, a bulwark against trolls and nature. It hadn't been enough. The neighbouring houses were large, inelegant detached houses undergoing continuous improvement and extension. Øystein, called Ø in his phone contacts list, had said that cog-jointed timbers were a statement of the bourgeoisie's longing for nature, simplicity and health. What Harry saw was sick, perverted, a family under siege from a serial killer. Nonetheless, she had chosen to keep the house.

Harry walked to the door and pressed the bell.

Heavy footsteps sounded from inside. And Harry realised that he should have phoned first.

The door opened.

The man standing before him had a blond fringe, the type of fringe that had been full in its prime and had undoubtedly brought him advantages, and which therefore one took into later life hoping that the somewhat more straggly version would still work. The man was wearing an ironed light blue shirt of the kind Harry guessed he had also worn in his youth.

'Yes?' the man said. Open, friendly features. Eyes looking as if they had not met anything other than friendliness. A small polo player sewn into the breast pocket.

Harry felt his throat go dry. He cast a glance at the nameplate under the doorbell.

Rakel Fauke.

Yet the man with the attractive, weak face was standing there and holding the door open as though it were his. Harry knew he had several options for a great opening gambit, but the one he chose was: 'Who are you?'

The man in front of him produced the facial expression Harry had never been able to achieve. He frowned and smiled at the same time. The superior person's condescending amusement at the inferior person's impudence.

'Since you are on the outside and I am on the inside it would seem more natural that you should say who you are. And what you want.'

'As you wish,' Harry said with a loud yawn. Of course, he could blame that on jet lag. 'I'm here to speak to the lady whose name is by the doorbell.'

'And you are from?'

'The Jehovah's Witnesses,' Harry said, checking his watch.

The man automatically shifted his eyes from Harry to look for the obligatory second man in the team.

'My name's Harry and I come from Hong Kong. Where is she?'

The man arched an eyebrow. '*The* Harry?'

'Since it has been one of Norway's least trendy names for the last fifty years, we can probably assume it is.'

The man studied Harry now, with a nod and a half-smile on his lips as though his brain was playing back the information it had received about the character in front of him. But with no suggestion that he was going to move from the doorway or answer any of Harry's questions.

'Well?' Harry said, shifting weight from one leg.

'I'll tell her you were here.'

Harry's foot was swift. Out of instinct he flipped the sole upward so that the door hit it instead of the shoe upper. That was the kind of trick his new occupation had taught him. The man looked down at Harry's foot and then at him. The condescending amusement was gone. He was about to say something. A withering remark that would re-establish order. But Harry knew he would change his mind. When he saw the look on Harry's face that made people change their minds.

'You'd better—' the man said. Stopped. Blinked once. Harry waited. For the confusion. The hesitation. The retreat. Blink number two. The man coughed. 'She's out.'

Harry stood stock-still. Let the silence ring out. Two seconds. Three seconds.

'I . . . er, don't know when she'll be back.'

Not a muscle stirred in Harry's countenance while the man's face leapt from one expression to another as if searching for one to hide behind. And ended up where it had started: with the friendly one.

'My name's Hans Christian. I . . . apologise for having to be so negative. But a lot of bizarre enquiries regarding the case have come in, and it's essential that Rakel has some peace now. I'm her solicitor.'

'Hers?'

'Theirs. Hers and Oleg's. Would you like to come in?'

Harry nodded.

On the living-room table there were piles of papers. Harry went over to them. Case documents. Reports. The height of the pile suggested they had not stinted on their searches.

'Dare I ask what has brought you here?' Hans Christian asked.

Harry flicked through the papers. DNA tests. Witness statements. 'Well, do you?'

'Do I what?'

'Why are *you* here? Haven't you got an office where you can prepare the defence?'

'Rakel wants to be involved. She is a lawyer herself. Listen, Hole. I know very well who you are and I know you've been close to Rakel and Oleg, but—'

'And how close are you exactly?'

'Me?'

'Yes, it sounds as if you've assumed responsibility for their all-round care.'

Harry ignored the overtone to his voice and knew that he had revealed himself, knew the man was watching him in amazement. And knew he had lost the upper hand.

'Rakel and I are old friends,' Hans Christian said. 'I grew up close to here, we studied law together, and . . . well. When you spend the best years of your life together there are bonds of course.'

Harry nodded. Knew that he should keep his mouth shut. Knew that everything he said would make things worse.

'Mm. With bonds of that kind it's strange I never saw or heard about you when Rakel and I were together.'

Hans Christian was unable to answer. The door opened. And there she was.

Harry felt a claw close around his heart and wrench it round.

Her figure was the same: slim, erect. The face was the same: heart-shaped with dark brown eyes and the broadish mouth that liked to laugh so much. The hair was almost the same: long, though the darkness was perhaps a tad lighter. But the eyes were changed. They were the eyes of a hunted animal, widened, wild. But when they fell on Harry it was as if something returned. Something of the person she had been. Of what they had been.

'Harry,' she said. And at the sound of her voice, the rest came, everything came back.

He took two long strides and held her in his arms. The scent of her hair. Her fingers on his spine. She was the first to let go. He retreated a step and looked at her.

'You look good,' he said.

'You too.'

84

'Liar.'

She smiled quickly. Tears had already formed in her eyes.

They stayed standing like that. Harry let her study him, let her absorb his older face with its new scar. 'Harry,' she repeated, tilted her head and laughed. The first tear trembled on her eyelashes and fell. A stripe ran down her soft skin.

Somewhere in the room a man with a polo player on his shirt coughed and said something about having to go to a meeting.

Then they were alone.

While Rakel was making coffee he saw her gaze fix on his metal finger, but neither of them made a comment. There was an unspoken agreement that they would never mention the Snowman. So Harry sat at the kitchen table and instead talked about his life in Hong Kong. Told her what he was able to tell. What he wanted to tell. That the job as 'debt consultant' for Herman Kluit's outstanding accounts consisted in meeting customers with payments that had fallen behind and jogging their memories in a friendly way. In brief, the consultation involved advising them to pay as soon as was practical and feasible. Harry said his major and basically sole qualification was that he measured 1 metre 92 centimetres in his stockinged feet, had broad shoulders, bloodshot eyes and a newly acquired scar.

'Friendly, professional. Suit, tie, multinationals in Hong Kong, Taiwan and Shanghai. Hotels with room service. Elegant office blocks. Civilised, Swiss-style private banks with a Chinese twist. Western handshakes and courtesy phrases. And Asian smiles. By and large they pay the next day. Herman Kluit is content. We understand each other.'

She poured coffee for both of them and sat down. Took a deep breath.

'I got a job with the International Court of Justice in The Hague, with offices in Amsterdam. I thought that if we left this house behind us, this town, all the attention . . .'

Me, Harry thought.

'. . . the memories, everything would be alright. And for a while it was.

85

But then it started. At first, the senseless bouts of temper. As a boy Oleg never raised his voice. He was grumpy, yes, but never . . . like that. Said I'd ruined his life by taking him away from Oslo. He said that because he knew I had no defence. And when I started to cry, he started to cry. Asked me why I'd pushed you out. You'd saved us from . . . from . . .'

He nodded so that she didn't have to say the name.

'He began to come home late. Said he was meeting friends, but they were friends I had never met. One day he admitted he'd been to a coffee shop in Leidseplein and smoked hash.'

'The Bulldog Palace with all the tourists?'

'Right. I suppose that's part of the Amsterdam experience, I thought. But I was afraid at the same time. His father . . . well, you know.'

Harry nodded. Oleg's aristocratic Russian genes from his father. Highs, furies and lows. Dostoevsky land.

'He sat in his room a lot listening to music. Heavy, gloomy stuff. Well, you know these bands . . .'

Harry nodded again.

'But your records, too. Frank Zappa. Miles Davis. Supergrass. Neil Young. Supersilent.'

The names came so quickly and naturally that Harry suspected she had been eavesdropping.

'Then, one day I was hoovering his room and I found two pills with smileys on.'

'Ecstasy?'

She nodded. 'Two months later I applied for and got a job at the Office of the Attorney General and moved back here.'

'To safe old innocent Oslo.'

She shrugged. 'He needed a change of scene. A new start. And it worked. He's not the type to have lots of friends, as you know, but he met a couple of old pals and got on well at school until . . .' Her voice fell apart at the seams.

Harry waited. He took a swig of coffee. Braced himself.

'He could be away for several days in a row. I didn't know what to do.

He did as he wanted. I rang the police, psychologists, sociologists. He wasn't legally an adult, yet there was nothing anyone could do unless there was evidence of taking drugs or law-breaking. I felt so helpless. Me! Who always thought it was the parents who were at fault, who always had a solution at hand when other parents' children went off the rails. Don't be apathetic, don't repress. Action!'

Harry looked at her hand beside his on the coffee table. The delicate fingers. The fine veins on the pale hand that was normally tanned so early in the autumn. But he didn't obey his impulse to cover her hand with his. Something was in the way. Oleg was in the way.

She sighed.

'So I went to the city centre and searched for him. Night after night. Until I found him. He was standing on a corner of Tollbugata and was pleased to see me. Said he was happy. He had a job and was sharing a flat with some friends. He needed his freedom. I shouldn't ask so many questions. He was "travelling". This was his version of a gap year, sailing round the world, like all the other kids on Holmenkollen Ridge. Sailing round the world of Oslo city centre.'

'What was he wearing?'

'What do you mean?'

'Nothing. Go on.'

'He said he would be home again soon. And would finish his studies at school. So we agreed he would come back and have Sunday lunch with me.'

'And did he?'

'Yes. And when he'd left I saw that he had been in my bedroom and stolen my jewellery box.' She took a long, quivering breath. 'The ring you bought me in Vestkanttorget was in the box.'

'Vestkanttorget?'

'Don't you remember?'

Harry's brain rewound at top speed. There were a few black holes, some white ones he had repressed and large, blank expanses alcohol had consumed. But also areas with colour and texture. Like the day they were walking around the second-hand market in Vestkanttorget. Was Oleg with them? Yes, he was. Of course. The photograph. The self-timer. The autumn leaves. Or was that another day? They had ambled from stall to stall. Old toys, crockery, rusty cigar boxes, vinyl records with and without sleeves, lighters. And a gold ring.

It had looked so lonely there. So Harry had bought it and put it on her finger. To give it a new home, he had said. Or some such thing. Something flippant he knew she would perceive as shyness, as a disguised declaration of love. And perhaps it was – at any rate they had both laughed. About the act, about the ring, about their both knowing the other knew. And about all of that being fine. For everything they wanted and yet did not want lay in this cheap, tatty ring. A vow to love each other as passionately and for as long as they could, and to part when there was no love left. When she had parted it had been for other reasons of course. Better reasons. But, Harry established, she had taken care of their tawdry ring, kept it in the box with the jewellery she had inherited from her Austrian mother.

'Shall we go out while there's still some sun?' Rakel asked.

'Yes,' Harry said, returning her smile. 'Let's do that.'

They walked up the road that coiled to the top of the ridge. The deciduous trees in the east were so red they looked as if they were on fire. The light played on the fjord making it resemble molten metal. But it was, as usual, the man-made features of the town below that fascinated Harry. The anthill perspective. The houses, parks, roads, cranes, boats in the harbour, lights that had begun to come on. The cars and trains hurrying hither and thither. The sum of our activities. And the question only the person with the time to stop and look down at the busy ants can allow himself to ask: Why?

'I dream of peace and quiet,' Rakel said. 'No more than that. What about you? What do you dream about?'

Harry shrugged. 'Finding myself in a narrow corridor and an avalanche coming and burying me.'

'Wow.'

'Well, you know me and my claustrophobia.'

'We often dream about what we fear and desire. Disappearing, being buried. In a way it offers security, doesn't it?'

Harry thrust his hands deeper in his pockets. 'I was buried under an avalanche three years ago. Let's say it's as simple as that.'

'So you didn't escape your ghosts even though you went all the way to Hong Kong?'

'Oh yes, I did,' Harry said. 'The trip thinned the ranks.'

'Really?'

'Well, it is in fact possible to put things behind you, Rakel. The art of dealing with ghosts is to dare to look at them long and hard until you know that is what they are. Ghosts. Lifeless, powerless ghosts.'

'So,' Rakel said in a tone that made him realise she didn't like the topic of conversation. 'Any women in your life?' The question came easily, so easily that he didn't believe it.

'Well.'

'Tell me.'

She had donned her sunglasses. It was hard to assess how much she wanted to hear. Harry decided on a swap. If he wanted to hear.

'She was Chinese.'

'Was? Is she dead?' She sent him a playful smile. He thought she looked as if she could take the heat. But he would have preferred it if she had been a bit more sensitive.

'A businesswoman in Shanghai. She nurses her *guanxi*, her network of useful connections. Plus her affluent, ancient Chinese husband. And – when it suits her – me.'

'In other words, you exploit her caring nature.'

'I wish I could say that.'

'Oh?'

'She makes fairly specific demands on where and when. And how. She likes—'

'Enough!' Rakel said.

Harry smiled wryly. 'As you know, I've always had a weakness for women who know what they want.'

'Enough, I said.'

'Message received.'

They continued to walk in silence. Until Harry finally said the words hovering around them in bold.

'What about this Hans Christian guy?'

'Hans Christian Simonsen? He's Oleg's solicitor.'

'I never heard of a Hans Christian Simonsen while I was doing murder cases.'

'He's from this area. We were in the same year at law school. He came and offered his services.'

'Mm. Right.'

Rakel laughed. 'I seem to remember he invited me out once or twice when we were students. And that he wanted us to do a jazz-dance course together.'

'God forbid.'

Rakel laughed again. Christ, how he had longed for that laughter.

She nudged him. 'As you know, I've always had a weakness for men who know what they want.'

'Uh-huh,' Harry said. 'And what have they ever done for you?'

She didn't answer. She didn't need to. Instead she formed the furrow between her broad, black eyebrows he had often stroked with his forefinger whenever he noticed it. 'Sometimes it's more important to have a lawyer who is dedicated rather than one who is so experienced he knows the outcome in advance.'

'Mm. You mean someone who knows it's a lost cause.'

'You mean I should have used one of the tired old plodders?'

'Well, the best *are* in fact pretty dedicated.'

'This is a petty drugs murder, Harry. The best are busy with prestige cases.'

'So, what has Oleg told his dedicated solicitor about what happened?'

Rakel sighed. 'That he can't remember anything. Beyond that, he doesn't want to say anything about anything at all.'

'And that's what you're basing your defence on?'

'Listen, Hans Christian's a brilliant solicitor in his field. He knows what's involved. He's taking advice from the best. And he's working day and night, he really is.'

'You're exploiting his caring nature in other words?'

This time Rakel did not laugh. 'I'm a mother. It's simple. I'm willing to do whatever it takes.'

They stopped where the forest began and sat on separate spruce trunks. The sun sank to the treetops in the west like a weary Independence Day balloon.

'I know why you've come of course,' Rakel said. 'But what exactly have you got planned?'

'To find out if Oleg's guilty beyond any reasonable doubt.'

'Because?'

Harry shrugged. 'Because I'm a detective. Because this is the way we've organised this anthill. No one can be convicted until we're sure.'

'And you're not sure?'

'No, I'm not sure.'

'And that's the only reason you're here?'

The shadows from the spruce trees crept over them. Harry shivered in his linen suit; his thermostat had evidently not adjusted to 59.9 degrees north yet.

'It's strange,' he said. 'But I have trouble remembering anything except fragmented moments of all the time we were together. When I look at a photograph that's how I remember it. The way we were in the photo. Even if I know it's not true.'

He looked at her. She was sitting with her chin in one hand. The sun glittered on her narrowed eyes.

'But perhaps that's why we take snaps,' Harry continued. 'To provide false evidence to underpin the false claim that we were happy. Because the thought that we weren't happy at least for some time during our lives is unbearable. Adults order children to smile in the photos, involve them in the lie, so we smile, we feign happiness. But Oleg could never smile unless he meant it, could not lie, he didn't have the gift.' Harry turned back to the sun, caught the last rays, extended like yellow fingers between the highest branches on the crest of the ridge. 'I found a photo of the three of us on his locker door in Valle Hovin. And do you know what, Rakel? He was smiling in that photo.'

Harry focused on the spruce trees. The little colour remaining was quickly sucked out of them, and now they stood like ranks of black uniformed silhouette-guardsmen. Then he heard her come over, felt her hand under his arm, her head against his shoulder, her hot cheek through his linen suit, and breathed in the perfume of her hair. 'I don't need any photograph to remember how happy we were, Harry.'

'Mm.'

'Perhaps he taught himself to lie. It happens to us all.'

Harry nodded. A gust of wind made him shiver. When was it he had taught himself to lie? Was it when Sis asked if their mother could see them from heaven? Had he learned so early? Was that why he found it so easy to lie when he pretended he didn't know what Oleg had been doing? Oleg's lost innocence was not that he had learned to lie, not that he had learned to inject heroin or steal his mother's jewels. It was that he had learned, in a risk-free and effective way, how to sell drugs that consume the soul, cause the body to disintegrate and send the buyer into dependency's cold, dripping hell. If Oleg was innocent of Gusto's murder he would still be guilty. He had sent them by plane. To Dubai.

Fly Emirates.

Dubai is in the United Arab Emirates.

There are no Arabs, only pushers in Arsenal shirts selling violin. Shirts they had been given along with instructions on how to sell dope in the right way: one money man, one dope man. A conspicuous and yet run-of-the-mill shirt showing what they sold and to which organisation they belonged. Not one of the standard ephemeral gangs who were always brought down by their own greed, stupidity, torpor and foolhardiness, but an organisation that took no unnecessary risks, did not expose its backers and still seemed to have a monopoly on the junkies' favourite new drug. And Oleg was one of them. Harry didn't know a great deal about football, but he was pretty sure that Van Persie and Fàbregas were Arsenal players. And absolutely sure that no Spurs supporter would have considered owning an Arsenal shirt if it hadn't been for a special reason. Oleg had managed to teach him that much.

There was a good reason for Oleg talking to neither him nor the police. He was working for someone or something no one knew anything about. Someone or something that made everyone stay shtum. That was where Harry had to begin.

Rakel had started crying and buried her face in his neck. The tears warmed his skin as they ran down inside his shirt, over his chest, over his heart.

Darkness fell quickly.

Sergey was lying on his bed, staring at the ceiling.

The seconds passed, one by one.

This was the slowest part: the waiting. And he did not even know for sure if it was going to happen. If it was going to be necessary. He had slept badly. Dreamed badly. He had to know. So he had rung Andrey, asked if he could talk to Uncle. But Andrey had answered that *ataman* was not available. No more than that.

That was how it had always been with Uncle. And, for the majority of his life, Sergey had not even known that he existed. It was only after he – or his Armenian straw man – had appeared and created order that Sergey had begun to make enquiries. It was an eye-opener how little the others in the family knew about this relation. Sergey had established that Uncle had come from the west and married into the family in the 1950s. Some said he came from Lithuania, from a kulak family, the peasant landowning class that Stalin had actively deported, and that Uncle's family had been sent to Siberia. Others said he was part of a small group of Jehovah's Witnesses that had been transported to Siberia from Moldavia in 1951. An ageing aunt said that although Uncle had been a well-read, linguistically talented and courteous man he had adapted immediately to their simple lifestyle and had espoused ancient Siberian urka traditions as if they were his own. And that perhaps it was precisely his ability to adapt, along with his obvious business acumen, which soon enabled other urkas to accept him as a leader. Within a short time he was running one of the most profitable smuggling operations in the whole of southern Siberia. His enterprise in the eighties was so wide-ranging that in the end the authorities could no longer be bribed to turn a blind eye. When the police struck, while the Soviet Union was collapsing around them, it was with a raid so violent and so bloody, according to a neighbour who remembered Uncle, that it was more reminiscent of a blitzkrieg than the hand of the law. At first Uncle was reported killed. It was said he had been shot in the back and the police, fearing reprisals, had secretly disposed of the body in the River Lena. One of the officers had stolen his flick knife and had not been able to stop boasting about it. Nevertheless, a year later, Uncle gave a sign of life, and by then he was in France. He said he had gone into hiding, and the only thing he wanted to know was if his wife was pregnant or not. She was not, and with that no one in Tagil heard a word from him for several years. Not until Uncle's wife died. Then he appeared for the funeral, Father said. He paid for everything, and a Russian Orthodox funeral does not come cheap. He also gave money to those of her relatives who needed a handout. Father was not among them, but it was him Uncle had gone to when he wanted a rundown on what family his wife had left in Tagil. And that was when his nephew, little Sergey, had been brought to his attention. The next morning Uncle was gone, as mysteriously and inexplicably as he had arrived. The years passed, Sergey became a teenager, an adult, and most people probably thought Uncle – whom they remembered as seeming old even when he went to Siberia – was long dead and buried. But then, when Sergey was arrested for smuggling hash, a man had made a sudden appearance, an Armenian who had presented himself as Uncle's straw man, sorted out matters for Sergey and arranged Uncle's invitation to Norway.

Sergey checked his watch. And confirmed that exactly twelve minutes had passed since he last checked. He closed his eyes and tried to visualise him. The policeman.

In fact, there was another detail about the story of his uncle's alleged death. The officer who had stolen his knife had been found soon afterwards in the Taiga forest, what was left of him, that is – the rest had been eaten by a bear.

It was dark both outside and inside when the telephone rang.

It was Andrey.

10

TORD SCHULTZ UNLOCKED THE DOOR to his house, stared into the darkness and listened to the dense silence for a while. Sat down on the sofa without switching on the light and waited for the reassuring roar of the next plane.

They had let him go.

A man who introduced himself as an inspector had entered his cell, crouched in front of him and asked why the hell he had hidden flour in his trolley bag.

'Flour?'

'That's what the Kripos lab say they've found.'

Tord Schultz had repeated the same thing he said when he was arrested, the emergency procedure, he didn't know how the plastic bag had come into his possession or what it contained.

'You're lying,' the inspector had said. 'And we're going to keep an eye on you.'

Then he had held the cell door open and nodded as a signal that he should leave.

Tord gave a start as a piercing ring filled the bare, darkened room. He got up and groped his way to the telephone on a wooden chair beside the training bench.

It was the operations manager. He told Tord that he had been taken off international flights for the foreseeable future and moved to domestic flights.

Tord asked why.

His boss said there had been a management meeting to discuss his situation.

'You must appreciate we cannot have you on foreign flights with this suspicion hanging over you.'

'So why don't you ground me?'

'Well.'

'Well?'

'If we suspend you and the arrest leaks out to the press they'll immediately conclude we think you're guilty and it will be grist to their mill . . . no pun intended.'

'And you don't?'

There was a silence before the answer came.

'It would damage the airline if we admitted we suspected one of our pilots of being a drug smuggler, don't you think?'

The pun *was* intended.

The remainder of what he said was drowned in the noise of a TU-154.

Tord put down the receiver.

He groped his way back to the sofa and sat down. Ran his fingertips over the glass coffee table. Felt stains of dried mucus, spit and coke. What now? A drink or a line? A drink *and* a line?

He got up. The Tupolev was coming in low. Its lights flooded the whole living room and Tord stared for a second at his reflection in the window.

Then it was dark again. But he had seen it. Seen it in his eyes, and he knew he would see it on colleagues' faces. The contempt, the condemnation and – worst of all – the sympathy.

Domestic. We're going to keep an eye on you. *I see you.*

If he couldn't fly abroad he would have no value for them any more. All he would be was a desperate, debt-ridden, cocaine-addicted risk. A man on police radar, a man under pressure. He didn't know much, but more than enough to be aware that he could destroy the infrastructure they had built. And they would do what had to be done. Tord Schultz wrapped his hands around the back of his head and groaned aloud. He was not born to fly a fighter jet. It had gone into a spin, and he didn't have it in him to regain control; he just sat watching the rotating ground getting closer. And knew his sole chance of survival was to sacrifice the jet. He would have to activate the ejector seat. Fire himself out. Now.

He would have to go to someone high up in the police, someone he could be sure was above the drug gangs' corruption money. He would have to go to the top.

Yes, Tord Schultz thought. He breathed out and felt muscles he had not noticed were tense, relax. He would go to the top.

First of all, though, a drink.

And a line.

Harry was given the room key by the same boy in reception.

He thanked him and took the stairs in long strides. There had not been a single Arsenal shirt to be seen on the way from the Metro station in Egertorget to Hotel Leon.

As he approached room 301 he slowed down. Two of the bulbs in the corridor had gone, which made it so dark he could barely see the light under his door. In Hong Kong electricity prices were so high he had abandoned the bad Norwegian habit of leaving lights on when he went out, but he could not be sure that the cleaner had left it on. If she had, she'd also forgotten to lock the door.

Harry stood with the key in his right hand as the door opened of its own accord. In the light from the solitary ceiling lamp he saw a figure. It was standing with its back to him, bent over his suitcase on the bed. As the door hit the wall with a little thud the figure turned calmly, and a man with an oblong, furrowed face looked at Harry with St Bernard eyes. He was tall, stooped and wore a long coat, a woollen jumper and a dirty priest's collar around his neck. His long, unkempt hair was broken up on either side of his face by the biggest eyes Harry had ever seen. The man had to be seventy, at least. They could not be more dissimilar, yet Harry's first thought was that it was like looking at a reflection.

'What the hell are you doing?' Harry asked from the corridor. Routine procedure.

'What's it look like?' The voice was younger than the face, sonorous with the distinct Swedish tone that Swedish dance bands and revival preachers adore for some unaccountable reason. 'I broke in to check if you had anything of value, of course.' It wasn't just a Swedish tone, he was speaking Swedish. He raised both hands aloft. The right one held a universal adapter, the left a paperback edition of Philip Roth's *American Pastoral*.

'You've got nothing at all, have you.' He threw the items on the bed. Peered into the little suitcase, and glanced enquiringly at Harry. 'Not even a shaver.'

'What the . . .' Harry ignored routine procedures, strode into the room and smacked the suitcase lid down.

'Easy, my son,' said the man, holding up his palms. 'Don't take it personally. You're new to this establishment. The question was only who would rob you first.'

'Who? Do you mean . . .?'

The old man proffered his hand. 'Welcome. I'm Cato. I live in 310.'

Harry looked down at the grimy frying pan of a hand.

'Come on,' Cato said. 'My hands are the only part of me it is advisable to touch.'

Harry said his name and shook his hand. It was surprisingly soft.

'Priest's hands,' the man said in answer to his thoughts. 'Got anything to drink, Harry?'

Harry nodded towards his suitcase and the open wardrobe doors. 'You already know.'

'That you haven't got anything, yes. I mean on you. In your jacket pocket, for example.'

Harry took out a Game Boy and tossed it on the bed where all his other possessions were strewn.

Cato angled his head and looked at Harry. His ear folded against his shoulder. 'With that suit I might have thought you were one of the by-the-hour guests, not a resident. What are you doing here, anyway?'

'I still think that should be my line.'

Cato put a hand on Harry's arm and looked him in the eyes. 'My son,' he said in his sonorous voice, stroking the cloth with two fingertips. 'That is a very nice suit. How much did you pay?'

Harry was about to say something. A combination of courtesy, rebuff and threat. But he realised it was pointless. He gave up. And smiled.

Cato smiled back.

Like a reflection.

'No time to chat. I've got to go to work now.'

'Which is?'

'There you are. You're a bit interested in your fellow mortals as well. I proclaim the Word of God to the hapless.'

'Now?'

'My calling has no church times. Goodbye.'

With a gallant bow the old man turned and departed. As he passed through the doorway Harry saw one of his unopened packs of Camel protruding from Cato's jacket pocket. Harry closed the door after him. The smell of old man and ash hung in the room. He went to push up the window. The sounds of the town filled the room at once: the faint, regular drone of traffic, jazz from an open window, a distant police siren rising and falling, a hapless individual screaming his pain between houses, followed by breaking glass, the wind rustling through dry leaves, the click-clack of women's heels. Sounds of Oslo.

A slight movement caused him to look down. The glow from the yard lamp fell on the skip. There was the gleam of a brown tail. A rat was sitting on the edge and sniffing up at him with a shiny nose. Harry was reminded of something his thoughtful employer, Herman Kluit, had said, and which perhaps, or perhaps not, was a reference to his job: 'A rat is neither good nor evil. It does what a rat has to do.'

* * *

This was the worst part of an Oslo winter. The part before ice has settled on the fjord and the wind blows through the city-centre streets, salty and freezing cold. As usual I stood in Dronningens gate selling speed, Stesolid and Rohypnol. I stamped my feet on the ground. I had lost sensation in my toes and pondered whether the day's profits should go on the hideously expensive Freelance boots I'd seen in the window of Steen & Strøm. Or on ice, which I had heard was for sale down at Plata. Perhaps I could filch some speed – Tutu wouldn't notice – and buy the boots. But on reflection I thought it was safer to nick the boots and make sure Odin got what was his. After all, I was better off than Oleg, who'd had to start from scratch selling hash in the frozen hell by the river. Tutu had given him the pitch under Nybrua Bridge where he competed with people from all the fucked-up places round the world, and was probably the only person to speak fluent Norwegian from Anker Bridge to the harbour.

I saw a guy in an Arsenal shirt further up the street. Usually Bisken, a pimply Sørlander who wore a studded dog collar, stood there. New man but the procedure was the same: he was gathering a group together. For the time being he had three punters waiting. God knows what they were so frightened of. The cops had given up in this area, and if they hauled in pushers off the street it was only for appearances' sake because some politician had been shooting his mouth off again.

A guy dressed as if he was going to confirmation passed the group and I saw him and Arsenal Shirt exchange barely perceptible nods. The guy stopped in front of me. Wearing a trench coat from Ferner Jacobsen, a suit from Ermengildo Zegna and a side parting from the Silver Boys. He was big.

'Somebody wants to meet you.' He spoke English with a sort of Russian growl.

I reckoned it would be the usual. He had seen my face, thought I was a rent boy and wanted a blow job or my teenage ass. And I had to confess that on days like today I did consider a change of profession; heated car seats and four times the hourly rate.

'No thanks,' I answered in English.

'Right answer is Yes please,' the guy said, grabbing my arm and lifting me rather than dragging me off to a black limousine, which at that moment pulled soundlessly up by the pavement. The rear door opened, and as resistance was useless I began to think about a proper price. Paid rape is better than unpaid, after all.

I was shoved onto the back seat, and the door was slammed with a soft, expensive click. Through the windows, which from the outside had seemed black and impenetrable, I saw that we were moving west. Behind the wheel sat a little guy with much too small a head for all the big things that should fit in it: a huge nose, a white, lipless shark-mouth and bulging eyes that looked as if they had been stuck on with crap glue. He too had a posh funeral suit and a parting like a choirboy's. He looked at me in the rear-view mirror. 'Sales good, eh?'

'What sales, fuckwit?'

The little guy gave a friendly smile and nodded. In my mind, I had decided not to give them a bulk discount if they asked me, but now I could see in his eyes it wasn't me they were after. There was something else, which for the moment I couldn't interpret. The City Hall appeared and was gone. The American Embassy. The Palace Gardens. Further west. Kirkeveien. Norwegian Broadcasting Corporation. And then houses and rich men's addresses.

We stopped in front of a large timber construction on a hill and the funeral directors escorted me to the gate. As we waded through the shingle to the oak door I had a look around. The property was as big as a football pitch with apple and pear trees, a bunker-like cement tower similar to the stores they have in desert countries, a double garage with iron bars that gave the impression it housed public emergency vehicles. A two- to three-metre-high fence enclosed the whole caboodle. I already had an inkling where we were going. Limousine, English with a growl, 'Sales good?', fortress sweet home.

In the lobby the bigger of the two suits frisked me, then he and the little one went to a corner where there was a small table with a red felt cloth and loads of old icons and crucifixes hanging all over the wall. They drew their shooters from their shoulder holsters, put them on the red felt and placed a cross on each pistol. Then a door to a lounge opened.

'*Ataman*,' he said, pointing the way to me.

The old boy must have been at least as old as the leather armchair he was sitting in. I stared. Gnarled elderly fingers around a black cigarette.

There was a lively crackle coming from the enormous fireplace, and I made sure to position myself near enough for the heat to reach my back. The light from the flames flickered over his white silk shirt and old-man face. He put down the cigarette and raised his hand as though he expected me to kiss the large blue stone he wore on his ring finger.

'Burmese sapphire,' he said. 'Six point six carat, four and a half thousand dollars per carat.'

He had an accent. It was not easy to hear, but it was there. Poland? Russia? Something to the east anyway.

'How much?' he said, resting his chin on the ring.

It took me a couple of seconds to understand what he meant.

'Just under thirty thousand,' I said.

'How much under?'

I pondered. 'Twenty-nine thousand seven hundred is pretty close.'

'The exchange rate for the dollar is five eighty-three.'

'Around a hundred and seventy thousand.'

The old boy nodded. 'They said you were good.' His old-man eyes shone bluer than the fricking Burmese sapphire.

'They've got brains,' I said.

'I've watched you in action. You have a lot to learn, but I can see you're smarter than the other imbeciles. You can see a customer and know what he's willing to pay.'

I shrugged. I wondered what he was willing to pay.

'But they also said you steal.'

'Only when it's worth my while.'

The old boy laughed. Well, since it was the first time I had met him, I thought it was a half-hearted coughing fit, like from lung cancer. There was a kind of gurgling noise deep in his throat, like the nice old chug-chug of a sailing boat.

Then he fixed his cold, blue Jew-eyes on me and said in a tone that suggested he was telling me about Newton's Second Law: 'You should be able to manage the next calculation as well. If you steal from me I will kill you.'

The sweat was pouring down my back. I forced myself to meet his gaze. It was like staring into the fricking Antarctic. Nothing. Freezing cold wasteland. But I knew what he wanted. Number one: money.

'The biker gang will let you sell ten grams on your own for every fifty grams you sell for them. Seventeen per cent. For me you sell only my stuff and you're paid in cash. Fifteen per cent. You have your own street corner. There are three of you. Money man, dope man and scout. Seven per cent for the dope man, three per cent for the scout. You settle up with Andrey at midnight.' He nodded towards the smaller choirboy.

Street corner. Scout. *The* fricking *Wire*.

'Deal,' I said. 'Sling me the shirt.'

The old boy smiled, the sort of reptilian smile that serves to tell you roughly where in the hierarchy you are. 'Andrey will sort it out.'

We continued to chat. He asked about my parents, friends, whether I had anywhere to live. I told him I lived with my foster-sister and lied no more than was necessary, for I had the feeling he already knew the answers. Only once was I out of my depth, when he asked why I spoke a kind of outdated Oslo East dialect when I had grown up in a well-educated family north of town, and I answered it was because of my father, the real one, he was from the East End of town. Fuck knows if that's right, but it's what I've always imagined, Dad, you walking around Oslo East, down on your luck, unemployed, hard up, a freezing flat, not a good place to bring up a kid. Or perhaps I talked the way I did to annoy Rolf and the posh neighbours' kids. And then I discovered it gave me a kind of upper hand, a bit like a tattoo; people got scared, shied away, gave me a wide berth. While I was droning on about my life the old boy was studying my face and kept rapping the sapphire ring on the armrest, again and again, relentlessly, as if it were some kind of countdown. When there was a break in the questioning and the only sound was the rapping, I felt as if we were going to explode unless I broke the silence.

'Cool shack,' I said.

That sounded so blonde I blushed.

'It was the head of the Gestapo's residence in Norway from 1942 to 1945. Hellmuth Reinhard.'

'S'pose the neighbours don't bother you.'

'I own the house next door as well. Reinhard's lieutenant lived there. Or vice versa.'

'Vice versa?'

'Not everything here is so easy to grasp,' the old boy said. Grinned his lizard smile. The Komodo dragon.

I knew I had to be careful, but could not resist. 'There's one thing I don't understand. Odin pays me seventeen per cent, and that's pretty much standard with the others as well. But you want a team of three people and you're giving twenty-five per cent in total. Why?'

The old boy's eyes stared intently at one side of my face. 'Because three is safer than one, Gusto. My sellers' risks are my risks. If you lose all the pawns it's just a question of time before you're checkmate, Gusto.' He seemed to repeat my name to revel in the sound.

'But the profit—'

'Don't concern yourself with that,' he retorted sharply. Then he smiled and his voice was soft again. 'Our goods come straight from the source, Gusto. It's six times purer than the so-called heroin that's diluted first in Istanbul, next in Belgrade and then in Amsterdam. Yet we pay less per gram. Understand?'

I nodded. 'You can dilute it seven or eight times more than the others.'

'We dilute it, but less than the others. We sell something that can be called heroin. You already know that, and it was why you were so quick to say yes to a lower percentage.' The light from the flames glistened on his white teeth. 'Because you know you're going to sell the best product in town, you're going to turn over three to four times as much as you do of Odin's flour. You know that because you see it every day: buyers walking straight past the line of heroin pushers to find the one wearing . . .'

'. . . the Arsenal shirt.'

'The customers will know your goods are the best on day one, Gusto.'
Then he accompanied me out.

As he had been sitting with a woollen blanket over his knees, I had assumed he was a cripple or something, but he was surprisingly light on his feet. He stopped in the doorway, clearly not wishing to show his face outside. Placed a hand on my arm, above the elbow. Gently squeezed my triceps.

'See you soon, Gusto.'

I nodded. I knew there was something else he wanted. *I've seen you in action.* From the inside of a limousine with smoked windows, studying me as if I was a fricking Rembrandt. That was how I knew I would get what I wanted.

'The scout has to be my foster-sister. And the dope man a guy called Oleg.'

'Sounds alright. Anything else?'

'I want number 23 on my shirt.'

'Arshavin,' the tall choirboy mumbled with contentment. 'Russian.' Obviously he had never heard of Michael Jordan.

'We'll see,' chuckled the old boy. He looked up at the sky. 'Now Andrey will show you something and you can get started.' His hand kept patting my arm and his smile was like a permanent bloody fixture. I was scared. And excited. Scared and excited like a Komodo dragon hunter.

The choirboys drove down to the deserted marina in Frognerkilen. They had keys to a gate, and we drove between the small boats laid up for the winter. At the tip of one wharf we came to a halt and got out. I stood staring down into the calm, black water while Andrey opened the boot.

'Come here, Arshavin.'

I went over and peered into the boot.

He was still wearing the studded dog collar and his Arsenal shirt. Bisken had always been ugly, but the sight of him almost made me throw up. There were large black holes of congealed blood across his pimply face, one ear was torn in half and one eye socket no longer had an eye but something resembling rice pudding. After finally managing to tear myself away from the mush I saw there was also a little hole in the shirt above the 'm' of Emirates. As in bullet hole.

'What happened?' I stuttered.

'He talked to the cop in the beret.'

I knew who he meant. There was an undercover cop – or so he thought at any rate – skulking round Kvadraturen.

Andrey waited, let me have a good look, before asking: 'Got the message?'

I nodded. I couldn't stop staring at the wasted eye. What the fuck had they done to him?

'Peter,' Andrey said. Together, they lifted him out of the boot, removed the Arsenal shirt and chucked him off the edge of the jetty. The black water swallowed him without a sound and closed its jaws. Gone.

Andrey slung the shirt over to me. 'This is yours now.'

I poked my finger through the bullet hole. Turned the shirt and looked at the back.

52. Bendtner.

11

IT WAS 6.30 A.M., a quarter of an hour before sunrise according to the back page of *Aftenposten*. Tord Schultz folded the newspaper and left it on the seat beside him. Glanced across the deserted atrium towards the exit again.

'He's usually here early,' said the Securitas guard behind the reception desk.

Tord Schultz had caught a dawn train into Oslo and watched the town awaken as he walked from Central Station eastwards along Grønlandsleiret. He had passed a dustcart. The men treated the rubbish bins with a roughness that Tord thought said more about attitude than efficiency. F-16 pilots. A Pakistani greengrocer had carried boxes of vegetables to the front of his shop, stopped, wiped his hands on his apron and smiled a good morning to him. Hercules pilot. After Grønland Church he had turned left. An enormous glass facade, built and designed in the 1970s, towered up above him. Police HQ.

At 6.37 the door opened. The guard coughed, and Tord raised his head. He received a confirmatory nod and got to his feet. The man coming towards him was smaller than he was.

He walked with a fast springy step and had longer hair than Tord would have expected of a man responsible for the largest narcotics unit in Norway.

As he came closer Tord noticed the pink and white stripes in the almost girlishly attractive, suntanned face. He remembered a stewardess who had had a pigment defect, a white patch spreading down from her solarium-scorched neck, between her breasts to her shaved sex. It had made the rest of her skin look like a tight-fitting nylon stocking.

'Mikael Bellman?'

'Yes, how can I help you?' The man smiled without slowing down.

'A private chat.'

'I'm afraid I have to prepare for a morning meeting, but if you ring—'

'I *have* to talk to you now,' Tord said, surprised at the insistent tone in his voice.

'Is that so?' The head of Orgkrim had already swiped his ID card at the gate, but stopped to scrutinise him.

Tord Schultz approached. Lowered his voice although the Securitas guard was still the only other person in the atrium. 'My name's Tord Schultz, I'm a pilot for Scandinavia's biggest airline, and I have information about drug smuggling into Norway via Gardermoen.

'I see. How much are we talking about?'

'Eight kilos a week.'

Tord could feel the man's eyes examining him physically. Knew that the man's brain was gathering and processing all available data: body language, clothes, posture, facial expression, the wedding ring he for some reason was still wearing on his finger, the ring he didn't have in his ear, the polished shoes, the vocabulary, the firmness of gaze.

'Perhaps we'd better get you registered,' Bellman said, nodding to the guard.

Tord Schultz slowly shook his head. 'I'd rather this meeting remained confidential.'

'Rules state that everyone should be registered, but I can reassure you that the information stays here at Police HQ.' Bellman signalled to the Securitas guard.

In the lift on the way up, Schultz stroked his finger over the name on the sticker the guard had printed and told him to wear on his lapel.

'Anything wrong?' Bellman asked.

'Not at all,' Tord said. But he continued rubbing, hoping he could erase his name.

Bellman's office was surprisingly small.

'Size doesn't matter,' Bellman said in a tone suggesting he was used to the reaction. 'Great things have been accomplished from here.' He pointed to a picture on the wall. 'Lars Axelsen, head of what was the Robberies Unit. Smashed the Tveita gang in the nineties.'

He motioned Tord to sit down. Took out a notebook, met Tord's glare and put it away again.

'Well?' he said.

Tord inhaled. And talked. He started with the divorce. He needed that. Needed to start with the why. Then he moved on to the when and where. Then to who and how. And in the end he talked about the burner.

Throughout the narration Bellman sat leaning forward, following carefully. Only when Tord talked about the burner did his face lose its concentrated, though professional, expression. After the initial surprise a red hue suffused the white pigment stains. It was a strange sight, as though a flame had been lit on the inside. He lost eye contact with Bellman, who was staring bitterly at the wall behind him, perhaps at the picture of Lars Axelsen.

After Tord had finished, Bellman sighed and raised his head.

Tord noticed there was a new look to his eyes. Hard and defiant.

'I apologise,' the section head said. 'On behalf of myself, my profession and the police force. I apologise for not having disposed of the bedbug.'

Bellman must have been saying that to himself, Tord thought, and not to him, a pilot who had been smuggling eight kilos of heroin a week.

'I appreciate that you're concerned,' Bellman said. 'I wish I could say you have nothing to fear. But bitter experience tells me that when this kind of corruption is exposed it goes down a lot further than one individual.'

'I understand.'

'Have you told anyone else about this?'

'No.'

'Does anyone know you are here and talking to me?'

'No, no one.'

'No one at all?'

Tord looked at him. Smiled wryly without saying what he was thinking: who was there to tell?

'OK,' Bellman said. 'This is an important, serious and extremely delicate matter you've brought to my attention. I'll have to proceed very warily so as not to warn those who must not be warned. That means I'll have to take the matter higher. You know, I ought to put you on remand for what you have told me, but imprisonment now could expose both you and us. So until the situation has been clarified you should go home and stay there. Do you understand? Don't tell anyone about this meeting, don't go outdoors, don't open the door to strangers, don't answer phone calls from unfamiliar numbers.'

Tord nodded slowly. 'How long will it take?'

'Three days max.'

'Roger that.'

Bellman appeared to be about to say something, but stopped and hesitated before finally deciding.

'This is something I've never been able to understand,' he said. 'That some people are willing to destroy the lives of others for money. Well, perhaps if you're a poor Afghan peasant . . . But a Norwegian with the salary of a chief pilot . . .'

Tord Schultz met his eyes. He had prepared himself for this; it almost felt like relief when it came.

'Nevertheless, coming here of your own free will and laying your cards on the table is brave. I know what you're risking. Life won't be easy from now on, Schultz.'

With that, the head of Orgkrim stood up and proffered his hand. And the same thought went through Tord's mind as when he had seen him approaching in reception: Mikael Bellman was the perfect height for a fighter pilot.

* * *

As Tord Schultz was leaving Police HQ, Harry Hole was ringing Rakel's doorbell. She opened up, wearing a dressing gown and narrow slits for eyes. She yawned.

'I'll look better later in the day,' she said.

'Nice that one of us will,' Harry said, stepping inside.

'Good luck,' she said, standing in front of the living-room table piled with documents. 'It's all there. Case reports. Photos. Newspaper cuttings. Witness statements. He's thorough. I have to go to work.'

By the time the door had slammed behind her Harry had brewed up his first cup of coffee and made a start.

After reading for three hours he had to have a break to fight the despondency stealing over him. He took the cup and stood by the kitchen window. Told himself he was here to question guilt, not to confirm innocence. *Doubt* was enough. And yet. The evidence was unambiguous. And all his years of experience as a murder investigator worked against him: things were surprisingly often exactly as they looked.

After three more hours the conclusion was the same. There was nothing in the documents that hinted at a different explanation. That didn't mean there wasn't one, but it wasn't here, he told himself.

He left before Rakel came home, telling himself he had jet lag, he had to sleep. But he knew why. He couldn't bring himself to say that from what he had read it was harder to cling to a doubt, the doubt that was the way, the truth, the life and the only hope of redemption.

So he grabbed his coat and left. Walked all the way from Holmenkollen, past Ris, over Sogn and Ullevål and Bolteløkka to Schrøder's. Considered going in but decided against it. Headed east instead, over the river to Tøyen.

And when he pushed open the door to the Watchtower, daylight had already started to fade. Everything was as he remembered. Pale walls, pale cafe decor, large windows that let in the maximum amount of light. And in this light the afternoon clientele sat around the tables with coffee and sandwiches. Some customers hung their heads over plates as if they had just reached the finishing line after a fifty-kilometre race, some carried on staccato conversations in impenetrable junkie-speak, others you wouldn't have been surprised to see drinking an espresso among the bourgeois pram armada at United Bakeries.

Some had been provided with new second-hand clothes they either kept in plastic bags or were wearing. Others looked like insurance agents or provincial schoolmistresses.

Harry headed for the counter, and a rotund, smiling girl in a Salvation Army hoodie offered him free filter coffee and wholewheat bread with brown cheese.

'Not today, thank you. Is Martine here?'

'She's working in the clinic.'

The girl pointed her finger at the ceiling and the Salvation Army first-aid room above.

'But she should be finished—'

'Harry!'

He turned.

Martine Eckhoff was as small as ever. The smiling kitten face had the same disproportionately broad mouth and a nose that was no more than a knoll in her tiny face. And her pupils looked as if they had run to the edge of the brown irises, forming the shape of a keyhole. She had once explained to him it was congenital and known as iris coloboma.

Martine stretched up and gave him a long, lingering hug. And when she had finished she still would not let go of him, but held both of his hands while looking up at him. He saw a shadow flit across her smile when she saw the scar on his face.

'How . . . how thin you are.'

Harry laughed. 'Thank you. But while I've got thinner—'

'I know,' Martine cried. 'I've got fatter. Everyone's got fatter, though, Harry. Except you. By the way, I do have an excuse for being fat . . .'

She patted her stomach where the black lambswool jumper was stretched to its limit.

'Mm. Did Rikard do this to you?'

She laughed and nodded with enthusiasm. Her face was red, the heat was coming off her like a plasma screen.

They walked over to the only free table. Harry sat down and watched the black hemisphere of a stomach trying to lower itself onto a chair. It looked incongruous against the backdrop of capsized lives and apathetic hopelessness.

'Gusto,' he said. 'Do you know anything about the case?'

She heaved a deep sigh. 'Of course. Everyone here does. He was part of the community. He didn't come here often, but we saw him now and then. The girls working here were in love with him, every last one. He was so good-looking!'

'What about Oleg, the guy who it's claimed killed him?'

'He came sometimes, with a girl.' She frowned. 'Claimed? Is there some doubt about it then?'

'That's what I'm trying to establish. A girl you say?'

'Lovely, but a wan little thing. Ingunn? Iriam?' She turned to the counter. 'Hey! What's the name of Gusto's foster-sister?' And before anyone had a chance to answer she answered herself: 'Irene!'

'Red hair and freckles?' Harry asked.

'She was so pale that if it hadn't been for her hair she would have been invisible. I mean that. In the end the sun shone right through her.'

'In the end?'

'Yes, we've just been speaking about that. It's a while since she's been here. I've asked lots of the people who come here if she's left town or what, but no one seems to know where she is.'

'Do you remember anything happening around the time the murder took place?'

'Nothing special except for that particular evening. I heard the police sirens and knew they were probably for some of our young parishioners, when one of your colleagues here received a phone call and stormed out.'

'Thought it was an unwritten rule that undercover officers weren't allowed to work here in the cafe.'

'I don't think he was working, Harry. He sat alone at the table over there, supposedly reading *Klassekampen*. It might sound rather vain, but I think he came here to watch *moi*.' She coquettishly laid her hand flat against her chest.

'You still attract lonely police officers, I suppose.'

She laughed. 'I was the one who checked you over, or have you forgotten?'

'A girl from a Christian family like you?'

'In fact his staring made me go all clammy, but he stopped when my pregnancy became visible. Anyway, that night he slammed the door after him, and I watched him head for Hausmanns gate. The crime scene was only a few hundred metres away from here. Straight afterwards rumours began to circulate that Gusto had been shot. And that Oleg had been arrested.'

'What do you know about Gusto, apart from the fact that he was attractive to women and came from a foster-family?'

'He was called the Thief. He sold violin.'

'Who did he work for?'

'He and Oleg used to sell for the bikers up in Alnabru, Los Lobos. But they joined Dubai, I think. Everyone who was approached did. They had the purest heroin, and when violin made an appearance it was the Dubai pushers who had it. And I suppose it still is.'

'What do you know about Dubai? Who is he?'

She shook her head. 'I don't even know if it is a who or a what.'

'So visible on the streets and yet so invisible behind the scenes. Does nobody know?'

'Probably, but those who do won't say.'

Someone called Martine's name.

'Stay where you are,' Martine said, struggling up from the chair. 'I'll be back in a sec.'

'Actually, I've got to be off,' Harry said.

'Where?'

There was a second's silence as they both realised he didn't have a sensible answer to her question.

Tord Schultz sat at the kitchen table by the window. The sun shone low, and there was still enough daylight for him to see everyone walking on the road between the houses. But he couldn't see the road. He took a bite of bread with cervelat.

Planes flew over rooftops. Landed and took off. Landed and took off.

Tord Schultz listened to the various engine sounds. It was like a timeline: the old engines that sounded *right*, which had the exact growl, the warm glow, which evoked the good memories, which gave meaning, which were a soundtrack to when things had a meaning: job, punctuality, family, a woman's caresses, recognition from colleagues. The new generation of engines moved more air, but were hectic, flew faster on less fuel, had greater efficiency, less time for inessentials. Also the essential inessentials. He glanced at the big clock on the fridge again. It ticked like a frightened little heart, fast and frenetic. Seven. Twelve hours left. Soon it would be dark. He heard a Boeing 747. The classic. The best. The sound grew and grew until it was a roar making the windowpanes tremble and the glass clink against the half-empty bottle on the table. Tord Schultz closed his eyes. It was the sound of optimism about the future, raw power, well-founded arrogance. The sound of invincibility to a man in his best years.

After the noise was gone and it was suddenly still in the house he noticed that the silence was different. As if the air had a different density.

As if it were occupied.

He turned right round, to the living room. Through the door he could see the weight-training bench and the furthest end of the coffee table. He looked at the parquet floor, at the shadows from the part of the living room he couldn't see. He held his breath and listened. Nothing. Just the clock ticking on the fridge. So he took another bite of the bread, a swig from the glass and leaned back in the chair. A big plane was on the way in. He could hear it coming from behind. It drowned the sound of time ticking away. And he was thinking it would have to pass between the house and the sun as a shadow fell over him and the table.

Harry walked along Urtegata and down Platous gate to Grønlandsleiret. Heading for Police HQ on autopilot. He stopped in Bots Park. Looked at the prison, at the solid grey walls.

'Where?' she had asked.

Was he really in any doubt as to who killed Gusto Hanssen?

An SAS plane left Oslo for Bangkok, direct, every day before midnight. Flew from there to Hong Kong five times a day. He could go to Hotel Leon right now. Pack his bag and check out. It would take precisely five minutes. The airport express to Gardermoen. Buy a ticket at the SAS counter. A meal and newspapers in the relaxing, impersonal transit atmosphere of an airport.

Harry turned. Saw the red concert poster from the day before was gone.

He continued down Oslo gate and was walking past Minne Park by Gamlebyen cemetery when he heard a voice from the shadows by the gate.

'Two hundred to spare?' it said in Swedish.

Harry half stopped, and the beggar stepped out. His coat was long and ragged, and the beam from the spotlight caused his large ears to cast shadows over his face.

'I assume you're asking for a loan?' Harry said, fishing out his wallet.

'Collection,' Cato said, extending his hand. 'You'll never get it back. I left my wallet at Hotel Leon.' There wasn't a whiff of spirits or beer on the old man's breath, just the smell of tobacco and something that reminded him of childhood, playing hide-and-seek at his grandfather's, when Harry hid in the wardrobe and inhaled the sweet, mouldy smell of clothes that had hung there for years. They must have been as old as the house itself.

Harry located a five-hundred note and handed it to Cato.

'Here.'

Cato stared at the money. Ran his hand over it. 'I've been hearing this and that,' he said. 'They say you're police.'

'Oh?'

'And that you drink. What's your poison?'

'Jim Beam.'

'Ah, Jim. A pal of my Johnnie. And you know the boy, Oleg.'

'Do *you* know him?'

'Prison's worse than death, Harry. Death is simple, it liberates the soul. But prison eats away at your soul until there is nothing human left of you. Until you become a phantom.'

'Who told you about Oleg?'

'My congregation is large and my parishioners are numerous, Harry. I listen. They say you're hunting that person. Dubai.'

Harry checked his watch. There was usually plenty of room on the flights at this time of the year. From Bangkok he could also go to Shanghai. Zhan Yin had texted that she was alone this week. They could go to the country house together.

'I hope you don't find him, Harry.'

'I didn't say I was—'

'Those who do, die.'

'Cato, tonight I'm going to—'

'Have you heard about the Beetle?'

'No, but—'

'Six insect legs that bore into your face.'

'I have to go, Cato.'

'I've seen it myself.' Cato dropped his chin onto his priest's collar. 'Under Älvsborg Bridge by Gothenburg harbour. A policeman searching for a heroin gang. They smacked a brick studded with nails in his face.'

Harry realised what the man was talking about. *Zjuk*. The Beetle.

The method had originally been Russian and used on informers. First of all, the informer's ear was nailed to the floor beneath a roof beam. Then six long nails were hammered halfway into a brick, the brick was tied to a rope slung around the beam and the informer held the rope end between his teeth. The point – and the symbolism – was that so long as the informer kept his mouth shut he was alive. Harry had seen the result of *zjuk* carried out by the Tapei Triad on a poor sod they found in a backstreet of Tanshui. They had used broad nail heads that didn't make such big holes on their way in. When the paramedics came and pulled the brick off the dead man the face came with it.

Cato stuffed the five-hundred note in his trouser pocket with one hand and placed the other on Harry's shoulder.

'I understand you want to protect your son. But what about the other guy? He also had a father, Harry. They call it self-sacrifice when parents fight for their children, but really they're protecting themselves, the ones who have been cloned. And that doesn't require any moral courage; it's just genetic egotism. As a child my father used to read the Bible to us, and I thought Abraham was a coward when God told him to sacrifice his son and he obeyed. Growing up, I understood that a truly selfless father is willing to sacrifice his child if it serves a higher goal than father and son. For that does exist.'

Harry threw his cigarette down in front of him. 'You're mistaken. Oleg is not my son.'

'He isn't? Why are you here then?'

'I'm a policeman.'

Cato laughed. 'Sixth commandment, Harry. Don't lie.'

'Isn't that the eighth?' Harry trod on the smouldering cigarette. 'And as far as I recall, the commandment says you shouldn't bear false witness against your neighbour, which would mean it's fine to lie a bit about yourself. But perhaps you didn't complete your theology studies?'

Cato shrugged. 'Jesus and I have no formal qualifications. We are men of the Word. But like all medicine men, fortune-tellers and charlatans we can sometimes inspire false hopes and genuine comfort.'

'You're not even a Christian, are you?'

'Let me say here and now that faith has never done me any good, only doubt. So that is what has become my testament.'

'Doubt.'

'Exactly.' Cato's yellow teeth glistened in the darkness. 'I ask: Is it so certain that a God doesn't exist, that he doesn't have a design?'

Harry laughed quietly.

'We're not so different, Harry. I have a false priest's collar; you have a false sheriff's badge. How unshakeable is your faith in your gospel actually? To protect those who have found their way and make sure those who have lost theirs are punished according to their sins? Aren't you also a doubter?'

Harry tapped a cigarette from the packet. 'Unfortunately there is no doubt in this case. I'm going home.'

'If that is so, I wish you a good trip. I have a service to hold.'

A car hooted and Harry turned automatically. Two headlights blinded him before sweeping round the corner. The brake lights resembled the glow of cigarettes in the darkness as the police vehicle slowed down to enter the Police HQ garages. And when Harry turned back Cato had gone. The old priest seemed to have melted into the night; all Harry could hear were footsteps heading for the cemetery.

In fact it did take only five minutes to pack and check out of Hotel Leon.

'There's a small discount for customers who pay cash,' said the boy behind the counter. Not everything was new.

Harry flicked through his wallet. Hong Kong dollars, yuan, US dollars, euros. His mobile phone rang. Harry lifted it to his ear while fanning out the notes and offering them to the boy.

'Speak.'

'It's me. What are you doing?'

Shit. He had planned to wait and phone her from the airport. Make it as simple and brutal as possible. A quick wrench.

'I'm checking out. Can I ring you back in a couple of minutes?'

'I just wanted to say that Oleg has contacted his solicitor. Erm . . . Hans Christian, that is.'

'Norwegian kroner,' said the boy.

'Oleg says he wants to meet you, Harry.'

'Hell!'

'Sorry? Harry, are you there?'

'Do you take Visa?'

'Cheaper for you to go to an ATM and withdraw cash.'

'Meet me?'

'That's what he says. As soon as possible.'

'That's not possible, Rakel.'

'Why not?'

'Because—'

'There's an ATM only a hundred metres down Tollbugata.'

'Because?'

'Take my card, OK?'

'Harry?'

'First of all, it's not possible, Rakel. He's not allowed visitors, and I won't get round that a second time.'

'And second of all?'

'I don't see the point, Rakel. I've read the documents. I . . .'

'You what?'

'I think he shot Gusto Hanssen, Rakel.'

'We don't take Visa. Have you got anything else? MasterCard, American Express?'

'No! Rakel?'

'Then let's say dollars and euros. The exchange rate's not very favourable, but it's better than the card.'

'Rakel? Rakel? Shit!'

'Something the matter, herr Hole?'

'She rang off. Is this enough?'

12

I STOOD IN SKIPPERGATA WATCHING the rain bucket down. The winter had never managed to get a grip, and there had been a lot of rain instead. Although it had not dampened demand. Oleg, Irene and I turned over more in one day than I had done in a whole week for Odin and Tutu. To the nearest round figure, I earned six thousand a day. I had counted all the Arsenal shirts in the centre. The old boy must have been making more than two million kroner a week, and that was a conservative calculation.

Every night, before we settled up with Andrey, Oleg and I carefully added up all the takings and made it tally with the goods. There was never as much as a krone missing. It wouldn't have been worth it.

And I could trust Oleg one hundred per cent, I don't think he had the imagination to think of stealing, or else he had not understood the concept. Or perhaps his head and his heart were too full of Irene. It was almost comical to see him wagging his tail when she was around. And how utterly blind she was to his adoration. Because Irene could see only one thing.

Me.

It neither bothered me nor pleased me, that was just how it was and always had been.

I knew her so well, knew exactly how I could make her little OMO-pure heart thump, her sweet mouth smile and – if that was what I wanted – her blue eyes fill with big tears. I could have let her go, opened the door and said there you are. But I'm a thief, and thieves don't give away anything they think they might be able to convert into cash. Irene belonged to me, but two million a week belonged to the old boy.

It's funny how six thousand a day develops legs when you take crystal meth like ice cubes in your drinks and wear clothes that are not bought from Cubus. That was why I was still dossing in the rehearsal room with Irene, who slept on a mattress behind the drums. But she was managing, didn't touch so much as a spiked fag, ate veggie shit and had opened a fricking bank account. Oleg was living with his mother, so he must have been rolling in money. He had cleaned himself up, was doing some studying and had even begun to train at Valle Hovin.

While I was standing in Skippergata and thinking and doing mental arithmetic I saw a figure coming towards me in the pouring rain. Glasses misted up, thin hair plastered to his skull, wearing the type of all-weather jacket your fat, ugly girlfriend bought you both for Christmas. Well, either the girlfriend was ugly or she didn't exist. I could see that from his gait. He limped. They've probably invented a word to camouflage it, but I call it a club foot, but then I say 'spastic' and 'negro' as well.

He stopped in front of me.

Now the thing is, I was no longer surprised at the kind of people who bought heroin, but this man definitely did not belong to the usual category of punter.

'How much—?'

'Three hundred and fifty for a quarter.'

'—would you pay for a gram of heroin?'

'Pay? We sell, fuckwit.'

'I know. Just doing a bit of research.'

I looked at him. A journalist? A social worker? Or perhaps a politician? While I was working for Odin and Tutu a similar sort of bozo had come over and said he was on the council and some committee called RUNO, and asked me very politely whether I would go to a meeting about 'Drugs and Youth'. They wanted to hear 'voices from the street'. I turned up for a laugh and listened to them rabbit on about European Cities Against Drugs and a big international plan for a drug-free Europe. I was given a soft drink and a bun and laughed until I cried. But the person leading the meeting was this MILF, peroxide blonde, with features like a man, huge jugs and the voice of a sergeant major. For a moment I wondered whether she'd had more than her tits done. After the meeting she came over to me, said she was secretary to the Councillor for Social Services and that she would like to talk more about these things, could we meet at her place if I had 'the opportunity' one day. She was a MILF without the M, it turned out. Lived alone on a farm, wore tight riding breeches when she opened the door and wanted 'it' to take place in a stable. Didn't bother me if she'd really had her dick done. They had tidied up nicely and installed a pair of milkers that bounced up a storm. But there's something odd about screwing a woman who howls like a model aircraft two metres from sturdy, ruminating horses, which watch you with a semi-interested stare. Afterwards I had to pick straw from between my buttocks, and I asked her if she had a thousand kroner to lend me. We continued to meet until I started to earn six thousand a day, and between shags she had time to explain that a secretary did not sit writing letters for her councillor but dealt with practical politics. Even if she was a slave right now she was the person who made things happen. And when the right people understood that, it would be her turn to be a councillor. What I learned from her talk about the City Hall was that all politicians – high or low – wanted the same two things: power and sex. In that order. Whispering 'cabinet minister' in her ear at the same time as getting two fingers up could make her squirt all the way to the pigsty. I'm not kidding. And in the face of the guy in front of me I could read some of the same sick, intense longings.

'Fuck off.'

'Who's your boss? I want to talk to him.'

Take me to your leader? The guy was either nuts or plain stupid.

'Piss off.'

The guy didn't budge, stood there with a peculiar crease at the hip and pulled something from the pocket of his all-weather jacket. A plastic bag containing white powder — seemed like it could have been half a gram or so.

'This is a sample. Take it to your boss. The price is eight hundred kroner a gram. Careful with the dosage, divide this into ten. I'll be back the day after tomorrow, same time.'

The man passed me the bag, turned and limped down the street.

Normally I would have chucked the bag in the nearest bin. I couldn't even sell the shit to make money for me; I had a reputation to tend to. But there was something about the gleam in the madman's eye. As though he knew something. So, when the working day was over and we had settled up with Andrey, I went with Oleg and Irene to Heroin Park. There, we asked if anyone felt like being a test pilot. I had done this before with Tutu. If there were new goods in town you went to where the most desperate junkies hung out, the ones willing to test anything so long as it's free, who don't care if it kills them because death is round the corner anyway.

Four volunteered, but said they wanted an eighth of real heroin on top. I said that was not on offer and was left with three. I doled out the goods.

'Not enough!' shouted one of the junkies with the diction of a stroke patient. I told him to shut up if he wanted dessert.

Irene, Oleg and I sat watching as they searched for veins between encrusted blood and injected themselves with surprisingly effective movements.

'Oh Jesus,' one of them groaned.

'Fffff . . .' another howled.

Then it went still. Total silence. It was like sending a rocket into space and losing all contact. But I already knew, I could see the ecstasy in their eyes before they disappeared: Houston, we have no problem. When they landed back on earth it was dark. The trip had lasted for more than five hours, double the length of a normal heroin trip. The test panel were unanimous. They had never experienced anything with such a kick. They wanted more, the rest of the bag, now, please, and staggered towards us like the zombies in *Thriller*. We burst out laughing and ran away.

When we sat on my mattress in the rehearsal room half an hour later, I had a bit of thinking to do. A seasoned junkie typically uses a quarter of a gram of street heroin per shot while Oslo's most hardened junkies had got as high as fricking virgins on a quarter of that! The guy had given me pure junk. But what was it? It looked and smelt like heroin, had the consistency of heroin, but to trip out for five hours on such a small dose? Whatever, I knew I was sitting on a gold mine. Eight hundred kroner per gram, which could be diluted three times and sold for fourteen hundred. Fifty grams a day. Thirty thousand straight in your pocket. In mine. In Oleg's and Irene's.

I raised the business proposition to them. Explained the figures.

They looked at each other. They didn't seem to be as enthusiastic as I had expected.

'But Dubai . . .' Oleg said.

I lied and told them there was no danger so long as we didn't trick the old boy. First, we would go and say we were stopping, that we had met Jesus or some such bollocks. Then wait a bit before starting up on our own in a small way.

They looked at each other again. And I suddenly realised there was something to it, something which I had not picked up on before.

'It's just that . . .' Oleg said, his eyes struggling to find a focus on the wall. 'Irene and I, we . . .'

'You what?'

He squirmed like an impaled worm and in the end glanced at Irene for help.

'Oleg and I have decided to live together,' Irene said. 'We're saving up to put a deposit on a flat in Bøler. We'd thought of working through till the summer and then . . .'

'And then?'

'Then we were going to finish school,' Oleg said. 'And then start studying.'

'Law,' Irene said. 'Oleg's got such good grades.' She smiled the way she used to do when she thought she had said something stupid, but her usually pale cheeks were hot and red with pleasure.

They had been sneaking round and palling up behind my fricking back! How had I managed to miss that?

'Law,' I said, opening the bag which still contained more than a gram. 'Isn't that for people who want to make it to the top in the gendarmes?'

Neither of them answered.

I found the spoon I ate cornflakes with and wiped it on my thigh.

'What are you doing?' Oleg asked.

'This has to be celebrated,' I said, pouring the powder onto the spoon. 'Besides, we have to test the product ourselves before we recommend it to the old boy.'

'So it's fine then?' Irene exclaimed with relief in her voice. 'We carry on as before?'

'Of course, my dear.' I put the lighter under the bowl of the spoon. 'This is for you, Irene.'

'Me? But I don't think—'

'For my sake, sis.' I looked up at her and smiled. Smiled the smile she knew I knew she had no antidote for. 'Boring getting high on your own, you know. Sort of lonely.'

The melted powder bubbled in the spoon. I didn't have any cotton wool, so I considered whether to strain it through a broken-off cigarette filter. But it looked so clean. White, even consistency. So I let it cool for a couple of seconds before drawing it into the syringe.

'Gusto—' Oleg began to say.

'We'd better be careful we don't OD, there's enough for three here. You're invited as well, my friend. But perhaps you only feel like watching?'

I didn't need to look up. I knew him too well. Pure of heart, blinded with love and clad in the armour suit of courage that had made him dive from fifteen-metre-high masts into Oslo fjord.

'OK,' he said and began to roll up his sleeve. 'I'm in.'

The same armour suit that would take him down to the bottom and drown him like a rat.

I woke up to pounding on the door. My head felt as if a coal mine had been operating inside it, and I dreaded taking the plunge and opening one eye. The morning light seeped through the crack between the wooden boards nailed to the windows and frame. Irene was lying on her mattress, and I saw Oleg's white Puma Speed Cat trainers sticking out between two amplifiers. I could hear whoever it was had started using their feet.

I got up and tottered towards the door trying to remember any messages about band practice or equipment that had to be collected. I opened a fraction and instinctively put my foot against the door. It didn't help. The shove knocked me backwards into the room and I fell over the drums. One hell of a racket. After shifting the cymbal stands and the snare drum I looked up into the kisser of my dear foster-brother, Stein.

Delete dear.

He had grown bigger, but the Parachute Regiment haircut and the dark, hate-filled flinty eyes were the same. I saw him open his mouth and say something, but my ears were ringing with the sound of the cymbals. Automatically I put my hands in front of my face as he came for me. But he rushed past, stepped over the drum kit and went to Irene on the mattress. She gave a little scream as he grabbed an arm and dragged her to her feet.

He held her tight while stuffing a few possessions into her rucksack. She had stopped resisting by the time he pulled her to the door.

'Stein . . .' I started.

He stopped in the doorway and regarded me with a questioning expression, but I had nothing to add.

'You've done enough damage to this family,' he said.

He looked like fricking Bruce Lee as he swung his leg and kicked the iron door shut. The air quivered. Oleg stuck his head up above the amplifier and said something, but I was still deaf.

I stood with my back to the fireplace and felt the heat making my skin tingle. The flames and an antique bloody table lamp constituted the only light in the room. The old boy sat in the leather chair examining the man we had brought with us in the limousine from Skippergata. He was still wearing his all-weather jacket. Andrey stood behind the man untying the blindfold round his eyes.

'Well,' the old boy said. 'So you supply this product which I have heard so much about.'

'Yes,' the man said, putting on his glasses and squinting round the room.

'Where does it come from?'

'I'm here to sell it, not to provide information about it.'

The old boy stroked his chin with thumb and finger. 'In that case I'm not interested. Taking others' stolen property always leads to dead bodies in this game. And dead bodies are trouble and bad for business.'

'This is not stolen property.'

'I venture to suggest I have a fairly good overview of supply channels, and this is not a product anyone has seen before. So I repeat: I will not buy anything until I have the assurance that this will not rebound on us.'

'I've allowed myself to be brought here blindfolded because I understand the need for discretion. I hope you can show me the same sensitivity.'

The heat had made his glasses mist up, but he kept them on. Andrey and Peter had searched him in the car while I had searched his eyes, body language, voice, hands. All I found was loneliness. There was no fat, ugly girlfriend, only this man and his fantastic dope.

'For all I know, you could be a policeman,' the old boy said.

'With this?' the man said, pointing to his foot.

'If you import goods, how come I haven't heard of you before?'

'Because I'm new. I don't have a record and no one knows me, neither in the police nor in this business. I have a so-called respectable profession and have so far lived a normal life.' He made a cautious grimace which I realised was supposed to be a smile. 'An abnormally normal life, some might claim.'

'Hm.' The old boy stroked his chin repeatedly. Then he grabbed my hand and pulled me to his chair so that I was standing beside him and looking at the man.

'Do you know what I think, Gusto? I think he makes this product himself. What do you think?'

I deliberated. 'Maybe,' I said.

'You know, Gusto, you don't exactly need to be an Einstein in chemistry.

There are detailed recipes on the Net for how to turn opium into morphine and then to heroin. Let's say you get hold of ten kilos of raw opium. Then you find yourself some boiling equipment, a fridge, a bit of methanol and a fan, and hey presto, you've got eight and a half kilos of heroin crystals. Dilute it and you have one point two kilos of street heroin.'

The man in the all-weather jacket coughed. 'It requires a bit more than that.'

'The question', the old boy said, 'is how you get hold of the opium.'

The man shook his head.

'Aha,' the old boy said, stroking the inside of my arm. 'Not opiate. Opioid.'

The man didn't answer.

'Did you hear what he said, Gusto?' The old boy pointed a finger at the club foot. 'He makes totally synthetic dope. He doesn't need any help from nature or Afghanistan, he applies simple chemistry and makes everything on the kitchen table. Total control and no risky smuggling. And it's at least as powerful as heroin. We've got a clever guy among us, Gusto. That sort of enterprise commands respect.'

'Respect,' I mumbled.

'How much can you produce?'

'Two kilos a week maybe. It depends.'

'I'll take the lot,' the old boy said.

'The lot?' The man's voice was flat and contained no real surprise.

'Yes, everything you produce. May I make you a business proposition, herr . . .?'

'Ibsen.'

'Ibsen?'

'If you don't mind.'

'Not at all. He was also a great artist. I would like to propose a partnership, herr Ibsen. Vertical integration. We corner the market and set the price. Better margin for both of us. What do you say?'

Ibsen shook his head.

The old boy tilted his head with a smile on the lipless mouth. 'Why not, herr Ibsen?'

I watched the little man straighten up; he seemed to grow in the baggy, all-year-round, world's-most-boring-person jacket.

'If I give you the monopoly, herr . . .'

The old boy pressed his fingertips together. 'You can call me whatever you like, herr Ibsen.'

'I don't want to be dependent on a single buyer, herr Dubai. It's too risky. And it means you can force prices down. On the other hand, I don't want too many buyers, because then the risk that the police will trace me is greater. I came to you because you're known to be invisible, but I want one more buyer. I have already been in contact with Los Lobos. I hope you can understand.'

The old boy laughed his chug-chug laugh. 'Listen and learn, Gusto. Not only is he a pharmacist, he's also a businessman. Good, herr Ibsen, let's say that then.'

'The price . . .'

'I'll pay what you asked. You'll find this is a business in which you don't waste time haggling, herr Ibsen. Life's too short and death too close at hand. Shall we say the first delivery next Tuesday?'

On the way out the old boy acted as if he needed to support himself on me. His nails scratched the skin on my arm.

'Have you thought about exporting, herr Ibsen? The checks on exporting drugs from Norway are non-existent, you know.'

Ibsen didn't answer. But I saw it now. What he wanted. Saw it as he stood over his club foot with a pivoted hip. Saw it in the reflection from his sweaty, shiny forehead below the thinning hair. The condensation had gone from his glasses, and his eyes had the same gleam I had seen in Skippergata. Payback, Dad. He wanted some payback. Payback for all the things he hadn't received: respect, love, admiration, acceptance, everything it is claimed you can't buy. Although you can, of course. Isn't that right, Dad? Life owes you stuff, but sometimes you have to be your own sodding debt collector. And if we have to burn in hell for it, heaven's going to be sparsely populated. Isn't that right, Dad?

*   *   *

Harry sat by the road looking out. Watched the planes taxiing in and taxiing out to the runway.

He would be in Shanghai within eighteen hours.

He liked Shanghai. Liked the food, liked walking down the Bund along the River Huangpu to Peace Hotel, liked going into the Old Jazz Bar and listening to the ancient jazz musicians creaking their way through standards, liked the thought that they had been sitting there and playing without an audible break since the revolution in '49. Liked her. Liked what they had, and what they didn't have, but ignored.

The ability to ignore. It was a wonderful quality, not something he was naturally blessed with, but which he had practised over the last three years. Not banging your head against the wall if you didn't have to.

How unshakeable is your faith in your gospel actually? Aren't you also a doubter?

He would be in Shanghai in eighteen hours.

Could be in Shanghai within eighteen hours.

Shit.

She answered on second ring.

'What do you want?'

'Don't ring off again, OK?'

'I'm here.'

'Listen, how strong a hold have you got on that Nils Christian?'

'Hans Christian.'

'Is he besotted enough for you to persuade him to help me with a very dubious stunt?'

13

IT HAD RAINED ALL NIGHT, and from where Harry was standing, in front of Oslo District Prison, he could see a fresh layer of leaves lying like a wet yellow tarpaulin over the park. He had not slept much after he had gone straight from the airport to Rakel's. Hans Christian had come, not protested too much and gone again. Afterwards Rakel and Harry drank tea and talked about Oleg. About how it had been before. About how it had been, but not about how it could have been. In the early hours Rakel had said Harry could sleep in Oleg's room. Before Harry went to bed he had used Oleg's computer to search for, and find, old articles about the police officer found dead beneath Älvsborg Bridge in Gothenburg. It confirmed what Cato had told him, and Harry also found a piece in the ever-sensationalist *Göteborgstidningen* leaking rumours about the dead man being a burner, which it defined as a person criminals used to destroy evidence against them. It was only two hours since Rakel had woken him with a steaming cup of coffee and a whisper. She had always done that, started the day with whispers, to him and Oleg, as if to soften the transition from dreams to reality.

Harry peered into the CCTV camera, heard the low buzz and pushed open the door. Then he entered quickly. Held the briefcase up in front of him for all to see and laid his ID card on the counter while turning his good cheek.

'Hans Christian Simonsen . . .' the prison officer mumbled without looking up, running her eye down the list in front of her. 'There, yes. For Oleg Fauke.'

'Correct,' Harry said.

Another officer led him through the corridors and across the open gallery in the middle of the prison. The officer talked about how warm the autumn had been and rattled the huge bunch of keys whenever he opened a new door. They walked through the common room, and Harry saw a ping-pong table with two rackets and an open book on top, and a kitchenette, in which a wholemeal loaf and a bread knife had been left out along with spreads of various kinds. But no inmates.

They stopped by a white door and the officer unlocked it.

'I thought cell doors were open at this time of day,' Harry said.

'The others are, but this prisoner's doing a 171,' the officer said. 'He's allowed out only one hour a day.'

'Where are all the others then?'

'God knows. Perhaps they've got the Hustler Channel on TV again.'

After the officer had let him in, Harry stood by the door until he heard the footsteps outside fading in the distance. The cell was the usual kind. Ten square metres. A bed, a cupboard, a desk and chair, bookshelves, a TV. Oleg sat at the desk and looked up in surprise.

'You wanted to meet me,' Harry said.

'I thought I wasn't allowed visitors,' Oleg said.

'This isn't a visit. It's a consultation with your defence counsel.'

'Defence counsel?'

Harry nodded. And saw the light dawn in Oleg's eyes. Smart boy.

'How . . .?'

'The type of murder you're suspected of committing doesn't qualify you for a high-security prison. It wasn't so difficult.' Harry opened the briefcase, took out the white Game Boy and passed it to Oleg. 'Here you are. It's for you.'

Oleg ran his fingers over the display. 'Where did you find it?'

Harry thought he could see the suggestion of a smile on the boy's serious face. 'Vintage model with battery. I found it in Hong Kong. My plan was to crush you at Tetris the next time we met.'

'Never!' Oleg laughed. 'Not at that, and not at underwater swimming.'

'That time in Frogner Lido? Mm. I seem to recall I was a metre ahead of you—'

'A metre *behind* more like! Mum was a witness.'

Harry sat still so as not to destroy anything, soaked up the happiness at seeing the pleasure in his face.

'What did you want to talk to me about, Oleg?'

The clouds drew back over his face. He fidgeted with the Game Boy, turned it over and over as if looking for the start button.

'Take all the time you need, Oleg, but it's often easiest to start at the beginning.'

The boy raised his head and looked at Harry. 'Can I trust you? No matter what?'

Harry was about to say something, but stopped. Just nodded.

'You have to get something for me . . .'

It was like someone twisting a knife in Harry's heart. He already knew how Oleg would continue.

'They've only got boy and speed here, but I need violin. Can you help me, Harry?'

'Was that why you asked me to come?'

'You're the only person who's managed to get round the ban on visitors.' Oleg stared at Harry with his solemn, dark eyes. A tiny twitch in the thin skin below one eye revealed the desperation.

'You know I can't, Oleg.'

'Course you can!' His voice sounded hard and metallic between the cell walls.

'What about the people you sold for, can't they supply you?'

'Sold what?'

'Don't lie to me!' Harry smacked his hand down on the briefcase lid. 'I found an Arsenal shirt in your locker at Valle Hovin.'

'Did you break in . . .?'

'I found this as well.' Harry slung the photograph of the family on the desk. 'The girl in the picture, do you know where she is?'

'Who . . .?'

'Irene Hanssen. Your girlfriend.'

'How . . .?'

'You were seen together at the Watchtower. There's a jumper smelling of wild flowers and a junkie kit for two in the locker. Sharing your stash is more intimate than sharing the marital bed, isn't it. Plus your mother told me she saw you in town, looking like a happy idiot. My diagnosis: in love.'

Oleg's Adam's apple went up and down.

'Well?' Harry said.

'I don't know where she is! OK? She just disappeared. Perhaps her brother picked her up again. Perhaps she's in rehab somewhere. Perhaps she caught a plane and buggered off from all this shit.'

'Or perhaps the news is not so good,' Harry said. 'When did you last see her?'

'I don't remember.'

'You remember to the hour.'

Oleg closed his eyes. 'One hundred and twenty-two days ago. Long before the stuff with Gusto, so what's this got to do with the case?'

'It all slots together, Oleg. A murder is a white whale. A missing person is a white whale. If you've seen a white whale twice it's the same whale. What can you tell me about Dubai?'

'It's the biggest town, but not the capital, of the United Arab Emir—'

'Why are you protecting them, Oleg? What is it you can't tell me?'

Oleg had found the start button on the Game Boy and flicked it to and fro. Then he flipped off the battery cover at the back, raised the lid of the metal bin beside the desk and dropped the batteries inside before passing the toy back to Harry.

'Dead.'

Harry looked at the Game Boy and slipped it into his pocket.

'If you can't get me violin, I'll shoot up the diluted shit they've got here. Heard of fentanyl and heroin?'

'Fentanyl is a recipe for an OD, Oleg.'

'Right. So you can tell Mum afterwards it was *your* fault.'

Harry didn't answer. Oleg's pathetic attempt to manipulate him didn't make him angry, it made him want to embrace the boy and hold him tight. Harry didn't need to see the tears in Oleg's eyes to know the struggle that was taking place in his body and head, he could feel the gnawing hunger in the boy, it was physical. And then there is nothing else, no morality, no love, no consideration, just the eternally pounding thought of the rush, the high, peace. Harry had once in his life been on the verge of accepting a heroin shot, but a chance second of clear-sightedness had made him decline. Perhaps it was the certainty that heroin would do what alcohol still had not been able to do: kill him. Perhaps it was the girl who had told him how she had been hooked from the first shot because nothing, nothing she had experienced or imagined, could surpass the ecstasy of it. Perhaps it was his pal from Oppsal who had gone to rehab to have his tolerance set to zero, because he hoped that when he injected himself afterwards it would be something like the first sweet shot. And who said that when he saw his three-month-old son's vaccination mark in his thigh, he began to cry because it had triggered such a strong craving for dope that he had been willing to sacrifice everything, to go straight from the clinic to Plata.

'Let's make a deal,' Harry said, conscious of his own thick voice. 'I'll get you what you ask and you tell me all you know.'

'Great!' Oleg said, and Harry saw his pupils widen. He had read somewhere that with heavy heroin users parts of their brains could be activated even before the syringe was inserted, that they were already physically high while the melted powder was being pumped up a vein. And Harry also knew it was these parts of Oleg's brain that were speaking now, that there was no other answer than 'Great!', whether it was a lie or the truth.

'But I don't want to buy it on the street,' Harry said. 'Have you got any violin in your stash?'

Oleg seemed to hesitate for a second. 'You've been to my stash.'

Harry remembered again that it was not true that nothing was sacred to a heroin user. The stash was sacred.

'Come on, Oleg. You don't keep dope where other junkies have access. Where's your other stash, your reserves?'

'I've only got one.'

'I'm not going to steal anything from you.'

'I haven't got another stash, I'm telling you!'

Harry could hear he was lying. But that was not so important; it only meant presumably he didn't have any violin there.

'I'll be back tomorrow,' Harry said, getting up, knocking on the door and waiting. But no one came. In the end he wrenched the handle. The door opened. Definitely not a high-security prison.

Harry walked back the way he had come. There was no one in the corridor, nor in the common room where Harry noticed the food was still out, but the bread knife had been tidied away. He continued to the door leading out of the unit and into the gallery and discovered to his surprise that it was open, too.

Only at reception did he find locked doors. He mentioned the fact to the prison officer behind the glass, and she raised an eyebrow and glanced at the monitors above her. 'No one will get any further than here anyway.'

'Apart from me, I hope.'

'Eh?'

'Nothing.'

Harry had walked almost a hundred metres through the park down towards Grønlandsleiret when it struck him. The empty rooms, the open doors, the bread knife. He froze. His heart accelerated so fast he felt nauseous. He heard a bird singing. The smell of grass. Then he turned and sprinted back to the prison. Felt his mouth go dry with fear and his heart pound adrenalin around his body.

14

VIOLIN HIT OSLO LIKE A fricking asteroid. Oleg had explained to me the difference between a meteorite and a meteoroid and all the other junk that could hit us on the head at any moment, and this was an asteroid, a huge ugly brute that could flatten the earth with . . . Shit, you know what I mean, Dad, don't laugh. We stood selling eighths, quarters, whole grams and five grams all at once from morning to night. The city centre was turned upside down. And then we raised the price again. And the queues stretched even further. And then we put up the price again. And the queues were just as long. And then we put up the price again. And that was when all hell broke loose.

A gang of Kosovar Albanians robbed our team behind the Stock Exchange. There were two Estonian brothers operating without a scout, and the Kosovar Albanians used baseball bats and knuckledusters. Took the money and the dope and smashed their hips. Two nights later a Vietnamese gang struck in Prinsens gate, ten minutes before Andrey and Peter were due to collect the day's takings. They attacked the dope man in the backyard without the money man or the scout noticing. It was a bit like: 'What next?'

The question was answered two days later.

Oslo folk who were up early and on their way to work caught sight of a slit-eye dangling upside down from Sanner Bridge before the cops came.

He was dressed as a lunatic, with a straitjacket and a gag in his mouth. The rope round his ankles was just long enough for him not to be able to hold his head above the water. At least after his stomach muscles failed him.

That same evening Oleg and I were given a shooter by Andrey. It was Russian, Andrey trusted only Russian things. He smoked black Russian cigarettes, used a Russian mobile phone (I'm not kidding, Dad. Gresso, expensive luxury number made from African blackwood, but apparently waterproof and didn't send out signals when it was switched on, so the cops couldn't trace it) and swore by Russian pistols. Andrey explained that the brand name of the shooter was Odessa, which was a cheap version of a Stechkin, as if we knew anything about either of them. Nonetheless, the Odessa's speciality was that it could fire fricking salvos. It had a magazine capable of holding twenty rounds of Makarov, nine by eighteen millimetre calibre, the same as Andrey and Peter and some of the others used. We were given a box of bullets, and he showed us how to load, put on the safety catch and fire the strange, clumpy gun. He said we had to hold it tight and aim a bit lower than we thought in order to hit. And that we shouldn't aim at the head, which was what we thought, but anywhere on the upper torso. If we twisted the little lever on the side to C it would fire salvos, and a little pressure on the trigger was enough to loose off three to four shots. But he assured us that nine times out of ten you just had to show the gun. After he had left, Oleg said it looked like the shooter on the cover of some Foo Fighters record, and he was buggered if he was going to shoot anyone, we should chuck it in the bin. So I said I would have it.

The newspapers ran riot. They screamed about gang warfare, blood in the streets, fricking LA, and so on. The opposition politicians went on about a failed crime policy, failed drug policy, failed chairman of the City Council, failed City Council. One Centre Party loony said Oslo was a failed town and should be wiped off the map, it was a disgrace to the country. The person who got the most stick was the Chief of Police, but as we know shit sinks, and after a Somali had shot dead two relatives in the tribe at point-blank range down by Plata, in broad daylight, and no one was arrested, the head of Orgkrim handed in his resignation. The Councillor for Social Services

– who was also head of the Police Commission – said that crime, drugs and the police were primarily the state's responsibility, but she saw it as her duty to ensure that Oslo's citizens could walk through the streets in safety. That was kind of her. And behind her stood her secretary. It was my old friend. MILF without the M. She looked serious and businesslike. Though all I saw was a hot bitch with riding breeches round her knees.

One night Andrey came early, said we were finished for the day and I should go with him to Blindern.

When he drove straight past the old boy's place I began to think very nasty thoughts. But then, fortunately, Andrey turned into the neighbour's plot, which of course he also owned. Andrey escorted me in. The house was not as empty as it looked from the outside. Behind the peeling walls and cracked windowpanes it was furnished and heated. The old boy was sitting in a room with bookshelves from floor to ceiling, and some of that classical-type music was belting out of large speakers on the floor. I sat on the only other chair in the room, and Andrey closed the door as he left.

'I've decided to ask you to do something for me, Gusto,' said the old boy, placing a hand on my knee.

I glanced at the closed door.

'We're at war,' he said, getting up. He went to the shelves and pulled out a thick book with a brown, stained cover. 'This text is from six hundred years before Christ was born. I can't read Chinese, so I have only this French translation, which was made more than two hundred years ago by a Jesuit named Jean Joseph Marie Amiot. I went to an auction and had my bid of one hundred and ninety thousand accepted. The book's about how to fool the enemy in war and it's the most quoted work on the subject. Stalin, Hitler and Bruce Lee had it as their bible. And do you know what?' He replaced the book and pulled out another. 'I prefer this one.' He threw the book over to me.

It was a thin volume with a shiny, blue cover, evidently quite new. I read the title: *Chess For Beginners*.

'Sixty kroner at a sale,' the old boy said. 'We're going to perform a move called castling.'

'Castling?'

'A sideways switch of king and castle to provide a defence. We're going to form an alliance.'

'With a castle?'

'Think City Hall castle.'

I thought.

'City Council,' said the old boy. 'The Councillor for Social Services has a secretary called Isabelle Skøyen, who in effect runs the town's drug policy. I've checked a source and she's perfect. Intelligent, efficient and extremely ambitious. The reason she has not climbed higher, according to my source, is her lifestyle, which is bound to attract headlines. Just a question of time. She parties, speaks her mind and has lovers in Oslo East and Oslo West.'

'Sounds absolutely dreadful,' I said.

The old boy sent me an admonitory look before continuing. 'Her father was spokesperson for the Centre Party, but was thrown out when he tried to enter national politics. And my source tells me Isabelle has inherited his dreams and since the odds are best for the Socialist Party she's left her father's little party of farmers. In short, everything about Isabelle Skøyen is flexible and can be adapted to suit her ambition. Furthermore, she is single with a not insubstantial debt on the family farm.'

'So what are we going to do?' I asked as if I were part of the violin administration.

The old boy smiled as though he considered the remark charming. 'We're going to threaten her to come to the negotiating table, where we will entice her into an alliance. And you're in charge of the threats, Gusto. That's why you're here now.'

'Me? Threaten a woman politician?'

'Precisely. A woman politician you've copulated with, Gusto. A council employee who has used her position and status for sexual exploitation of a teenager with considerable social problems.'

At first I couldn't believe my ears. Until he produced a photo from his jacket and placed it on the table in front of me. It looked as if it had been taken from behind a tinted car window. It was of Tollbugata and showed a young boy getting into a Land Rover. The number plate was visible. The boy was me. The car belonged to Isabelle Skøyen.

A cold shiver ran down my spine. 'How do you know . . .?'

'My dear Gusto, I told you I was keeping an eye on you. What I want you to do is to contact Isabelle Skøyen on the private number I am sure you have and tell her this story we have prepared for the press. And then ask for an extremely private meeting between the three of us.'

He walked over to the window and looked at the drab weather.

'You'll find she has a gap in her calendar.'

15

IN THE COURSE OF THE last three years in Hong Kong Harry had done more running than in the whole of his former life. Yet in the thirteen seconds he spent covering the hundred metres to the prison entrance, his brain was playing various scenarios with a common theme: he was too late.

He rang and resisted the temptation to shake the door while waiting for it to open. At last there was a buzz, and he ran to reception.

'Forgotten something?' the officer asked.

'Yes,' Harry said and waited for her to let him through the locked door. 'Sound the alarm!' he shouted, dropped the briefcase and ran. 'Oleg Fauke's cell.'

His footsteps echoed through the empty gallery, the empty corridors and the much too empty common room. He was not out of breath, yet his breathing sounded like roaring inside his head.

Oleg's scream reached him as he emerged from the last corridor. The door to his cell was half open, and seconds before he got there it felt like the nightmare, the avalanche, the feet that would not move fast enough.

Then he was inside and absorbing the scene.

The desk was on its side, paper and books were strewn across the floor. At the other end of the room, with his back to the cupboard, stood Oleg.

The black Slayer T-shirt was drenched in blood. He was holding the metal lid of the waste-paper bin in front of him. His mouth was open, and he was screaming and screaming. Harry saw the back of a Gym Tech singlet, above it a broad, sweaty bull neck, above that a shiny skull and above that a raised hand holding a bread knife. Metal resounded against metal as the blade struck the bin lid. The man must have noticed the change of light in the room, for the next moment he whirled round. Lowered his head and held the knife low, pointing it towards Harry.

'Out!' he hissed.

Harry avoided the temptation of looking at the knife; instead he focused on the feet. He noted that behind the man Oleg had slid to the floor. Compared with martial arts practitioners Harry had a lamentably small repertoire of offensive moves. He had only two. And also only two rules. One: there are no rules. Two: attack first. And when Harry acted it was with the automatic movements of someone who has learned, practised and repeated only two methods of attack. Harry stepped towards the knife so that the man was forced to retreat in order to swing at him. And by the time the man had wound up his arm Harry had raised his right leg and angled his hip. As the knife was on its way forward, Harry's foot was on its way down. It struck the man's knee above the patella. And since the human anatomy is not very well protected against violence from that angle, the quadriceps immediately gave way, followed by the knee-joint ligaments and – as the kneecap was pressed down in front of the tibia – also the patellar tendon.

The man fell to the ground with a howl. The knife clattered to the floor as his hands groped for his kneecap. And his eyes saucered when he found it in a completely new position.

Harry kicked the knife away and raised his foot to finish off the attack as he had been taught: stamp on the opponent's thigh muscles to cause such massive internal bleeding that he would not be able to get up again. But he saw that the job was already done and lowered his foot.

He heard the sound of running feet and the rattle of keys from outside in the corridor.

'Over here!' Harry shouted, stepping over the screaming man towards Oleg.

He heard panting from the door.

'Get that man out and get hold of a doctor.' Harry had to yell to drown the continuous screams.

'Bloody hell, what—'

'Never mind that now, get hold of the doctor.' Harry tore the Slayer T-shirt and searched through the blood for the wound. 'And the doctor should come here first. He's only got a wonky knee.'

Harry held Oleg's face between his bloodstained hands while listening to the screaming man being dragged away.

'Oleg? Are you there? Oleg?'

The boy's eyes rolled and the word that escaped his lips was so faint that Harry barely heard it. And felt his chest constrict.

'Oleg, it'll be alright. He hasn't stabbed anything you really need.'

'Harry—'

'And soon it'll be Christmas Eve. They're going to give you morphine.'

'Shut up, Harry.'

Harry shut up. Oleg opened his eyes. There was a feverish, desperate sheen to them. His voice was hoarse, but quite clear now.

'You should have let him complete the job, Harry.'

'What are you saying?'

'You have to let me do this.'

'Do what?'

No answer.

'Do what, Oleg?'

Oleg placed a hand behind Harry's head, pulled him down and whispered: 'You can't stop this, Harry. It's all happened. It has to run its course. If you get in the way, more will die.'

'Who's going to die?'

'It's too big, Harry. It'll swallow you up, swallow everyone up.'

'Who's going to die? Who are you protecting, Oleg? Is it Irene?'

Oleg closed his eyes. His lips barely moved. Then not at all. And Harry thought he looked like he had when he was eleven and had just fallen asleep after a long day. Then he spoke.

'It's you, Harry. They're going to kill you.'

As Harry was leaving the prison the ambulances had arrived. He thought of how things used to be. The town as it used to be. His life as it used to be. While he had been using Oleg's computer he had also looked for Sardines and Russian Amcar Club. He hadn't found any signs to suggest they had been resurrected. Resurrection may be generally too much to hope for. Perhaps life doesn't teach you much, apart from this one thing: there is no way back.

Harry lit a cigarette, and before he took the first drag, the brain already celebrating the fact that nicotine would accompany the blood, he heard the sound being played back, the sound he knew he would hear for the rest of the evening and night, the almost inaudible word that had first crossed Oleg's lips in the cell:

'Dad.'

PART TWO

16

THE MOTHER RAT LICKED THE metal. It tasted of salt. She gave a start as the fridge sprang into life and began to hum. The church bells were still ringing. There was a way into the nest she hadn't tried. Hadn't dared to try since the human blocking the entrance was not yet dead. But the high-frequency howls of her young were making her desperate. So she did. She darted up the jacket sleeve of the human. There was a vague smell of smoke. Not smoke from a cigarette or a bonfire, but something else. Something in gas form that had been in the clothes, but had been washed out so that only a few molecules of air were left between the innermost threads in the cloth. She approached the elbow, but it was too narrow there. She stopped and listened. In the distance there was the sound of a police siren.

There were all those brief moments and choices, Dad. Those I thought were unimportant, here today, gone tomorrow, as it were. But they pile up. And before you know it they have become a river that drags you along with it. That leads you to where you are going. And that was where I was going. In fricking July. No, I wasn't going there! I wanted to go elsewhere, Dad.

As we turned in towards the main building Isabelle Skøyen stood on her drive, in her tight riding breeches, legs akimbo.

'Andrey, you wait here,' the old boy said. 'Peter, you check the area.'

We got out of the limousine to a cowshed smell, the buzz of flies and distant cowbells. She shook hands stiffly with the old boy, ignored me and invited us in for a coffee, 'a' being the operative word.

In the corridor hung pictures of nags with the best bloodlines, the most racing cups and fuck knows what. The old boy walked along by the photos and asked if one was an English thoroughbred and praised the slim legs and impressive chest. I wondered whether he was talking about a horse or her. Nevertheless, it worked. Isabelle's expression thawed a little and she became less curt.

'Let's sit in the lounge and talk,' he said.

'I think we'll go to the kitchen,' she said and the ice was back in her voice.

We sat down, and she put the coffee pot in the middle of the table.

'You pour for us, Gusto,' the old boy said, looking out of the window. 'Nice farm you have here, fru Skøyen.'

'There's no "fru" here.'

'Where I grew up we called all women who could run a farm "fru" whether they were widows, divorced or unmarried. It was considered a mark of respect.'

He turned to her with a broad smile. She met his eyes. And for a couple of seconds it was so quiet all you heard was the retard fly banging against the window trying to get out.

'Thank you,' she said.

'Good. For the moment let's forget these photos, fru Skøyen.'

She stiffened on her chair. In the phone conversation I'd had with Isabelle she had at first attempted to laugh off the suggestion that we could send the photographs of her and me to the press. She said she was a single, sexually active woman who had taken a younger man, so what? First of all, she was an insignificant secretary to a councillor, and second this was Norway. Hypocrisy was what they pursued at American presidential elections. So I had painted the threat in bright colours with concise strokes. She had paid me, and I could prove it. She was a punter, and prostitution and drugs were issues she tackled in the press on behalf of the Social Services Committee, didn't she?

Two minutes later we had agreed a time and place for this meeting.

'The press writes enough about politicians' private lives as it is,' the old boy said. 'Let's talk about a business proposal instead, fru Skøyen. A good proposal may, unlike blackmail, afford advantages to both parties. Agreed?'

She frowned. The old boy beamed. 'By business proposal I don't mean of course that money is involved. Even though this farm probably doesn't run itself. That would be corruption. What I'm offering you is a purely political transaction. Covert, I'll grant you that, but this is something practised every day at City Hall. And it is in the people's best interests, isn't it?'

Skøyen nodded again, on her guard.

'This deal will have to stay between you and us, fru Skøyen. It will primarily benefit the town, although if you have political ambition, I can see a possible advantage for you personally. Given that is the case, it will of course make the path to a leading chair at City Hall much shorter. Never mind a role in national politics.'

Her coffee cup had stopped halfway to her mouth.

'I haven't even considered asking you to do something unethical, fru Skøyen. I just want to illustrate where we have common interests and then leave it to you to do what I think is right.'

'I do what *you* think is right?'

'The City Council is in a tough spot. Even before last month's unfortunate developments, the steering committee's aim was to get Oslo off the list of Europe's worst towns for heroin use. You were to reduce drugs turnover, addiction among young people and not least the number of overdoses. Right now nothing seems more unlikely. Isn't that right, fru Skøyen?'

She didn't answer.

'What's needed is a hero, or a heroine, to tidy the mess from the bottom upwards.'

She nodded slowly.

'What she has to do is to clear up the gangs and the cartels.'

Isabelle snorted. 'Thanks, but that's been tried in every town in Europe. New gangs spring up again like weeds. Where there's demand there will always be new suppliers.'

'Exactly,' he said. 'Just like weeds. I see you have a field of strawberries, fru Skøyen. Do you use a mulch?'

'Yes, strawberry clover.'

'I can offer you a mulch,' the old boy said. 'Strawberry clover wearing Arsenal shirts.'

She looked at him. I could see her greedy brain working at maximum revs. The old boy looked pleased.

'Mulch, my dear Gusto,' he said, taking a swig of coffee, 'is a weed you plant and allow to grow unhindered to prevent other weeds from appearing. Because strawberry clover is a lesser evil than the alternatives. Do you understand?'

'I think so,' I said. 'Where weeds will grow anyhow it's a good idea to plant a weed that doesn't destroy the strawberries.'

'Exactly. And in this little analogy the City Council's vision of a cleaner Oslo is the strawberries, and all the gangs selling dangerous heroin and creating anarchy on the streets are the weeds. While we and violin are the mulch.'

'And so?'

'And so you first have to do the weeding. And then you can leave the strawberry clover in peace.'

'And what is it that is actually so much better for the strawberries?' she asked.

'We don't shoot anyone. We operate discreetly. We sell a drug that does not end in overdoses. With a monopoly in the strawberry field we can raise the prices so high that there are fewer and fewer young people recruited. Without our total profit going down, it has to be admitted. Fewer users and fewer sellers. Junkies will no longer fill the parks and our city-centre streets. In brief, Oslo will be a delight to behold for tourists, politicians and voters.'

'I'm not on the Social Services Committee.'

'Not yet, fru Skøyen. But then weeding is not for committees. For that they have a secretary. To make all the small, daily decisions which in their entirety constitute the real action taken. Naturally you follow the council's adopted policies, but you are the person who has daily contact with the police, who discusses their activities and ventures in Kvadraturen for example. You will of course have to define your role a bit more, but you seem to have a certain talent for that. A little interview about drug policies in Oslo here, a statement about drug overdoses there. So that when success is a fact the press and your party colleagues will know who is the brain behind –' he put on his Komodo dragon grin – 'the market's proud winner of this year's biggest strawberries.'

We all sat very still. The fly had given up its attempt to escape when it discovered the sugar bowl.

'This conversation has never taken place,' Isabelle said.

'Of course not.'

'We've never even met.'

'Sad but true, fru Skøyen.'

'And how do you imagine . . . the weeding should be conducted?'

'We can offer a helping hand. There's a long tradition of snitching to eliminate rivals in this industry, and we'll supply you with the necessary information. You will naturally provide the Social Services Committee with suggestions for the Police Commission, but you will need a confidant in the police. Perhaps someone who can benefit from being part of this success story. A person . . .'

'An ambitious person who can be pragmatic so long as it's in the town's best interests?' Isabelle Skøyen raised her cup to a *skål*. 'Shall we go and sit in the lounge?'

Sergey was lying supine on the bench as the tattooist studied the drawings in silence.

When he had arrived punctually at the little shop the tattooist had been busy designing a big dragon on the back of a boy who was lying there with his teeth clenched while a woman, who was clearly the mother, was comforting him and asking if the tattoo needed to be so big. She paid when it was finished and on the way out asked the boy if he was happy now he had an even cooler tattoo than Preben and Kristoffer.

'This one will fit on your back better,' the tattooist said, pointing to one of the drawings.

'*Tupoy*,' Sergey muttered. Idiot.

'Eh?'

'Everything has to be exactly the same as the drawing. Do I have to tell you every time?'

'Yeah, well, I can't do it all today.'

'Yes, you can, do it all. Double pay.'

'Urgent, is it?'

Sergey responded with a brief nod. Andrey had rung him every day, kept him up to date. So when he had called today, Sergey had not been prepared. Prepared for what Andrey had to say.

The necessary had become necessary.

And Sergey had known there was no way out.

He had immediately brought himself up short: no way *out*? Who wanted out?

Perhaps he'd thought of escape because Andrey had warned him. Told him that the policeman had managed to disarm an inmate they had paid to kill Oleg Fauke. Fair enough, the inmate was only a Norwegian and hadn't killed anyone with a knife before, but it meant that this wasn't going to be as easy as the last time. Shooting their dope seller, the boy, had been a simple execution. This time he would have to sneak up on the policeman, wait till he had him where he wanted and take him when he least expected it.

'I don't want to be a killjoy but the tattoos you've already got are not exactly quality workmanship. The lines are unclear, and the ink's poor. Shouldn't we freshen them up a little?'

Sergey didn't answer. What did the guy know about quality workmanship? The lines were unclear because the tattooist in prison had to use a sharpened guitar string attached to an electric shaver as a needle, and the ink was made from melted shoe sole mixed with urine.

'Drawing,' Sergey said, pointing. 'Now!'

'And you're sure you want a pistol? It's your choice, but my experience is that people are shocked by violent symbols. Just so you're warned.'

The guy clearly knew nothing about Russian criminals' tattoos. Didn't know that the cat meant he had been convicted for stealing, the church with two cupolas meant he had two convictions. Didn't know that the burn marks on his chest were from a magnesium powder dressing he had held directly on his skin to remove a tattoo. The tattoo had been of female genitals and had been given to him while he had been doing a second stint in prison by members of the Georgian Black Corn gang who thought he owed them money after a card game.

Nor did the tattooist know that the pistol in the drawing, a Makarov, the Russian police's service weapon, denoted that he, Sergey Ivanov, had killed a policeman.

He knew nothing, and that was fine, it was best for everyone if he stuck to tattooing butterflies, Chinese symbols and colourful dragons on well-fed Norwegian youths who thought their catalogue tattoos were a statement about something.

'Shall we begin then?' the tattooist asked.

Sergey hesitated. The tattooist had been right, this was urgent. But why was it so urgent, why couldn't he wait until the policeman was dead? Because if he was caught after the murder and sent to a Norwegian prison, where unlike in Russia there were no tattooists, he wouldn't be able to get the bloody tattoo he needed.

But there was another answer to the question as well.

Was he getting the tattoo before the murder because, deep down, he was afraid? So afraid he was not sure he would be able to go through with it? That was why he had to have the tattoo now, to burn all the bridges behind him, remove all possibilities of a retreat so that he *had* to carry out the murder? No Siberian urka can live with a lie carved into his skin, that goes without saying. And he had been happy, he *knew* that he had been happy, so what were these thoughts, where did they come from?

He knew where they came from.

The dope seller. The boy with the Arsenal shirt.

He had started to appear in his dreams.

'Yes, let's begin,' Sergey said.

17

'THE DOCTOR RECKONS OLEG WILL be on his feet again within a few days,' Rakel said. She was leaning against the fridge holding a cup of tea.

'Then he'll have to be moved to somewhere absolutely no one can get their hands on him,' Harry said.

He was standing by her kitchen window and looking down on the town, where the cars of the afternoon rush hour were crawling like glow-worms along the main roads.

'The police must have such places for witness protection,' she said.

Rakel had not become hysterical. She had taken the news of the knife attack on Oleg with a kind of resigned composure. As though it was something she had been half expecting. At the same time Harry could see the indignation on her face. Her fight face.

'He has to be in a prison, but I'll talk to the public prosecutor about a move,' Hans Christian Simonsen said. He had come as soon as Rakel had rung, and he sat at the kitchen table with circles of sweat under the arms of his shirt.

'See if you can circumvent official channels,' Harry said.

'What do you mean?' the solicitor asked.

'The doors were unlocked, so at least one of the prison guards must

159

have been in on this. As long as we're in the dark about who was involved, we have to assume that everyone could have been.'

'Aren't you being a touch paranoid now?'

'Paranoia saves lives,' Harry said. 'Can you fix that, Simonsen?'

'I'll see what I can do. What about where he is now?'

'He's in Ullevål Hospital, and I've made sure there are two officers I trust looking after him. One more thing: Oleg's attacker is in hospital, but he will end up with restricted rights afterwards.'

'No post or visitors?' Simonsen asked.

'Yep. Can you make sure we find out what he says in his statement to the police or his solicitor?'

'That's trickier.' Simonsen scratched his head.

'They probably won't get a word out of him, but try anyway,' Harry said, buttoning his coat.

'Where are you going?' Rakel asked, holding his arm.

'To the source,' Harry said.

It was eight o'clock in the evening, and the traffic in the capital of the country with the world's shortest working day had eased long ago. The boy standing on the steps at the bottom of Tollbugata was wearing shirt number 23. Arshavin. He had his hoodie drawn over his head and wore a pair of oversized white Air Jordan trainers. The Girbaud jeans were ironed and so stiff they could almost stand up by themselves. Full gangsta gear, everything was copied down to the last detail from the latest Rick Ross video, and Harry assumed that when the trousers slipped down the right boxer shorts would be revealed, no scars from knives or bullets, but at least one violence-glorifying tattoo.

Harry walked over to him.

'Violin, a quarter.'

The boy looked down at Harry without taking his hands from the pockets of his zip hoodie and nodded.

'Well?' Harry said.

'You'll have to wait, *boraz*.' The boy spoke with a Pakistani accent which

Harry presumed he dropped when he was eating his mother's meatballs in their one hundred per cent Norwegian home.

'I haven't got time to wait for you to get a group together.'

'Chillax, it'll be quick.'

'I'll pay you a hundred more.'

The boy measured Harry with his eyes. And Harry knew roughly what he was thinking: an ugly businessman in a weird suit, regulated consumption, scared to death that colleagues and family will chance by. A man asking to be screwed.

'Six hundred,' the boy said.

Harry sighed and nodded.

'*Idra*,' the boy said and began to walk.

Harry presumed the word meant he had to follow.

They rounded the corner and went through an open gate into a backyard. The dope man was black, probably a North African, and he was leaning against a stack of wooden pallets. His head was bobbing up and down to the beat of the music from an iPod. One earplug hung down by his side.

'Quarter,' said Rick Ross in the Arsenal shirt.

The dope man took something from a deep pocket and passed it to Harry palm down so that it couldn't be seen. Harry looked at the bag he'd been given. The powder was white, but with tiny, dark flecks.

'I have a question,' Harry said, putting the bag into his jacket pocket.

The other two braced themselves, and Harry saw the dope man's hand move behind his back. He guessed he had a small-calibre pistol in his trouser waistband.

'Either of you seen this girl?' He held up the photo of the Hanssen family.

They peered and shook their heads.

'I've got five thousand for anyone who can give me a lead, a rumour, anything.'

They looked at each other. Harry waited. Then they shrugged and turned back to Harry. Perhaps they allowed the question because they had experienced this before, a father searching for his daughter in Oslo's junkie community. Nonetheless, they lacked the requisite cynicism or imagination to invent a story to cash in on a reward.

'OK,' Harry said. 'But say hello to Dubai for me and tell him I have some information that may be of interest. Concerning Oleg. Say he can come to Hotel Leon and ask for Harry.'

The next moment it was out. And Harry was right, it looked like a Cheetah-series Beretta. Nine millimetre. Snub-nosed, nasty piece of work.

'Are you *baosj*?'

Kebab Norwegian. Police.

'No,' Harry said, trying to swallow the nausea that always rose whenever he looked down the muzzle of a gun.

'You're lying. You don't shoot violin, you're an undercover cop.'

'I'm not lying.'

The dope man nodded to Rick Ross, who went to Harry and pulled up the sleeve of his jacket. Harry tried to take his eyes off the gun. There was a low whistle. 'Looks like Norskie here shoots up after all,' Rick Ross said.

Harry had used a standard sewing needle, which he'd held over a lighter flame. He'd made deep incisions and wriggled it around in four or five places on his forearm and rubbed ammonium soap into the wounds to give them a more inflamed red colour. Finally he had perforated the vein on his elbow so that blood appeared under the skin and created some impressive bruises.

'I think he's lying anyway,' the dope man said, moving his legs apart and grabbing the stock of the gun with both hands.

'Why? Look, he's got a syringe and aluminium foil in his pocket as well.'

'He's not frightened.'

'What the fuck do you mean? Look at the guy!'

'He's not frightened enough. Hey, *baosj*, show us a syringe now.'

'Have you gone schitz, Rage?'

'Shut up!'

'Chillax. Why so angry?'

'Don't think Rage liked you using his name,' Harry said.

'You shut up too! A shot! And use your own bag.'

Harry had never melted or injected before, at least not when sober, but he had used opium and knew what was involved: melting the substance into a fluid form and drawing it into a syringe. How difficult could that be? He crouched down, poured powder into the foil, some fell to the ground and he licked his finger, dabbed it up and rubbed it into his gums, tried to seem keen. It tasted bitter like other powders he had tested as a policeman. But there was another taste as well. An almost imperceptible tang of ammonium. No, not ammonium. He remembered now, the tang reminded him of the smell of overripe papaya. He flicked the lighter, hoping they attributed his slight clumsiness to the fact that he was working with a gun to his head.

Two minutes later he had the syringe charged and ready.

Rick Ross had regained his gangsta coolness. He had rolled his sleeves up to his elbows and was posing with legs wide, arms crossed and head tipped back.

'Shoot,' he commanded. He twitched and held up a defensive palm. 'Not you, Rage!'

Harry looked at the two of them. Rick Ross had no marks on his bare forearms, and Rage looked a bit too alert. Harry pumped his left fist up towards his shoulder twice, flicked his forearm and inserted the needle at the prescribed thirty-degree angle. And hoped it looked professional to someone who did not inject himself.

'Ahh,' Harry groaned.

Professional enough for them not to think about how far the needle penetrated a vein or just the flesh.

He rolled his eyes and his knees gave way.

Professional enough for them to fall for a faked orgasm.

'Don't forget to tell Dubai,' he whispered.

Then he staggered to the street and swayed westwards towards the Royal Palace.

Only in Dronningens gate did he straighten up.

In Prinsens gate he got the delayed effect. Caused by those parts of the drug that had found blood, that had reached the brain via the roundabout routes of capillaries. It was like a distant echo of the rush from a needle straight into an artery. Yet Harry felt his eyes filling with tears. It was like being reunited with a lover you thought you would never see again. His ears filled, not with heavenly music, but heavenly light. And all at once he knew why they called it violin.

It was ten o'clock at night, and the lights were out in the Orgkrim offices, and the corridors were empty. But in Truls Berntsen's office the computer screen cast a blue light on the policeman sitting with his feet on the desk. He had put fifteen hundred on Man City to win and was about to lose it. But now they had a free kick. Eighteen metres and Tévez.

He heard the door open, and his right index finger automatically hit the escape button. But it was too late.

'Hope it's not my budget paying for streaming.'

Mikael Bellman took a seat on the only other chair. Truls had noticed that as Bellman had risen through the ranks he had changed the pronunciation they had grown up with in Manglerud. It was only when he talked to Truls that he sometimes went back to their roots.

'Have you read the paper?'

Truls nodded. Since there had been nothing else to read he had kept going after the crime and sport pages were finished. He had seen a good deal about the council secretary Isabelle Skøyen. She had begun to be photographed at premieres and social events after Verdens Gang had run a profile that summer of her entitled 'The Street Sweeper'. She had been credited as the architect behind the clean-up of Oslo's streets, at the same time launching herself as a national politician. At any rate her steering committee had made progress. Truls thought he had noticed her neckline plunging in step with opposition support, and her smile in the photographs was soon as broad as her backside.

'I've had a very unofficial conversation with the Police Commissioner,' Bellman said. 'She's going to appoint me as Chief of Police, reporting to the Minister of Justice.'

'Shit!' Truls shouted. Tévez had smashed the free kick against the crossbar.

Bellman got up. 'By the way, thought you'd like to know. Ulla and I are going to invite a few people over next Saturday.'

Truls felt the same stab in his heart as always whenever he heard Ulla's name.

'New house, new job, you know. And you helped to build the terrace.'

Helped? Truls thought. I constructed the whole bloody thing.

'So unless you're very busy . . .' Bellman said, motioning towards the screen. 'You're invited.'

Truls thanked him and accepted. The way he had done ever since they were boys, agreed to play gooseberry, to be a spectator of Mikael Bellman and Ulla's obvious happiness. Agreed to another evening when he would have to hide who he was and how he felt.

'One other matter,' Bellman said. 'Do you remember the guy I asked you to delete from the visitors' register in reception?'

Truls nodded without batting an eyelid. Bellman had rung him and explained that a certain Tord Schultz had dropped by to give him information about drug smuggling and tell him they had a burner in their ranks. He was worried about the man's safety and the name was to be removed from the register in case this burner was working at HQ and had access.

'I've tried to call him several times, but there's no answer. I'm a bit concerned. Are you absolutely sure Securitas removed his name and no one else found out?'

'Absolutely, Chief of Police,' Truls said. City were back in defence and scooped the ball away. 'By the way, have you heard any more from that annoying inspector at the airport?'

'No,' Bellman said. 'Seems as if he's accepted it must have been potato flour. Why?'

'Just wondering, Chief of Police. Regards to the dragon at home.'

'I'd rather you didn't use that term, OK?'

Truls shrugged. 'It's what you call her.'

'I mean the Chief of Police stuff. Won't be official for a couple of weeks.'

* * *

165

The operations manager sighed. The air traffic control officer had phoned to say the Bergen flight was delayed because the captain had not turned up or rung in, and they had to scramble a new one fast.

'Schultz is having a rough time right now,' said the manager.

'He's not answering his phone, either,' said the officer.

'I was afraid of that. He might be doing some solo trips in his free time.'

'So I've heard, yes. But this is not free time. We almost had to cancel the flight.'

'Bit of a bumpy road at the moment, as I said. I'll talk to him.'

'We all have bumpy roads, Georg. I'll have to write a full report, you understand?'

The operations manager paused. But gave up. 'Of course.'

As they rang off an image appeared in the operations manager's memory. One afternoon, barbecue, summer. Campari, Budweiser and enormous steaks straight from Texas, flown in by a trainee. No one saw him and Else sneak into a bedroom. She groaned softly, softly enough not to be heard over the screams of children playing, the incoming flights and carefree laughter outside the open window. Planes coming and going. Tord's ringing laughter, after another classic flying story. And Tord's wife's low groans.

18

'YOU'VE BOUGHT VIOLIN?'

Beate Lønn stared in disbelief at Harry, who was sitting in the corner of her office. He had dragged the chair away from the bright morning light into the shadow where he folded his hands round the mug she had passed him. He had hung his jacket over the back of the chair, and sweat lay like cling film over his face.

'You haven't . . .?'

'You crazy?' Harry slurped the boiling hot coffee. 'Alkies can't get up to that kind of business.'

'Good, because otherwise I would think that was a botched shot,' she said, pointing.

Harry looked at his forearm. Apart from the suit, he had only three pairs of underpants, a change of socks and two short-sleeved shirts. He had thought of buying whatever clothes he needed in Oslo, but so far there hadn't been a free moment. And this morning he had woken up with what seemed so much like a hangover that from habit he almost threw up in the toilet. The result of injecting into flesh was the shape and colour of the USA when Reagan was re-elected.

'I'd like you to analyse this for me,' Harry said.

'Why?'

'Because of the crime-scene photos showing the bag you found on Oleg.'

'Yeah?'

'You've got fantastic cameras. You can see the powder was pure white. This powder's got brown bits. I want to know what it is.'

Beate took a magnifying glass from the drawer and leaned over the powder Harry sprinkled onto the cover of *Forensic Magazine*.

'You're right,' she said. 'The samples we've had in have been white, but in fact over recent months there hasn't been a single confiscation, so this is interesting. Especially since an inspector from the police at Gardermoen rang the other day and said something similar.'

'What?'

'They found a bag of powder in a pilot's hand luggage. The inspector wondered how we'd come to the conclusion that it was potato flour. He had seen the brown grains in the powder with his own eyes.'

'Did he think the pilot was smuggling in violin?'

'Since there hasn't been a single confiscation of violin on the borders, the inspector has probably never seen it. White heroin is rare. Most of the stuff that winds up here is brown, so the inspector probably thought the two had been mixed. By the way, the pilot wasn't coming in, he was going out.'

'*Out?*'

'Yes.'

'Where to?'

'Bangkok.'

'He was taking potato flour to Bangkok?'

'Perhaps it was for some Norwegians to make white sauce for their fish balls.' She smiled while blushing at her attempt to be funny.

'Mm. Something quite different. I've just read about an undercover man who was found dead in Gothenburg harbour. There were rumours he'd been a burner. Were there any rumours about him in Oslo?'

Beate shook her head. 'No. On the contrary. He was more famous for being overkeen to catch the bad guys. Before he was killed, he talked about having a big fish on the hook and wanting to reel it in solo.'

'Solo.'

'He didn't want to say any more, he didn't trust anyone else. Sound like someone you know, Harry?'

He smiled, got up and threaded his arms into his jacket sleeves.

'Where are you going?'

'To visit an old friend.'

'Didn't know you had any.'

'It's a manner of speaking. I rang the head of Kripos.'

'Heimen?'

'Yes. I asked if he could give me a list of people Gusto had spoken to on his mobile before the murder. He answered that, first off, it was such an open-and-shut case they didn't have a list. Secondly, if they did they would never give it to a . . . let me see . . .' Harry closed his eyes and counted on his fingers. '. . . discharged cop, alkie or traitor like me.'

'As I said, I didn't know you had any old friends.'

'So now I'll have to try elsewhere.'

'OK. I'll have this powder analysed today.'

Harry stopped in the doorway. 'You said that recently violin had been turning up in Gothenburg and Copenhagen. Does that mean it appeared there after Oslo?'

'Yes.'

'Isn't it usually the other way round? New dope goes to Copenhagen first and then spreads north?'

'You're probably right. Why?'

'Not quite sure yet. What did you say that pilot's name was?'

'I didn't. Schultz. Tord. Anything else?'

'Yes. Have you considered that the undercover man may have been right?'

'Right?'

'To keep his mouth shut and not to trust anyone. He may have known there was a burner somewhere.'

Harry looked around the large, airy cathedral of a reception area at Telenor HQ in Fornebu. At the desk ten metres away two people stood waiting.

He saw them receiving passes and being collected by the person they were visiting at the barriers. Telenor had obviously tightened up their procedures, and his plan of more or less gatecrashing Klaus Torkildsen's office was no longer viable.

Harry assessed the situation.

Torkildsen would certainly not appreciate the visit. For the simple reason that he had been caught exposing himself, which he had managed to keep secret from his employer, but which Harry had used for several years to pressurise him into giving him access to information, sometimes way beyond what a telephone company was legally entitled to do. Nevertheless, without the authority a police ID card endowed, Torkildsen would probably not even see Harry.

To the right of the four gates leading to the lifts was a larger gate which had been opened to let in a group of visitors. Harry made a swift decision. He strode up to the group and edged to the middle of the throng, which was shuffling towards the Telenor representative holding the gate open. Harry turned to his neighbour, a small man with Chinese features.

'*Nin hao.*'

'Excuse me?'

Harry saw the name on the visitor's pass. Yuki Nakazawa.

'Oh, Japanese.' Harry laughed and patted the little man several times on the shoulder, as if he were an old friend. Yuki Nakazawa returned a tentative smile.

'Nice day,' Harry said, still with his hand on the man's shoulder.

'Yes,' Yuki said. 'Which company are you?'

'TeliaSonera,' Harry said.

'Very, very good.'

They passed the Telenor employee and from the corner of his eye Harry could see him coming towards them and knew roughly what he would say. And he was right.

'Sorry, sir. I can't let you in without a name badge.'

Yuki Nakazawa looked at the man in surprise.

* * *

Torkildsen had been given a new office. After walking a kilometre through an open-plan office Harry finally saw a familiar large physique in a glass cage.

Harry went straight in.

The man was sitting with his back to him, a telephone pressed to his ear. Harry could see the shower of spittle stand out against the window. 'Now you get the bloody SW2 server up and running!'

Harry coughed.

The chair swivelled round. Klaus Torkildsen was even fatter. A surprisingly elegant, tailored suit succeeded in partially hiding the rolls of flab, but nothing could hide the expression of sheer fear that spread across his extraordinary face. What was so extraordinary about it was that with such an expanse at their disposal, the eyes, nose and mouth had deemed it appropriate to assemble on a small island amid an ocean of face. His eyes descended to Harry's lapel.

'Yuki . . . Nakazawa?'

'Klaus.' Harry beamed and stretched out his arms for a hug.

'What the hell are you doing here?' Torkildsen whispered.

Harry dropped his arms. 'I'm happy to see you too.'

He perched on the edge of the desk. Same place he had always sat. Invade and find higher ground. Simple and effective way to rule. Torkildsen gulped, and Harry saw large, shiny beads of sweat forming on his brow.

'The mobile network in Trondheim,' Torkildsen grumbled, indicating the phone. 'Should have had the server up and running last week. Can't trust anyone any bloody more. I'm pushed for time. What do you want?'

'The list of calls to and from Gusto Hanssen's mobile since May.' Harry grabbed a pen and wrote the name on a yellow Post-it.

'I'm management now. I don't work on the floor.'

'No, but you can still get me the numbers.'

'Have you got any authorisation?'

'If I had I would've gone straight to a police contact instead of you.'

'So why wouldn't your police solicitor authorise this?'

The old Torkildsen would not have dared to ask this. He had become tougher. Had more confidence. Was it the new promotion? Or something else? Harry saw the back of a photo frame on the desk. The kind of personal photo used to remind yourself you had someone. So, unless it was a dog, it was a woman. Perhaps even with a child. Who would have thought it? The old flasher had got himself a woman.

'I no longer work for the police,' Harry said.

Torkildsen smirked. 'Yet you still want info on conversations?'

'I don't need much, just this mobile.'

'Why should I? If anyone found out I'd passed this kind of info on I'd get the boot. And it wouldn't be hard to see if I'd been in the system.'

Harry didn't answer.

Torkildsen gave a bitter laugh. 'I understand. It's the same old cowardly blackmail number. If I don't give you info, contrary to regulations, you'll make sure my colleagues get to hear about my conviction.'

'No,' Harry said. 'No, I won't talk. I'm simply asking you for a favour, Klaus. It's personal. My ex-girlfriend's boy risks life imprisonment for something he didn't do.'

Harry saw Torkildsen's double chin jerk and create a wave of flesh that rippled down his neck until it was absorbed into the greater body mass and was gone. Harry had never addressed Klaus Torkildsen by his Christian name before today. Torkildsen looked at him. Blinked. Concentrated. The beads of sweat glinted, and Harry could see the cerebral calculator adding, subtracting and – at length – reaching a result. Torkildsen threw up his arms and leaned back in the chair, which creaked under the weight.

'Sorry, Harry, I would have liked to help you. But right now I can't afford that sort of sympathy. Hope you understand.'

'Of course,' Harry said, rubbing his chin. 'It's completely understandable.'

'Thank you,' Torkildsen said, clearly relieved and beginning to struggle up from his chair, so as to escort Harry out of the glass cage and his life.

'Right,' Harry said. 'If you don't get me the numbers it won't just be your colleagues who find out about your flashing but your wife as well. Any kids? Yes? One, two?'

Torkildsen slumped back in the chair. Staring at Harry in disbelief. The old, trembling Klaus Torkildsen. 'You . . . you said you wouldn't . . .'

Harry shrugged. 'Sorry. But right now I can't afford that sort of sympathy.'

It was ten minutes past ten at night and Schrøder's was half full.

'I wouldn't have wanted you to come to my workplace,' Beate said. 'Heimen rang me and said you'd been asking about a list of phone calls, and he'd heard you'd been to see me. He warned me not to get mixed up in the Gusto case.'

'Well,' Harry said, 'it's good you could come here.' He established eye contact with Rita who was serving beer at the other end of the room. He held up two fingers. She nodded. It was three years since he had been here, but she still understood the sign language of her ex-regular: a beer for the companion, a coffee for the alcoholic.

'Was your friend any help with the list?'

'Lots of help.'

'So what did you find out?'

'Gusto must have been broke at the end; his account had been blocked several times. He didn't use his phone much, but he and Oleg had a few short conversations. He called his foster-sister, Irene, quite a bit, but the conversations suddenly finished some weeks before he died. Otherwise the calls were mostly to Pizza Xpress. I'll go to Rakel's afterwards and google these other names. What can you tell me about the analysis?'

'The substance you bought is almost identical to early samples of violin we have examined. But there is a small difference in the chemical compound. And then there are the brown flecks.'

'Yes?'

'It's not an active pharmaceutical ingredient. It's quite simply the coating that's used on pills. You know, to make them easier to swallow or to give them a better taste.'

'Is it possible to trace it to the producer?'

'In theory, yes. But I've checked, and it transpires that medicine manufacturers generally make their own coating, which means there are several thousand of them over the globe.'

'So we won't make any headway there?'

'Not with the coating,' Beate said. 'But on the inside of some fragments there are still remains of the pill. It was methadone.'

Rita brought the coffee and beer. Harry thanked her, and she left.

'I thought methadone was liquid and came in bottles.'

'The methadone used in the so-called medicine-assisted rehabilitation of drug addicts comes in bottles. So I rang up St Olav's Hospital. They research opioids and opiates and told me that methadone pills are used for the treatment of pain.'

'And in violin?'

'They said it was possible that modified methadone could be used in its manufacture, yes.'

'That only means violin is not made from scratch, but how does that help us?'

Beate curled her hand round the beer glass. 'Because there are very few producers of methadone pills. And one of them is based in Oslo.'

'AB? Nycomed?'

'The Radium Hospital. They have their own research institute and have manufactured a methadone pill to treat severe pain.'

'Cancer.'

Beate nodded. One hand transported the glass to her mouth while the other picked up something lying on the table.

'From the Radium Hospital?'

Beate nodded again.

Harry picked up the pill. It was round, small and had an R stamped into the brown glazing.

'Do you know what, Beate?'

'No.'

'I think Norway has created a new export.'

* * *

'Do you mean to say that someone in Norway is producing and exporting violin?' Rakel asked. She was leaning with her arms crossed against the door frame of Oleg's room.

'There are at least a couple of facts that suggest someone might be,' Harry said, keying in the next name on the list he had been given by Torkildsen. 'Firstly, the ripples spread outwards from Oslo. No one at Interpol had seen or heard about violin before it appeared in Oslo, and it is only now that you can find it on the streets of Sweden and Denmark. Secondly, the substance contains chopped-up methadone pills which I swear are made in Norway.' Harry pressed search. 'Thirdly, a pilot was arrested at Gardermoen with something which might have been violin, but was then swapped.'

'Swapped?'

'In which case we have a burner in the system. The point is that this pilot was leaving the country for Bangkok.'

Harry smelt the aroma of her perfume and knew she had moved from the door and was standing by his shoulder. The sheen from the computer screen was the only light in the dark room.

'Foxy. Who's that?' Her voice was next to his ear.

'Isabelle Skøyen. City Council. One of the people Gusto rang. Or to be precise, she rang him.'

'The blood donor T-shirt's a size too small for her, isn't it?'

'It's probably part of a politician's job to advertise giving blood.'

'Are you actually a politician if you're just a council secretary?'

'Anyway, the woman says she's AB rhesus negative, and then it's simply your civic duty.'

'Rare blood, yes. Is that why you've been looking at that picture for so long?'

Harry smiled. 'There were lots of hits here. Horse breeder. "The Street Sweeper."'

'She's the one credited with putting all the drug gangs behind bars.'

'Not all of them obviously. I wonder what she and Gusto could have had to talk about.'

'Well, she heads the Social Services Committee's work against drugs, so maybe she used him to gather general information.'

'At half past one in the morning?'

'Whoops!'

'I'd better ask her.'

'Yes, I'm sure you'd like that.'

He craned his head towards her. Her face was so close he could hardly focus on her.

'Do I hear what I think I hear, my love?'

She laughed softly. 'Not at all. She looks cheap.'

Harry inhaled slowly. She hadn't moved. 'And what makes you think I don't like cheap?' he asked.

'And why are you whispering?' Her lips moved so close to his he could feel the stream of air with her words.

For two long seconds the computer's fan was all that could be heard. Then she suddenly straightened up. Sent Harry an absent-minded, far-off look and placed her hands against her cheeks as if to cool them down. Then she turned and left.

Harry leaned back, closed his eyes and cursed softly. Heard her clattering about in the kitchen. Breathed in a couple of times. Decided that what had just happened, had not happened. Tried to collect his thoughts. Then he went on.

He googled the remaining names. Some came up with ten-year-old results of skiing competitions or a report of a family get-together, others not even that. They were people who no longer existed, who had been withdrawn from modern society's almost all-embracing floodlights, who had found shady nooks where they sat waiting for the next dose or else nothing.

Harry sat looking at the wall, at a poster of a guy with plumage on his head. 'Jónsi' was written underneath. Harry had a vague memory that it had something to do with the Icelandic band Sigur Rós. Ethereal sounds and relentless falsetto singing. Quite a long way from Megadeath and Slayer. But of course Oleg may have changed his taste. Or have been influenced. Harry settled back with his hands behind his head.

Irene Hanssen.

He had been surprised by the list of calls. Gusto and Irene had spoken on the phone almost every day, then abruptly stopped. After that he hadn't even tried to ring her. As if they had fallen out. Or maybe Gusto had known that Irene could not be reached by phone. But then, a few hours before he was shot, Gusto had rung the landline at her home address. And had got an answer. The conversation had lasted one minute and twelve seconds. Why did he think that was odd? Harry tried to unravel his way back to where the thought had originated. But had to give up. He dialled the landline number. No answer. Tried Irene's mobile. A voice told him that the account was temporarily blocked. Unpaid bills.

Money.

It started and finished with money. Drugs always did. Harry tried to remember the name Beate had told him. The pilot who had been arrested with powder in his hand luggage. The police memory still worked. He typed TORD SCHULTZ into directory enquiries.

A mobile number came up.

Harry opened a drawer in Oleg's desk to find a pen. He lifted *Masterful Magazine* and his eye fell on a newspaper cutting in a plastic folder. He immediately recognised his own, younger face. He took out the folder and flicked through the other cuttings. They were all of cases Harry had worked on and where Harry's name had been mentioned or his picture appeared. There was also an old interview in a psychology journal where he had answered – not without some irritation he seemed to remember – questions about serial killings. Harry closed the drawer. Cast around. He felt a need to smash something. Then he switched off the computer, packed the little suitcase, went into the hall and put on his suit jacket. Rakel came out. She brushed an invisible speck of dust from his lapel.

'It's so strange,' she said. 'I haven't seen you for ages, I had just begun to forget you, and then, here you are again.'

'Yes,' he said. 'Is that a good thing?'

A fleeting smile. 'I don't know. It's both good and bad. Do you understand?'

Harry nodded and pulled her to him.

'You're the worst thing that's ever happened to me,' she said. 'And the best. Even now, merely by being here, you can make me forget everything else. No, I'm not sure that's good.'

'I know.'

'What's that?' she asked, pointing to the suitcase.

'I'm checking in to Hotel Leon.'

'But . . .'

'We'll talk tomorrow. Goodnight, Rakel.'

Harry kissed her on the forehead, opened the door and went out into the warm autumn evening.

The boy in reception said he didn't need to fill in another registration form and offered Harry the same room as last time, 301. Harry said that was fine so long as they fixed the broken curtain pole.

'Is it broken again?' the boy said. 'It was the previous lodger. He had a bit of a temper, I'm afraid.' He passed Harry the room key. 'He was a policeman as well.'

'Lodger?'

'Yes, he was one of the permanent ones. An agent, undercover as you call him.'

'Mm. Sounds like his cover wasn't up to much, if *you* knew.'

The boy smiled. 'Let me go and see if I have a curtain pole in the storeroom.' The boy left.

'Beret Man was very like you,' a deep Swedish voice said. Harry turned.

Cato was sitting in a chair in what with a little charity could be termed the lobby. He looked drawn and was slowly shaking his head. 'Very like you, Harry. Very passionate. Very patient. Very obstinate. Unfortunately. Not as tall as you, of course, and he had grey eyes. But the same police look about them, and just as lonely. And he died in the same place as you will. You should have gone, Harry. You should have caught the plane.' He gesticulated something incomprehensible with his long fingers. His expression was so mournful that for a moment Harry wondered if the old man was going to cry. He staggered to his feet as Harry turned to the boy.

'Is what he says true?'

'What who says?' the boy asked.

'Him,' Harry said, turning to point at Cato. But he was already gone. He must have flitted into the darkness by the stairs.

'Did the undercover cop die here, in my room?'

The boy stared at Harry before answering. 'No, he went missing. He was washed ashore by the Opera House. Afraid I don't have a curtain pole, but what about this nylon line? You can thread it through the curtains and tie it to the pole attachments.'

Harry nodded slowly.

It was gone two o'clock in the morning. Harry was still awake and on his last cigarette. On the floor lay the curtains and the thin nylon line. He could see the woman on the other side of the yard; she was dancing a soundless waltz, without a partner. Harry listened to the sounds of the town and watched the smoke curling up towards the ceiling. Studied the winding routes it took, the apparently random figures it made and tried to see a pattern in it.

19

IT TOOK TWO MONTHS FROM the meeting between the old boy and Isabelle for the clean-up to begin.

The first ones to be busted were the Vietnamese. The newspapers said the cops had struck in nine places simultaneously, found five heroin stores and arrested thirty-six Vietcong. The week after it was the Kosovar Albanians' turn. The cops used elite Delta troops to raid a flat in Helsfyr which the gypsy chief thought no one knew about. Then it was the turn of the North Africans and Lithuanians. The guy who was head of Orgkrim, a good-looking model-type with long eyelashes, said in the papers they had been given anonymous tip-offs. Over the next few weeks street sellers, everything from coal-black Somalis to milky-white Norwegians, were busted and banged up. But not a single one of us wearing an Arsenal shirt. It was already clear that we had more elbow room and the queues were getting longer. The old boy was recruiting some of the unemployed street sellers, but keeping his end of the bargain: heroin dealing had become less visible in Oslo city centre. We cut down on heroin imports as we earned so much more on violin. Violin was expensive, so some tried to switch to morphine, but they soon came back.

We were selling faster than Ibsen could make it.

One Tuesday we ran out at half past twelve, and since it was strictly forbidden to use mobiles – the old boy thought Oslo was fricking Baltimore – I went down to the station and rang the Russian Gresso phone from one of the call boxes. Andrey said he was busy, but he would see what he could do. Oleg, Irene and I sat on the steps in Skippergata waving away punters and chilling. An hour later I saw a figure come limping towards us. It was Ibsen in person. He was furious. Yelling and cursing. Until he caught sight of Irene. Then it was as if the storm was over and his tone became more conciliatory. Followed us to the backyard where he handed over a plastic bag containing a hundred packages.

'Twenty thousand,' he said, holding out his paw. 'This is cash on delivery.' I took him aside and said that next time we ran out we could go to his place.

'I don't want visitors,' he said.

'I might pay more than two hundred a bag,' I said.

He eyed me with suspicion. 'Are you planning to start up on your own? What would your boss say to that?'

'This is between you and me,' I said. 'We're talking chicken-feed. Ten to twenty bags for friends and acquaintances.'

He burst out laughing.

'I'll bring the girl,' I said. 'Her name's Irene, by the way.'

He stopped laughing. Looked at me. Club Foot tried to laugh again, but couldn't. And now everything was written in big letters in his eyes. Loneliness. Greed. Hatred. And desire. Fricking desire.

'Friday evening,' he said. 'At eight. Does she drink gin?'

I nodded. From now on she did.

He gave me the address.

Two days later the old boy invited me to lunch. For a second I thought Ibsen had grassed on me, because I could remember his expression. We were served by Peter and sat at the long table in the cold dining room while the old boy told me he had cut out heroin imports across the country and from Amsterdam and now only imported from Bangkok via a couple of pilots. He talked about the figures, checked I understood and repeated the usual question: was I keeping away from violin? He sat there in the semi-gloom gazing at me, then he called Peter and told him to drive me home. In the car I considered asking Peter whether the old boy was impotent.

Ibsen lived in a typical bachelor pad in a block on Ekeberg. Big plasma screen, little fridge and nothing on the walls. He poured us a cheap gin with lifeless tonic, without a slice of lemon, but with three ice cubes. Irene watched the performance. Smiled, was sweet, and left the talking to me. Ibsen sat with an idiotic grin on his face gawping at Irene, though he did manage to close his gob whenever saliva threatened to leak out. He played fricking classical music. I got my packages and we agreed I would drop by again in a fortnight. With Irene.

Then came the first report about the falling number of ODs. What they didn't write was that first-time users of violin, after only a few weeks, were queueing with staring eyes and visible fits of the shakes from withdrawal symptoms. And as they stood there with their crinkled hundred-krone notes and found out that the price had gone up again, they cried.

After the third visit to Ibsen he took me aside and said that next time he wanted Irene to come alone. I said that was fine, but then I wanted fifty packages and the price was a hundred kroner apiece. He nodded.

Persuading Irene required some effort, and for once the old tricks didn't work. I had to be hard. Explain this was my chance. Our chance. Ask if she wanted to stay sleeping on a mattress in a rehearsal room. And in the end she mumbled that she didn't. But she didn't want to . . . And I said she didn't have to, she should just be nice to the lonely old man, he probably didn't have much fun with that foot of his. She nodded and said I had to promise not to tell Oleg. After she left for Ibsen's pad I felt so down I diluted a bag of violin and smoked what was left in a cigarette. I woke up to someone shaking me. She stood over my mattress crying so much the tears were running down onto my face and making my eyes sting. Ibsen had tried it on, but she had managed to get away.

'Did you get the packages?' I asked.

That was obviously the wrong question. She broke down completely. So I said I had something to make everything alright again. I fixed up a syringe and she stared at me with big, wet eyes as I found a blue vein in her fine, white skin and inserted the needle. I felt the spasms transplant themselves from her body to mine as I pressed the plunger. Her mouth opened in a silent orgasm. Then the ecstasy drew a bright curtain in front of her eyes.

Ibsen might be a dirty old man, but he knew his chemistry.

I also knew that I had lost Irene. I could see it in her face when I asked about the packages. It could never be the same. That night I saw Irene glide into blissful oblivion along with my chances of becoming a millionaire.

The old boy continued to make millions. Yet still he wanted more, faster. It was as if there was something he had to catch, a debt that was due soon. He didn't seem to need the money; the house was the same, the limousine was washed but not changed and the staff remained at two: Andrey and Peter. We still had one competitor – Los Lobos – and they too had extended their street-selling operations. They hired the Vietnamese and Moroccans who were not already banged up, and they sold violin not only in the town centre but also at Kongsvinger, in Tromsø, Trondheim and – so the rumour went – in Helsinki. Odin and Los Lobos may have earned more than the old boy, but the two of them shared this market, there were no fights for territory, they were both getting very rich. Any businessman with his brain fully connected would have been happy with the status fricking quo.

There were just two clouds in the bright blue sky.

One was the undercover cop with the stupid hat. We knew the police had been told that the Arsenal shirts were not a priority target for the moment, but Beret Man was snouting around anyway. The other was that Los Lobos had started selling violin in Lillestrøm and Drammen at a cheaper price than in Oslo, which meant some punters were catching the train there.

One day I was summoned by the old boy and told to take a message to a policeman. His name was Truls Berntsen, and it had to be done with discretion. I asked why he couldn't use Andrey or Peter, but the old boy explained that he didn't want to have any contact that might lead the police back to him. It was one of his principles. And even if I had information that could expose him I was the only person beside Peter and Andrey he trusted. Yes, in many ways he did trust me. The Dope Baron trusts the Thief, I thought.

The message was that he had arranged a meeting with Odin to discuss Lillestrøm and Drammen. They would meet at McDonald's in Kirkeveien, Majorstuen, on Thursday evening at seven. They had booked the whole of the first floor for a private children's party. I could visualise it, balloons, streamers, paper hats and a fricking clown. Whose face froze when he saw the birthday guests: beefy bikers with murder in their eyes and studs on their knuckles, two and a half metres of Cossack concrete, and Odin and the old boy trying to stare each other to death over the french fries.

Truls Berntsen lived alone in a block of flats in Manglerud, but when I called round early one Sunday morning, no one was at home. The neighbour, who'd obviously heard Berntsen's bell ring, stuck his head out from the veranda and shouted that Truls was at Mikael's, building a terrace. And while I was on my way to the address he had given me I was thinking that Manglerud had to be a terrible place. Everyone clearly knew everyone.

I had been to Høyenhall before. This is Manglerud's Beverly Hills. Vast detached houses with a view over Kværnerdalen, the centre and Holmenkollen. I stood in the road looking down over the half-finished skeleton of a house. In front were some guys with their shirts off, can of beer in hand, laughing and pointing to the formwork which was obviously going to be the terrace. I immediately recognised one of them. The good-looking model-type with long eyelashes. The new head of Orgkrim. The men stopped talking as they caught sight of me. And I knew why. They were police officers, every single one of them, who smelt a bandit. Tricky situation. I hadn't asked the old boy, but the thought had struck me that Truls Berntsen was the alliance in the police he had advised Isabelle Skøyen to form.

'Yes?' said the man with the eyelashes. He was in very good shape as well. Abs like cobblestones. I still had the opportunity to back away and visit Berntsen later in the day. So I don't quite know why I did what I did.

'I have a message for Truls Berntsen,' I said, loud and clear.

The others turned to a man who had put his beer down and waggled over on bow legs. He didn't stop until he was so close to me that the others couldn't hear us. He had blond hair, a powerful, prognathous jaw that hung like a tilting drawer. Hate-filled suspicion shone from the small piggy eyes.

If he had been a domestic pet he would have been put down on purely aesthetic grounds.

'I don't know who you are,' he whispered, 'but I can guess, and I don't want any fucking visits of this kind. OK?'

'OK.'

'Quick, out with it.'

I told him about the meeting and the time. And that Odin had warned he would be turning up with his whole gang.

'He daren't do anything else,' Berntsen said and grunted.

'We have information that he's just received a huge supply of horse,' I said. The guys on the terrace had resumed their beer-drinking, but I could see the Orgkrim boss casting glances at us. I spoke in a low voice and concentrated on passing on every detail. 'It's stored in the club at Alnabru, but will be shipping out in a couple of days.'

'Sounds like a few arrests followed by a little raid.' Berntsen grunted again, and it was only then I realised it was meant to be laughter.

'That's all,' I said, turning to go.

I had only gone a few metres down the road when I heard someone shout. I didn't need to turn to know who it was. I had seen it in his gaze at once. This is after all my speciality. He came up alongside, and I stopped.

'Who are you?' he asked.

'Gusto.' I stroked the hair out of my eyes so that he could see them better. 'And you?'

For a second he regarded me with surprise, as though it was a tough question. Then he answered with a little smile: 'Mikael.'

'Hi, Mikael. Where do you train?'

He coughed. 'What are you doing here?'

'What I said. Delivering a message to Truls. Could I have a swig of your beer?'

The strange, white stains on his face seemed to light up all of a sudden. His voice was taut with anger when he spoke again. 'If you've done what you came to do I suggest you clear off.'

I met his glare. A furious glare. Mikael Bellman was so stunningly handsome that I felt like placing a hand on his chest. Feeling the sun-warmed sweaty skin under my fingertips. Feeling the muscles that would automatically tense in shock at my audacity. The nipple that hardened as I squeezed it between thumb and forefinger. The wonderful pain as he punched me to save his good name and reputation. Mikael Bellman. I felt the desire. My own fricking desire.

'See you,' I said.

The same night it struck me. How I would succeed in what I guess you never managed. For if you had, you wouldn't have dumped me, would you. How I would become whole. How I would become human. How I would become a millionaire.

20

THE SUN GLITTERED SO INTENSELY on the fjord that Harry had to squint through his ladies' sunglasses.

Oslo was not only having a facelift in Bjørvika, it was also having a silicone tit of a new district stuck out into the fjord where once it had been flat-chested and boring. The silicone wonder was called Tjuvholmen and looked expensive. Expensive apartments with expensive fjord views, expensive boat moorings, expensive bijou shops with exclusive items, art galleries with parquet flooring from jungles you had never heard of, galleries which are more spectacular than the art on the walls. The nipple on the most prominent edge of the fjord was a restaurant with the kind of prices that had caused Oslo to overtake Tokyo as the most expensive city in the world.

Harry went in and a friendly head waiter greeted him.

'I'm looking for Isabelle Skøyen,' Harry said, scanning the room. It seemed to be packed to the rafters.

'Do you know what name the table's reserved under?' the waiter asked with a little smile that told Harry all the tables had been booked weeks ago.

The woman who had answered when Harry rang the Social Services Committee office in City Hall had at first been willing to tell him only that Isabelle Skøyen was out having lunch. But when Harry had said that was

187

why he was ringing, he was sitting at the Continental waiting for her, the secretary had in her horror blurted out that the lunch was at Sjømagasinet!

'No,' Harry said. 'Is it alright if I go and have a look?'

The waiter hesitated. Studied the suit.

'Don't worry,' Harry said. 'I can see her.'

He strode past the waiter before the final judgement was passed.

He recognised the face and the pose from the pictures on the Net. She was leaning against the bar with her elbows on the counter, facing the dining room. Presumably she was waiting for someone but looked more as if she were appearing on stage. And when Harry looked at the men around the tables he understood she was probably doing both. Her coarse, almost masculine face was split into two by an axe-blade of a nose. Nevertheless, Isabelle Skøyen did have a kind of conventional attraction other women might call 'elegance'. Her eyes were heavily made up, a constellation of stars round the cold, blue irises, which lent her a predatory, lupine look. For that reason her hair was a comical contrast: a blonde doll's mane arranged in sweet garlands on either side of her manly face. But it was her body that made Isabelle Skøyen such an eye-catcher.

She was a towering figure, athletic, with broad shoulders and hips. The tight-fitting black trousers emphasised her big, muscular thighs. Harry decided that her breasts were bought, supported by an unusually clever bra or simply impressive. His Google search had revealed that she bred horses on a farm in Rygge; had been divorced twice, the last from a financier who had made a fortune four times and lost it three; had been a participant in national shooting competitions; was a blood donor, in trouble for having given a political colleague the boot because he 'was such a wimp'; and she more than happily posed for photographers at film and theatre premieres. In short: a lot of woman for your money.

He moved into her field of vision, and halfway across the floor her stare still hadn't relinquished him. Like someone who considers it their right to look. Harry went up to her, fully aware that he had at least a dozen pairs of eyes on his back.

'You are Isabelle Skøyen,' he said.

She looked as if she was about to give him short shrift, but changed her mind, angled her head. 'That's the thing about these overpriced Oslo restaurants, isn't it? Everyone is someone. So . . .' She dragged out the 'o' as her gaze took him in from top to toe. 'Who are you?'

'Harry Hole.'

'There's something familiar about you. Have you been on TV?'

'Many years ago. Before this.' He pointed to the scar on his face.

'Oh yes, you're the policeman who caught the serial killer, aren't you?'

There were two ways to play this. Harry chose to be direct.

'I was.'

'And what do you do now?' she asked without interest, her gaze wandering over his shoulder, to the exit. Pressed her red lips together and widened her eyes a couple of times. Warm-up. Must be an important lunch.

'Clothes and shoes,' Harry said.

'I can see. Cool suit.'

'Cool boots. Rick Owens?'

She looked at him, apparently rediscovering him. Was about to say something, but her glance caught a movement behind him. 'My lunch date's here. See you again perhaps, Harry.'

'Mm. I had hoped we might have a chat now.'

She laughed and leaned forward. 'I like the move, Harry. But it's twelve o'clock, I'm as sober as a judge and I already have a lunch date. Have a nice day.'

She walked away on her click-clacking heels.

'Was Gusto Hanssen your lover?'

Harry said it in a low tone, and Isabelle Skøyen was already three metres away. Nevertheless, she stiffened, as if she had found a frequency that cut through the noise of heels, voices and Diana Krall's background crooning, and beamed into her eardrum.

She turned.

'You rang him four times the same night, the last was at twenty-six minutes to two.' Harry had taken a bar stool. Isabelle Skøyen retraced the three metres. She towered over him. Harry was reminded of Little Red Riding Hood and the Wolf. And she was not Little Red Riding Hood.

'What do you want, Harry boy?' she asked.

'I want to know everything you know about Gusto Hanssen.'

The nostrils on Axe-Nose flared and her majestic breasts rose. Harry noticed that her skin had large black pores, like dots in a comic strip.

'As one of the few people in this town concerned about keeping drug addicts alive I'm also one of the few to remember Gusto Hanssen. We lost him, and that's sad. These calls are because I have his mobile number saved on my phone. We had invited him to a meeting of the RUNO committee. I have a good friend whose name is similar, and sometimes I hit the wrong key. That sort of thing can happen.'

'When did you last meet him?'

'Listen here, Harry Hole,' she hissed under her breath, stressing Hole and lowering her face even closer to his. 'If I've understood correctly you are not a policeman, but someone who works with clothes and shoes. I see no reason to talk to you.'

'Thing is,' Harry said, leaning back against the counter, 'I'm very keen to talk to someone. So if it isn't you, it'll be a journalist. And they're always so pleased to talk about celebrity scandals and the like.'

'Celebrity?' she said, turning on a radiant smile aimed not at Harry but a suit-clad man standing by the head waiter and waving back with his fingers. 'I'm just a council secretary, Harry. The odd photo in the papers doesn't make you a celebrity. Look how soon you're forgotten.'

'I believe the papers see a rising star in you.'

'Do you indeed? Perhaps, but even the worst tabloids need something concrete, and you have nothing. Calling the wrong number is—'

'—the sort of thing that can happen. What cannot happen, however . . .' Harry took a deep breath. She was right; he had nothing on her. And that was why it was not a great idea to play it direct. '. . . is that blood of the type AB rhesus negative appears by chance in two places on the same murder case. One person in two hundred has that group. So when the forensics report shows the blood under Gusto's nails is AB rhesus negative and the papers say that's your group, an ageing detective cannot help but put two and two together. All I need to do is ask for a DNA test, then we'll know with a hundred per cent certainty who Gusto stuck his claws into before he died. Does that sound like a somewhat above-average interesting newspaper headline, Skøyen?'

The council secretary kept blinking, as though her eyelids were trying to activate her mouth.

'Tell me, isn't the Crown Prince in the Socialist Party?' Harry asked, scrunching up his eyes. 'What's his name again?'

'We can have a chat,' Isabelle Skøyen said. 'Later. But then you'll have to swear to keep your mouth shut.'

'When and where?'

'Give me your number and I'll phone you after work.'

Outside, the fjord glinted and flashed. Harry put on his sunglasses and lit a cigarette to celebrate a well-accomplished bluff. Sat on the edge of the harbour, enjoying every drag, refused to feel the gnawing that persisted, and focused on the meaninglessly expensive toys the world's richest working class had moored alongside the quay. Then he stubbed out the butt, spat in the fjord and was ready for the next visit on the list.

Harry confirmed to the female receptionist at the Radium Hospital that he had an appointment, and she gave him a form. Harry filled in name and telephone number, but left 'Firm' blank.

'Private visit?'

Harry shook his head. He knew this was an occupational habit with good receptionists: seeing the lie of the land, collecting information about people who came and went and those who worked on the premises. If, as a detective, he needed the low-down on everyone in an organisation he made a beeline for the receptionist.

She pointed Harry to the office at the end of the corridor. On his way there Harry passed closed office doors and glass panes looking onto large rooms, people wearing white coats inside, benches littered with flasks and test-tube stands and big padlocks for steel cabinets Harry guessed would be an El Dorado for any drug addict.

At the end Harry stopped and, to be on the safe side, read the nameplate before knocking on the door: Stig Nybakk. He had barely knocked once when a voice reverberated: 'Come in!'

Nybakk was standing behind the desk with a telephone to his ear, but waved Harry in and indicated a chair. After three 'Yes's, two 'No's, one 'Well, I'm damned' and a hearty laugh, he rang off and fixed a pair of sparkling eyes on Harry, who true to form had slumped in a chair with his legs stretched out.

'Harry Hole. You probably don't remember me, but I remember you.'

'I've arrested so many people,' Harry said.

More hearty laughter. 'We went to Oppsal School. I was a couple of years below you.'

'Young kids remember the older ones.'

'That's true enough. But to be frank I don't remember you from school. You were on TV and someone told me you'd been to Oppsal and you were a pal of Tresko's.'

'Mm.' Harry studied the tips of his shoes to signal he wasn't interested in moving into private territory.

'So you ended up as a detective? Which murder are you investigating now?'

'I'm investigating a drugs-related death,' Harry started, to keep as close as possible to the truth. 'Did you get a look at the stuff I sent you?'

'Yes.' Nybakk lifted the receiver again, tapped in a number and scratched feverishly behind his ear while waiting. 'Martin, can you come in here? Yes, it's about the test.'

Nybakk rang off, and there followed three seconds of silence. Nybakk smiled; Harry knew his brain was scanning to find a topic to fill the pause. Harry said nothing. Nybakk coughed. 'You used to live in the yellow house down by the gravel track. I grew up in the red house at the top of the hill. Nybakk family?'

'Right,' Harry lied, demonstrating again to himself how little he remembered of his childhood.

'Have you still got the house?'

Harry crossed his legs. Knowing he couldn't have the match called off before this Martin came. 'My father died a few years ago. Sale dragged a bit, but—'

'Ghosts.'

'Pardon?'

'It's important to let the ghosts out before you sell, isn't it? My mother died last year, but the house is still empty. Married? Kids?'

Harry shook his head. And played the ball into the other half of the field. 'But you're married, I can see.'

'Oh?'

'The ring.' Harry nodded towards his hand. 'I used to have an identical one.'

Nybakk held up the hand with the ring and smiled. 'Used to? Are you separated?'

Harry cursed inside. Why the hell did people have to chit-chat? Separated? Course he was separated. Separated from the person he loved. Those he loved. Harry coughed.

'There you are,' Nybakk said.

Harry turned. A stooped figure wearing a blue lab coat squinted at him from the door. Long, black fringe that hung over a pale, almost snow-white, high forehead. Eyes set deep in his skull. Harry had not even heard him coming.

'This is Martin Pran, one of our best scientists,' Nybakk said.

That, Harry thought, is the Hunchback of Notre-Dame.

'Eh, Martin?' Nybakk said.

'What you call violin is not heroin but a drug similar to levorphanol.'

Harry noted the name. 'Which is?'

'A high-explosive opioid,' Nybakk intervened. 'Immense painkiller. Six to eight times stronger than morphine. Three times more powerful than heroin.'

'Really?'

'Really,' Nybakk said. 'And it has double the effect of morphine. Eight to twelve hours. If you take just three milligrams of levorphanol we're talking a full anaesthetic. Half of it through injection.'

'Mm. Sounds dangerous.'

'Not quite as dangerous as one might imagine. Moderate doses of pure opioids like heroin don't destroy the body. No, it's primarily the dependency that does it.'

'Right. Heroin addicts die like flies.'

'Yes, but for two main reasons. First of all, heroin is mixed with other substances that turn it into nothing less than poison. Mix heroin and cocaine, for example, and—'

'Speedball,' Harry said. 'John Belushi—'

'May he rest in peace. The second usual cause of death is that heroin inhibits respiration. If you take too large a dose you simply stop breathing. And as the level of tolerance increases you take larger and larger doses. But that's the interesting thing about levorphanol – it doesn't inhibit respiration nearly as much. Isn't that right, Martin?'

The Hunchback nodded without raising his eyes.

'Mm,' Harry said, watching Pran. 'Stronger than heroin, longer effect, and little chance of OD'ing. Sounds like a junkie's dream substance.'

'Dependency,' the Hunchback mumbled. 'And price.'

'Excuse me?'

'We see it with patients,' Nybakk sighed. 'They get addicted like that.' He snapped his fingers. 'But with cancer patients dependency is a non-issue. We increase the type of painkiller and dosage according to a chart. The aim is to prevent pain, not to chase its heels. And levorphanol is expensive to produce and import. That might be the reason we don't see it on the streets.'

'That's not levorphanol.'

Harry and Nybakk turned to Martin Pran.

'It's modified.' Pran lifted his head. And Harry thought he could see his eyes shining, as if a light had just been switched on.

'How?' Nybakk asked.

'It will take time to discover how, but it does appear that one of the chlorine molecules has been exchanged for a fluorine molecule. It may not be that expensive to produce.'

'Jesus,' Nybakk said. 'Are we talking Dreser?'

'Possibly,' Pran said with an almost imperceptible smile.

'Good heavens!' Nybakk exclaimed, scratching the back of his head with both hands in his enthusiasm. 'Then we're talking the work of a genius. Or an enormous flash in a pan.'

'Afraid I'm not quite with you here, boys,' Harry said.

'Oh, sorry,' Nybakk said. 'Heinrich Dreser. He discovered aspirin in 1897. Afterwards he worked on modifying diacetymorphine. Not a lot needs to be done, molecule here, molecule there, and hey presto, it fastens on to other receptors in the human body. Eleven days later, Dreser had discovered a new drug. It was sold as cough medicine right up until 1913.'

'And the drug was?'

'The name was supposed to be a pun on a brave woman.'

'Heroine,' Harry said.

'Correct.'

'What about the glazing?' Harry asked, turning to Pran.

'It's called a coating,' the Hunchback retorted. 'What about it?' He faced Harry but his eyes were elsewhere, on the wall. Like an animal hunting for a way out, Harry thought. Or a herd animal that did not want to meet the hierarchical challenge of the creature looking you straight in the eye. Or simply a human with slightly above-average social inhibitions. But there was something else that caught Harry's attention, something about the way he was standing, his crooked posture.

'Well,' Harry said, 'Forensics says that the brown specks in violin originate from the finely chopped glazing of a pill. And it's the same . . . coating you use on methadone pills that are made here at the Radium Hospital.'

'So?' Pran riposted.

'Is it conceivable that violin is made here in Norway by someone with access to your methadone pills?'

Stig Nybakk and Martin Pran exchanged glances.

'Nowadays we deliver methadone pills to other hospitals as well, so quite a few people have access,' Nybakk said. 'But violin is high-level chemistry.' He expelled air between flapping lips. 'What do you reckon, Pran? Have we got the competence in Norwegian scientific circles to discover such a substance?'

Pran shook his head.

'What about by fluke?' Harry asked.

Pran shrugged. 'It is of course possible that Brahms wrote *ein deutsches Requiem* by fluke.'

The room fell silent. Not even Nybakk appeared to have anything to add.

'Well,' Harry said, getting up.

'Hope that was of some help,' Nybakk said, extending his hand to Harry across the desk. 'Say hello to Tresko. I suppose he still does nights at Hafslund Energy, keeping his finger on the electricity switch for the town?'

'Something like that.'

'Doesn't he like daylight?'

'He doesn't like hassle.'

Nybakk gave a tentative smile.

On his way out Harry stopped twice. Once to examine the empty laboratory in which the light had been turned off for the day. The second time was outside the door displaying Martin Pran's nameplate. There was light under the door. Harry carefully pressed the handle. Locked.

The first thing Harry did when he got into the rental car was to check his mobile phone. He saw one missed call from Beate Lønn, but still nothing from Isabelle Skøyen. By Ullevål Stadium Harry realised he had timed his journey out of town badly. The nation with the shortest working hours was on its way home. It took him fifty minutes to reach Karihaugen.

Sergey was sitting in his car drumming his fingers on the wheel. In theory, his workplace was situated on the right side of rush-hour traffic, but when he was on the evening shift he ended up stuck in the gridlock leaving town anyway. The cars edged towards Karihaugen like cooling lava. He had googled the policeman. Clicked on old news stories. Murder cases. He had taken out a serial killer in Australia. Sergey had noticed that because the same morning he had been watching a programme from Australia on Animal Planet. It was all about the intelligence of crocodiles in the Northern Territory, about how they learned the habits of their prey. When men camped in the bush they usually took a path along a billabong to collect water after waking in the morning. On the path they were safe from crocodiles lying in the water and watching. If they stayed a second night the same would be repeated the next day. If they stayed a third night they would walk along the path once more, but this time they wouldn't see a crocodile. Not until it rushed out of the bush and dragged its prey into the water.

The policeman had seemed ill at ease in the pictures on the Net. As though he didn't like being photographed. Or watched.

The phone rang. It was Andrey. He got straight to the point.

'He's staying at Hotel Leon.'

The south Siberian dialect was in fact like a machine gun, staccato, but Andrey made it sound soft and flowing. He said the address twice, slowly and clearly, and Sergey memorised it.

'Good,' he said, trying to sound keen. 'I'll ask for his room number. And unless it's at the end of a corridor I'll wait there, at the end. So that when he leaves his room for the stairs or the lift he'll have to turn his back on me.'

'No, Sergey.'

'No?'

'Not in the hotel. He'll be ready for us at Leon.'

Sergey started with surprise. 'Ready?'

He changed lane and slipped in behind a rental car as Andrey explained that the policeman had contacted two sellers and invited *ataman* to Hotel Leon. It stank of a trap from some distance. *Ataman* had given clear orders that Sergey was to do the job somewhere else.

'Where?'

'Wait for him in the street outside the hotel.'

'But where shall I *do* it?'

'You can choose,' Andrey said. 'But my personal favourite is an ambush.'

'Ambush?'

'Always an ambush, Sergey. And one more thing . . .'

'Yes?'

'He's beginning to advance into areas where we don't want him to advance. That means this is becoming a matter of urgency.'

'What . . . does that mean?'

'*Ataman* says you should take whatever time you need, but no more. Today is better than tomorrow. Which is better than the day after. Understand?'

When they rang off Sergey was still in the traffic jam. He had never felt so alone in all his life.

Rush hour was at its peak, and the tailback did not lighten until Berger, just before the Skedsmo intersection. By then Harry had been sitting in the car for an hour and had scanned all the radio channels before ending up with NRK Classical out of sheer protest. Twenty minutes later he saw the turn-off to Gardermoen. He had rung Tord Schultz's number a dozen times during the day without getting through. Schultz's colleague, whom he eventually located at the airline, said he had no idea where Tord could be and that he generally stayed at home when he wasn't flying. And confirmed the address Harry had found on the Net.

Darkness was falling when Harry inferred from the road sign that he was in the right place. He drove slowly between the identical shoeboxes on either side of the newly asphalted road. From the houses which were illuminated enough for him to be able to read the numbers he worked out which was Tord Schultz's. It lay in total darkness.

Harry parked the car. Looked up. Silver came out of the black sky, a plane, as soundless as a bird of prey. Lights swept across rooftops, and the plane disappeared behind him carrying the noise after it like a bridal train.

Harry walked up to the front door, placed his face against the glass panel and rang. Waited. Rang again. Waited for a minute.

Then he kicked in the panel.

He passed his hand through, found the latch and opened the door.

Stepping over the shards of glass, he continued into the living room.

The first thing that struck him was the darkness, that it was darker than a room should be, even unlit. He realised that the curtains were drawn. Thick blackout curtains of the kind they used at the military camp in Finnmark to keep out the midnight sun.

The second thing that struck him was the sense that he was not alone. And since Harry's experience was that such feelings were almost always accompanied by quite tangible sensory impressions he concentrated on what they could be, and repressed his own natural reaction: a faster pulse rate and the need to go back the same way he had come. He listened, but all he could hear was a clock ticking somewhere, probably in an adjacent room. He sniffed. A pungent, stale smell, but there was something else, distant, but familiar. He closed his eyes. As a rule he could see them before they came. Over the years he had developed coping strategies to ward them off. But now they were on him before he could bolt the door. The ghosts. It smelt of a crime scene.

He opened his eyes and was dazzled. The light. It swept across the living-room floor. Then came the sound of the plane, and in the next second the room was plunged into darkness again. But he had seen. And it was no longer possible to repress the faster pulse and the urge to get out.

It was the Beetle. *Zjuk*. It hovered in the air in front of his face.

21

THE FACE WAS A MESS.

Harry had switched on the living-room light and was looking down at the dead man.

His right ear had been nailed to the parquet floor and his face displayed six black, bloody craters. He didn't need to search for the murder weapon: it hung at head height right in front of him. At the end of a rope suspended from a beam was a brick. From the brick protruded six blood-covered nails.

Harry crouched down and stretched out his hand. The man was cold, and rigor mortis had definitely set in, despite the heat of the room. The same applied to livor mortis; the combination of gravity and the absence of blood pressure had allowed the blood to settle at the body's lowest points and lent the underside of the arms a slightly reddish colour. The man had been dead for more then twelve hours, Harry guessed. The white, ironed shirt had rucked up and some of the stomach could be seen. It did not yet have the green hue which showed that bacteria had started to consume him, a feast which generally started after forty-eight hours and spread outwards from the stomach.

In addition to the shirt, he was wearing a tie, which had been loosened, black suit trousers and polished shoes. As though he had come straight from a funeral or a job with a dress code, Harry thought.

He took out his phone and wondered whether to ring the Ops Room or Crime Squad directly. He tapped in the number for the Ops Room while looking around. He hadn't noticed any signs of a break-in, and there was no evidence of a struggle in this room. Apart from the brick and the corpse there was no evidence of any kind, and Harry knew that when the SOC people came they would not find a shred. No fingerprints, no shoe prints, no DNA. And the detectives would be none the wiser; no neighbours who had seen anything, no surveillance cameras at nearby petrol stations with shots of familiar faces, no revealing telephone conversations to or from Schultz's line. Nothing. While Harry waited for an answer he went into the kitchen. Instinctively he trod with care and avoided touching anything. His glance fell on the kitchen table and a plate with a half-eaten piece of bread and cervelat. Over the back of the chair was a suit jacket matching the trousers on the corpse. Harry searched the pockets and found four hundred kroner, a visitor's pass, a train ticket and an airline ID card. Tord Schultz. The professional smile on the face in the picture resembled the remains of the one he had seen in the living room.

'Switchboard.'

'I have a body here. The address is—'

Harry noticed the visitor's pass.

'Yes?'

There was something familiar about it.

'Hello?'

Harry picked up the visitor's pass. At the top was OSLO POLITIDISTRIKT. Beneath it was TORD SCHULTZ and a date. He had visited a police HQ or a station two days ago. And now he was dead.

'Hello?'

Harry rang off.

Sat down.

Pondered.

He spent ninety minutes searching the house. Afterwards he wiped all the places where he might have left prints and removed the plastic bag he had put around his head with an elastic band so as not to drop hairs. It was an established rule that all detectives and other officers who might conceivably enter a crime scene should register their fingerprints and DNA. If he left any clues it would take the police five minutes to find out that Harry Hole had been there. The fruits of his labours were three small packages of cocaine and four bottles of what he assumed was contraband booze. Otherwise there was exactly what he presumed: nothing.

He closed the door, got in the car and drove off.

Oslo Politidistrikt.

Shit, shit, shit.

When he reached the city centre, he parked and sat staring out of the windscreen. Then he rang Beate's number.

'Hi, Harry.'

'Two things. I'd like to ask you a favour. And give you an anonymous tip-off that there is another man dead in this case.'

'I've just been told.'

'So you know?' Harry said in surprise. 'The method is called *Zjuk*. Russian for "beetle".'

'What are you talking about?'

'The brick.'

'Which brick?'

Harry breathed in. 'What are *you* talking about?'

'Gojke Tošić.'

'Who's that?'

'The guy who attacked Oleg.'

'And?'

'He's been found dead in his cell.'

Harry looked straight into a pair of headlights coming towards him. 'How . . .?'

'They're checking now. Looks like he hanged himself.'

'Delete *himself*. They killed the pilot as well.'

'What?'

'Tord Schultz is lying on the living-room floor of his house by Gardermoen.'

Two seconds passed before Beate answered. 'I'll inform the Ops Room.'

'OK.'

'What was the second thing?'

'What?'

'You said you wanted to ask me for a favour?'

'Oh, yes.' Harry pulled the visitor's pass from his pocket. 'I wonder whether you could check the visitors' register in reception at Police HQ. See who Tord Schultz visited two days ago.'

Silence again.

'Beate?'

'Are you sure this is something I'll want to be mixed up in, Harry?'

'I'm sure this is something you won't want to be mixed up in.'

'Sod you.'

Harry rang off.

Harry left his vehicle in the multi-storey car park at the bottom of Kvadraturen and headed for Hotel Leon. He passed a bar, and the music floating through the open door reminded him of the evening he arrived: Nirvana's inviting 'Come As You Are'. He was not aware that he had entered the bar until he was standing in front of the counter in the winding intestine of a room.

Three customers sat hunched on bar stools. It looked like a month-old wake no one had broken up. There was a smell of corpses and creaking flesh. The barman sent Harry an order-now-or-go-to-hell look while slowly removing a cork from a bottle opener. He had three large Gothic letters tattooed across a broad neck. EAT.

'What's it to be?' he shouted, managing to drown out Kurt Cobain, who was asking Harry to come as a friend.

Harry moistened his lips, which had suddenly gone dry. Looked at the barman's hands twisting. It was a corkscrew of the simplest kind, one that requires a firm, trained hand, but only a couple of turns to penetrate, followed by a quick pull. The cork was pierced right through. This however was not a wine bar. So what else did they serve? He saw the distorted image of himself in the mirror behind the barman. The disfigured face. But it was not only his face; all of their faces, all the ghosts, were there. And Tord Schultz was the latest to join. His gaze scanned the bottles on the mirror shelf and like a heat-seeking rocket found its target. The old enemy. Jim Beam.

Kurt Cobain didn't have a gun.

Harry coughed. Just one.

No gun.

He gave his order.

'Eh?' shouted the bartender, leaning forward.

'Jim Beam.'

There is no gun.

'Gin what?'

Harry swallowed. Cobain repeated the word 'memoria'. Harry had heard the song a hundred times before, but he realised he had always thought Cobain sang 'The more' followed by something else.

In memoriam. Where had he seen it? On a gravestone?

He saw a movement in the mirror. At that moment the phone in his pocket began to vibrate.

'Gin what?' shouted the barman, placing the corkscrew on the counter.

Harry pulled out his mobile. Looked at the display. R. He took the call.

'Hi, Rakel.'

'Harry?'

Another movement behind him.

'All I can hear is noise, Harry. Where are you?'

Harry turned and walked with hurried strides to the exit. Inhaled the exhaust-polluted yet fresher air outside.

'What are you doing?' Rakel asked.

'Wondering whether to turn left or right,' Harry said. 'And you?'

'I'm going to bed. Are you sober?'

'What?'

'You heard me. And I can hear you. I notice when you're stressed. And that sounds like a bar.'

Harry took out a pack of Camel. Tapped out a cigarette. Saw his hand was shaking. 'It's good you rang, Rakel.'

'Harry?'

He lit his cigarette. 'Yeah?'

'Hans Christian's arranged for Oleg to be held in custody at a secret location. It's in Østland, but no one knows where.'

'Not bad.'

'He's a good man, Harry.'

'Don't doubt it.'

'Harry?'

'I'm here.'

'If we could plant some evidence. If I took the rap for the murder. Would you help me?'

Harry inhaled. 'No.'

'Why not?'

The door opened behind Harry. But he didn't hear any footsteps walking away.

'I'll ring you from the hotel. OK?'

Harry rang off and strode down the street without a backward glance.

Sergey watched the man jog across the street.

Watched him go into Hotel Leon.

He had been so close. So close. First of all in the bar and now here on the street.

Sergey's hand was still pressed against the deer-horn handle of the knife in his pocket. The blade was out and cutting the lining. Twice he had been on the point of stepping forward, grabbing his hair with his left hand, knife in, carving a crescent. True, the policeman was taller than he had imagined, but it wouldn't be a problem.

Nothing would be a problem. And as his pulse slowed he could feel his calm return. The calm he had lost, the calm his terror had repressed. And again he could feel himself looking forward, looking forward to the completion of his task, to becoming at one with the story that was already told.

For this was the place, the place for the ambush. Sergey had seen the eyes of the policeman when he was staring at the bottles. It was the same look his father had when he returned home from prison. Sergey was the crocodile in the billabong, the crocodile that knew the man would take the same path to get something to drink, that knew it was only a question of waiting.

Harry lay on the bed in room 301, he blew smoke at the ceiling and listened to her voice on the phone.

'I know you've done worse things than planting evidence,' she said. 'So, why not? Why not for a person you love?'

'You're drinking white wine,' he said.

'How do you know it's not red wine?'

'I can hear.'

'So, explain why you won't help me.'

'May I?'

'Yes, Harry.'

Harry stubbed out the cigarette in the empty coffee cup on the bedside table. 'I, lawbreaker and discharged police officer, consider that the law means something. Does that sound weird?'

'Carry on.'

'Law is the fence we've erected at the edge of the precipice. Whenever someone breaks the law they break the fence. So we have to repair it. The guilty party has to atone.'

'No, *someone* has to atone. Someone has to take the punishment to show society that murder is unacceptable. Any scapegoat can rebuild the fence.'

'You're gouging out chunks of the law to suit you. You're a lawyer. You know better.'

'I'm a mother, I work as a lawyer. What about you, Harry? Are you a policeman? Is that what you've become? A robot, a slave of the anthill and ideas other people have had? Is that where you are?'

'Mm.'

'Have you got an answer?'

'Well, why do you think I came to Oslo?'

Pause.

'Harry?'

'Yes?'

'Sorry.'

'Don't cry.'

'I know. Sorry.'

'Don't say sorry.'

'Goodnight, Harry. I . . .'

'Goodnight.'

Harry woke. He had heard something. Something that drowned the sound of his running footsteps in the corridor and the avalanche. He looked at his watch. 01.34. The broken curtain pole leaned against the window frame and formed the silhouette of a tulip. He got up and went to the window and peered down into the backyard. A bin lay on its side, still rattling around. He rested his forehead against the glass.

22

IT WAS EARLY, AND THE morning rush-hour traffic was creeping along at a whisper towards Grønlandsleiret as Truls walked up to Police HQ. He caught sight of the red poster on the linden tree just before he arrived at the doors with the curious portholes. Then he turned, walked calmly back. Past the slow-moving queues in Oslo gate to the cemetery.

The cemetery was as deserted as usual at this time. At least with respect to the living. He stopped in front of the headstone to A. C. Rud. There were no messages written on it, ergo it had to be pay day.

He crouched down and dug the earth beside the stone. Caught hold of the brown envelope and pulled it out. Resisted the temptation to open it and count the money there and then, stuffed it in his jacket pocket. He was about to get up, but a sudden sense that he was being watched made him stay in the crouch for a couple of seconds, as if meditating about A. C. Rud and the transient nature of life or some such bullshit.

'Stay where you are, Berntsen.'

A shadow had fallen over him. And with it a chill, as if the sun was hidden behind a cloud. Truls Berntsen felt as though he were in free fall, and his stomach lurched into his chest. So this was what it would be like. Being exposed.

'We have a different type of job for you this time.'

Truls felt terra firma beneath his feet again. The voice. The slight accent. It was him. Truls glanced to his side. Saw the figure standing with bowed head two gravestones away, apparently praying.

'You have to find out where they've hidden Oleg Fauke. Look straight ahead!'

Truls stared at the stone in front of him.

'I've tried,' he said. 'But the move hasn't been recorded anywhere. Nowhere I can access at any rate. And no one I've spoken to has heard anything about the guy, so my guess is they've given him another name.'

'Talk to those in the know. Talk to the defence counsel. Simonsen.'

'Why not the mother? She must—'

'No women!' The words came like a whiplash. Had there been other people in the cemetery they would surely have heard them. Then, calmer: 'Try the defence counsel. And if that doesn't work . . .'

In the ensuing pause Berntsen heard the whoosh through the cemetery treetops. It must have been the wind; that was what had suddenly made everything so cold.

'. . . then there's a man called Chris Reddy,' the voice continued. 'On the street he's known as Adidas. He deals in—'

'Speed. Adidas means amphet—'

'Shut up, Berntsen. Just listen.'

Truls shut up. And listened. The way he had shut up whenever anyone with a similar voice had told him to shut up. Listened when they told him to dig muck. Told him . . .

The voice gave an address.

'You've heard a rumour that Adidas has been going round boasting he shot Gusto Hanssen. So you take him in for questioning. And he makes a no-holds-barred confession. I'll leave it to you to agree on the details so that it's a hundred per cent credible. First, though, try to make Simonsen talk. Have you understood?'

'Yes, but why would Adidas—'

'Why is not your problem, Berntsen. Your sole question should be "how much".'

Truls Berntsen swallowed. And kept swallowing. Dug shit. Swallowed shit. 'How much?'

'That's right, yes. Sixty thousand.'

'Hundred thousand.'

No answer.

'Hello?'

But all that could be heard was the whisper of the morning congestion.

Bernsten sat still. Glanced to the side. No one there. Felt the sun beginning to warm him again. And sixty thousand was good. It was.

There was still mist on the ground as Harry swung up in front of the main building on Skøyen farm at ten in the morning. Isabelle Skøyen stood on the steps, smiling and slapping a little riding whip against the thigh of her black jodhpurs. While Harry was getting out of the car he heard the gravel crunch under her boots.

'Morning, Harry. What do you know about horses?'

Harry slammed the car door. 'I've lost a lot of money on them. Does that help?'

'So you're a gambler as well?'

'As well?'

'I've done a bit of detective work too. Your achievements are offset by your vices. That, at least, is what your colleagues claim. Did you lose the money in Hong Kong?'

'Happy Valley racecourse. It only happened once.'

She began to walk towards a low, red building, and he had to quicken his pace to keep up with her. 'Have you ever done any riding, Harry?'

'My grandfather had a sturdy old horse in Åndalsnes.'

'Experienced rider then.'

'Another one-off. My grandfather said horses weren't toys. He said riding for pleasure showed a lack of respect for working animals.'

She stopped in front of a wooden stand holding two narrow leather saddles. 'Not a single one of my horses has ever seen or will ever see a cart or plough. While I saddle up I suggest you head over there . . .' She pointed to the farmhouse. 'You'll find some suitable clothes belonging to my ex-husband in the hall wardrobe. We don't want to ruin your elegant suit, do we?'

In the wardrobe Harry found a sweater and a pair of jeans that were in fact big enough. The ex-husband must have had smaller feet, though, because he couldn't get any of the shoes on, until he found a pair of used blue Norwegian Army trainers at the back.

When he re-emerged in the yard Isabelle was ready and waiting with two saddled horses. Harry opened the passenger door of the hired car, sat inside with his legs out, changed shoes, removed the insoles, left them on the car floor and reached for his sunglasses from the glove compartment. 'Ready.'

'This is Medusa,' Isabelle said, patting a large sorrel on the muzzle. 'She's an Oldenburger from Denmark, perfect breed for dressage. Ten years old and the boss of the herd. And this is Balder, he's five years old, a gelding, so he'll follow Medusa.'

She passed him the reins to Balder and swung herself up on Medusa.

Harry put his left foot in the left stirrup and rose into the saddle. Without waiting for a command the horse began to walk briskly after Medusa.

Harry had understated the case when he said he had ridden only once, but this was quite different from his grandfather's steadfast battleship of a jade. He had to balance in the saddle, and when he squeezed his knees against the slim horse's sides he could feel its ribs and the movement of its muscles. And when Medusa accelerated on the path across the field and Balder responded, even this minor increase in pace made Harry feel he had a Formula One animal between his legs. At the end of the field they joined a path that disappeared into the forest and onto the ridge. Where the path forked round a tree Harry tried to steer Balder to the left, but the horse ignored him and followed in Medusa's hoof prints to the right.

'I thought stallions were the leaders of a herd,' Harry said.

'As a rule they are,' Isabelle said over her shoulder. 'But it's all about character. A strong, ambitious and smart mare can outcompete all of them if she wants.'

'And you want.'

Isabelle Skøyen laughed. 'Of course. If you want something you have to be willing to compete. Politics is all about acquiring power.'

'And you like competing?'

He saw her shrug her shoulders in front of him. 'Competition is healthy. It means the strongest and the best make the decisions, and that's to the benefit of the whole herd.'

'And she can also mate with whoever she likes?'

Isabelle didn't answer. Harry watched her. Her back was willowy and her firm buttocks appeared to be massaging the horse, moving from side to side with gentle hip movements. They came into a clearing. The sun was shining, and beneath them lay scattered puffs of mist across the countryside.

'We'll let them have a rest,' Isabelle Skøyen said, dismounting. After they had tethered the horses to a tree, Isabelle lay down on the grass and waved for Harry to follow. He sat beside her and adjusted his sunglasses.

'Are those glasses for men?' she teased.

'They protect against the sun,' Harry said, taking out a pack of cigarettes.

'I like that.'

'What do you like?'

'I like men who are secure with their masculinity.'

Harry looked at her. She was leaning on her elbows and had undone a button on her blouse. He hoped his sunglasses were dark enough. She smiled.

'So, what can you tell me about Gusto?' Harry said.

'I like men who are genuine,' she said. The smile broadened.

A brown dragonfly whizzed past on the last flight of the autumn. Harry didn't like what he saw in her eyes. What he had seen ever since he arrived. Expectant relish. And none of the tormented unease there ought to be in someone facing a career-threatening scandal.

'I don't like falseness,' she said. 'Such as bluffing, for example.'

Triumph shone from her blue mascara-wreathed eyes.

'I rang a police contact, you see. And apart from telling me a little about the legendary detective Harry Hole, he was able to tell me that no blood had been analysed in the Gusto Hanssen case. The sample had apparently been destroyed. There are no nails with my blood type under them. You were bluffing, Harry.'

Harry lit a cigarette. No blood in his cheeks or ears. He wondered if he had become too old to blush.

'Mm. If all the contact you had with Gusto was some innocent interviews why were you so frightened I would send the blood to be tested?'

She chuckled. 'Who says I was frightened? Perhaps I just wanted you to come out here. Enjoy the nature and so on.'

Confirming that he was not too old to blush, Harry lay down and blew smoke up into the ludicrously blue sky. Closed his eyes and tried to find some good reasons not to fuck Isabelle Skøyen. There were many.

'Was that wrong?' she asked. 'All I'm saying is that I'm a single adult woman with natural needs. That doesn't mean I'm not serious. I would never get involved with anyone I didn't consider my equal, such as Gusto.' He heard her voice coming closer. 'With a tall adult man, on the other hand . . .' She laid a hot hand on his stomach.

'Did you and Gusto lie where we're lying now?' Harry asked softly.

'What?'

He wriggled up onto his elbows and nodded towards the blue trainers. 'Your wardrobe was full of exclusive men's shoes, size 42. These barges were the only 45s.'

'So what? I can't guarantee that I haven't had a male visitor who takes size 45 at some point.' Her hand stroked backwards and forwards.

'This trainer was made a while ago for the Armed Services, and when they changed model, the surplus stock was taken over by charitable organisations who distributed them to the needy. In the police we call them junkie shoes as they were doled out by the Salvation Army at the Watchtower. The question is of course how a casual visitor, a size 45, would leave behind a pair of shoes. The obvious explanation is that he probably acquired a new pair.'

Isabelle Skøyen's hand stopped moving. So Harry continued.

'I've seen a picture of the crime scene. When Gusto died he was wearing a cheap pair of trousers, but a very expensive pair of shoes. Alberto Fasciani, unless I'm much mistaken. A generous gift. How much did you pay for them? Five thousand?'

'I have no idea what you're talking about.' She pulled away her hand.

Harry regarded his erection with disapproval; it was already pressing against the inside of the borrowed trousers. He stretched his feet.

'I left the insoles in the car. Did you know that foot sweat is excellent for DNA testing? We'll probably find some microscopic remains of skin, too. And there can't be that many shops in Oslo that sell Alberto Fasciani shoes. One, two? Anyway, it'll be a simple job to cross-check against your credit card.'

Isabelle Skøyen had sat up. She stared into the distance.

'Can you see the farms?' she asked. 'Aren't they beautiful? I love cultivated landscapes. And I hate forests. Apart from planted ones. I hate chaos.'

Harry studied her profile. The axe-nose looked downright dangerous.

'Tell me about Gusto Hanssen.'

She shrugged. 'Why? You've obviously worked most of it out.'

'Who do you want questioning you? Me or *Verdens Gang*.'

She gave a short laugh. 'Gusto was young and good-looking. That kind of stallion is a great sight, but it has dubious genes. Biological father's a criminal and mother's a drug addict, according to the foster-father. Not a horse you breed, but one that's fun to ride if you . . .' She took a deep breath. 'He came here and we had sex. Now and then I gave him money. He met other people as well, it was nothing special.'

'Did that make you jealous?'

'Jealous?' Isabelle shook her head. 'Sex has never made me jealous. I met other people, too. And after a while someone special. Then I dropped Gusto. Or maybe he had already dropped me. He no longer seemed to need the pocket money anyway. But then he contacted me again. He became a nuisance. I think he had financial problems. And also a drug problem.'

'What was he like?'

'He was selfish, unreliable, charming. A self-confident bastard.'

'And what did he want?'

'Do I look like a psychologist, Harry?'

'No.'

'No. People don't interest me that much.'

'Really?'

Isabelle Skøyen shook her head. Looked into the distance. Her eyes glistened.

'Gusto was lonely,' she said.

'How do you know?'

'I know what loneliness is, OK? And he was full of self-loathing.'

'Self-confidence and self-loathing?'

'It's not a contradiction. You know what you can achieve, but that doesn't mean you see yourself as someone others can love.'

'And what's that down to?'

'I told you, I'm not a psychologist.'

'No, that's right.'

Harry waited.

She cleared her throat.

'His parents had given him away. What do you think that does to a boy? Behind all the gestures and the hard face he was someone who didn't think he was worth much. Just as little as those who had given up on him. Isn't it simple logic, herr Quasi Policeman?'

Harry looked at her. Nodded. Noticed his gaze made her uncomfortable. But he refrained from asking her the questions she obviously knew were on his lips: what was her story? How lonely, how self-loathing was she behind the facade?

'How about Oleg? Did you meet him?'

'The one who was arrested for the murder? Never. But Gusto mentioned an Oleg a couple of times, said he was his best friend. I think he was his only friend.'

'What about Irene?'

'He mentioned her too. She was like a sister.'

'She *was* a sister.'

'Not in blood, Harry. It's never the same.'

215

'Isn't it?'

'People are naive and believe they are capable of selfless love. But it's all about passing on genes that are as close as possible to your own. I see this in horse breeding every day, believe me. And, yes, people are like horses, we're herd animals. A father will protect his biological son, a brother his biological sister. In any conflict we instinctively take the side of those who look most like us. Imagine you're in the jungle and walk round a corner and suddenly see another white man, dressed like you, grappling with a semi-naked black man in warpaint. They've both got knives and are fighting to the death. You've got a gun. What's your first instinct? To shoot the white man to save the black man? It's not, is it.'

'Mm. And what's your proof?'

'The proof is that our loyalty is biologically determined. Circles that spread out from the centre, which is ourselves and our genes.'

'So you'd shoot one of them to protect your genes?'

'Without a second thought.'

'What about killing both to be on the safe side?'

She looked at him. 'What do you mean?'

'What were you doing the night Gusto was killed?'

'What?' She scrunched up one eye in the sun and beamed at him. 'Do you suspect me of killing Gusto, Harry? And that I was after this . . . Oleg?'

'Just answer me.'

'I remember where I was because it was in my mind when I was reading about the murder in the paper. I was sitting in a meeting with representatives of the Police Narco Unit. They should be reliable witnesses. Do you want names?'

Harry shook his head.

'Anything else?'

'Well, this Dubai. What do you know about him?'

'Dubai, hm. As little as everyone else. There's talk, but the police aren't making any headway. It's typical; the professionals behind the scams always get away.' Harry looked for a change in the size of pupils, the colour of her cheeks. If Isabelle Skøyen was lying, she was good.

'I ask because you've cleared the streets of all the dope dealers apart from Dubai and a couple of minor gangs.'

'Not me, Harry. I'm just a council secretary following the orders of the Social Services Committee and the council's policies. And what you call clearing the streets, strictly speaking, is a police job.'

'Mm. Norway is a little fairy-tale land. But I've spent the last few years in the real world, Skøyen. And the real world is driven by two types of people. Those who want power and those who want money. The first want a statue, the second enjoyment. And the currency they use when negotiating with each other to get what they want is called corruption.'

'I've got things to do, Hole. Where do you want this to go?'

'Where others have obviously lacked the courage or the imagination to go. If you live in a town for a long time you usually see the situation as a mosaic of details you know well. But someone who returns to the town and doesn't know the details only sees the picture. And the picture is that the situation in Oslo is favourable for two groups: the dealers who have the market to themselves and the politicians who are credited with having cleared up.'

'Are you saying I'm corrupt?'

'Are you?'

He saw the fury flash into her eyes. Genuine, without a doubt. He wondered only whether it was the anger of the just or the ensnared. Then, out of the blue, she laughed. A trilled, surprisingly girlish laugh.

'I like you, Harry.' She got up. 'I know men, and they're wimps when it comes to the crunch. But I think you might be an exception.'

'Well,' Harry said, 'at least you know where you are with me.'

'Reality calls, my dear.'

Harry turned to see the roll of Isabelle Skøyen's voluminous beam-end as she headed for the horses.

He followed. Got his feet in the stirrups. Mounted Balder. Looked up and met Isabelle's eyes. There was a small provocative smile in the middle of that hard, handsomely chiselled face. She pouted a kiss. Made an obscene sucking sound and dug her heels into Medusa's sides. And her back swayed as the great beast leapt forward.

Balder reacted without warning, but Harry managed to hold on tight.

Isabelle led again, and wet clods of earth from Medusa's hooves rained down. Then the mare upped her pace, and Harry saw Isabelle's ponytail standing upright as she disappeared round a bend. He gripped the reins further up, the way his grandfather had taught him, without tightening them. The path was so narrow that branches whipped at him, but he crouched down in the saddle and squeezed his knees hard against the horse. He knew he would not be able to stop, so he concentrated on keeping his feet in the stirrups and his head low. At the margins of his vision, trees flashed past in yellow and red stripes. Automatically he rose in the saddle and put his weight on his knees and the stirrups. Beneath him muscles rippled and undulated. He had the feeling he was sitting on a boa constrictor. And now they had slipped into a kind of rhythm, accompanied by the thunderous drumming of the hooves on the ground. A sense of horror competed with a sense of obsession. The path straightened, and fifty metres in front of them Harry saw Medusa and Isabelle. For a moment it was as if the image was freeze-framed, as if they had stopped, as if horse and rider were floating above the ground. Then Medusa resumed her gallop. Another second passed before Harry realised.

And it had been a valuable second.

At Police College he had read scientific reports showing that in catastrophes the human brain tries to process enormous quantities of data in seconds. For some officers this can lead to a paralysis; for others to a feeling that time is going slower, that life passes before them, and they manage to make an astonishing number of observations and evaluations of the situation. Such as that at a speed of almost seventy kilometres an hour they had covered twenty metres and there were only thirty metres and ninety seconds left to the chasm that Medusa had just crossed.

That it was impossible to see how wide it was.

That Medusa was a trained, fully grown dressage horse with an experienced dressage rider while Balder was younger and smaller and had a novice of close on ninety kilos on his back.

That Balder was a herd animal and of course Isabelle Skøyen knew that.

That it was too late to stop.

Harry relaxed his hands on the reins and dug his heels into Balder's sides. Felt a last surge of pace. Then all went still. The drumming stopped. They were floating. Far beneath them he saw a treetop and a stream. Then he was thrust forward and banged his head against the horse's neck. They fell.

23

WERE YOU A THIEF AS well, Dad? Because I'd always known I was going to be a millionaire. My motto has been to steal only when it's worthwhile, so I had been patient and waited. And waited. Waited so long that when the opportunity finally offered itself I thought I bloody deserved it.

The plan was as simple as it was brilliant. While Odin's biker gang was meeting the old boy at McDonald's, Oleg and I would steal part of their heroin store in Alnabru. First of all, there would be no one in the clubhouse as Odin would take the muscle they had with them. Second, Odin would never find out that he had been robbed as he would be arrested at McDonald's. When he was sitting in the witness box he would in fact thank Oleg and me for reducing the number of kilos the heavies had found in the raid. The only problem would be the cops and the old boy. If the cops realised that someone had been a step ahead of them and nabbed the stash, and this came to the old boy's ears, we would be fucked. The problem solved itself in the way the old boy had taught me: castling, a strategic alliance. I went straight to the block of flats in Manglerud, and this time Truls Berntsen was at home.

He stared at me sceptically as I explained, but I wasn't concerned. Because I had seen it in his eyes. The greed. Another of these people after payback, who believe that money can buy them medicine for despair, loneliness and bitterness. That there is not only something called justice, but that it's a consumer product, sort of. I explained we needed his expertise to cover any clues we left for the police, and to burn anything they found. Perhaps even direct suspicion on others if necessary. I saw the glint in his eye when I said we would take five of the twenty kilos in the stash. Two for me and him, one for Oleg. I watched him doing the calculations, one point two mil times two, two point four for him.

'And this Oleg is the only other person you've spoken to?' he asked.

'Cross my heart.'

'Have you got any weapons?'

'An Odessa between us.'

'Eh?'

'The H&M version of a Stechkin.'

'OK. It's unlikely the detectives will give the number of kilos a thought if there are no signs of a break-in, but I suppose you're scared Odin will come after you?'

'No,' I said, 'I don't give a shit about Odin. It's my boss I'm scared of. I have no idea how, but I just know he knows to the gram how much heroin they have stored there.'

'I want half,' he said. 'You and Boris can share the rest.'

'Oleg.'

'Be happy I've got a bad memory. And it works both ways. It'll take me half a day to find you and nothing to destroy you.' He lovingly rolled the 'r' in destroy.

It was Oleg who worked out how we should camouflage the robbery. It was so simple and obvious I don't know why I hadn't thought of it myself.

'We swap what we pinch with potato flour. The police will report how many kilos they confiscate, not the purity of its content, right?'

The plan was, as I said, as brilliant as it was simple.

The same night that Odin and the old boy were having a birthday party at McDonald's and discussing the price of violin in Drammen and Lillestrøm, Berntsen, Oleg and I were standing in the darkness outside the fence round the bikers' clubhouse in Alnabru. Berntsen had taken control, and we were wearing nylon stockings, black jackets and gloves. In our rucksacks we had shooters, a drill, a screwdriver, a jemmy and six kilos' worth of plastic bags packed with potato flour. Oleg and I had explained where Los Lobos had placed their surveillance cameras, but by climbing over the fence and running to the wall on the left we stayed in the blind spot the whole time. We knew that we could make as much noise as we wanted as the heavy traffic on the E6 below would drown everything, so Berntsen drilled through the wall while Oleg kept lookout and I hummed 'Been Caught Stealing', which was on the soundtrack of Stein's GTA game, and he said it was by a band called Jane's Addiction, and I remembered because it was a cool name, cooler than the songs actually. Oleg and I were in familiar territory and the layout of the clubhouse was simple: it consisted of one large lounge area. But as all the windows had been cleverly covered with wooden shutters the plan was to drill a peephole, then we would be sure the clubhouse was unoccupied before we entered. Berntsen had insisted on this, he had refused to believe that Odin would leave twenty kilos of heroin, with a street value of twenty-five million, unguarded. We knew Odin better, but gave in. Safety first.

'There we are,' Berntsen said, holding the drill, which died with a snarl.

I put my eye to the hole. Couldn't see fuck. Either someone had switched off the light or else we hadn't drilled right through. I turned to Berntsen who was wiping the drill. 'What kind of bloody insulation is this?' he said, holding up a finger. It looked like egg yolk and fricking hair.

We walked a couple of metres further down and bored a new hole. I peered through. And there was the good old clubhouse. With the same old leather chairs, the same bar and the same picture of Karen McDougal, Playmate of the Year, arranged over some customised motorbike. I never found out what gave them the biggest hard-on: women or bikes.

'All clear,' I said.

The back door was festooned with hinges and locks.

'I thought you said there was *one* lock!' Berntsen said.

'So there was,' I said. 'Odin's obviously developing a bit of paranoia.'

The plan had been to drill the lock off and screw it back on before leaving, so that there would be no signs of a break-in. That was still possible but not in the time we had calculated. We got down to work.

After twenty minutes Oleg checked his watch and said we had to hurry. We didn't know exactly when the raid was due, only that it would happen at some point after the arrests, and the arrests would have to take place pretty quickly as Odin wouldn't want to hang around when he realised the old boy wasn't coming.

We spent half an hour cleaning up the crap, three times as much as calculated. We took out our shooters, pulled the stockings down over our faces and went in, Berntsen first. We had hardly got inside the door when he fell onto one knee and held the shooter in front of him with both hands like a member of the fricking SWAT team.

A guy was sitting on a chair by the west wall. Odin had left Tutu as a watchdog. In his lap he had a sawn-off shotgun. But the watchdog was sitting with his eyes closed, gob open and head against the wall. Rumours were circulating that Tutu stammered even when he snored, but he was sleeping as sweetly as a baby now.

Berntsen got to his feet again and tiptoed towards Tutu, gun first. Oleg and I followed, also on tiptoe.

'There's only one hole,' Oleg whispered to me.

'What?' I whispered back.

But then I realised.

I could see the last drill hole. And worked out where the first must have been.

'Oh shit,' I whispered. Even though I realised there was no longer any reason to whisper.

Berntsen had reached Tutu. He gave him a nudge. Tutu rolled sideways off the chair and fell to the floor. He lay face down on the concrete and we could see the circular entry into the back of his head.

'Drill went right through, OK,' Berntsen said. He poked his finger into the hole in the wall.

'Bloody hell,' I whispered to Oleg. 'What are the chances of that happening, eh?'

But he didn't answer. He was staring at the body as though he didn't know whether to vomit or cry.

'Gusto,' he said finally, 'what have we done?'

I don't know what got into me, but I started laughing. It was impossible to hold back. The übercool hip gyration from the cop with the massive underbite, the despair on Oleg's face, flattened behind the stocking, and Tutu, who turned out to have a brain after all, with his mouth hanging open. I laughed so much I howled. Until I was slapped and saw sparks in front of my eyes.

'Shape up unless you want another,' Berntsen said, rubbing his palm.

'Thank you,' I said and meant it. 'Let's find the dope.'

'First we have to figure out what to do with Drillo here,' Berntsen said.

'It's too late,' I said. 'Now they'll find out there's been a break-in anyway.'

'Not if we get Tutu into the car and screw the locks on again,' Oleg whined in a reedy, tear-filled voice. 'If they discover some of the dope's gone they'll think he ran off with it.'

Berntsen looked at Oleg and nodded. 'Bright partner you've got there, Wussto. Let's get going.'

'Dope first,' I said.

'Drillo first,' Berntsen said.

'Dope,' I repeated.

'Drillo.'

'I intend to become a millionaire this evening, you pelican.'

Berntsen raised a hand. 'Drillo.'

'Shut up!' It was Oleg. We stared at him.

'It's simple logic. If Tutu isn't in the boot before the police come we lose both the dope and our freedom. If Tutu, but not the dope, is in the boot we lose only the money.'

Berntsen turned to me. 'Sounds like Boris agrees with me, Wussto. Two against one.'

'OK,' I said. 'You carry the body and I'll search for the dope.'

'Wrong,' Berntsen said. 'We carry the body and you wash up the gunge after us.' He pointed to the sink on the wall beside the bar.

I poured water into a bucket while Oleg and Berntsen grabbed a leg each and dragged Tutu towards the door, leaving a thin trail of blood. Under

Karen McDougal's provocative gaze I scrubbed brain and blood off the wall and then the floor. I had just finished and was about to start searching for dope when I heard a sound from the door that opened onto the E6. A sound I tried to persuade myself was going somewhere else. The fact that the sound was getting louder and louder could be a figment of my imagination. Police sirens.

I checked the bar, the office and the toilet. It was a simple room, no second storey, no cellar, not many places to hide twenty kilos of horse. Then my eyes fell on the toolbox. On the padlock. Which had not been there before.

Oleg shouted something from the door.

'Give me the jemmy,' I shouted back.

'We've got to get out now! They're down the road!'

'Jemmy!'

'Now, Gusto!'

I knew it was in there. Twenty-five million kroner, right in front of me, in a shitty wooden box. I started kicking the lock.

'I'll shoot, Gusto!'

I turned to Oleg. He was pointing the bloody Odessa at me. Not that I thought he would hit me from that range, it was well over ten metres, but just the idea that he would train a weapon on me.

'If they catch you, they'll catch us!' he shouted with tears in his throat.

'Come on!'

I battered away at the lock again. The sirens were getting louder and louder. The thing about sirens, though, is that they always sound closer than they are.

I heard a crack like a whip above me on the wall. I looked back at the door, and my blood ran cold. It was Berntsen. He was standing there with a smoking police shooter in his hand.

'Next one won't miss,' he said calmly.

I gave the box one last kick. Then I ran.

We had hardly clambered over the fence and removed the stockings when we found ourselves looking into the headlights of the police cars. We walked casually towards them.

Then they sped past us and turned in front of the clubhouse.

We continued up the hill to where Berntsen had parked his car. Got in and drove off. As we passed the clubhouse I turned and looked at Oleg on the rear seat. Blue light swept across his face, inflamed from the tears and the tight stocking. He looked completely drained, staring into the darkness as if ready to die.

Neither of us said anything until Berntsen pulled in at a bus stop in Sinsen.

'You screwed up, Wussto,' he said.

'I couldn't know about the locks,' I said.

'It's called preparation,' Berntsen said. 'Casing the joint. Sound familiar? We're going to find an open door with a lock that's been unscrewed.'

I realised that by 'we' he meant the cops. Odd fish.

'I took the lock and the hinges,' Oleg sniffled. 'It's going to look as though Tutu ran hell for leather when he heard the sirens, didn't even have time to lock up. And the screw marks could be after a break-in at any point over the last year, right?'

Berntsen looked at Oleg in the mirror. 'Learn from your pal, Wussto. Actually, don't. Oslo doesn't need any more smart thieves.'

'Right,' I said. 'But perhaps it's not such a bloody smart idea to park on double yellow lines at a bus stop with a body in the back, either.'

'Agreed,' Berntsen said. 'Off you go then.'

'The body . . .'

'I'll sort Drillo out.'

'Where . . .?'

'None of your business. Out!'

We got out and watched Berntsen's Saab spin off.

'From now on, we've got to keep away from that guy,' I said.

'Why?'

'He's killed a man, Oleg. He has to remove all the physical evidence. First he'll have to find a place to hide the body. But after that . . .'

'He'll have to remove the witnesses.'

I nodded. Felt as depressed as fuck. Then I ventured an optimistic thought: 'Sounded like he had a great stash in mind for Tutu, didn't it?'

'I was going to spend the money on moving to Bergen with Irene,' Oleg said.

I looked at him.

'I've got a place to do law at uni there. Irene's in Trondheim with Stein. I was thinking of going up there and persuading her to join me.'

We caught the bus to town. I couldn't stand Oleg's blank gaze any longer, it had to be filled with something.

'Come on,' I said.

While I fixed him a shot in the rehearsal room I saw him sending me impatient glances, as if he wanted to take over, as if he thought I was clumsy. And when he rolled up his sleeve I knew why. The boy had needle marks all over his forearm.

'Just until Irene comes back,' he said.

'Have you got your own stash as well?' I asked.

He shook his head. 'It's been stolen.'

That was the night I taught him where and how to make a proper stash.

Truls Berntsen had been waiting for more than an hour at the multi-storey car park when a vehicle finally turned into the vacant spot with a sign showing it was reserved for the firm of solicitors Bach & Simonsen. He had decided this was the right place; only two cars had come to this part of the car park in the hour he had been here, and there were no surveillance cameras. Truls checked the number plate was the same as he had found on AUTOSYS. Hans Christian Simonsen had long lie-ins. Or perhaps he wasn't asleep, perhaps he had some woman or other. The man getting out had a blond, boyish fringe, the kind Oslo West prats used to have when he was growing up.

Truls Berntsen put on his sunglasses, stuffed his hands in his coat pockets and squeezed the grip of the gun, a Steyr, Austrian, semi-automatic. He had left behind the standard police revolver so that the solicitor wouldn't have any unnecessary leads. He walked quickly to cut off Simonsen while he was still standing between the cars. A threat works best if it's fast and aggressive. If the victim has no time to mobilise any other thoughts than fear of life and limb, you will get what you want straight away.

It was as if he had fizz powder in his blood – there was a hiss and a pounding in his ears, groin and throat. He visualised what was going to happen. The gun in Simonsen's face, so close that the barrel would be all he remembered. 'Where's Oleg Fauke? Answer me, quick and precise, or else I'll kill you right now.' The reply. Then: 'If you warn anyone or say this conversation has taken place we'll be back to kill you. Got that?' Yes. Or numb nods. Maybe involuntary urination. Truls smiled at the thought. Increased his pace. The pounding had spread to his stomach.

'Simonsen!'

The solicitor looked up. And his face brightened. 'Oh, hi there! Berntsen. Truls Berntsen, isn't it?'

Truls's right hand froze in his coat pocket. And he must have worn a crestfallen expression because Simonsen gave a hearty laugh. 'I've got a good memory for faces, Berntsen. You and your boss, Mikael Bellman, investigated the embezzlement business at Heider Museum. I was the defence counsel. You won the case, I'm sorry to say.'

Simonsen laughed again. Jovial, naive West Oslo laughter. The laughter of people who have grown up with everyone wishing everyone else well, in a place with the wealth necessary for them to be able to do that. Truls hated all the Simonsens in this world.

'Anything I can help you with, Berntsen?'

'I . . .' Truls Berntsen fumbled for words. But this was not his strong suit, deciding what to do face to face with . . . with what? People who were verbally quicker on their feet than he was? It had been fine that time in Alnabru, then it had been two boys and he had taken command. But Simonsen had a suit, education, a different way of speaking, superiority, he . . . oh shit!

'I just wanted to say hello.'

'Hello?' Simonsen said with a question mark in his intonation and face.

'Hello,' Berntsen said, forcing a smile. 'Shame about the case. You'll beat us next time.'

Then he headed for the exit with an accelerated step. Feeling Simonsen's eyes on his back. Digging muck, eating shit. Sod the lot of them.

Try the solicitor, and if that doesn't work there's a man called Chris Reddy whom everyone knows as Adidas.

The speed dealer. Truls hoped he would have a pretext for violence during the arrest.

Harry swam towards the light, towards the surface. The light became stronger and stronger. Then he broke through. Opened his eyes. And stared straight up at the sky. He was lying on his back. Something came into his field of vision. A horse's head. And another.

He shaded his eyes. Someone was sitting on a horse, but he was dazzled by the light.

The voice came from far away.

'I thought you said you'd ridden before, Harry.'

Harry groaned and struggled to his feet as he recalled what exactly had happened. Balder had sailed across the chasm and landed on the ground with his front legs, Harry had been thrown forward, banging into Balder's neck, losing the stirrups and sliding down one side while holding on tightly to the reins. He vaguely remembered dragging Balder with him, but kicked out at him so as not to have half a ton of horse on top of him.

His back felt as if it was out, but otherwise he seemed to be in one piece.

'Grandfather's nag didn't jump over canyons,' Harry said.

'Canyons?' Isabelle Skøyen laughed, passing him Balder's reins. 'That's no more than a little crevice of five metres. I can jump further *without* a horse. Didn't know you were the jittery type, Harry. First back to the farm?'

'Balder,' Harry said, patting the horse's muzzle as they watched Isabelle Skøyen and Medusa racing down towards the open field, 'are you conversant with the equine gait "an amble"?'

* * *

Harry stopped at a petrol station on the E6 and bought a coffee. He got back into the car and looked in the mirror. Isabelle had given him a plaster for the graze on his forehead, the opportunity to join her at the premiere of *Don Giovanni* at the Opera House ('. . . impossible to find a date taller than my chin when I wear heels . . . looks bad in the newspapers . . .') and a firm departing hug. Harry took out his mobile and picked up the message.

'Where have you been?' Beate asked.

'Bit of fieldwork,' Harry said.

'There wasn't much to help us at the crime scene in Gardermoen. My people have hoovered the place. Nada. The only thing we found out is that the nails are a standard steel variety, with extra-large sixteen-millimetre aluminium heads, and that the brick probably comes from a property in Oslo built at the end of the 1800s.'

'Oh?'

'We found pig's blood and horse hair in the mortar. There was a well-known Oslo bricklayer who used to mix it in, there's loads of it in the city-centre apartment blocks. You can make mortar with anything.'

'Mm.'

'So, no lead there, either.'

'Either?'

'Yes, that visit you were talking about. It must have been to somewhere else, not Police HQ, because no Tord Schultz has been registered. The visitor's pass only says Oslo Politidistrikt and there are similar ones in several police stations.'

'OK. Thank you.'

Harry searched his pockets until he found what he was after. Tord Schultz's visitor's pass. And his, the one he'd been given when he visited Hagen at Crime Squad on the first day in Oslo. He placed them beside each other on the dashboard. Studied them. Drew his conclusions and stuffed them back in his pocket. Turned the ignition key, breathed in through his nostrils, confirmed he could still smell horse and decided to visit an old rival at Høyenhall.

24

IT STARTED TO RAIN AT about five, and when Harry rang the bell of the large house at six it was as dark as a Christmas night in Høyenhall. The house bore all the signs of being newly built; there were still the remains of building materials stacked beside the garage, and under the steps he saw paint pots and insulation packaging.

Harry saw a figure move behind the decorative bevelled glass and felt the hairs rising on the back of his neck.

Then the door opened, quick, fierce, the movements of a man who has nothing to fear from anyone. Nevertheless, he stiffened when he saw Harry.

'Evening, Bellman,' Harry said.

'Harry Hole. Well, I must say.'

'Say what?'

Bellman chuckled. 'It's a surprise to see you here at my door. How did you find out where I live?'

'Everyone knows the monkey, but the monkey knows no one. In most other countries the head of Organised Crime would have a bodyguard, did you know that? Am I interrupting anything?'

'Not at all,' Bellman said, scratching his chin. 'I'm wondering whether to invite you in or not.'

'Well,' Harry said, 'it's wet out here. And I come in peace.'

'You don't know what the word means,' Bellman said, pulling back the door. 'Wipe your feet.'

Mikael Bellman led Harry through the hall, past the tower of cardboard boxes, a kitchen in which there were as yet no white goods, and into a living room. Not luxurious in the way he had seen some houses in Oslo West, but solid and spacious enough for a family. The view of Kværner Valley, Oslo Central Station and the city centre was fantastic. Harry noticed that.

'The plot cost nearly as much as the house,' Bellman said. 'You'll have to excuse the mess. We've just moved in. We're having a housewarming party next week.'

'And you forgot to ask me?' Harry said, taking off his wet jacket.

Bellman smiled. 'I can offer you a drink now. What about—'

'I don't drink,' Harry smiled back.

'Oh, damn,' Bellman said without any sign of remorse, 'one forgets so quickly. See if you can a find a chair somewhere, and I'll see if I can find a coffee pot and two cups.'

Ten minutes later they were sitting by the windows overlooking the terrace and the view. Harry got straight down to business. Mikael Bellman listened without interrupting, even when Harry could see disbelief in his eyes. When Harry had finished Bellman summed up.

'So you think that the pilot, Tord Schultz, was trying to smuggle violin out of the country. He was arrested, but released after a burner carrying police ID had exchanged the violin for potato flour. And that Schultz was executed in his home after release, probably because his employer had discovered that he'd visited the police and was scared he would tell what he knew.'

'Mm.'

'And you support your claim that he had been to Police HQ with the fact that he had a visitor's pass with Oslo Politidistrikt written on?'

'I compared it with the pass I got when I visited Hagen. The print on the bar of the 'H's is faint on both. Definitely the same printer.'

'I won't ask you how you got hold of Schultz's visitor's pass, but how can you be so certain that this was not a normal visit? Perhaps he wanted to explain the potato flour, make sure we believed him.'

'Because his name has been deleted from the visitors' book. It was important that this visit was kept secret.'

Mikael Bellman sighed. 'It's what I've always thought, Harry. We should have worked with each other, not against each other. You would have liked Kripos.'

'What are you talking about?'

'Before I say anything else, I have a favour to ask you. Please keep quiet about what I'm going to tell you.'

'OK.'

'This case has already put me in an embarrassing situation. It was me Schultz visited. And, you're quite right, he did want to tell me what he knew. Among other things he told me what I had long suspected: that we have a burner among us. Someone, I believe, who works at HQ, close to Orgkrim cases. I told him to wait at home while I spoke to my superior. I had to tread warily so as not to alarm the burner. But caution often means things move slowly. I spoke to the retiring Chief of Police, but he left it to me to find a way to tackle this.'

'Why?'

'As I said, he is retiring. He has no wish to have a case involving a corrupt police officer as a parting gift.'

'So he wanted to keep it under wraps until he was gone?'

Bellman stared into his coffee cup. 'It's very likely that I will be the new Chief of Police, Harry.'

'You?'

'And I might as well kick off with a shit case, he probably thought. The problem is I was too slow on the trigger. I racked my brains. We could have got Schultz to reveal the burner's identity straight away. But then all the others would have gone into hiding. I thought, what if we put a wire on Schultz, make him lead us to the others we were after first? Who knows, perhaps all the way to the present Mr Big in Oslo.'

'Dubai.'

Bellman nodded. 'The problem was: who could I trust at HQ and who couldn't I? I had just hand-picked a small group of officers, checked them out thoroughly, then news came in of an anonymous tip-off . . .'

'Tord Schultz had been found dead,' Harry said.

Bellman eyed him sharply.

'And now,' Harry said, 'your problem is that if it gets out you've slipped up that could put a spoke in your appointment as Chief of Police.'

'Well, there is that,' Bellman said. 'But that's not what worries me most. The problem is that nothing of what Schultz told me can be used. We're no further than before. This alleged policeman who visited Schultz in his cell and may have exchanged the dope . . .'

'Yes?'

'He identified himself as a policeman. The inspector at Gardermoen appears to remember his name was Thomas something or other. We have five Thomases at Police HQ. None of them at Orgkrim, by the way. I sent over the photos of our Thomases, but he didn't recognise any of them. So, for all we know, the burner may not even be in the police.'

'Mm. So a person with false police ID. Or, more likely, someone like me, an ex-policeman.'

'Why?'

Harry shrugged. 'It takes a policeman to trick a policeman.'

The front door clicked.

'Darling!' Bellman called. 'We're in here.'

The lounge door opened, and the sweet, suntanned face of a woman in her thirties appeared. Her blonde hair was tied up in a ponytail, and Harry was reminded of Tiger Woods's ex-wife.

'I've dropped the kids off at Mum's. Are you coming, honeybunch?'

Bellman coughed. 'We have a visitor.'

She tilted her head. 'I can see that, honey.'

Bellman looked at Harry with a resigned what-can-you-do? expression.

'Hi,' she said and sent Harry a teasing look. 'Dad and I have got another load on the trailer. Feel like . . .?'

'Bad back and a sudden longing for home,' Harry mumbled, draining his coffee cup and jumping to his feet.

'One more thing,' Harry said as he and Bellman stood outside in the porch. 'The visit I told you about, to the Radium Hospital?'

'Yes?'

'There's a man there, a scientist. Martin Pran. Just a gut instinct, but I wonder if you could check him out for me.'

'For you?'

'Sorry, old habit. For the police. For the country. For humanity.'

'Gut instinct?'

'By and large that's all I have to offer as far as this case is concerned. If you could let me know what you find . . .'

'I'll consider it.'

'Thank you, Mikael.' Harry could feel how strange the man's Christian name felt on his tongue. Wondered if he'd ever said it before. Mikael opened the door to the rainy weather, and cold air gusted in.

'Sorry to hear about the boy,' Bellman said.

'Which one?'

'Both.'

'Mm.'

'Know what? I met Gusto Hanssen once. He came here.'

'Here?'

'Yes. A stunningly attractive boy. The kind . . .' Bellman searched for the words. Gave up. 'Were you in love with Elvis when you were a boy? Man crush, as the Americans say.'

'Well,' Harry said, taking out a pack of cigarettes. 'No.'

He could have sworn he saw a flicker of red in Mikael Bellman's white pigment stains.

'The boy had that kind of face. And charisma.'

'What did he want here?'

'To talk to a policeman. I had a gang of colleagues helping out. When you only have a police salary you have to do most things yourself, you know.'

235

'Who did he talk to?'

'Who?' Bellman looked at Harry, although his eyes were fixed elsewhere, on something he had seen. 'I don't remember. These dopeheads are always ready to grass on somebody if it'll give them a thousand kroner for a shot. Goodnight, Harry.'

Harry was walking through Kvadraturen. A camper van stopped further up the street by a black prostitute. The door opened and three boys – they couldn't have been older than twenty – jumped out. One filmed while a second turned to the woman. She shook her head. Probably didn't want to do a gang-bang film which would go on YouPorn. They had Internet where she came from as well. Family, relatives. Perhaps they thought the money she sent home was from her waitressing job. Or perhaps they didn't, and preferred not to ask. As Harry went closer one of the boys spat on the tarmac in front of her and said in a shrill, drunken voice: 'Cheap nigger ass.'

Harry met the black woman's tired gaze. They nodded as if they both saw something they recognised. The two other boys noticed Harry and straightened up. Big, well-fed boys. Apple cheeks, biceps from a fitness studio, maybe done a year's kick-boxing or karate.

'Good evening, kind folk,' Harry smiled, without slowing his pace.

Then he was past and heard the camper door slam and the engine rev up.

It was the same tune that always rang out. 'Come As You Are'. The invitation.

Harry slowed his pace. For a moment.

Then he increased it again, walked on without a backward glance.

Harry was woken next morning by the ringing of his mobile. He sat up, squinted into the light from the curtainless window, stretched out his arm for the jacket hanging over the chair, rummaged through the pockets until he found the phone.

'Speak.'

'It's Rakel.' She was breathless with excitement. 'They've released Oleg. He's free, Harry!'

25

HARRY STOOD IN THE MIDDLE of the hotel room, bathed in the morning light. Apart from the phone covering his right ear he was naked. In the room across the yard a woman sat watching him with sleepy eyes, her head angled as she slowly chewed a slice of bread.

'Hans Christian wasn't told until he turned up at work fifteen minutes ago,' Rakel said. 'They released Oleg late yesterday afternoon. Someone else has confessed to the murder of Gusto Hanssen. Isn't that fantastic, Harry?'

Yes indeed, thought Harry. It was fantastic. As in un-believe-able.

'Who confessed?'

'Someone called Chris Reddy, alias Adidas. He's a junkie. He shot Gusto because he owed him money for amphetamines.'

'Where's Oleg now?'

'We don't know. We've only just been told.'

'Think, Rakel! Where could he be?' Harry's voice sounded sterner than he had meant.

'What . . . what's the matter?'

'The confession. The confession's the matter, Rakel.'

'What about it?'

'Don't you understand? The confession's a fabrication!'

'No, no, no. Hans Christian says it's detailed and extremely credible. That's why they've already released Oleg.'

'This Adidas says he shot Gusto because he was owed money. So he's an ice-cold, cynical murderer. Who suffers pangs of conscience and simply has to confess?'

'But when he saw the wrong person was about to be convicted for—'

'Forget it! A desperate drug addict has one thing in his head: getting high. There isn't any room for a conscience, believe me. This Adidas is so desperate that, for suitable compensation, he's more than willing to confess to a murder and then withdraw his confession later, after the main suspect has been released. Don't you see the plot here? If the cat knows it can't get close to the caged bird—'

'Stop!' Rakel screamed, in tears now.

But Harry didn't stop. '—the bird has to come out of the cage.'

He heard her crying. Knew that he had probably put into words what she had half considered herself.

'Can't you say something to reassure me, Harry?'

He didn't answer.

'I don't want to be frightened any more,' she whispered.

Harry took a deep breath. 'We've managed before, and we'll manage again, Rakel.'

He rang off. And it struck him again. He had become a brilliant liar.

The woman in the window on the other side waved lazily to him with three fingers.

Harry ran a hand over his face.

Now it was just a question of who found Oleg first, Harry or them.

Think.

Oleg had been released yesterday afternoon, somewhere in Østland. A drug addict with a craving for violin. He would have made a beeline for Oslo, Plata, if he didn't have reserves stashed away. He wouldn't be able to get into Hausmanns gate, the crime scene was still sealed off. So where would he sleep, with no money, no friends? Urtegata? No, Oleg knew he would be seen there, and rumours would fly.

There was only one place Oleg could be.

Harry glanced at his watch. It was vital he got there before the bird had flown.

The stadium was as deserted as the last time he was at Valle Hovin. The first thing Harry saw as he rounded the corner to the dressing-room area was that one of the panes at street level had been smashed. He peered in. Glass was scattered across the floor. So he strode to the door, unlocked it with the key he still had and entered.

And was struck by a goods train.

Harry gasped for air as he lay floundering on the floor with something on top of him. Something stinking, wet and desperate. Harry twisted away, tried to get out of the grip. He resisted his reflex action to hit out; instead he grabbed an arm, a hand, bent it backwards. Struggled to his knees while using this grip to force the assailant's face to the ground.

'Ow. Shit! Let go!'

'It's me. It's Harry, Oleg.'

He let go and helped Oleg up, dropped him onto the dressing-room bench.

The boy looked dreadful. Pale. Thin. Bulging eyes. And he stank of an indefinable mixture of dental surgery and excrement. But he wasn't high.

'I thought . . .' Oleg said.

'You thought I was them.'

Oleg covered his face with his hands.

'Come on,' Harry said. 'Let's go outside.'

They sat in the sports stand. Sat with the pale light shining on the cracked concrete deck. Harry thought of all the times he had sat there watching Oleg skate, hearing the steel blades singing before they bit into the ice again, the floodlights' reflections on the sea-green and eventually milky-white surface.

They sat close, as if there were a crush in the stand.

Harry listened to Oleg's breathing for a while before beginning.

'Who are they, Oleg? You have to trust me. If I can find you, so can they.'

'And how did you find me?'

'Process known as deduction.'

'I know what it is. Eliminate the impossible and see what you're left with.'

'When did you get here?'

Oleg shrugged. 'Last night sometime. Nine-ish.'

'Why didn't you ring your mother when you were released? You know it's seriously dangerous for you out here now.'

'She would only have taken me somewhere, hidden me. She and that Nils Christian.'

'Hans Christian. They're going to find you, you know.'

Oleg looked down at his hands.

'I thought you'd come to Oslo for a fix,' Harry said. 'But you're clean.'

'I have been for more than a week.'

'Why?'

Oleg didn't answer.

'Is it her? Is it Irene?'

Oleg looked at the concrete, as if he could see himself down there. Could hear the high singing tone as he pushed off on one skate. He nodded slowly. 'I'm the only person who's trying to find her. She has no one else but me.'

Harry didn't say anything.

'The jewellery box I stole from Mum . . .'

'Yes?'

'I sold it for dope. Apart from the ring you bought her.'

'Why didn't you sell that as well?'

Oleg smiled. 'First of all, it isn't worth much.'

'What?' Harry sat up with a horrified expression. 'Was I conned?'

Oleg laughed. 'A gold ring with a black nick in? That's called verdigris copper. With a bit of lead added for weight.'

'So why didn't you leave it?'

'Mum didn't wear it any more. So I wanted to give it to Irene.'

'Copper, lead and gold paint.'

Oleg shrugged. 'It felt right. I remember how happy Mum was when you put it on her finger.'

'What else do you remember?'

'Sunday. Vestkanttorget. The sun angling down and us wading through rustling autumn leaves. You and Mum smiling and laughing at something. I wanted to hold your hand. But of course I wasn't a little boy any more. You bought the ring at a stall where they sold house-clearance goods.'

'You can remember all this?'

'Yes. And I thought if Irene is only half as happy as Mum . . .'

'Was she?'

Oleg looked at Harry. Blinked. 'I don't remember. We must have been high when I gave it to her.'

Harry gulped.

'He's got her,' Oleg said.

'Who?'

'Dubai. He's got Irene. He's holding her hostage so I won't talk.'

Harry stared at Oleg, who bowed his head.

'That's why I haven't said anything.'

'You *know* this? And they've threatened you with what will happen to Irene if you talk?'

'They don't need to. They know I'm not stupid. Besides, they've got to shut her up as well. They've got her, Harry.'

Harry shifted position. He remembered they used to sit exactly like this before important races. Heads bowed, in silence, in a kind of communal concentration. Oleg hadn't wanted any advice. And Harry didn't have any. But Oleg had liked just sitting there.

Harry coughed. This was not Oleg's race.

'If we're to have a chance of saving Irene you have to help me find Dubai,' Harry said.

Oleg looked at Harry. Tucked his hands under his thighs and fidgeted with his feet. The way he used to do. Then he nodded.

'Start with the murder,' Harry said. 'Take all the time you need.'

Oleg closed his eyes for a few seconds. Then he opened them again.

'I was high, I'd shot up violin by the river behind our place in Hausmanns gate. It was safer. If I had a fix in the flat and some of the others were desperate, they would jump on me to steal it. You understand?'

Harry nodded.

'The first thing I saw, coming up the stairs, was the door to the office opposite. It had been broken into. Again. I didn't think any more about it. I went into our sitting room and there was Gusto. And a man in a balaclava. He was pointing a gun at Gusto. And I don't know if it was the dope or what talking, but I knew it wasn't a robbery. Gusto was going to be killed. So I reacted instinctively. I threw myself at his gun hand. But I was too late and he managed to fire one shot. I fell to the ground and when I looked up again I was lying beside Gusto with a gun barrel at my head. The man didn't say a word, and I was sure I was going to die.' Oleg stopped, took a deep breath. 'But it was as if he couldn't make up his mind. Then he drew a finger across his throat to indicate what would happen if I blabbed.'

Harry nodded.

'He repeated the message and I indicated that I understood. Then he left. Gusto was bleeding like a stuck pig, and I knew he needed help fast. But I didn't dare move, I was sure the man with the gun was still standing outside because I hadn't heard his steps on the stairs. And that if he saw me he might change his mind and shoot me after all.'

Oleg's feet were pumping up and down.

'I tried taking Gusto's pulse, tried talking to him, said I would fetch help. But he didn't answer. And then I couldn't feel his pulse any more. And I couldn't stand being there any longer. I fled.' Oleg straightened up as though he had a pain in his back, folded his hands and put them behind his head. As he went on his voice became thicker. 'I was high, I couldn't think straight. I went down to the river. I thought about swimming. Perhaps I would be lucky and drown. Then I heard the sirens. And then they were there . . . And all I could think of was the finger across the throat. And that I had to keep my mouth shut. Because I know what they're like, those people, I've heard them speaking about what they do.'

'And what do they do?'

'They go for where you're most vulnerable. At first I was frightened for Mum.'

'But it was simpler to take Irene,' Harry said. 'No one would react to a girl off the street disappearing for a while.'

Oleg looked at Harry. Swallowed. 'So you believe me?'

Harry shrugged. 'It's easy to pull the wool over my eyes as far as you're concerned, Oleg. I suppose that's how it is when you're . . . when you . . . you know.'

Tears came into Oleg's eyes. 'But . . . but it's so utterly implausible. All the evidence . . .'

'Things are falling into place,' Harry said. 'The residue on your arm you got when you threw yourself forward. His blood when you took his pulse. And that was when you left your fingerprints on him. The reason no one saw anyone else leave after the shooting is that the killer went into the office, out of the window and down the fire escape facing the river. That was why you didn't hear any footsteps on the stairs.'

Oleg had fixed pensive eyes somewhere on Harry's chest. 'But why was Gusto killed? And who killed him?'

'I don't know. But I think he was killed by someone you know.'

'Someone I know?'

'Yes. That's why he used gestures instead of speaking. So that you wouldn't recognise his voice. And the balaclava suggests he was frightened others in the drugs world might recognise him as well. He could be someone most of you living there have seen before.'

'But why did he spare me?'

'No idea.'

'I don't understand it. They tried to kill me in prison later. Even though I hadn't uttered a word.'

'Perhaps the killer hadn't been given detailed instructions about what to do with possible witnesses. He hesitated. On the one hand, you might recognise him by his shape, body language, gait if you'd seen him lots of times before. On the other, you were so high you probably weren't taking in a great deal.'

'Dope saves lives?' Oleg said with a tentative smile.

'Yes. Though his boss may not have agreed with his decision when he delivered the report afterwards. But by then it was too late. So to make sure you didn't blab they kidnapped Irene.'

'They knew I would keep my mouth shut for as long as they had Irene, so why kill me?'

'I turned up,' Harry said.

'You?'

'Yes. They knew I was here in Oslo from the second I landed. They knew I was the one who could make you talk. Having Irene wasn't enough. So Dubai gave orders that you were to be silenced in prison.'

Oleg nodded slowly.

'Tell me about Dubai,' Harry said.

'I've never met him. But I think I've been to his house once.'

'And where's that?'

'I don't know. Gusto and I were picked up by his lieutenants and driven to a house, but I was blindfolded.'

'You know it was Dubai's house, do you?'

'That's what Gusto told me. And it smelt occupied. Sounded like a house with furniture, carpets and curtains if you—'

'I do. Go on.'

'We were led into a cellar and that was when the blindfold was taken off. A dead man lay on the floor. They said that was what they did to people who tried to trick them. Have a good look, they said. Then we had to tell them what had happened at Alnabru. Why the door hadn't been locked when the police arrived. And why Tutu had disappeared.'

'Alnabru?'

'I'm coming to that.'

'OK. This man, how had he been killed?'

'What do you mean?'

'Did he have stab wounds to the face? Or was he shot?'

'Well, I didn't know what he'd died of until Peter stepped on his stomach. Then water ran out of the corners of his mouth.'

Harry moistened his lips. 'Do you know who the dead man was?'

'Yes. An undercover cop who used to hang around where we were. We called him Beret Man because of the cap he wore.'

'Mm.'

'Harry?'

'Yes?'

Oleg's feet were drumming wildly on the concrete. 'I don't know much about Dubai. Not even Gusto would talk about him. But I do know that if you try to catch him you'll die.'

PART THREE

26

THE RAT SCRABBLED AROUND THE floor impatiently. The human heart was beating, but it was getting fainter and fainter. She stopped by the shoe again. Bit into the leather. Soft but thick, solid leather. She ran over the body again. The clothes smelt of more than shoes, they smelt of sweat, food and blood. He – because she could smell it was a he – was lying in the same position, he hadn't stirred, he was still blocking the entrance. She scratched at the man's stomach. Knew it was the shortest route. Faint heartbeat. It wouldn't be long now before she could begin.

It's not that you have to stop living, Dad. But that you have to die to put an end to the shit. There should be a better way, don't you think? A pain-free exodus into the light instead of this damned cold darkness that seems to close in on you. Someone should definitely have put a pinch of opiate into the Makarov bullets, should have done what I did for Rufus, the mangy dog, should have bought me a single ticket to Euphoria, bon voyage for Christ's sake! But everything that's good in this shit world is either on prescription, sold out or so expensive you have to flog your soul to taste it. Life is a restaurant you can't afford. Death the bill for the food you didn't even have the chance to eat. So you order the most expensive thing on the menu, you're in for it anyway, right, and you might get a mouthful.

OK, I'll stop whingeing, Dad, so don't go now, you haven't heard the rest. The rest is good. Where were we? Yes, just a couple of days after the burglary in Alnabru Peter and Andrey came for Oleg and me. They tied a scarf round Oleg's eyes and drove us to the old boy's house and took us down to the cellar. I had never been there before. We were led into a long, narrow, low corridor where we had to bow our heads. Our shoulders scraped against the sides. I gradually twigged that it wasn't a cellar but a subterranean tunnel. An escape passage perhaps. Which hadn't helped Beret Man. He looked like a drowned rat. Well, he *was* a drowned rat.

Then they took Oleg back to the car while I was summoned to the old boy. He sat in a chair opposite me, with no table in between.

'Were you two there?' he asked.

I looked him straight in the eye. 'If you're asking whether we were in Alnabru the answer's no.'

He studied me in silence.

'You're like me,' he said at length. 'It's impossible to see when you're lying.'

I wouldn't swear to it, but I thought I detected a smile.

'Well, Gusto, did you understand what that was, downstairs?'

'It was the undercover cop. Beret Man.'

'Correct. And why?'

'I don't know.'

'Have a guess.'

I imagine the guy must have been a crap teacher in a former life. But, whatever, I answered: 'He'd nicked something.'

The old boy shook his head. 'He found out I lived here. He knew he had no basis for a search warrant. After the arrest of Los Lobos and the recent seizure of Alnabru he saw the writing on the wall, he would never get a search warrant, however good his case was . . .' The old boy grinned. 'We'd given him a warning we thought would stop him.'

'Oh?'

'Cops like him rely on their false identity. They think it's impossible to discover who they are. Who their family is. But you can find everything in police archives, provided you have the right passwords. Which you do if, for example, you hold a trusted position in Orgkrim. And how did we warn him?'

I answered without a second's thought. 'Bumped off his kids?'

The old boy's face darkened. 'We're not monsters, Gusto.'

'Sorry.'

'Besides, he didn't have any children.' Chug-chug laugh. 'But he had a sister. Or perhaps it was just a foster-sister.'

I nodded. It was impossible to see if he was lying.

'We said she would be raped then put out of her misery. But I misjudged him. Instead of thinking he had other relatives to keep an eye on, he went on the attack. A very lonely, but desperate attack. He managed to break in here last night. We were not prepared for that. He probably loved this sister a lot. He was armed. I went down to the cellar, and he followed. And then he died.' He tilted his head. 'Of what?'

'Water was coming out of his mouth. Drowning?'

'Correct. But drowned where?'

'Was he brought here from a lake or something?'

'No. He broke in, and he drowned. So?'

'Then I don't know—'

'Think!' The word cracked like a whiplash. 'If you want to survive you have to be able to think, draw conclusions from what you can see. That's real life.'

'Fine, fine.' I tried to think. 'The cellar's not a cellar but a tunnel.'

The old boy crossed his arms. 'And?'

'It's longer than this property. It could of course come out in a field.'

'But?'

'But you told me you own a neighbouring property, so it probably goes there.'

The old boy smiled with satisfaction. 'Guess how old the tunnel is.'

'Old. The walls were green with moss.'

'Algae. After the Resistance movement had made four failed attacks on this house the Gestapo boss had a tunnel built. They succeeded in keeping it secret. When Reinhard came home in the afternoon he came in through the front door here so that everyone could see. He switched on the light and then walked through the tunnel to his real home next door and sent the German lieutenant everyone thought lived over there, over here. And this lieutenant strutted around, often close to windows, wearing the same kind of uniform as his Gestapo boss.'

'He was a decoy.'

'Correct.'

'Why are you telling me this?'

'Because I want you to know what real life is like, Gusto. Most people in this country don't know anything about it, don't know how much it costs to survive in real life. But I'm telling you all this because I want you to remember that I trusted you.'

He looked at me as if what he was saying was very important. I pretended to understand; I wanted to go home. Perhaps he could see that.

'Nice to see you, Gusto. Andrey will drive you both back.'

When the car passed the university there must have been some student gig taking place on campus. We could hear the thrashing guitars of a rock band playing on an outdoor stage. Young people streamed towards us down Blindernveien. Happy, expectant faces, as if they had been promised something, a future or some such thing.

'What's that?' asked Oleg, who was still blindfolded.

'That,' I said, 'is unreal life.'

'And you've no idea how he drowned?' Harry asked.

'No,' Oleg said. 'The foot-pumping had increased; his whole body was vibrating.

'OK, so you were blindfolded, but tell me everything you can remember about the journey to and from this place. All the noises. When you got out of the car, for example, did you hear a train or a tram?'

'No. But it was raining when we arrived, so basically that is what I heard.'

'Heavy rain, light rain?'

'Light. I hardly felt it as we left the car. But that was when I heard it.'

'OK, if light rain doesn't usually make much noise it might when it falls on leaves?'

'Possibly.'

'What was under your feet going towards the front door? Tarmac? Flagstones? Grass?'

'Shingle. I think. Yes, there was a crunch. That's how I knew where Peter was. He's the heaviest, so he crunched most.'

'Good. Steps by the door?'

'Yes.'

'How many?'

Oleg groaned.

'OK,' Harry said. 'Was it still raining by the door?'

'Yes, of course.'

'I mean, was it in your hair?'

'Yes.'

'So no porch-type structure then.'

'Are you planning to search for places in Oslo without a porch?'

'Well, different parts of Oslo were built in different periods, and they have a number of common features.'

'And what's the period for timber houses, shingle paths and steps to a door without an overhang or nearby tramlines?'

'You sound like a chief superintendent.' Harry did not reap the smile or laughter he had hoped he would. 'When you left did you notice any sounds close by?'

'Such as?'

'Such as the peeping of the pedestrian crossing.'

'No, nothing like that. But there was music.'

'Recorded or live?'

'Live, I think. The cymbals were clear. You could hear the guitars, sort of floating and fading on the wind.'

'Sounds live. Well remembered.'

'I only remember because they were playing one of your songs.'

'*My* songs?'

'From one of your records. I remember because Gusto said this was unreal life, and I thought that must have been an unconscious train of thought. He must have heard the line they had just sung.'

'Which line?'

'Something about a dream. I've forgotten, but you used to play that song all the time.'

'Come on, Oleg, this is important.'

Oleg looked at Harry. His feet stopped tapping. He closed his eyes and tried humming a tune. '*It's just a dreamy Gonzales . . .*' He opened his eyes, his face was red. 'Something like that.'

Harry hummed it to himself. And shook his head.

'Sorry,' Oleg said, 'I'm not sure, and it lasted only a few seconds.'

'That's fine,' Harry said, patting the boy's shoulder. 'Tell me what happened at Alnabru then.'

Oleg's foot started up again. He took two breaths, two deep mouthfuls of air, as he had learned to do on the start line before he crouched down. Then he spoke.

Afterwards Harry sat for a long time rubbing the back of his neck. 'So you drilled a man to death?'

'We didn't. A policeman did.'

'Whose name you don't know. Or where he worked.'

'No, both Gusto and he were careful about that. Gusto said it was best if I didn't know.'

'And you've no idea what happened to the body?'

'No. Are you going to report me?'

'No.' Harry took his pack of cigarettes and flipped out a smoke.

'Do I get one?' Oleg asked.

'Sorry, son. Bad for your health.'

'But—'

'On one condition. That you let Hans Christian hide you and leave it to me to find Irene.'

Oleg stared at the blocks of flats on the hill behind the stadium. Flowerboxes still hung from the balconies. Harry studied his profile. The Adam's apple going up and down the slim neck.

'Deal,' he said.

'Good.' Harry passed him a cigarette and lit up for both of them.

'Now I understand the metal finger,' Oleg said. 'It's so that you can smoke.'

'Yep,' Harry said, holding the cigarette between the titanium prosthesis and his index finger while selecting Rakel's number. He didn't need to ask for Hans Christian's number as he was there with her. The solicitor said he would come at once.

Oleg bent double as if it had suddenly become colder. 'Where's he going to hide me?'

'I don't know, and I don't want to know either.'

'Why not?'

'I have such sensitive testicles. I spill the beans at the very mention of the words *car battery*.'

Oleg laughed. It was short, but it was laughter. 'I don't believe that. You'd let them take your life before you said a word.'

Harry eyed the boy. He could crack weak jokes all day if only to see those glimpses of a smile.

'You've always had such high expectations of me, Oleg. Too high. And I've always wanted you to see me as better than I am.'

Oleg looked down at his hands. 'Don't all boys see their fathers as heroes?'

'Maybe. And I didn't want you to expose me as a deserter, someone who clears off. But things happened as they did anyway. What I wanted to say was that even if I wasn't there for you, that doesn't mean you weren't important to me. We can't live the lives we would like to. We're prisoners of . . . things. Of who we are.'

Oleg lifted his chin. 'Of junk and shit.'

'That too.'

They inhaled in unison. Watching the smoke drift in gusts towards the vast, open, blue sky. Harry knew that nicotine couldn't appease the cravings in the boy, but at least it was a distraction. And that was all it was about, for the next few minutes.

'Harry?'

'Yes?'

'Why didn't you come back?'

Harry took another drag before answering. 'Because your mother thought I wasn't good for you or her. And she was right.'

Harry continued to smoke as he stared into the distance. Knowing Oleg would not want him to look at him now. Eighteen-year-old boys don't like being watched when they're crying. Nor would he want him to put an arm around his shoulder and say something. He would want him to be there. Without straying. To think alongside him about the impending race.

When they heard the car approach they walked down the stand and into the car park. Harry saw Hans Christian place a hand on Rakel's arm as she was about to charge out of the car.

Oleg turned to Harry, puffed himself up, hooked his thumb round Harry's and nudged his right shoulder with his. But Harry didn't let him get away so easily and pulled him close. Whispered in his ear: 'Win.'

Irene Hanssen's last known address was her family home. The house was in Grefsen, semi-detached. A small overgrown garden with apple trees, no apples, and a swing.

A young man Harry guessed to be about twenty opened the door. The face was familiar, and Harry's police brain searched for a tenth of a second before it had two hits on the database.

'My name's Harry Hole. And you are Stein Hanssen perhaps?'

'Yes?'

His face had the combination of innocence and alertness of a young man who had experienced both good and bad, but still vacillated between overly revealing openness and overly inhibiting caution in his confrontation with the world.

'I recognise you from a photo. I'm a friend of Oleg Fauke's.'

Harry looked for a reaction in Stein Hanssen's grey eyes, but it failed to materialise.

'You may have heard that he's been released? Someone has confessed to the killing of your foster-brother.'

Stein Hanssen shook his head. Still minimal expression.

'I'm an ex-policeman. I'm trying to find your sister, Irene.'

'How come?'

'I want to be sure she's OK. I've promised Oleg I would.'

'Great. So that he can continue to feed her drugs?'

Harry shifted his weight. 'Oleg's clean now. As you may know, that takes its toll. But he's clean because he wanted to try to find her. He loves her, Stein. But I'd like to try to find her for all our sakes, not only for his. And I'm reckoned to be quite handy at finding people.'

Stein Hanssen looked at Harry. Hesitated. Then he opened the door.

Harry followed him into the living room. It was tidy, nicely furnished and seemed completely unoccupied.

'Your parents . . .'

'They don't live here now. And I'm only here when I'm not in Trondheim.'

He had a conspicuous trilled 'r', the kind that was once regarded as a status symbol for families who could afford nannies from Sørland. The kind of 'r' that makes your voice easy to remember, Harry thought without knowing why he did.

There was a photograph on the piano, which looked as if it had never been used. The photograph must have been six or seven years old. Irene and Gusto were younger, smaller versions of themselves, sporting clothes and hairstyles that Harry assumed would have been deadly embarrassing for them to see now. Stein stood at the back with a serious expression. The mother stood with her arms crossed and wore a condescending, almost sarcastic, smile. The father was smiling in a way that made Harry think it had been his idea to have this family photo taken. At least, he was the only person showing any enthusiasm.

'So that's the family?'

'Was. My parents are divorced now. My father moved to Denmark. Fled is probably a more precise word. My mother's in hospital. The rest . . . well, you obviously know the rest.'

Harry nodded. One dead. One missing. Big losses for one family.

Harry sat down unbidden in one of the deep armchairs. 'What can you tell me that might help me find Irene?'

'I haven't a clue.'

Harry smiled. 'Try.'

'Irene moved to my place in Trondheim after going through an experience she wouldn't tell me about. But which I'm sure Gusto was behind. She idolised Gusto, would do anything for him, imagined he cared because now and then he would pat her on the cheek. But after a few months there was a phone call and she said she had to return to Oslo. Refused to divulge why. That's four months ago, and since then I've neither seen nor heard from her. When, after more than two weeks, I hadn't been able to contact her, I went to the police and reported her missing. They took note, did a bit of checking, then nothing else happened. No one cares about a homeless junkie.'

'Any theories?' Harry asked.

'No. But she hasn't gone of her own free will. She's not the type to clear off like . . . like some others.'

Harry had no idea whom he actually meant, yet the jibe hit home.

Stein Hanssen scratched a scab on his forearm. 'What is it you all see in her? Your daughter? Do you think you can *have* your daughters?'

Harry looked at him in surprise. 'You? What do you mean?'

'You oldies drooling over her. Just because she looks like a fourteen-year-old Lolita.'

Harry recalled the picture on the wardrobe door. Stein Hanssen was right. And the thought took root in Harry. He might be wrong, Irene might be the victim of a crime that had nothing to do with this case.

'You study in Trondheim. At the University of Science and Technology?'

'Yes.'

'What subject?'

'Information technology.'

'Mm. Oleg also wanted to study. Do you know him?'

Stein shook his head.

'Never spoken to him?'

'We must have met a couple of times. Very short meetings, you might say.'

Harry scrutinised Stein's forearm. It was an occupational hazard for

Harry. But apart from the scab there were no other marks. Of course not, Stein Hanssen was a survivor, one of those who would cope. Harry got to his feet.

'Anyway, I'm sorry about your brother.'

'Foster-brother.'

'Mm. Could I take your mobile number? In case anything crops up.'

'Like what?'

They looked at each other. The answer hung in the air between them, unnecessary to elucidate, unbearable to articulate. The scab had burst and a line of blood was trickling down towards his hand.

'I know one thing that might help,' Stein Hanssen said when Harry was outside on the step. 'The places you're planning to search for her. Urtegata. Møtestedet Kafé. The parks. The hostels. Junkie hovels. Red-light district. Forget it. I've been there.'

Harry nodded. Put on his sunglasses. 'Keep your mobile switched on, OK?'

Harry went to Lorry Kafé for lunch, but on the steps felt a sudden craving for beer and about-turned in the doorway. Instead he went to a new place opposite the Literature House. Left after a quick scan of the clientele, and ended up in Pla where he ordered a Thai variant of a tapa.

'Drink? Singha?'

'No.'

'Tiger?'

'Have you only got beer?'

The waiter took the hint and returned with water.

Harry had king prawns and chicken but declined sausage Thai-style. Then he called Rakel at home and asked her to go through the CDs he had taken to Holmenkollen over the years and which had been left there. Some he had wanted to listen to for his own pleasure, and some he had wanted to redeem them with. Elvis Costello, Miles Davis, Led Zeppelin, Count Basie, Jayhawks, Muddy Waters. They hadn't saved anyone.

She kept what, without any tangible irony, she called 'Harry music' in its own section on the rack.

'I'd like you to read all the titles,' he said.

'Are you joking?'

'I'll explain later.'

'OK. The first is Aztec Camera.'

'Have you—'

'Yes, I've organised them alphabetically.' She sounded embarrassed.

'That's a boy thing.'

'It's a Harry thing. And they're your CDs. Can I read them now?'

After twenty minutes they had got to W and Wilco without Harry picking up on any associations. Rakel heaved a sigh, but went on.

'"When You Wake Up Feeling Old".'

'Mm. no.'

'"Summerteeth".'

'Mm. Next.'

'"In a Future Age".'

'Hang on!'

Rakel hung on.

Harry started laughing.

'Was that funny?' Rakel asked.

'The chorus on "Summerteeth". It goes like this . . . *It's just a dream he keeps having.*'

'That doesn't sound great, Harry.'

'Yes, it does! I mean, the original does. So beautiful that I've played it several times for Oleg. But he thought the lyrics went "It's just a dreamy Gonzales".' Harry laughed again. And began to sing: '*It's just a dreamy Gonz—*'

'Please, Harry.'

'OK. Could you go onto Oleg's computer and find something on the Net for me?'

'What?'

'Google Wilco and find their home page. See if they've had any concerts in Oslo this year. And if so, where exactly.'

Rakel came back after six minutes.

'One.' She told Harry where.

'Thank you,' Harry said.

'You've got that voice again.'

'Which voice?'

'The hyped-up one. The boy's voice.'

Like a hostile armada, the ominous steel-grey clouds came rolling over Oslo fjord at four o'clock. Harry turned from Skøyen towards Frogner Park and parked on Thorvald Erichsens Vei. After ringing Bellman's mobile three times without any luck he had called Police HQ and been told that Bellman had left early to do some training with his son at Oslo Tennis Club.

Harry watched the clouds. Then he went in and surveyed OTC's facilities.

A superb clubhouse, shale courts, hard courts, even a centre court with stands. Yet only two of the twelve courts were in use. In Norway you played football and skied. Declaring yourself a tennis player attracted whispers and suspicious glances.

Harry found Bellman on a shale court. He was plucking balls out of a basket and hitting them gently at a boy who might have been practising backhand cross-court shots; it was hard to say, because the balls were going all over the place.

Harry went through the gate behind Bellman, onto the court and stood beside him. 'Looks like he's struggling,' Harry said, taking out his pack of cigarettes.

'Harry,' Mikael Bellman said, without stopping or taking his eyes off the boy. 'He's getting there.'

'There's a certain similarity. Is he . . .?'

'My son. Filip. Ten.'

'Time flies. Talented?'

'He's got a bit of his father in him, but I have faith. He just needs to be pushed.'

'I didn't think that was legal any more.'

'We want the best for our children, Harry, but may do them a disservice. Move your feet, Filip!'

'Did you find out about Martin Pran?'

'Pran?'

'The hunchback weirdo at the Radium Hospital.'

'Oh, yes, the gut instinct. Yes and no. That is, yes, I checked. And no, we've got nothing on him. Nothing at all.'

'Mm. I was thinking about asking for something else.'

'Down on your knees! What would that be?'

'A warrant to dig up Gusto Hanssen to see if there was any blood under his nails for a new test.'

Bellman took his eyes off his son, evidently to check whether Harry was serious.

'There's a very plausible confession, Harry. I think I can say with some confidence that warrant would be rejected.'

'Gusto did have blood under his nails. The sample went missing before it was tested.'

'That sort of thing happens.'

'Very rarely.'

'And whose blood is it, in your opinion?'

'Don't know.'

'You don't know?'

'No. But if the first sample was sabotaged that means it spells danger for someone.'

'This dealer who confessed, for example. Adidas?'

'Real name: Chris Reddy.'

'Anyway, aren't you done with this case now that Oleg Fauke has been released?'

'Anyway, shouldn't he have both hands on the racket for backhand?'

'Do you know anything about tennis?'

'Seen a bit on TV.'

'One-handed backhands develop character.'

'I don't even know if the blood has anything to do with the killing. Perhaps someone's frightened of being linked with Gusto?'

'Such as?'

'Dubai maybe. Besides, I don't think Adidas killed Gusto.'

'Why not?'

'A hardened dealer suddenly confessing out of the blue?'

'See your point,' Bellman said. 'But it is a confession. And a good one.'

'And it's just a drugs killing,' Harry continued, ducking a stray ball. 'And you've got enough cases to crack.'

Bellman sighed. 'It's the same as it's always been, Harry. Our resources are under too much pressure for us to be able to prioritise cases for which we already have a solution.'

'*A* solution? What about *the* solution?'

'As boss one is obliged to acquire slippery formulations.'

'OK, so let me offer you two case solutions. In exchange for help with finding a house.'

Bellman stopped hitting balls. 'What?'

'A killing in Alnabru. A biker called Tutu. A source informed me he got a drill through his head.'

'And the source is willing to testify?'

'Maybe.'

'And the second?'

'The undercover guy who washed up by the Opera House. Same source saw him dead on Dubai's cellar floor.'

Bellman scrunched up one eye. The pigment stains flared up and Harry was reminded of a tiger.

'Dad!'

'Go and fill the water bottle in the dressing room, Filip.'

'The dressing room's locked, Dad!'

'And the code is?'

'The year the king was born, but I don't remember—'

'Remember and quench your thirst, Filip.'

The boy shuffled through the gate, arms hanging by his sides.

'What do you want, Harry?'

'I want a team combing the area around Frederikkeplassen, at the

263

university, over a radius of one kilometre. I want a list of all the detached houses that fit this description.' He passed Bellman a sheet of paper.

'What happened at Frederikkeplassen?'

'Just a concert.'

Realising he wasn't going to be told any more, Bellman looked down at the paper and read aloud: '"Old timber house with long shingle drive, deciduous trees and steps by the front door, no overhang"? Sounds like a description of half the houses in Blindern. What are you after?'

Harry lit a smoke. 'A rat's nest. An eagle's lair.'

'And if we find it, what then?'

'You and your officers need a search warrant to be able to do anything while a normal civilian like me could get lost one autumn evening and be forced to take refuge in the nearest house.'

'OK, I'll see what I can do. But explain to me first why you're so keen to catch this Dubai.'

Harry shrugged. 'Professional deformation perhaps. Get the list and email it to the address at the bottom. Then we'll see what I can get for you.'

Filip returned without water as Harry was leaving, and on his way to the car he heard a ball hit the racket frame and a low curse.

Distant cannons rumbled in the armada of clouds, and it was as dark as night when Harry got into his car. He started the engine and rang Hans Christian Simonsen.

'Harry here. What are the current penalties for grave desecration?'

'Er, four to six years, I would guess.'

'Are you willing to risk that?'

A tiny pause. Then: 'To what end?'

'To catch the person who killed Gusto. And perhaps the person who's after Oleg.'

'And if I'm not willing?'

A very tiny pause. 'I'm in.'

'OK, find out where Gusto is buried and get some spades, a torch, nail scissors and two screwdrivers. We'll do it tomorrow night.'

As Harry drove across Solli plass the rain came. It lashed the rooftops, lashed the streets, lashed the man standing in Kvadraturen opposite the open door to the bar.

The boy in reception sent Harry a dour look as he came in.

'Would you like to borrow an umbrella?'

'Not unless your hotel's leaking,' Harry said, running a hand through his brush-like hair and sending a fine spray through the air. 'Any messages?'

The boy laughed as if it were a joke.

As Harry was climbing the stairs to the second floor he thought he heard footsteps further down and stopped. Listened. Silence. Either it had been the echo of his own steps he had heard, or else the other person had stopped as well.

Harry walked on slowly. In the corridor he increased his speed, inserted the key in the lock and opened the door. Scanned the darkened room and peered across the yard to the woman's illuminated room. No one there. No one there, no one here.

He switched on the light.

As it came on he saw his reflection in the window. And someone else standing behind him. At once he felt a heavy hand squeeze his shoulder.

Only a phantom can be so fast and silent, Harry thought, whirling round, but he knew it was already too late.

27

'I SAW THEM. ONCE. It was like a wake.'

Cato still had his large, dirty hand resting on Harry's shoulder.

Harry heard himself gasp and felt his lungs pressing against the inside of his ribs.

'Who?'

'I was talking to someone selling the devilry. His name was Bisken and he wore a leather dog collar. He came to me because he was frightened. The police had hauled him in for possession of heroin, and he had told Beret Man where Dubai lived. Beret Man had promised him protection and an amnesty if he would testify in court. And while I was standing there they came in a black car. Black suits, black gloves. He was old. Broad face. He looked like a white aborigine.'

'Who?'

'I saw him, but . . . he wasn't there. Like a phantom. And when Bisken saw him he didn't move, didn't try to run or struggle when they took him with them. After they'd gone it was as if I'd dreamt it all up.'

'Why didn't you tell me this before?'

'Because I'm a coward. Have you got a ciggy?'

Harry gave him the pack, and Cato fell into the chair.

'You're chasing a ghost, and I don't want to be involved.'

'But?'

Cato shrugged and held out his hand. Harry passed him the lighter.

'I'm an old, dying man. I have nothing to lose.'

'Are you dying?'

Cato lit his cigarette. 'It's not acute, perhaps, but we're all dying, Harry. I just want to help you.'

'With what?'

'Don't know. What plans have you got?'

'Can I trust you?'

'Christ, no, you can't trust me. But I'm a shaman. I can also make myself invisible. I can come and go without anyone noticing.'

Harry rubbed his chin. 'Why?'

'I told you why.'

'I'm asking again.'

Cato looked at Harry, first with a reproachful glare. Then, when that didn't help, he heaved a deep sigh of annoyance. 'Perhaps I had a son once myself. One I didn't treat as well as I should have. Perhaps it's a new opportunity. Don't you believe in fresh opportunities, Harry?'

Harry eyed the old man. The furrows in his face looked even deeper in the darkness, like valleys, like slashes from a knife. Harry thrust out his hand, and reluctantly Cato took the cigarettes from his pocket and handed them back.

'I appreciate it, Cato. I'll tell you if I need you. But what I'm going to do now is link Dubai to Gusto's death. From there the tracks will lead directly on to the burner in the police and the killing of the undercover cop who was drowned in Dubai's house.'

Cato slowly shook his head. 'You have a pure and courageous heart, Harry. Perhaps you'll go to heaven.'

Harry poked a cigarette between his lips. 'So there'll be a kind of happy ending after all then.'

'Which has to be celebrated. May I offer you a drink, Harry Hole?'

'Who's paying?'

'Me, of course. If you stump up. You can say hello to your Jim, I can say hello to my Johnnie.'

'Get thee hence.'

'Come on. Jim's a good man deep down.'

'Goodnight. Sleep well.'

'Goodnight. And don't sleep too well, in case—'

'Goodnight.'

It had been there all the time, but Harry had succeeding in suppressing it. Up until now, up until Cato's invitation. It was enough, it was impossible to ignore the gnawing now. It had started with the violin fix, that had set it in motion, had released the dogs again. And now they were baying and clawing, barking themselves hoarse and gnashing at his intestines. Harry lay on the bed with his eyes closed, listening to the rain and hoping sleep would come and carry him away.

It didn't.

He had a phone number in his mobile he had apportioned two letters. AA. Alcoholics Anonymous. Trygve, an AA member and sponsor he had used several times before at critical points. Three years. Why start now, now there was everything to play for and he needed more than ever to be sober? It was madness. He heard a scream outside. Followed by laughter.

At ten past eleven he got up and left. He barely registered the rain splashing down on his skull as he crossed the street to the open door. And this time he didn't hear the footsteps behind him, for Kurt Cobain's voice filled his auditory canals, the music like an embrace, and he stepped inside, sat on the stool by the counter and called to the barman.

'Whis . . . key. Jim . . . Beam.'

The barman stopped wiping down the counter, put the cloth beside the corkscrew and lifted the bottle from the mirror shelf. Poured. Set the glass on the counter. Harry placed his forearms either side of the glass and stared into the golden-brown liquid. And for that moment nothing else existed.

Not Nirvana, not Oleg, not Rakel, not Gusto, not Dubai. Not Tord

Schultz's face. Not the figure that muffled the street noise as it came in. Nor the movement behind him. Nor the singing tone of the springs as the blade shot out. Nor the heavy breathing of Sergey Ivanov standing a metre from him with legs together and hands held low.

Sergey looked at the man's back. He had both arms resting on the counter. It couldn't be more perfect. The hour had come. His heart was pounding. Pounding wildly with fresh blood, as it had done the first time he had fetched the heroin packages from the cockpit. All fear was gone. Because he knew now, he was alive. He was alive and about to kill the man before him. *Take* his life, make it part of his own. The very idea of it made him grow; it was as though he had already consumed the enemy's heart. Now. The movements. Sergey took a deep breath, stepped forward and placed his left hand on Harry's head. As if in blessing. As if he were going to baptise him.

28

SERGEY IVANOV COULDN'T GET A HOLD. Simply could not get a hold. The damn rain had soaked the man's skull and hair, and the short spikes slipped through his fingers preventing him from snatching his head back. Sergey's left hand shot forward again, grasped the man's forehead and pulled it to him as he brought the knife round his throat. The man's body jerked. Sergey slashed with the knife, felt it make contact, felt it slice through skin. There! The hot jet of blood on his thumb. Not as deep as he expected, but three more heartbeats and it would all be over. He raised his gaze to the mirror to see the fountain. He saw a bared row of teeth and beneath that a gaping wound from which blood was streaming down the front of the shirt. And the man's eyes. It was that look – a cold, angry predatory glare – that made him realise the job was not yet done.

When Harry had felt the hand on his head he had known instinctively. Known it was not a drunken customer or an old acquaintance, but them. The hand slid off and that gave Harry a tenth of a second to look in the mirror, to see the glint of steel. He already knew where it was heading. Then the hand was around his forehead and jerking him backwards. It was too late to put a hand between throat and blade, so Harry stood on the foot rail and levered himself upwards while squeezing his chin against his chest. He felt no pain as the knife sliced his skin, didn't feel it until it cut through to the chin and penetrated the sensitive membrane around the bone.

Then he met the other man's eyes in the mirror. He pulled Harry's head back towards his own, making them resemble two friends posing for a picture. Harry felt the blade being pressed against his chin and chest, trying to find a way into one of the two neck arteries, and he knew that within a few seconds it would succeed.

Sergey wrapped the whole of his arm around the man's forehead and jerked with all his might. The man's head tilted backwards, and in the mirror he saw the blade finally find the gap between chin and chest and slide in. The steel bit into the throat and moved to the right, towards the neck artery, the arteria carotis. *Blin!* The man had managed to lift his right hand and stick a finger between knife and artery. But Sergey knew the razor-sharp edge would sever a finger. It was just a question of applying enough pressure. He pulled. And pulled.

Harry could feel the pressure from the knife, but knew it wouldn't make any headway. The highest strength-to-weight ratio of any metal. Nothing cut through titanium, whether it was made in Hong Kong or not. But the guy was strong, soon he would realise that the blade wasn't biting.

He groped with his free hand in front of him, knocking over his drink, and found something.

It was a T-shaped corkscrew. Of the simplest kind, with a short helix. He grabbed the handle with the point protruding between first and second fingers. Felt panic surge as he heard the knife blade slide over the prosthesis. He forced his eyes down to see in the mirror. See where he should aim. Raised his hand to the side and struck backwards, behind his head.

He noticed the other man's body stiffen as the tip of the corkscrew perforated the skin on the side of his neck. But it was an innocuous, superficial wound and it didn't stop him. He was beginning to shift the knife to the left. Harry concentrated. The corkscrew demanded a firm, practised hand. However, a couple of turns was all it needed to penetrate deep into the cork. Harry twisted twice. Felt it slip through the flesh. Bore its way in. Felt soft resistance. The oesophagus. Then he pulled.

It was like pulling the bung from the side of a full barrel of red wine.

Sergey Ivanov was fully conscious and saw the whole process in the mirror as the first heartbeat sent a jet of blood to the right. His brain registered, analysed and formed a conclusion: the man whose throat he was trying to cut had found a main artery with a corkscrew, pulled the vessel from his neck and it was now pumping out his life blood. Sergey had three further thoughts before the second heartbeat came and consciousness went.

He had let down his uncle.

He would never see his beloved Siberia again.

He was going to be buried with a tattoo that lied.

On the third beat of his heart he fell. And by the time the song finished, Sergey Ivanov was dead.

Harry got up from the stool. In the mirror he saw the cut running across his chin. But that wasn't the worst; there were deep cuts to his throat from which blood was trickling and had already discoloured his entire collar.

The three other customers in the bar had gone. He looked down at the man lying on the floor. Blood was still flowing from the gash in his neck, but it wasn't pumping. Which meant that his heart had stopped beating and there was no point trying to revive him. And even if there had been life left in him, Harry knew this person would never have revealed who had sent him. Because he saw the tattoos protruding above the shirt. He didn't know any of the symbols, but he knew they were Russian. Black Corn maybe. They were different from the typically Western tattoo belonging to the barman, who was pressed up against the mirror shelf and staring with pupils so black with shock they seemed to cover the whites of his eyes. Nirvana had faded out and there was total silence. Harry looked at the whiskey glass lying on its side.

'Sorry about the mess,' he said.

Then he picked up the cloth from the counter, wiped first where his hands had been, then the glass, then the handle of the corkscrew, which he put back. He checked that none of his own blood had ended up on the counter or the floor. Then he bent over the dead man and wiped his bloody hand, the long, ivory knife handle and the thin blade. The weapon – for it was a weapon and useless for anything else – was heavier than any knife he had ever held. The edge was as sharp as a Japanese sushi knife. Harry hesitated. Then he folded the blade into the shaft, heard a soft click as it locked, flicked the safety catch and dropped it into his jacket pocket.

'OK to pay with dollars?' Harry asked, using the cloth to pick a twenty-dollar bill from his wallet. 'Legal tender in the United States, it says.'

Small whining noises came from the barman as if he wanted to say something, but had lost the power of speech.

Harry was about to go, then stopped. Turned to look at the bottle on the mirror shelf. Wetted his lips again. Stood unmoving for a second. Then his body seemed to twitch and he left.

Harry crossed the street in pouring rain. They knew where he was staying. They could have tailed him of course, but it could also have been the boy in reception. Or the burner who had got hold of his name via the routine registering of hotel guests. If he went in through the backyard he would be able to reach his room unnoticed.

The gate to the street was locked. Harry cursed.

The reception desk was unmanned as he entered.

On the stairs and in the corridor he left a trail of red dots, like Morse code, on the light blue linoleum.

Inside his room, he took the sewing kit from the bedside table to the bathroom, undressed and leaned over the washbasin, which was soon red from blood. He soaked a hand towel and washed his chin and neck, but the cuts to his neck soon filled up with more blood. In the cold, white light he managed to thread the cotton through the eye of the needle and put the needle through the white flaps of skin on his neck, first underneath and then above the wound. Sewed his way along, stopped to wipe away blood and carried on. The thread broke as he was almost finished. He swore, pulled the ends out and started again with the thread doubled. Afterwards he sewed the wound on his chin, which was easier. He washed the blood from his upper torso and took a clean shirt from his suitcase. Then he sat down on the bed. He was dizzy. But he was in a hurry, he doubted they would be far away, he had to act now before they found out he was alive. He called Hans Christian Simonsen's number and after the fourth ring he heard a sleepy: 'Hans Christian.'

'Harry. Where's Gusto buried?'

'Vestre Cemetery.'

'Have you got the gear ready?'

'Yes.'

'We'll do it tonight. Meet me on the pathway on the eastern side in an hour.'

'*Now?*'

'Yes. And bring some plasters.'

'Plasters?'

'A clumsy barber, that's all. Sixty minutes from now, OK?'

A slight pause. A sigh. And then: 'OK.'

As Harry was about to ring off he thought he heard a sleepy voice, someone else's voice. But by the time he had dressed he had already convinced himself that he had misheard.

29

HARRY WAS STANDING BENEATH a lone street lamp. He had been waiting for twenty minutes when Hans Christian, wearing a black tracksuit, came barrelling up the footpath.

'I parked in Monolittveien,' he said, out of breath. 'Is a linen suit standard garb for desecrating a grave?'

Harry raised his head, and Hans Christian's eyes widened. 'Good God, what do you look like? That barber—'

'Isn't recommended,' Harry said. 'Come on, let's get out of the light.'

Once they were in the darkness, Harry stopped. 'Plasters?'

'Here.'

Hans Christian studied the unlit houses on the hill behind them while Harry carefully placed plasters over the stitches on his neck and chin.

'Relax, no one can see us,' Harry said, grabbing one of the spades and setting off. Hans Christian hurried after him, pulled out a torch and clicked it on.

'Now they can see us,' Harry said.

Hans Christian clicked it off.

They strode through the war memorial grove, past the British sailors' graves and continued along the gravel paths. Harry established that death was not a great leveller; the headstones in this West Oslo cemetery were bigger and brighter than in the east of town. The gravel crunched whenever their feet hit it, they were walking faster and faster and in the end it sounded like one continuous noise.

They stopped at the gypsy's grave.

'It's second left,' Hans Christian whispered and tried to angle the map he had printed into the sparse moonlight.

Harry stared into the darkness behind them.

'Something up?' Hans Christian whispered.

'Just thought I heard footsteps. They stopped when we stopped.'

Harry raised his head, as if scenting the air.

'Echo,' he said. 'Come on.'

Two minutes later they were standing by a modest, black stone. Harry held the torch close to the stone before switching it on. The letters had been engraved and painted in gold.

Gusto Hanssen

14.03.1992 – 12.07.2011

Rest in Peace

'Bingo,' Harry whispered without ceremony.

'How are we—' Hans Christian began, but was interrupted by the sigh of Harry's spade entering the soft earth. He grabbed his own and got stuck in.

It was half past three, and the moon had gone behind a cloud when Harry's spade hit something hard.

Fifteen minutes later the white coffin was revealed.

They both grabbed a screwdriver, knelt down on the coffin and began to loosen the six screws in the lid.

'We won't get the lid off with both of us on top,' Harry said. 'One of us has to go up so the other can open the coffin. Volunteers?'

Hans Christian had already half crawled out.

Harry put one foot down beside the coffin and the other against the earth wall and squeezed his fingers under the lid. Then he exerted pressure and from force of habit began to breathe through his mouth. Before he even looked down he could feel the heat rising from the coffin. He knew the process of decomposition produced energy, but what made the hairs stand up on the back of his neck was the sound.

The rustle of fly larvae in flesh. He kneed the coffin lid to the side of the grave.

'Shine here,' he said.

White slithering larvae glistened in and around the corpse's mouth and nose. The eyelids had sunk as the eyeballs were the first parts to be consumed.

Harry shut out the sounds of Hans Christian being sick and switched on his analytical faculties: face discoloured, dark, impossible to determine whether the owner was Gusto Hanssen, but the hair colour and shape of face suggested it was.

But there was something that caught Harry's attention and caused him to stop breathing.

Gusto was bleeding.

Red roses were growing on the white shroud, roses of blood that were spreading.

Two seconds passed before Harry realised that the blood was coming from him. He clutched his neck. His fingers felt thick blood. The stitches had come undone.

'Your T-shirt,' Harry said.

'What?'

'I need some patching-up here.'

Harry heard the brief song of a zip, and a few seconds later a T-shirt floated down into the light. He grabbed it, saw the logo. Free Legal Aid. Christ, an idealist. Harry wound the T-shirt round his neck with no clear idea of how this would help, but it was all he could do for now. Then he bent over Gusto, grabbed the shroud with both hands and tore it open. The body was dark, slightly bloated and larvae were crawling out from the bullet holes in the chest.

Harry could see the wounds tallied with the report.

'Give me the scissors.'

'The scissors.'

'The nail scissors.'

'Damn,' Hans Christian coughed. 'I forgot them. Perhaps I've got something in the car. Shall I—'

'No need,' Harry said, taking the long flick knife from his jacket pocket. Undid the safety catch and pressed the release button. The blade shot out with a brutal power, so fierce it made the handle vibrate. He could feel the perfect balance of the weapon.

'I can hear something,' Hans Christian said.

'It's a Slipknot song,' Harry said. '"Pulse of the Maggots".' He was humming softly.

'No, damn it. Someone's coming!'

'Angle the torch so that I can see, and run for it,' Harry said, lifting up Gusto's hands and studying the nails on the right hand.

'But you—'

'Run for it,' Harry said. 'Now.'

Harry heard Hans Christian's steps fade into the distance. The nail on Gusto's middle finger was cut shorter. He examined the first finger and the third. Said calmly: 'I'm from the funeral home. We're doing a bit of after-hours.'

Then he turned his face up to the very young, uniform-clad guard standing by the edge of the grave looking down at him.

'The family wasn't very happy with the manicure.'

'Out you get!' the guard ordered with only a slight tremble in his voice.

'Why?' Harry said, taking a little plastic bag from his jacket pocket and holding it under the third finger while sedulously cutting. The blade sliced through the nail as if it were butter. Indeed a fantastic instrument. 'Unfortunately for you, your instructions state that you mustn't tackle intruders head-on.'

Harry used the tip of the blade to winkle out the dry remains of blood from under the short nail.

'If you do, you'll get the boot and Police College will reject you, and you won't be allowed to carry a big gun and shoot someone in self-defence.'

Harry turned his attention to the first finger.

'Do what your instructions tell you, ring an adult in the police. If you're lucky they'll be here in half an hour. But if we're realistic we'll probably have to wait for office hours tomorrow. There we are!'

Harry closed the bags, put them in his jacket pocket, replaced the coffin lid and clambered out of the grave. He brushed the soil off his suit and bent down to pick up the spade and torch.

Saw the headlamps of a car turning into the chapel.

'In fact they said they would come straight away,' said the young guard, retreating to a safe distance. 'I told them it was the grave of the guy who was shot, you see. Who are you?'

Harry switched off the torch and it was pitch black.

'I'm the one you should be rooting for.'

Then Harry set off at a run. He headed east, away from the chapel, back along the route they had come.

He took his bearings from a bright light he assumed was a lamp post in Frogner Park. If he could make it to the park he knew, in his current form, he could outrun most of them. He only hoped they didn't have any dogs. He hated dogs. Best to keep to the gravel paths so as not to stumble over headstones and bunches of flowers, but the crunching made it more difficult to hear any potential pursuers. By the war memorial Harry moved onto the grass. He couldn't hear anyone behind him. But then he saw it. A quivering beam of light on the treetops above. Someone was chasing him with a torch.

Harry emerged onto the path and headed for the park. Tried to shut out the pain round his neck and run in a relaxed, efficient way, concentrating on technique and breathing. Told himself he was pulling away. He ran towards the Monolith, knowing they would see him under the lamps on the pathway that continued over the hill and it would look as if he was making for the park's main gate on the eastern side.

Harry waited until he had topped the crest and was out of sight before heading south-west towards Madserud allé. Adrenalin had kept him going, but now he could feel his muscles stiffening. For a second, things went black and he thought he had lost consciousness. But then he was back, and a sudden feeling of nausea engulfed him, followed by overwhelming giddiness. He looked down. Blood was oozing from under his jacket sleeve and dripping between his fingers, like strawberry jam off a slice of bread at his grandfather's house. He wasn't going to last the distance.

He craned his head. Saw a figure pass through the light under the lamp at the top of the hill. A big man, but with a light running style. Tight-fitting black clothes. Not a police uniform. Could it be a Delta guy? In the middle of the night at such short notice? Because someone was digging in a cemetery?

Harry swayed but managed to steady himself. He had no hope of outrunning anyone in this state. He had to find a place to hide.

Harry aimed for one of the houses in Madserud allé. Left the path, sprinted down a grass slope, had to stretch out his arms so as not to fall, continued across the tarmac road, jumped over the low picket fence, carried on into the apple trees and round the back of the house. Where he threw himself into the long, wet grass. Took a deep breath, felt his stomach constrict, braced himself to vomit. Concentrated on breathing as he listened.

Nothing.

But it was just a matter of time before they would be here. And he needed a decent bandage for his neck. Harry got to his feet and walked to the terrace of the house. Peered through the glass in the door. Dark living room.

He kicked in the glass and slipped his hand inside. Good old naive Norway. The key was in the door. He slid into the gloom.

Held his breath. The bedrooms were probably on the first floor.

He switched on a table lamp.

Plush chairs. Cabinet TV. Encyclopedia. A table covered with family photographs. Knitting. So elderly occupants. And old people sleep well. Or was it badly?

Harry found the kitchen, switched on the light. Searched the drawers. Cutlery, cloths. Tried to remember where they had always kept that kind of thing when he was small. Opened the second-bottom drawer. And there it was. Standard tape, parcel tape, gaffer tape. He grabbed the roll of gaffer tape and opened two doors before he found the bathroom. Pulled off his jacket and shirt, held his head over the bath and the hand-held shower over his neck. Watched the white enamel gain a red filter in a second. Then he dried himself with the T-shirt and squeezed the edges of the wound together with his fingers while winding the silver tape round his neck several times. Tested to make sure it wasn't too tight. After all he needed some blood to go to the brain. Put on his shirt. Another attack of dizziness. He sat down on the edge of the bath.

He noticed a movement. Raised his head.

From the doorway an elderly woman's pale face was staring at him with enlarged, frightened eyes. Over her nightdress she was wearing a red, quilted dressing gown. It gave off a strange sheen and electric static whenever she moved. Harry guessed it was made of some synthetic material that no longer existed, was banned, carcinogenic, asbestos or something.

'I'm a police officer,' Harry said. Coughed. 'Ex-police officer. And in a bit of trouble right now.'

She said nothing, just stood there.

'Of course I'll pay for the broken glass.' Harry lifted his jacket off the bathroom floor and took out his wallet. Put some notes on the sink. 'Hong Kong dollars. They're . . . better than they sound.'

He essayed a smile and saw a tear running down wrinkled cheeks.

'Oh dear,' Harry said, feeling panic, a sense that he was on the slide, losing control. 'Don't be frightened. I really won't do anything to you. I'll leave this minute, OK?'

He forced his arm into the jacket sleeve and walked towards her. She backed away, taking tiny, shuffling steps, but not releasing him from her gaze. Harry held up the palms of his hands and made swiftly for the terrace door.

'Thank you,' he said. 'And sorry.'

Then he pushed open the door and went onto the terrace.

The power of the explosion suggested it was a heavy-calibre weapon. Then came the sound of the shot, the primer blast, and that was the confirmation. Harry fell to his knees as the next bullet splintered the back of the garden chair beside him.

A very heavy calibre.

Harry scrabbled back into the living room.

'Keep down!' he shouted as the living-room window shattered. Glass tinkled onto the parquet floor, the TV and the table covered with family photographs.

Bent double, Harry ran through the living room, the hall, to the front door. Opened it. Saw the muzzle of flame from the open door of a black limousine under a street lamp. He felt a stinging pain on his face, and a high-pitched, piercing metallic sound rang out. Harry turned automatically and saw that the wall-mounted doorbell had been shot to pieces. Large white splinters of wood stuck out.

Harry retreated. Lay down on the floor.

A heavier calibre than any of the police weapons. Harry thought of the tall figure he had seen running across the ridge. That had not been a police officer.

'You've got something in your cheek . . .'

It was the woman; she had to shout over the shrill ringing of the bell that had got stuck. She was standing behind him, at the back of the hall. Harry groped with his fingers. It was a splinter of wood. He pulled it out. Had time to think it was lucky it was on the same side as the scar: it shouldn't reduce his market value to any dramatic extent. Then there was another bang. This time it was the kitchen window. He was running out of Hong Kong dollars.

Over the ringing he could hear sirens in the distance. Harry raised his head. Through the hallway and living room he saw that lights had come on in the surrounding houses. The street was illuminated like a Christmas tree. He was going to be a floodlit moving target whichever route he took. The options were being shot or arrested. No, not even that. They heard the sirens as well, and knew time was running out for them. And he hadn't returned fire, so they must have assumed he was unarmed. They would follow him. He had to get away. He pulled out his mobile. Shit, why hadn't he taken the trouble to file his number under T? It wasn't as if his contacts list was exactly full.

'What's the number of directory enquiries again?' he shouted.

'The number . . . for . . . directory enquiries?'

'Yes.'

'Well.' She stuck a pensive finger in her mouth, tucked the red asbestos gown underneath her as she sat down on a wooden chair. 'There's 1880. But I think they're nicer on 1881. They're not as quick or stressed. They take their time and have a chat if you've—'

'Enquiries 1880,' said a nasal voice in Harry's ear.

'Asbjørn Treschow,' Harry said. 'With a *c* and an *h*.'

'We've got an Asbjørn Berthold Treschow in Oppsal, Oslo, and an Asbjø—'

'That's him! Could you give me his mobile number?'

Three seconds of an eternity later a familiar crabby voice answered.

'I don't want any.'

'Tresko?'

Protracted pause without an answer. Harry visualised his fat friend's astonished face.

'Harry? Long time—'

'Are you at work?'

'Yes.' The extended *e* indicated suspicion. No one rang Tresko for no reason.

'I need a quick favour.'

'Yes, I suppose you do. Doh, what about the hundred kroner you borrowed? You said—'

'I need you to turn off the electricity in the Frogner Park / Madserud allé area.'

'You what?'

'We've got a police emergency here. There's a guy gone nuts with a gun. We need cover of darkness. Are you still at the substation in Montebello?'

Another pause.

'So far, but are you still a cop?'

'Of course. Tresko, this is actually pretty urgent.'

'I don't give a shit. I don't have the authorisation to do that. You'll have to talk to Henmo, and he—'

'He's asleep and we don't have the time!' Harry shouted. At that moment another shot rang out and a cupboard in the kitchen was hit. A set of dishes slid out with a clatter and smashed on the floor.

'What on earth was that?' Tresko asked.

'What do you think? You can choose between the responsibility for a forty-second blackout or a pile of human bodies.'

Silence at the other end for a few moments. Then it came, slowly:

'Fancy that, eh, Harry? Now I'm sitting here and I'm in charge. You would never have believed that, would you, eh?'

Harry took a deep breath. Saw a shadow glide across the terrace. 'No, Tresko. I wouldn't have believed it. Can you—'

'You and Øystein never thought I'd amount to much, did you?'

'No, we made a big booboo there.'

'What about saying pleas—'

'Turn that fucking electricity off!' Harry yelled. And heard the dial tone. He got to his feet, took the elderly woman under his arm and half dragged her into the bathroom. 'Stay here,' he whispered, closing the door behind him and running to the open front door. He charged into the light, steeling himself for the deluge of bullets.

And then everything went black.

So black that he landed on the flagstones and rolled forward thinking for a confused instant that he was dead. Before he realised that Asbjørn 'Tresko' Treschow had flicked the switch, pressed the key or whatever it was they did at the substation. And that he had forty seconds.

Harry ran blind into the pitch black. Stumbled over the picket fence, felt tarmac under his feet and ran on. Heard shouting and sirens coming closer. But also the growl of a powerful car engine starting up. Harry kept to the right, could see enough to stay on the road. He was south of Frogner Park. There was a chance he would make it. He passed darkened detached houses, trees, forest. The district was still without electricity. The car engine was coming closer. He lurched left into the car park by the tennis courts. A puddle in the gravel almost brought him to grief, but he stumbled on. The only objects reflecting enough light to be seen were the white chalk stripes on the tennis courts behind the wire fence. Harry saw the outline of the OTC clubhouse. He sprinted to the wall in front of the dressing-room door and dived headlong as the light from two car headlamps swept across. He landed and rolled sideways on the concrete. It was a soft landing, but nevertheless it made him dizzy.

He lay as still as a mouse, waiting.

Heard nothing.

Stared up into the dark night.

Then, without warning, he was dazzled by light.

The outside lamp beneath the roof. The electricity was back.

Harry lay for two minutes listening to the sirens. Cars came and went on the road by the clubhouse. The search parties. The area was probably already surrounded. Soon they would be bringing in the dogs.

He couldn't move away, so he would have to break into the building.

He stood up, peered over the edge of the wall.

Saw the box with the red light and the keypad beside the door.

The year the king was born. God knows when that was.

He visualised a photo from a gossip mag and tried 1941. It beeped and he wrenched at the door handle. Locked. Hang on, hadn't the king just been born when the family went to London in 1940? 1939? Bit older maybe. Harry feared it would be three tries and you're out. 1938. Grabbed the handle. Shit. 1937? Green light. The door opened.

Harry slipped in and heard the door lock behind him.

Silence. Safe.

He switched on the light.

Dressing room. Narrow wooden benches. Iron cabinets.

It was only now that he realised how exhausted he was. He could stay here until dawn, until the hunt had been called off. He inspected the dressing room. A sink with a mirror. Four showers. One toilet. He opened a heavy wooden door at the end of the room.

A sauna.

He went in and let the door close behind him. The smell of wood. He lay down on one of the broad benches by the cold stove. Closed his eyes.

30

THERE WERE THREE OF THEM. They were running down a corridor, holding each other's hands, and Harry shouted that they would have to hold tight when the avalanche hit so they wouldn't be separated. He heard the snow coming behind them, first as a rumble, next as a roar. Then it was there, the white darkness, the black chaos. He clung on as hard as he could, yet still he felt their hands slipping from his.

Harry woke with a start. Looked at his watch and saw he had been asleep for three hours. He let out his breath in a long wheeze as though he had been holding it. His body felt battered and bruised. His neck ached. He had a thundering headache. And he was sweating. Was so drenched in sweat that his suit had dark patches. He didn't need to turn to see the reason. The stove. Someone had switched on the sauna.

He got to his feet and staggered into the dressing room. There were clothes lying on the benches, and he heard the sound of racket strings on balls outside. They wanted a sauna after the tennis.

Harry went to the sink. Looked at himself in the mirror. Red eyes, bloated red face. The ridiculous necklace of silver gaffer tape; the edge had dug into the soft skin. He threw water over his face and walked into the morning sun.

Three men, all pensioner-tanned with thin pensioner-legs, stopped playing and stared at him. One of them straightened his glasses.

'We're a man short for doubles, young man. Feel like . . .?'

Harry stared ahead and concentrated on speaking calmly.

'Sorry, boys. Tennis elbow.'

Harry felt their eyes on his back as he walked down towards Skøyen. There should be a bus around here somewhere.

Truls Berntsen knocked on the unit head's door.

'Come in!'

Bellman was standing with the phone to his ear. He looked calm, but Truls knew Mikael too well. The hand that kept going to his well-tended hair, the slightly accelerated manner of talking, the concentrated furrow in his brow.

Bellman cradled the receiver.

'Stressful morning?' Truls asked, passing Bellman a steaming cup of coffee.

The unit head looked at the cup with surprise, but took it.

'The Chief of Police,' Bellman said, nodding towards the phone. 'The papers are on his back about this old lady in Madserud allé. Her house has been shot half to bits, and he wants me to explain what happened.'

'What did you answer?'

'Ops Room sent out a patrol car after the guard at Vestre Cemetery informed us there were people digging up Gusto Hanssen. The culprits had escaped by the time the car arrived, but then some shooting broke out around Madserud allé. Someone was shooting at someone else who broke into the house. The lady's in shock, she just says the intruder was a polite young man, two and a half metres tall with a scar on his face.'

'Do you think the shooting is connected with the grave desecration?'

Bellman nodded. 'There were clods of mud on her living-room floor that certainly come from the cemetery. So now the Chief of Police is wondering if this is drugs-related, if this is another showdown between gangs. Whether I have the situation under control, that sort of thing.'

Bellman went to the window and stroked the ridge of his narrow nose with his first finger.

'Is that why you asked me to come?' Truls asked, taking a careful swig of coffee.

'No,' Bellman said with his back to Truls. 'I was wondering about the night we got that anonymous tip-off that the whole Los Lobos gang would be at McDonald's. You weren't on that arrest, were you?'

'No,' Berntsen said with a cough. 'I couldn't make it. I was ill that night.'

'Same illness as recently?' Bellman asked without turning.

'Eh?'

'Some officers were surprised that the door to the bikers' clubhouse wasn't locked when they arrived. And wondered how this Tutu who, according to Odin, was keeping watch there managed to get away. No one could have known we were coming. Could they?'

'As far as I know,' Truls said, 'there was only us.'

Bellman continued to stare out of the window and rocked on his heels. Hands behind his hips. Rocked back. And rocked forward.

Truls wiped his upper lip. Hoped the sweat wasn't visible. 'Anything else?'

Kept rocking. Backwards and forwards. Like a boy trying to see over something, but he's too short.

'That was all, Truls. And thank you . . . for the coffee.'

When Truls was back in his own office he went to the window. Saw what Bellman must have seen. The red poster was hanging from the tree.

It was twelve o'clock, and on the pavement outside Schrøder's there were the usual thirsty souls waiting for Rita to open up.

'Ooooh,' she said as she caught sight of Harry.

'Relax, I don't want any beer, just breakfast,' Harry said. 'And a favour.'

'I mean the neck,' Rita said, holding the door for him. 'It's gone all blue. And what's that . . .?'

'Gaffer tape,' Harry said.

Rita nodded and went to take orders. At Schrøder's the policy was that you kept yourself to yourself.

Harry sat down at his regular corner table by the window and rang Beate Lønn.

Got her voicemail. Waited until the beep.

'Harry here. I've bumped into an elderly lady I may have made something of an impression on, so I don't think I should approach police stations or the like for a while. I'm leaving two specimen bags here at Schrøder's. Come in person and ask for Rita. There's another favour I'd like to ask. Bellman's started a collection of addresses in Blindern. I'd like you, as discreetly as possible, to see if you could get copies of the teams' lists, before they're sent on to Orgkrim.'

Harry rang off. Then he called Rakel. Voicemail again.

'Hi, this is Harry. I need some clean clothes which fit, and there used to be some hanging up at your place from . . . from then. I'm going for a minor upgrade and checking into the Plaza, so if you could send some there in a taxi when you come home that would be . . .' He found himself automatically hunting for a word that might have a chance of making her smile. Like 'spiffing' or 'mega' or 'wi-icked'. But failed and settled on a conventional 'great.'

Rita arrived with coffee and a fried egg while Harry was calling Hans Christian. She sent him a reproving look. Schrøder's had a more or less unspoken rule that computers, board games and mobile phones were out of bounds. This was a place for drinking, preferably beer, eating, chatting or shutting up and at a pinch reading newspapers. Presumably reading books was a grey area.

Harry signalled that this would only take a few seconds, and Rita nodded graciously.

Hans Christian sounded relieved and horrified. 'Harry? Goodness me. Everything alright?'

'On a scale from one to ten . . .'

'Yes?'

'Did you hear about the shooting in Madserud allé?'

'Oh Lord! Was that you?'

'Have you got a weapon, Hans Christian?'

Harry thought he could hear him gulp.

'Do I need one, Harry?'

'You don't. I do.'

'Harry . . .'

'For self-defence only. Just in case.'

Pause. 'I've got an old hunting rifle my father left me. For hunting elk.'

'Sounds good. Could you get it, wrap it up and deliver it to Schrøder's within three quarters of an hour?'

'I can try. Wh- what are you going to do?'

'I,' Harry said, meeting Rita's admonishing eyes from the counter, 'am going to have breakfast.'

On his way to Gamlebyen Cemetery Truls Berntsen saw a black limousine parked outside the gate where he generally entered. And as he approached, the door opened on the passenger side and a man stepped out. He was wearing a black suit and had to be well over two metres tall. Powerful jaw, flat fringe and something indefinably Asian that Truls had always associated with the Sami, Finns and Russians. The jacket must have been made to measure, yet it was still too narrow on the shoulders.

He moved aside and gestured that Truls was to take his place in the passenger seat.

Truls stopped. If these were Dubai's men it was an unexpected breach of the rules regarding direct contact. He looked around. No one in sight.

He hesitated.

If they had decided to rid themselves of the burner, this is how they would do it.

He looked at the enormous man. It was impossible to read anything from his facial expression, and Truls could not decide whether it was a good or a bad sign that the man had taken the trouble to put on a pair of sunglasses.

Of course he could turn and flee. But what then?

'Q5,' Truls mumbled to himself under his breath.

The door was immediately closed after him. It was strangely dark inside, must have been the tinted windows. And the air conditioning must have been unusually effective, it felt as if it was several degrees below zero. In the driver's seat was a man with the face of a wolf. Black suit as well. Flat fringe. Probably Russian.

'Nice you could make it,' said a voice behind Truls. He didn't need to turn. The accent. It was him. Dubai. The man no one knew. No one *else* knew. But what good was it to Truls to know a name, to recognise a face? Furthermore, you don't bite the hand that feeds you.

'I want you to get hold of someone for us.'

'Get hold of?'

'Collect. And deliver to us. You don't need to bother yourself with the rest.'

'I've told you I don't know where Oleg Fauke is.'

'This isn't Oleg Fauke, Berntsen. This is Harry Hole.'

Truls Berntsen could scarcely believe his own ears. 'Harry Hole?'

'Don't you know who he is?'

'Course I do. He was at Crime Squad. Mad as a hatter. A drunk. Solved a couple of cases. Is he in town?'

'He's staying at Hotel Leon. Room 301. Collect him from there at twelve sharp tonight.'

'And how should I *collect* him?'

'Arrest him. Knock him down. Say you want to show him your boat. Do whatever you like, just get him to the marina at Kongen. We'll take the rest from there. Fifty thousand.'

The rest. He was talking about killing Harry Hole. He was talking about murder. Of a *policeman*.

Truls opened his mouth to say no, but the voice on the back seat was quicker.

'Euros.'

Truls Berntsen's jaw dropped with a shipwrecked 'no' somewhere between his brain and vocal cords. Instead he repeated the words he thought he had heard but scarcely believed.

'Fifty thousand *euros*?'

'Well?'

Truls looked at his watch. He had a bit more than eleven hours. He coughed.

'How do you know he'll be in his room at midnight?'

'Because he knows we're coming.'

'Eh? Don't you mean he *doesn't* know you're coming?'

The voice behind him laughed. It sounded like the motor on a wooden boat. Chug-chug.

31

IT WAS FOUR O'CLOCK AND Harry was standing under a shower on the eighteenth floor of the Radisson Plaza. He hoped the gaffer tape would hold in the hot water – at least it was dulling the pain for a short while. He had been allocated room number 1937, and something fluttered through his mind as he was given the key. The king's year of birth, Koestler, synchronicity and all that. Harry didn't believe it. What he believed in was the human mind's ability to find patterns. And where, in fact, there were none. That was why he had always been a doubter as a detective. He had doubted and searched, doubted and searched. Seen patterns, but doubted the guilt. Or vice versa.

Harry heard the phone peep. It was audible but discreet and pleasant. The sound of an expensive hotel. He turned off the shower and went to the bed. Lifted the receiver.

'There's a lady here,' the receptionist said. 'Rakel Fauske . . . My apologies. *Fauke*, she says. She has something she would like to give you.'

'Give her a lift key and send her up,' Harry said. He eyed his suit hanging in the wardrobe. It looked as though it had been through two world wars. He opened the door and wound a couple of metres of towel around his waist. Sat down on the bed listening. Heard a pling from the lift and then her footsteps. He could still recognise them. Quite firm but short steps, with a high frequency, as though she always wore a tight skirt. He closed his eyes for a second, and when he reopened them she was standing in front of him.

'Hi, naked man,' she smiled, dumping the bags on the floor and herself on the bed beside him. 'What's this?' She stroked the gaffer tape with her fingers.

'Just an improvised plaster,' he said. 'You didn't need to come in person.'

'I know,' she said. 'But I couldn't find any of your clothes. They must have gone missing during the move to Amsterdam.'

Been chucked out, Harry thought. Fair enough.

'But then I spoke to Hans Christian, and he had a wardrobe full of clothes he doesn't wear. Not quite your style, but you're not too far apart size-wise.'

She opened the bags, and he looked with horror as she took out a Lacoste shirt, four pairs of ironed underpants, a pair of Armani jeans with a crease, a V-neck sweater, a Timberland jacket, two shirts bearing polo players and even a pair of soft, brown leather shoes.

She began to hang them in the wardrobe, and he got up and took over. She observed him from the side, smiled as she tucked a lock of hair behind an ear.

'You wouldn't have bought any new clothes until that suit literally fell off you. Isn't that right?'

'Well,' Harry said, moving the hangers. The clothes were unfamiliar but there was a faint, familiar aroma. 'I have to concede that I was considering a new shirt and perhaps a pair of underpants.'

'Haven't you got any clean underpants?'

Harry looked at her. 'Define clean.'

'Harry!' She slapped his shoulder with a laugh.

He smiled. Her hand remained on his shoulder.

'You're hot,' she said. 'Feverishly hot. Are you sure whatever is under your so-called plaster isn't infected?'

He shook his head. Knowing full well, from the dull, pulsating pain, that the wound was inflamed. But with his many years of experience from

Crime Squad he knew something else as well. That the police had interviewed the barman and the customers at the Nirvana bar and would know the person who had killed the knifeman had left the place with deep cuts to his chin and neck. They would also have alerted all the doctors in town and run surveillance on A&E departments. And this was no time to be held on remand.

She stroked his shoulder, up as far as his neck and back again. Over his chest. And he thought she must be able to feel his heart beating and that she was like the Pioneer TV they had stopped producing because it was too good, and you could see it was good because the black bit of the picture was so black.

He had managed to open a window a fraction; they didn't want suicides on their hands at the hotel. And even up on the eighteenth floor they could hear the rush hour, the occasional car horn, and from somewhere else, perhaps another room, an inappropriate, belated summer song.

'Are you sure you want this?' he said without trying to cough away his hoarseness. They stood there; she with a hand on his shoulder, her eyes fixed on his like a concentrated tango partner.

She nodded.

Such a cosmic, intense black in the blackness that it sucked you in. He didn't even notice her raise her foot and close the door. He heard it close, so gently, that was all, the sound of an expensive hotel, like a kiss.

And while they made love he thought only of the darkness and the aroma. The darkness of her hair, eyebrows and eyes. And the aroma of the perfume he had never asked her about, but that was only hers, which was in her clothes, in her wardrobe, which had rubbed off on his clothes then, when they hung together with hers. And which was now in the wardrobe here. Because the other man's clothes had also hung in her wardrobe. And that was where she had found them, not at his house, perhaps it had not even been his idea, perhaps she had just taken them straight from the wardrobe and brought them here. But Harry said nothing. Because he knew he had her on loan, that was all. He had her right now, and it was either that or nothing. So he held his tongue. Made love to her the way he always had, with intensity and at his leisure. Not allowing himself to be influenced by her greed or impatience, but did it with such slow passion that she alternated between cursing him and gasping. Not because that was how he thought she wanted it, but because that was how he wanted it. Because he only had her on loan. He had only these few hours.

And when she came, stiffened and stared at him with that paradoxical, wronged expression, all the nights they had spent together came back, and he was close to tears.

Afterwards they shared a cigarette.

'Why won't you tell me that you're a couple?' Harry said, inhaling and passing her the cigarette.

'Because we aren't. It's a . . . a stop-gap thing.' She shook her head. 'I don't know. I don't know anything any more. I should stay away from everything and everyone.'

'He's a good man.'

'That's the point. I need a good man, so why don't I want a good man? Why are we so bloody irrational when we actually know what's best for us?'

'Humans are a perverted and damaged species,' Harry said. 'And there is no cure, only relief.'

Rakel cuddled up to him. 'That's what I like about you, the indomitable optimism.'

'I see it as my duty to spread sunshine, my love.'

'Harry?'

'Mm.

'Is there any way back? For us?'

Harry closed his eyes. Listened to the heartbeats. His own and hers.

'Not back, no.' He turned to her. 'But if you think you still have some future left in you . . .'

'Do you mean that?'

'This is just pillow talk, isn't it?'

'Muppet.' She kissed him on the cheek, passed him the cigarette and stood up. Got dressed.

'You can stay upstairs at mine, you know.'

He shook his head. 'It's best like this now.'

'Don't forget I love you,' she said. 'Never forget that. Whatever happens. Do you promise?'

He nodded. Closed his eyes. The door closed as gently again the second time. Then he opened his eyes. Looked at his watch.

It's best like this now.

What else could he have done? Gone back to Holmenkollen with her, ensuring Dubai had followed his trail there, and dragged Rakel into this confrontation, the way he had done with the Snowman? Because he could see it now, he could see they had been dogging his steps from the very first day. Sending an invitation to Dubai via his pushers had been superfluous. They would find him before he found them. And then they would find Oleg.

So, the sole advantage he had was that he could choose the place. The scene of the crime. And he had chosen. Not here in the Plaza, this was so that he could have some time out, a couple of hours' sleep and collect himself. The place was Hotel Leon.

Harry had considered contacting Hagen. Or Bellman. Explaining the situation to them. But it would give them no other choice but to arrest him. Even so, it was just a question of time before the police would put together the three descriptions they had been given by the barman in Kvadraturen, the security guard at Vestre Cemetery and the old lady in Madserud allé. A man, one ninety-two, wearing a linen suit, scar on one side of his face and a bandaged chin and neck. They would soon be putting out a call for Harry Hole. So it was urgent.

He got up with a groan, opened the wardrobe.

Put on the ironed underpants and a shirt with a polo player. Mulled over the Armani trousers. Shook his head with a soft expletive and donned his suit instead.

Then he pulled out the tennis bag lying on the hat shelf. Hans Christian had explained it was the only one he had with enough space for a rifle.

Harry bundled it over his shoulder and left. The door behind him closed with a soft kiss.

32

I DON'T KNOW IF IT'S possible to say exactly how the throne changed hands. Exactly when violin came to power and began to rule over us rather than vice versa. Everything had gone down the pan; the deal I had tried to make with Ibsen, the coup at Alnabru. And Oleg went around with that depressed Russian mug on him, complaining life without Irene was meaningless. After three weeks we shot up more than we earned, we were high when working and we knew it was all about to go tits up. As even then it meant less than the next fix. It sounds like a cliché, it is a cliché, and that's precisely how it is. So bloody simple and so absolutely impossible. I think I can safely say that I have never loved any human, I mean, really loved. But I was hopelessly in love with violin. For while Oleg was using violin as medicine to dull the pain of his broken heart, I was using violin as it is supposed to be used. To be happy. And I mean just that: fricking happy. It was better than food, sex, sleep, yes, it was even better than breathing.

And that was why it did not come as a shock when, one evening after the showdown, Andrey took me aside and said the old boy was concerned.

'I'm fine,' I said.

He explained that if I didn't sharpen up and go to work with a clear head every bloody day from now on the old boy said I would be forcibly packed off to rehab.

I laughed. Said I didn't realise this job had fringe benefits like health schemes and stuff. Did Oleg and I get dental treatment and pensions as well?

'Oleg doesn't.'

I saw in his eyes more or less what that meant.

I had no intention of kicking the habit yet. And neither did Oleg. So we didn't give a toss, and the following evening we were as high as the Post Office building, sold half of our stock, took the rest, stole a car and drove to Kristiansand. Played fricking Sinatra at full blast, 'I Got Plenty of Nothing', which was true, we didn't even have a bloody licence. In the end Oleg was singing too, but only to drown out Sinatra and *moi*, he claimed. We laughed and drank lukewarm beer, it was like the old days. We stayed at Hotel Ernst, which wasn't as dull as it sounds, but when we asked at reception where the dope dealers hung out, we got only a blank look in return. Oleg had told me about the town's festival, which had been wrecked by some idiot who was so desperate to be a guru he booked bands that were so cool they couldn't afford them. Nevertheless, the Christian folk in the town maintained that half of the population between eighteen and twenty-five had bought drugs because of the festival. But we didn't find any customers; we zoomed around on a dark evening in the pedestrian area where there was one – one! – drunken man and also fourteen members of a Ten Sing choir, who enquired whether we wanted to meet Jesus.

'If he wants some violin, yes,' I said.

But apparently Jesus didn't, so we went back to our hotel room and had a goodnight shot. I have no idea why, but we hung around in the back of beyond. Did nothing, just got high and sang Sinatra. One night I woke up with Oleg standing over me. He was holding a fricking dog in his arms. Said he'd been woken up by the squeal of brakes outside the window and that, when he looked out, this dog was lying in the street. I had a peep. It didn't look good. Oleg and I were agreed, its back was broken. Mangy with lots of sores as well. The poor creature had been beaten up, whether by an owner or other dogs who knows. But it was fine, it was. Calm, brown eyes looked at me as if it believed I could fix what was wrong. So I tried. Gave it food and water, patted its head and talked to the animal. Oleg said we should take it to a vet, but I knew what they would do, so we kept the dog in the hotel room, hung a DO NOT DISTURB sign on the door and let it lie in the bed. We took turns to stay awake and check it was breathing. It lay there getting hotter and hotter and with its pulse getting weaker. The third day I gave it a name. Rufus. Why not? Nice to have a name if you're going to peg it.

'It's suffering,' Oleg said. 'The vet'll put it to sleep with an injection. Won't hurt at all.'

'No one's going to inject Rufus with cheap dope,' I said, flicking the syringe.

'Are you mad?' Oleg said. 'That violin is worth two thousand kroner.'

Perhaps it was. At any rate Rufus left this fricking world business class.

I seem to remember the journey home was cloudy. Anyway there was no Sinatra, no one sang.

Back in Oslo, Oleg was terrified about what would happen. As for myself I was quite cool, strangely enough. It was as if I knew the old boy wouldn't touch us. We were two harmless junkies on our way down. Broke, unemployed and after a while out of violin. Oleg had found out that the expression 'junkie' was more than a hundred years old, from the time when the first heroin addicts stole junk metal from the harbour in Philadelphia and sold it to finance their consumption. And that was precisely what Oleg and I did. We began to sneak into building sites down by the harbour in Bjørvika and stole whatever we came across. Copper and tools were gold. We sold the copper to a scrap merchant in Kalbakken, the tools to a couple of Lithuanian tradesmen.

But as more people latched onto the scam, the fences grew in height, more nightwatchmen were employed, the cops showed up and the buyers went AWOL. So there we sat, our cravings lashing us like rabid slave drivers round the clock. And I knew I would have to come up with a decent idea, an *Endlösung*. So I did.

Of course I said nothing to Oleg.

I prepared the speech for a whole day. Then I rang her.

Irene had just returned home from training. She sounded almost happy to hear my voice. I talked without stopping for an hour. She was crying by the time I'd finished.

The following evening I went down to Oslo Central Station and was standing on the platform when the Trondheim train trundled in.

Her tears were flowing as she hugged me.

So young. So caring. So precious.

As I've mentioned, I've never really loved anyone. But I must have been close to it, because I was almost crying myself.

33

THROUGH THE NARROW OPENING OF the window in room 301 Harry heard a church bell strike eleven somewhere in the darkness. His aching chin and throat had one advantage: they kept him awake. He got out of bed and sat in the chair, tilted it back against the wall beside the window so that he was facing the door with the rifle in his lap.

He had stopped at reception and asked for a strong light bulb to replace the one that had gone in his room and a hammer to knock in a couple of nails sticking up from the door sill. Said he would fix them himself. Afterwards he had changed the weak bulb in the corridor outside and used the hammer to loosen and remove the door sill.

From where he was sitting he would be able to see the shadow in the gap beneath the door when they came.

Harry lit another cigarette. Checked the rifle. Finished the rest of the pack. Outside in the darkness the church bell chimed twelve times.

The phone rang. It was Beate. She said she had been given copies of four of the five lists from patrol cars trawling the Blindern district.

'The last patrol car had already delivered its list to Orgkrim,' she said.

'Thanks,' Harry said. 'Did you get the bags from Rita at Schrøder's?'

'Yes, I did. I've told Pathology to make it a priority. They're analysing the blood now.'

Pause.

'And?' Harry asked.

'And what?'

'I know that intonation, Beate. There's something else.'

'DNA tests take more than a few hours, Harry. It—'

'—can take days before we have a final result.'

'Yes, so for the time being it's incomplete.'

'How incomplete?' Harry heard footsteps in the corridor.

'Well, there's at least a five per cent chance there's no match.'

'You've been given an interim DNA profile and have a match on the DNA register, haven't you?'

'We use incomplete tests only to say who we can *eliminate*.'

'Who's the match for?'

'I don't want to say anything until—'

'Come on.'

'No. But I can say it's not Gusto's own blood.'

'And?'

'And it's not Oleg's. Alright?'

'Very alright,' Harry said, suddenly aware that he had been holding his breath.

A shadow under the door.

'Harry?'

Harry rang off. Pointed the rifle at the door. Waited. Three short knocks. Waited. Listened. The shadow didn't move. He tiptoed along the wall towards the door, out of any possible firing line. Put his eye to the peephole in the middle of the door.

He saw a man's back.

The jacket hung straight and was so short he could see the trouser waistband. A black piece of cloth hung from his back pocket, a cap perhaps. But he wasn't wearing a belt. His arms hung close to his sides. If the man was carrying a weapon it had to be in a holster, either on his chest or on the inside of his calf. Neither very common.

The man turned to the door and knocked twice, harder this time. Harry held his breath while studying the distorted image of a face. Distorted, and yet there was something unmistakable about it. A pronounced underbite. And he was scratching himself under the chin with a card he had hanging from his neck. The way police officers sometimes carried ID cards when they were going to make an arrest. Shit! The police had been quicker than Dubai.

Harry hesitated. If the guy had orders to arrest him he would also have a blue chit with a search warrant he had already shown the receptionist and he would have been given a master key. Harry's brain calculated. He tiptoed back, pushed the rifle in behind the wardrobe. Went back and opened the door. Said: 'What do you want and who are you?' while glancing up and down the corridor.

The man stared at him. 'What a state you're in, Hole. Can I come in?' He held up his ID card.

'Truls Berntsen. You used to work for Bellman, didn't you?'

'Still do. He sends his regards.'

Harry stepped aside and let Berntsen go first.

'Cosy,' Berntsen said, looking around.

'Take a seat,' Harry said, indicating the bed and sitting on the chair by the window.

'Chewing gum?' Berntsen said, offering a packet.

'Gives me cavities. What do you want?'

'As friendly as ever?' Berntsen grinned, rolled up the chewing gum, placed it in his drawer-like prognathous jaw and sat down.

Harry's brain was registering intonation, body language, eye movement, smell. The man was relaxed, yet threatening. Open palms, no sudden movements, but his eyes were collecting data, reading the situation, preparing for something. Harry already regretted stowing his rifle. Failure to hold a licence was the least of his problems.

'Thing is, we found blood on Gusto's shirt in connection with a grave desecration at Vestre Cemetery last night. And the DNA test shows it to be your blood.'

Harry watched as Berntsen neatly folded the silver paper that had been wrapped round the chewing gum. Harry remembered him better now. They had called him Beavis. Bellman's errand boy. Stupid and smart. And dangerous. Forrest Gump gone bad.

'I've no idea what you're talking about,' Harry said.

'No, I can imagine,' Berntsen said with a sigh. 'Mistake on the register perhaps? I'll have to drive you down to Police HQ to take another blood sample.'

'I'm searching for a girl,' Harry said. 'Irene Hanssen.'

'She's in Vestre Cemetery?'

'She's been missing since this summer at any rate. She's the foster-sister of Gusto Hanssen.'

'News to me. Nevertheless you'll have to come with me down to—'

'It's the girl in the middle,' Harry said. He had taken the Hanssen family photograph from his jacket pocket and passed it to Berntsen. 'I need a bit of time. Not much. Afterwards you'll understand why I've had to do things like this. I promise to report within forty-eight hours.'

'*48 Hours*,' Berntsen said, studying the picture. 'Good film. Nolte and that negro. McMurphy?'

'Murphy.'

'Right. Stopped being funny, he did. Isn't that strange? You have something, and then suddenly you've lost it. How do you think that feels, Hole?'

Harry looked at Truls Berntsen. He wasn't so sure about this Forrest Gump thing any more. Berntsen held the photograph up to the light. Squinted with concentration.

'Do you recognise her?'

'No,' said Berntsen, passing the picture back as he twisted round. Obviously it wasn't comfortable sitting on the item of clothing he had in his back pocket because he quickly moved it to his jacket pocket. 'We're going for a ride to Police HQ, where we will review your forty-eight hours.'

His tone was light. Too light. And Harry had already done his thinking. Beate had prioritised her DNA tests at the Pathology Unit and still did not have a final result. So how come Berntsen had a blood test result off Gusto's shroud? And there was another thing. Berntsen hadn't moved the item quickly enough. It wasn't a cap, it was a balaclava. The type used when Gusto was executed.

And the next thought followed hard on its heels. The burner.

Were the police perhaps not the first on the scene? Was it not Dubai's lackey?

Harry considered the rifle behind the wardrobe. But it was too late to escape now. In the corridor he heard footsteps approaching. Two people. One of them so big the floorboards creaked. The footsteps stopped outside the door. The shadows of two pairs of legs, standing akimbo, fell across the floor under the crack. He could of course have hoped they were police colleagues of Berntsen, that this was a real arrest. But he had heard the floor's lament. A big man, he guessed the size of the figure running after him through Frogner Park.

'Come on,' Berntsen said, getting up and standing in front of Harry. Scratched his chest inside his lapel in an apparently casual way. 'A little ride, just you and me.'

'We're not alone, it seems,' Harry said. 'I see you have backup.'

He nodded to the shadow under the door. Another shadow appeared. A straight, oblong shadow. Truls followed his gaze. And Harry saw it. The genuine astonishment on his face. The kind of astonishment types like Truls Berntsen cannot simulate. They weren't Berntsen's people.

'Move away from the door,' Harry whispered.

Truls stopped masticating the chewing gum and looked down at him.

Truls Berntsen liked to have his Steyr pistol in a shoulder holster, positioned in such a way that the gun lay flat against his chest. It made it harder to see when you stood face to face with someone. And as he knew that Harry Hole was an experienced detective, trained by the FBI in Chicago and so on, he also knew that Hole would automatically notice anything bulky in the usual places. Not that Truls reckoned he would need to use the pistol, but he had taken precautions. If Harry resisted he would escort him outside with the Steyr discreetly pointing at his back, having put on the balaclava so that any potential witnesses couldn't say whom they had seen with Hole before he disappeared off the face of the earth. The Saab was parked in a backstreet; he had even smashed the only street lamp so that no one would see the number plate. Fifty thousand euros. He had to be patient, build stone by stone. Get a house a bit higher up in Høyenhall with a view, looking down on them. Down on her.

Harry Hole had seemed smaller than the giant he remembered. And uglier. Pale, ugly, dirty and exhausted. Resigned, unfocused. This was going to be an easier job than he had anticipated. So when Hole whispered he should move away from the door Truls Berntsen's first reaction was irritation. Was the guy attempting to play games now everything looked to be going so well? But his second reaction was that this was the voice they used. Police officers in critical situations. No colouring, no drama, just a neutral, cold clarity with the least possible chance of a misunderstanding. And the greatest possible chance of survival.

So Truls Berntsen – almost without thinking – took a step to the side.

At that moment the top part of the door panel was blown into the room.

As Berntsen whirled round his instinctive conclusion was that the barrel must have been sawn off to have such wide coverage at such short range. He already had a hand inside his jacket. With the shoulder holster in its conventional position and without a jacket he would have drawn faster as the handle would have been sticking out.

Truls Berntsen fell backwards onto the bed with the gun freed and at the end of an outstretched arm as the remains of the door opened with a bang. He heard the glass shatter behind him before everything was drowned by a new explosion.

The noise filled his ears, and there was a snowstorm in the room.

In the doorway the silhouettes of two men stood in the snowdrift. The taller one raised his gun. His head almost touched the door frame, he must have been well over two metres. Truls fired. And fired again. Felt the wonderful recoil and even more wonderful certainty that this was for real, to hell with the consequences. The tall one jerked, seemed to flick his fringe before stepping back and disappearing from view. Truls shifted his pistol and his gaze. The second man stood there without moving. White feathers fluttered around him. Truls had him in his sights. But he didn't fire. He saw him more clearly now. Face like a wolf. The kind of face Truls had always associated with the Sami, Finns and Russians.

Now the guy calmly raised his gun. Finger wrapped around the trigger.

'Easy, Berntsen,' he said in English.

Truls Berntsen gave a long, drawn-out roar.

Harry fell.

He had lowered his head, crouched up and moved back as the first blast of the shotgun sprayed over his head. Back to where he knew the window was. Felt the pane almost bend before it remembered it was glass and gave way.

Then he was in free fall.

Time had jammed on the brakes, as though he was falling through water. Hands and arms working like slow paddles in a reflex attempt to stop the body rotating into the beginnings of a backward somersault. Semi-transmitted thoughts bounced between the brain's synapses:

He was going to land on his head and break his neck.

It was lucky he didn't have curtains.

The naked woman in the window opposite was upside down.

Then he was received by softness everywhere. Empty cardboard boxes, old newspapers, used nappies, milk cartons and day-old bread from the hotel's kitchen, wet coffee filters.

He lay on his back in the open skip amid a shower of glass. Flashes of light appeared from the window above him, like camera flashbulbs. Muzzles of flames. But it was eerily quiet, as though the flashes came from a TV with the volume turned down. He could feel the gaffer tape around his neck had torn. Blood was streaming out. And for one wild moment he considered staying where he was. Closing his eyes, going to sleep, drifting off. He seemed to be watching himself sit up, jump over the edge of the skip and race towards the gate at the end of the yard. Open it as he heard a protracted, furious roar from the window reach the street. Slip on a drain cover but manage to stay on his feet. See a black woman in tight jeans, on the game, who smiled instinctively and pouted at him, then reviewed the situation and averted her gaze.

Harry set off.

And decided that this time he would just run.

Until there was nowhere left to run.

Until it was over, until they had him.

He hoped it wouldn't be too long.

In the meantime he would do what hunted prey are programmed to do: flee, try to escape, try to survive for a few more hours, a few more minutes, a few more seconds.

His heart pounded in protest, and he began to laugh as he crossed the street in front of a night bus and continued down towards Oslo Central.

34

HARRY WAS LOCKED IN. He had just woken and noticed. On the wall immediately above him hung a poster of a skinned human body. Beside it, a neatly carved wooden figure depicting a man on a cross bleeding to death. And beside that, medicine cabinet after medicine cabinet.

He twisted round on the couch. Tried to continue where he had left off yesterday. Tried to see the picture. There were lots of dots, but he hadn't managed to connect them. And even the dots were for the time being mere assumptions.

Assumption one. Truls Berntsen was the burner. As an employee in Orgkrim he was probably in a perfect position to serve Dubai.

Assumption two. It was Berntsen Beate had found a match for on the DNA register. That was why she wouldn't say anything until she was one hundred per cent certain; the test on the blood under Gusto's nails suggested it was one of their own. And if that was correct Gusto had clawed Truls Berntsen the same day he was killed.

But then came the tricky part. If Berntsen was indeed working for Dubai and had been given the job of expediting Harry, why did the Blues Brothers appear and try to blow off both their heads? And if they were Dubai henchmen how come they and the burner were at each other's throats like that? Weren't they on the same side, or had it been no more than a badly coordinated operation? Perhaps it wasn't coordinated because Truls Berntsen had acted on his own to prevent Harry from delivering the evidence from Gusto's grave and exposing him?

There was a rattle of keys and the door opened.

'Morning,' Martine twittered. 'How do you feel?'

'Better,' Harry lied, looking at his watch. Six o'clock in the morning. He threw off the blanket and swung his legs onto the floor.

'Our infirmary is not intended for overnight stays,' Martine said. 'Lie down so that I can put a fresh bandage around your neck.'

'Thanks for taking me in last night,' Harry said. 'But, as I said before, giving me a place to hide is not without its dangers, so I think I should go.'

'Lie down!'

Harry looked at her. Sighed and obeyed. Shut his eyes and listened to Martine opening and closing drawers, the clatter of scissors on glass, the sound of the first people arriving for breakfast at the Watchtower cafe on the floor below.

While Martine undid the bandage she had applied the previous day Harry used his other hand to ring Beate and reach a minimalist message telling him to be brief, beep.

'I know the blood is from an ex-Kripos detective,' Harry said. 'Even if this is confirmed at the Pathology Unit today you should wait before telling anyone. On its own it's not enough to justify an arrest warrant, and if we shake his cage now we risk him burning the whole case and taking flight. So we should have him arrested for something else so that we can work in peace. Breaking into the bikers' place in Alnabru. Unless I'm much mistaken this is Oleg's accomplice. And Oleg will testify. So I'd like you to fax a photo of Truls Berntsen, now working at Orgkrim, to Hans Christian Simonsen's office and ask him to show it to Oleg for identification.'

Harry rang off, took a deep breath, felt it coming, suddenly and with such power that he gasped. He turned away, felt the contents of his stomach assessing a trip up north.

'Does it hurt?' Martine asked as she ran the alcohol-dipped cotton wool along his neck and chin.

Harry shook his head and nodded towards the open bottle of alcohol.

'Right,' Martine said, tightening the cap. 'Will it never get better?' she asked in a low voice.

'What?' Harry said hoarsely.

She didn't answer.

Harry's eyes jumped around the infirmary to find himself a distraction, something to refocus his mind, anything at all. They found the gold ring she had removed and placed on the couch before tending to his wounds. She and Rikard had been married for a few years now; the ring had chips and scratches, it wasn't shiny and new like Torkildsen's at Telenor. Harry experienced a sudden chill and his scalp began to itch. Of course it could have been just sweat.

'Genuine gold?' he asked.

Martine began to wind round the fresh bandage. 'It's a wedding ring, Harry.'

'So?'

'So of course it's gold. However poor or mean you are, you don't buy a wedding ring that's not gold.'

Harry nodded. His scalp itched and itched; he could feel the hairs on the back of his neck standing up. 'I did,' he said.

She laughed. 'In which case you're the only person in the whole world who did, Harry.'

Harry stared at the ring. That was what she had said. 'Like hell I'm the only . . .' he said slowly. The hairs on his neck were never wrong.

'Hey, wait, I haven't finished!'

'It's fine,' said Harry, who had already sat up.

'At least you should have some clean clothes. You stink of rubbish, sweat and blood.'

'The Mongolians used to rub animal excrement all over themselves before big battles,' Harry said, buttoning up his shirt. 'If you want to give me something, a cup of coffee wouldn't go . . .'

She sent him a resigned look. And went through the door and down the stairs shaking her head.

Harry hurriedly took out his mobile.

'Yes?' Klaus Torkildsen sounded like a zombie. Kids screaming in the background were probably the explanation.

'This is Harry H. If you do this for me I'll never pester you again, Torkildsen. I'd like you to check some base stations. I have to know all the places Truls Berntsen – address somewhere in Manglerud – was on the night of 12 July.'

'We can't pinpoint that down to the square metre or chart—'

'—movements minute by minute. I know all that stuff. Just do the best you can.'

Pause.

'Is that all?'

'No, there's another name.' Harry closed his eyes and racked his brain. Visualised the letters of the nameplate on the door at the Radium Hospital. Mumbled to himself. Then he said the name into the phone, loud and clear.

'Noted. And *never again* means?'

'Never again.'

'I see,' Torkildsen said. 'One more thing.'

'Yes?'

'The police asked for your number yesterday. You don't have one.'

'I have an unregistered Chinese number.'

'They seemed to be interested in tracing it. What's going on?'

'Sure you want to know, Torkildsen?'

'No,' Torkildsen said after another pause. 'I'll ring you when I've got something.'

Harry ended the call and pondered. He was wanted by the police. Even if they didn't find his name against the number, they could put two and two together if they checked Rakel's calls and saw a Chinese number appear. The phone gave away his location, and he would have to get rid of it.

When Martine returned with a cup of steaming hot coffee, Harry allowed himself two swigs and then asked straight out if he could borrow her phone for a couple of days.

She studied him with that pure, direct look of hers and said yes, if he'd thought the matter through.

Harry nodded, took the little red phone, kissed her on the cheek and carried his coffee down to the cafe. Five of the tables were already occupied, and more early-morning scarecrows were on their way. Harry sat at a free table and jotted down the numbers from his Chinese phone. Sent the important ones a short text message about his new temporary number.

Drug addicts are as inscrutable as other people, but in one area they are reasonably predictable, so when Harry left his Chinese mobile in the middle of the table and went to the toilet he was quite sure of the result. On his return the phone had vanished. It had gone on a journey the police would be able to follow around town via base stations.

Harry, for his part, walked out and down Tøyengata to Grønland.

A police car rolled up the hill towards him. He immediately lowered his head, took out Martine's phone and pretended he was in conversation as a pretext to shield most of his face.

The car passed. The next few hours would be about staying under cover.

More important, though, he knew something. He knew where to begin.

Truls Berntsen lay frozen under two layers of spruce twigs.

He had been playing the same film all night, over and over. Wolf-face, who had backed away carefully, repeating 'easy' like a prayer for a truce while they pointed their guns at each other. Wolf-face. The limousine driver outside Gamlebyen Cemetery. Dubai's man. When he had stooped to grab the big guy whom Truls had shot, he had to lower his pistol and Truls had realised the man was willing to risk his life to save his pal. Wolf-face must have been an ex-soldier, an ex-policeman, there was some kind of honour crap going on, at any rate. A groan came from the big guy at that moment. He was alive. Truls felt both relief and disappointment. But he had let Wolf-face do it, let him haul the man to his feet and had heard the squelch of blood in his shoes as they staggered down the corridor to the rear door. Once they were outside he had pulled on his balaclava and run out, through reception, to the Saab, driven straight up here, not daring to go home. For this was the safe place, the secret place. The place where no one could see him, the place only he knew and where he went when he wanted to see her.

The place was in Manglerud, in a popular hiking area, but the hikers kept to the paths and never came up to his rock, which in any case was surrounded by a dense scrub forest.

Mikael and Ulla Bellman's house stood on the ridge opposite the rock, and he had a perfect view of the living-room window where he had seen her sitting on so many evenings. Just sitting on the sofa, her beautiful face, her graceful body that had barely changed over the years, she was still Ulla – the most attractive girl in Manglerud. Sometimes Mikael was there too. He had seen them kissing and caressing each other, but they had always gone into the bedroom before anything else happened. He didn't know that he wanted to see any more anyway. For he liked to see her sitting there alone best of all. On the sofa with a book and her feet drawn underneath her. Now and then she would cast a glance at the window as though she could feel she was being observed. And on those occasions he felt himself getting excited by the notion that she might know. Know he was out there somewhere.

But now the living-room window was black. They had moved. She had moved. And there were no safe viewing points near the new house. He had checked. And the way things were it wasn't certain he was going to need one. Was going to need anything. He was a marked man.

They had tricked him into visiting Hole at Hotel Leon at midnight and then attacked.

They had tried to get rid of him. Tried to burn the burner. But why? Because he knew too much? But he was a burner, wasn't he. Burners do know too much, that goes without saying. He couldn't understand. Hell! It didn't matter *why*, he had to make sure he stayed alive.

He was so cold and tired his bones ached, but he didn't dare go home until it was light and he had checked the coast was clear. If he could get inside the door of his flat he had enough artillery to withstand a siege. He should have shot them both when he had the chance, but if they tried it on again they would see that it was not so bloody easy to nail Truls Berntsen.

317

Truls got up. Brushed the fir needles off his clothes, shivered and slapped his arms against his chest. Looked up at the house again. Dawn was beginning to break. He thought of the other Ullas. Like the little dark number at the Watchtower. Martine. He had in fact thought he could get her. She worked with dangerous people, and he was someone who could protect her. But she had ignored him, and as usual he hadn't had the guts to approach her and get the rejection over and done with. It was better to wait in hope, drag it out, torment yourself, see possible encouragement where less desperate men saw only universal friendliness. And then one day he had overheard someone say something to her, and he had realised she was pregnant. Bloody whore. They're all whores. Like this girl Gusto Hanssen had used as a lookout. Whore, whore, whore. He hated these women. And the men who knew how to make these women love them.

He jumped up and down slapping his arms around him, but knew he would never get the warmth back.

Harry had gone back to Kvadraturen. Found a seat inside Postcafé. That was the one that opened earliest, four hours before Schrøder's, and he had to queue with beer-thirsty customers until he could buy himself something that would pass for breakfast.

Rakel was his first call. He asked her to check Oleg's inbox.

'There's something from Bellman,' she said. 'Looks like a list of addresses.'

'OK,' Harry said. 'Forward it to Beate Lønn.' He gave her the email address.

Then he texted Beate, said the lists had been sent, and finished his breakfast. He moved to Gjæstgiveri in Stortorvet, and he had just been given a cup of well-percolated coffee when Beate rang.

'I've compared the lists I copied directly from the patrol cars with the list you forwarded. What's this list?'

'It's the list Bellman received and forwarded to me. I'd like to see if he's been given a correct report or if it's been doctored.'

'I see. All the addresses I had from before are on the list you and Bellman received.'

'Mm,' Harry said. 'Wasn't there one patrol car you didn't get a list from?'

'What's this about, Harry?'

'It's about me trying to get the burner to help us.'

'Help us to do what?'

'To point out the house where Dubai lives.'

Pause.

'I'll see if I can get hold of the last list,' Beate said.

'Thanks. Talk to you later.'

'Wait.'

'Yes?'

'Aren't you interested in the rest of the DNA profile of the blood under Gusto's nail?'

35

IT WAS SUMMER, AND I was the king of Oslo. I had half a kilo of violin in exchange for Irene and I had sold half on the street. It was supposed to be the starting capital for something big, a new network that would sweep the old boy off the court. First of all, though, the start had to be celebrated. I spent a tiny fraction of the sales money to buy myself a suit that matched the shoes I had been given by Isabelle Skøyen. I looked like a million dollars, and they didn't raise an eyebrow when I went into the fricking Grand and asked for a suite. We stayed there. We were twenty-four-hour partygoers. Exactly who 'we' were varied somewhat, but it was summer, Oslo, women, boys, it was like the old days, though with slightly heavier medication. Even Oleg brightened up and was his old self for a while. It turned out I had more friends than I could remember, and the dope went faster than you would believe. We were kicked out of the Grand and went to the Christiania. Then to the Radisson, Holbergs plass.

Of course it couldn't last for ever, but what the fuck does?

Once or twice I saw a black limousine on the opposite side of the street as I came out of the hotel, but there are lots of cars like that. However, this one didn't go anywhere.

And then came the inevitable day when the money ran out, and I had to sell more dope. I had made a stash in one of the broom closets on the floor below, inside the ceiling tiles, behind a bunch of electric cables. But either I must have shot my mouth off while I was high or else someone must have seen me going there. Because the stash had been cleaned out. And I had nothing in reserve.

We were back to square one. Apart from the fact that there was no 'we' any more. It was time to check out. And inject the day's first fix, which had to be bought on the street. But when I had to settle up for the room we'd had for more than two weeks I was fifteen thousand short.

I took the only sensible course of action.

I ran.

Ran straight through the lobby onto the street, through the park towards the sea. No one followed me.

Then I strolled down to Kvadraturen to do some shopping. There wasn't an Arsenal player in sight, just hollow-eyed zonkers shuffling around on the lookout for a dealer. I talked to someone wanting to sell me meth. He said there hadn't been any violin on the go for days, stocks had simply dried up. But there were rumours circulating that dopeheads were selling their last quarters of violin for five thousand kroner apiece in Plata, so that they could buy a week's supply of horse.

I didn't have five sodding thousand of course, so I knew I was in trouble. Three alternatives: flog, con or nick.

Flog first. But what did I actually have to flog, me who had even sold my foster-sister? I remembered. The Odessa. It was in the rehearsal room, and the Pakis in Kvadraturen would definitely fork out five thousand for a shooter that fired fricking salvos. So I jogged north, past the Opera House and Oslo Central. But it must have been burgled because there was a new padlock on the door and the amps had gone. Only the drums were left. I searched for the Odessa, but they must have taken that too. Bloody thieves.

Con next. I hailed a taxi, directed it west, up to Blindern. The driver nagged me for money from the moment I got in, so he knew the score. I told him to pull in where the road ends by the railway lines, jumped out and dodged the driver by running over the footbridge. I ran up through

Forskningsparken, ran even though no one was chasing me. Ran because I was in a hurry. Why, I didn't know.

I opened the gate, ran up the gravel path to the garage. Peered through the crack at the side of the iron shutter. The limousine was there. I knocked on the front door.

Andrey opened. The old boy wasn't at home, he said. I pointed to the neighbouring house behind the water tank, said he had to be there then, the limo was in the garage. He repeated that *ataman* was not at home. I said I needed money. He said he couldn't help me and that I was never to come here again. I said I needed violin, just this once. He said there was no violin at the moment, Ibsen was short of some ingredient or other, I would have to wait a couple of weeks. I said I would be dead by then. I had to have either money or violin.

Andrey was about to close the door, but I stuck out a foot.

I said that if I didn't get it I would tell people where he lived.

Andrey looked at me.

'Are you trying to get yourself killed?' he said with that comical accent. 'Remember Bisken?'

I stuck out my hand. Said the cops would pay well to find out where Dubai and his flunkeys lived. Plus a bit more to find out what happened to Bisken. And they would fork out most if I told them about the dead undercover guy on the cellar floor.

Andrey slowly shook his head.

So I told the Cossack bastard to *passhol v'chorte*, which I think is Russian for 'go to hell', and left.

Felt his eyes on my back all the way to the gate.

I had no idea why the old boy had let me get away with stealing the dope, as Oleg and I had done, but I knew I wouldn't get away with this. I didn't give a shit, though, I was at the end of my tether, all I heard were the hungry screams of my blood vessels.

I walked up to the path behind Vestre Aker Church. Stood there watching some old ladies coming and going. Widows on the way to graves, their husbands' and their own, carrying handbags groaning with cash. But I didn't

322

have it in me. Me, the Thief, stood quite still, sweating like a pig, scared to death by brittle-boned eighty-year-old women. It was enough to make you weep.

It was Saturday, and I was going through the friends I had who might be willing to lend me money. Didn't take long. None.

Then it struck me who ought to lend me money at least. If he knew what was good for him.

I sneaked onto the bus, travelled eastwards, back to the proper side of the river, and got off at Manglerud.

This time Truls Berntsen was at home.

He was standing in the doorway on the fifth floor of his block and heard me give him roughly the same ultimatum I had given in Blindernveien. If he didn't dig deep for five big ones, I would let it be known that he had killed Tutu and buried his body afterwards.

But Berntsen was cool. Asked me into his flat. He was sure we could come to some agreement, he said.

But there was something all wrong about his eyes.

So I didn't budge and said there was nothing to discuss, either he coughed up or else I would grass on him for money. He said the police didn't pay people to grass on officers. Five thousand was fine though, he said, we went way back, we were almost pals. Said he didn't have much cash at home, so we would have to drive to an ATM, the car was down in the garage.

I chewed on that one. Alarm bells were ringing, but the craving was a bloody nightmare, it shut out all sensible thoughts. So, even though I knew this was not good, I nodded.

'So, you've got the final result, have you?' Harry said, scanning the crowd in the cafe. No suspicious types. Or, to be more accurate, loads of suspicious types, but no one who could be presumed to be police.

'Yes,' Beate said.

Harry shifted his grip on the phone. 'I think I already know who clawed Gusto.'

'Oh?' There was surprise in Beate's voice.

'Yep. A man on a DNA register is usually a suspect or a convicted criminal or a policeman who might have contaminated a crime scene. In this case it's the last. His name's Truls Berntsen and he's an officer with Orgkrim.'

'How do you know it's him?'

'Well, the sum of things that have happened, you could say.'

'Fine,' Beate said. 'I don't doubt your reasoning is solid.'

'Thank you,' Harry said.

'And yet you're wrong,' Beate said.

'What?'

'The blood under Gusto's nails doesn't come from anyone called Berntsen.'

But while I was standing in front of Truls Berntsen's door – he had just gone to get the car keys – I looked down. At my shoes. Bloody fantastic shoes. Then I began to think about Isabelle Skøyen.

She wasn't dangerous like Berntsen was. And she was mad about me. Wasn't she? Perhaps?

Mad and a half.

So before Berntsen returned I leapt down seven steps at a time and pressed the lift button on each floor.

I jumped on the Metro for Oslo Central. At first I thought I should ring her, but changed my mind. She could always snub me on the phone, but never if I turned up in wonderful, drop-dead-gorgeous person. Saturday also meant her stable lad was off. Which in turn – since nags and pigs are pretty bad at getting food from the fridge – meant she was at home. So at Oslo Central I got into the season-ticket carriage on the Østfold line as the journey to Rygge cost a hundred and four forty, which I still didn't have. I walked from the station to the farm. It's quite a distance. Especially if it starts raining. It started to rain.

As I came into the yard I saw her car, one of those 4x4s people drive to barge their way through city-centre streets. I knocked at the farmhouse door. But no one opened it. I called, the echo resounding around the walls, but

324

no one answered. She could of course have gone for a ride on a horse. Fine, I knew where she kept her cash, and out in the country people still didn't always lock their doors. So I pressed the handle, and, yes, it was quite open.

I was on my way up to the bedroom when suddenly there she was. Big, standing legs apart on the stairs, wearing a bathrobe.

'What are you doing here, Gusto?'

'I wanted to see you,' I said, turning on the smile. Turned it right up.

'You need a dentist,' she said coldly.

I knew what she meant, I had some brown stuff on my teeth. They looked a bit rotten, but it was nothing a wire brush couldn't fix.

'What are you doing here?' she repeated. 'Money?'

That was the thing with Isabelle and me, we were the same, we didn't need to pretend.

'Five big ones?' I said.

'That won't work, Gusto, we've finished with that. Should I drive you back to the station?'

'Eh? Come on, Isabelle. What about a shag?'

'Shhh!'

It took me a second to suss the situation. Bit slow on the uptake, I was. Have to blame the fricking craving. There she stood, middle of the day, in a bathrobe but fully made up.

'You expecting someone?' I asked.

She didn't answer.

'New fuck buddy?'

'That's what happens when you go missing, Gusto.'

'I'm hot on comebacks,' I said and was so quick she lost balance as I grabbed her wrist and pulled her to me.

'You're wet,' she said and struggled, but no more than she did when she wanted it hard.

'It's raining,' I said, biting her earlobe. 'What's your excuse?' I already had a hand up under her bathrobe.

'And you stink. Let me go!'

My hand stroked her shaven pussy, found the crack. She was wet. Dripping wet. I could get two fingers up at once. Too wet. I felt something sticky. Pulled my hand away. Held it up. My fingers were covered with something white and slimy. I looked up at her in surprise. Saw the triumphant grin as she leaned over to me and whispered: 'As I said. If you go missing . . .'

I lost it, raised my hand to slap, but she grabbed it and stopped me. Strong bitch, that Skøyen.

'Go now, Gusto.'

I felt something in my eyes. If I hadn't known better I would have said it was tears.

'Five thousand,' I whispered in a thick voice.

'No,' she said. 'Then you'll come back. And we can't have that.'

'You cunt!' I shouted. 'You're forgetting a few seriously important points. Cough up or I'll go to the papers with your whole set-up. And by that I'm not referring to our shagging, but the fact that the whole clean-up-Oslo stuff is your and the old boy's doing. Fricking pseudo socialists. Dope money and politics in the same bed. How much do you think *Verdens Gang* will pay?'

I heard the bedroom door open.

'If I were you I'd make a run for it now,' Isabelle said.

I heard the creak of the floorboards in the blackness behind her.

I wanted to run, I really did. Yet I didn't move.

It came closer.

I imagined I could see the stripes on his face light in the dark. Fuck buddy. Tiger boy.

He coughed.

Then he stepped into the light.

He was so drop-dead gorgeous that, sick as I was, I could feel it again. The desire to place my hand on his chest. Feel the sun-warmed, sweaty skin under my fingertips. Feel the muscles that would automatically tense in shock at whatever bloody liberties I took.

'Who did you say?' Harry said.

Beate coughed and repeated: 'Mikael Bellman.'

'Bellman?'

'Yes.'

'Gusto had Mikael Bellman's blood under his nails when he died?'

'Looks like it.'

Harry leaned back. This changed everything. Or did it? It didn't need to have anything to do with the killing. But it had something to do with something. Something which Bellman had not wanted to talk about.

'Get out,' Bellman said with the kind of voice that isn't loud because it doesn't need to be.

'So it's you two, is it?' I said. 'I thought it was Truls Berntsen she had hired. Smart to go higher, Isabelle. What's the set-up? Is Berntsen just along as your slave, Mikael?'

I caressed rather than pronounced his first name. That was after all how we had introduced ourselves on his land that day, Gusto and Mikael. Like two boys, two potential play pals. I saw how it seemed to light something in his eyes, made them flare up. Bellman was quite naked; perhaps that was why I imagined he would not attack. He was too quick for me. He was on me and had my head in a vice.

'Let go!'

He pulled me to the top of the stairs. My nose was squeezed between his chest and armpit and I could smell both of them. And this was a thought that lodged itself in my brain: if he wanted me to get out why haul me up the stairs? I couldn't punch my way free, so I dug my nails in his chest and dragged my hands like claws towards me, felt one nail catch on his nipple. He swore and slackened his grip. I slipped out of the vice and jumped. Landed halfway down the stairs, but managed to stay on my feet. Charged down the hall, grabbed her car keys and ran into the yard. Course, the car wasn't locked either. The wheels churned up the gravel as I released the clutch. In the mirror I saw Mikael Bellman come running out of the door. Saw something glint in his hand. Then the wheels bit, I was thrust back against the seat and the car shot across the yard and onto the road.

* * *

327

'It was Bellman who took Truls Berntsen along to Orgkrim,' Harry said. 'Is it conceivable that Berntsen is doing the burner jobs under Bellman's instructions?'

'You're aware of what we're moving into here, Harry?'

'Yes,' Harry said. 'And from now on you don't have anything to do with it, Beate.'

'Try bloody stopping me!' The phone diaphragm crackled. Harry couldn't remember Beate Lønn ever swearing before. 'This is my police force, Harry. I don't want people like Berntsen dragging it down into the dirt.'

'OK,' Harry said. 'But let's not draw any hasty conclusions. The only evidence we have is that Bellman met Gusto. We don't even have anything concrete on Truls Berntsen yet.'

'So what are you going to do?'

'I'm going to start somewhere else. And if it's what I hope it is, the pieces will topple against each other like dominoes. The problem is staying free long enough to launch the plan.'

'Do you mean to say you have a plan?'

'Of course I have a plan.'

'A *good* plan?'

'I didn't say that.'

'But a plan?'

'Absolutely.'

'You're lying, aren't you?'

'Not half.'

I was racing into Oslo on the E18 when I realised how deep the mess I had landed myself in was.

Bellman had tried to drag me upstairs. To the bedroom. Where he had the pistol he chased me with. He was willing to fricking liquidate me to keep my mouth shut. Which could only mean he was up to his knees in shit. So, what would he do now? Get me busted of course. For stealing a car, drug dealing, not paying the hotel bill, there was quite a selection. Put me behind bars before I could blab to anyone. And as soon as I was banged up and gagged, there was little doubt about what would happen: they would make it look either like suicide or like another inmate had nobbled me. So the stupidest thing I could do would be to drive around in this car that they probably already had on their radar. So I put my foot down. The place I was going was on the east of town, and I could avoid going through the centre. I drove up the hill, headed for the quiet residential areas. Parked some distance away and started walking.

The sun had appeared again, and people were out and about, pushing prams, with disposable barbecues in those net bags hanging from the handles. Grinning at the sun as if it were happiness itself.

I chucked the car keys into a garden and walked up to the flats.

Found the name on the doorbell and rang.

'It's me,' I said when he eventually answered.

'I'm a bit busy,' said the voice in the intercom.

'And I'm a drug addict,' I said. It was meant as a joke, but I felt the impact of the words. Oleg thought it was funny when for a laugh I occasionally asked punters whether perhaps they were suffering from drug addiction and wanted some violin.

'What do you want?' the voice asked.

'I want some violin.'

The punters' line had become mine.

Pause.

'Haven't got any. Run out. No base to make any more.'

'Base?'

'Levorphanol base. Do you want the formula as well?'

I knew it was the truth, but he had to have some. Had to. I pondered. I couldn't go to the rehearsal room, they were bound to be waiting for me. Oleg. Good old Oleg would let me in.

'You've got two hours, Ibsen. If you haven't come to Hausmanns gate with four quarters I'll go straight to the cops and tell all. There's nothing for me to lose any more. Do you understand? Hausmanns gate 92. You go straight in and it's on the second floor.'

I tried to imagine his face. Terrified, sweating. The poor old perv.

'Fine,' he said.

That was the way. You just have to make them understand the gravity of the situation.

Harry was swallowing the rest of his coffee and staring into the street. Time to move on.

On his way across Youngstorget to the kebab shops in Torggata he received a call.

It was Klaus Torkildsen.

'Good news,' he said.

'Oh yeah?'

'At the time in question Truls Berntsen's phone was registered at four of the base stations in Oslo city centre, and that locates his position in the same area as Hausmanns gate 92.'

'How big is the area we're talking about?'

'Erm, a kind of hexagonal area with a diameter of eight hundred metres.'

'OK,' Harry said, absorbing the information. 'What about the other guy?'

'I couldn't find anything in his name exactly, but he had a company phone registered at the Radium Hospital.'

'And?'

'And, as I said, it's good news. That phone was in the same area at the same time.'

'Mm.' Harry entered a door, walked past three occupied tables and stopped in front of a counter on which was displayed a selection of unnaturally bright kebabs. 'Have you got his address?'

Klaus Torkildsen read it out, and Harry jotted it down on a serviette.

'Have you got another number for that address?'

'How do you mean?'

'I was wondering if he had a wife or a partner.'

Harry heard Torkildsen typing on a keyboard. Then came the answer: 'No. No one else with that address.'

'Thank you.'

'Have we got a deal then? We'll never speak again?'

'Yes. Apart from one final thing. I want you to check Mikael Bellman. Who he's spoken to over recent months, and where he was at the time of the killing.'

Loud laughter. 'The head of Orgkrim? Forget it! I can hide or explain away a search for a lowly officer, but what you're asking me to do would get me sacked on the spot.' More laughter, as if the idea were really a joke. 'I expect you to keep your end of the bargain, Hole.'

The line went dead.

When the taxi arrived at the address on the serviette a man was waiting outside.

Harry stepped out and went over to him. 'Ola Kvernberg, the caretaker?'

The man nodded.

'Inspector Hole. I rang you.' He saw the caretaker steal a glance at the taxi which was waiting. 'We use taxis when there are no patrol cars.'

Kvernberg examined the ID card the man held up in front of him. 'I haven't seen any signs of a break-in,' he said.

'But someone's rung in, so let's check. You've got a master key, haven't you?'

Kvernberg nodded and unlocked the main door while the policeman studied the names on the bells. 'The witness maintained he'd seen someone climbing up the balconies and breaking into the second floor.'

'Who rang in?' asked the caretaker on his way up.

'Confidential matter, Kvernberg.'

'You've got something on your trousers.'

'Kebab sauce. I keep thinking about getting them cleaned. Can you unlock the door?'

'The pharmacist's?'

'Oh, is that what he is?'

'Works at the Radium Hospital. Shouldn't we ring him at work before we enter?'

'I'd rather see if the burglar's here so we can arrest him, if you don't mind.'

The caretaker mumbled an apology and hastened to unlock the door. Hole went into the flat.

It was obvious that a bachelor was living here. But a tidy one. Classical CDs on their own CD shelf, in alphabetical order. Scientific journals about chemistry and pharmacy stacked in high but neat piles. On one bookshelf there was a framed photograph of two adults and a boy. Harry recognised the boy. He was stooping a little to one side with a sullen expression. He can't have been more than twelve or thirteen. The caretaker stood by the front door watching carefully, so for appearances' sake Harry checked the balcony door before going from room to room. Opening drawers and cupboards. But there was nothing compromising on view.

Suspiciously little, some colleagues would say.

But Harry had seen it before; some people don't have secrets. Not often, it's fair to say, but it happened. He heard the caretaker shifting weight from foot to foot in the bedroom door behind him.

'No signs of a break-in or anything taken,' Harry said, walking past him towards the exit. 'Maybe a false alarm.'

'I see,' said the caretaker, locking up after them. 'What would you have done if there had been a thief there? Taken him in the taxi?'

'We'd have probably called for a patrol car,' Harry smiled, pulling up and examining the boots on the stand by the door. 'Tell me, aren't these two boots *very* different sizes?'

Kvernberg rubbed his chin while scrutinising Harry.

'Yes, maybe. He's got a club foot. May I have another look at your ID?'

Harry passed his card to him.

'The expiry date—'

'The taxi's waiting,' Harry said, snatching the card back and setting off down the stairs at a jog. 'Thanks for your help, Kvernberg!'

I went to Hausmanns gate, and, course, no one had fixed the locks, so I went straight up to the flat. Oleg wasn't there. Nor anyone else. They were out getting stressed. Gotta getta fix, gotta getta fix. Several junkies living together, and the place looked like it. But there was nothing there, of course, just empty bottles, used syringes, bloodstained wads of cotton wool and empty fag packets. Fricking burnt earth. And it was while I was sitting on a filthy mattress and cursing that I saw the rat. When people describe rats they always say a huge rat. But rats are not huge. They're quite small. It's just that their tails can be quite long. OK, if they feel threatened and stand up on two legs they can seem bigger than they are. Apart from that, they're poor creatures who get stressed the same as us. Gotta getta fix.

I heard a church bell ring. And I told myself that Ibsen would be coming.

Had to come. Shit, I felt so bad. I had seen them standing and waiting when we went to work, so happy to see us it was moving. Trembling, their banknotes at the ready, reduced to being amateur beggars. And now I was there myself. Sick with longing to hear Ibsen's lame shuffle on the stairs, to see his idiotic mush.

I had played my cards like a fool. I wanted a shot, nothing else, and all I had achieved was to bring the whole pack of them down on me. The old boy and his Cossacks. Truls Berntsen with his drill and crazed eyes. Queen Isabelle and her fuck-buddy-in-chief.

The rat scampered along the skirting board. Out of sheer desperation I checked under the carpets and mattresses. Under one mattress I found a picture and a piece of steel wire. The picture was a crumpled and faded passport photo of Irene, so I guessed this had to be Oleg's mattress. But I couldn't understand what the wire was for. Until it slowly dawned on me. And I felt my palms go sweaty and my heart beat faster. After all, I had taught Oleg to make a stash.

36

HANS CHRISTIAN SIMONSEN WRIGGLED HIS way between tourists up the slope of the Italian white marble that made the Opera House look like a floating iceberg at the end of the fjord. When he was atop the roof he looked around and caught sight of Harry Hole sitting on a wall. He was on his own, as the tourists by and large went to the other side to enjoy the view of the fjord. But Harry was sitting and staring inwards at the old, ugly parts of town.

Hans Christian sat down beside him.

'HC,' Harry said without looking up from the brochure he was reading. 'Did you know that this marble is called Carrara marble and that the Opera House cost every Norwegian more than two thousand kroner?'

'Yes.'

'Do you know anything about *Don Giovanni?*'

'Mozart. Two acts. An arrogant young rake, who believes he is God's gift to women and men, cheats everyone and makes everyone hate themselves. He thinks he is immortal, but in the end a mysterious statue comes and takes his life as they are both swallowed up by the earth.'

'Mm. There's the premiere of a new production in a couple of days. It says here that in the final scene the chorus sings, "*Such is the end of the evildoer: the death of a sinner always reflects his life.*" Do you think that's true, HC?'

'I *know* it isn't. Death, sad to say, is no more just than life is.'

'Mm. Did you know a policeman was washed ashore here?'

'Yes.'

'Anything you don't know?'

'Who shot Gusto Hanssen?'

'Oh, the mysterious statue,' Harry said, putting down the brochure. 'Do you want to know who it is?'

'Don't you?'

'Not necessarily. The important thing to prove is who it *isn't*, that it isn't Oleg.'

'Agreed,' said Hans Christian, studying Harry. 'But hearing you say that doesn't tally with what I've heard about the zealous Harry Hole.'

'So perhaps people change after all.' Harry smiled quickly. 'Did you check the progress of the investigation with your police solicitor pal?'

'They haven't gone public with your name yet, but it has been sent to all airports and border controls. Put it this way, your passport's not worth a lot.'

'That's the Mallorca trip up in smoke.'

'You know you're wanted, yet you meet in Oslo's number-one tourist attraction?'

'Tried-and-tested small-fry logic, Hans Christian. It's safer in the shoal.'

'I thought you considered loneliness safer.'

Harry took out his pack of cigarettes, shook and held it out. 'Did Rakel tell you that?'

Hans Christian nodded and took a cigarette.

'How long have you two been together?' Harry asked with a grimace.

'A while. Does it hurt?'

'My throat? Little infection perhaps.' Harry lit Hans Christian's cigarette. 'You love her, don't you.'

The solicitor inhaled in a way which suggested to Harry that he had hardly smoked since the parties of his student days.

'Yes, I do.'

Harry nodded.

'But you were always there,' Hans Christian said, sucking on the cigarette. 'In the shadows, in the wardrobe, under the bed.'

'Sounds like a monster,' Harry said.

'Yes, I suppose it does,' Hans Christian said. 'I tried to exorcise you, but I failed.'

'You don't need to smoke the whole cigarette, Hans Christian.'

'Thank you.' The solicitor threw it away. 'What do you want me to do this time?'

'Burglary,' Harry said.

They drove straight after the onset of darkness.

Hans Christian picked up Harry from Bar Boca in Grünerløkka.

'Nice car,' Harry said. 'Family car.'

'I had an elkhound,' Hans Christian said. 'Hunting. Cabin. You know.'

Harry nodded. 'The good life.'

'It was trampled to death by an elk. I consoled myself with the thought that it must be a good way for an elkhound to die. In service as it were.'

Harry nodded. They drove up to Ryen and snaked round the bends to Oslo's best viewing points in the east.

'It's right here,' Harry said, pointing to an unlit house. 'Park at an angle so that the headlights are shining at the windows.'

'Shall I . . .?'

'No,' Harry said. 'You wait here. Keep your phone on and ring if anyone comes.'

Harry took the jemmy with him and walked up the shingle path to the house. Autumn, sharp night air, the aroma of apples. He had a moment of déjà vu. He and Øystein creeping into a garden and Tresko on the lookout by the fence. And then suddenly out of the dark a figure came hobbling towards them wearing an Indian headdress and squealing like a pig.

He rang.

Waited.

No one came.

Nonetheless Harry had the feeling someone was at home.

He slotted the jemmy inside the crack by the lock and carefully applied his weight. The door was old with soft, damp wood and an old-fashioned lock. Then he used his other hand to insert his ID card on the inside of the crooked snap latch. Pressed harder. The lock burst open. Harry slid inside and closed the door behind him. Stood in the darkness holding his breath. Felt a thin thread on his hand, probably the remains of a spider's web. There was a damp, abandoned smell. But also something else, something acrid. Illness, hospital. Nappies and medicine.

Harry switched on his torch. Saw a bare coat stand. He continued into the house.

The sitting room looked as if it had been dusted with powder; the colours seemed to have been sucked out of the walls and the furniture. The cone of light moved across the room. Harry's heart stopped when it was reflected back from a pair of eyes. Then went on beating. A stuffed owl. As grey as the rest of the room.

Harry ventured further into the house and was able to confirm afterwards that it was the same as the flat. Nothing out of the ordinary.

Until, that is, he reached the kitchen and discovered the two passports and the plane tickets on the table.

Although the passport photo had to be almost ten years old Harry recognised the man from his visit to the Radium Hospital. Her passport was brand new. In the photo she was almost unrecognisable, pale, hair hanging in lank strands. The tickets were to Bangkok, departure in ten days.

Harry went down to the basement. Headed for the only door he had not looked behind. There was a key in the lock. He opened it. The same smell he had noticed when he was in the hall met him. He flicked the switch inside the door, and a naked bulb lit the steps leading to the cellar. The feeling that someone was at home. Or 'Oh, yes, the gut instinct', which Bellman had said with light irony when Harry had asked whether he had checked Martin Pran's record. A feeling that Harry now knew had misled him.

Harry wanted to go down, but something was holding him back. The cellar. Similar to the one he had grown up with. When his mother had asked him to fetch potatoes, which they kept in the dark in two big bags, Harry had raced down trying not to think. Trying to imagine that he was running because it was so cold. Because they were in a hurry to prepare the meal. Because he *liked* running. It had nothing to do with the yellow man waiting down there; a naked, smiling man with a long tongue you could hear slithering in and out of his mouth. But that wasn't what stopped him. It was something else. The dream. The avalanche through the cellar corridor.

Harry repressed the thoughts and set his foot on the first step. There was an admonitory creak. He forced himself to tread slowly. Still with the jemmy in his hand. At the bottom, he began to walk along between the storerooms. A bulb in the ceiling cast meagre light. And created more shadows. Harry noticed that all the rooms were shut with padlocks. Who would lock a storeroom in their own cellar?

Harry inserted the pointed end of the jemmy under one hinge. Breathed in, dreading the noise. Pressed the jemmy back quickly, and there was a short crack. He held his breath, listened. The house seemed to be holding its breath as well. Not a sound.

Then he gently opened the door. The smell assailed his nostrils. His fingers found a switch on the inside, and the next moment Harry was bathed in light. Neon tube.

The storeroom was much larger than it had appeared from the outside. He recognised it. It was a copy of a room he had seen before. The lab at the Radium Hospital. Benches with glass flasks and test-tube stands. Harry lifted the lid off a big plastic box. The white powder was speckled with brown. Harry licked the tip of his index finger, dabbed it into the powder and rubbed it against his gums. Bitter. Violin.

Harry gave a start. A sound. He held his breath again. And there it was again. Someone sniffling.

Harry rushed back to turn off the light and hunched up in the dark, holding the jemmy ready.

Another sniffle.

Harry waited a few seconds. Then with quick, quiet steps, he walked out of the storeroom and headed to where the sounds had come from. A storeroom on the left. He moved the jemmy to his right hand. Tiptoed up to the door, which had a small peephole covered with wire netting, exactly like they'd had at home. With one difference: this door was reinforced with metal.

Harry held the torch ready, stood against the wall beside the door, counted down from three, switched on the beam and pointed it through the hole.

Waited.

After three seconds had passed and no one had either shot or launched themselves at the light, he put his head against the wire and peered inside. The beam roved over brick walls, illuminated a chain, flitted across a mattress and then found what it was looking for. A face.

Her eyes were closed. She was sitting quite still. As though she was used to this. Being inspected with a torch.

'Irene?' Harry asked tentatively.

At that moment the phone in Harry's pocket began to vibrate.

37

I LOOKED AT MY WATCH. I had searched the whole flat and still hadn't found Oleg's stash. And Ibsen should have been here twenty minutes ago. Just let him try not turning up, the perv! It was life for kidnapping and rape. The day Irene came to Oslo Central I had taken her to the rehearsal room, where I said Oleg was waiting for her. He wasn't, of course. But Ibsen was. He held her while I gave her a shot. I thought about Rufus. About how it was for the best. Then she calmed right down, and all we had to do was drag her into his car. He had my half-kilo in the boot. Did I have any regrets? Yes, I regretted I hadn't asked for a kilo! No, of course I had some regrets. I'm not entirely without feeling. But when I came over all 'Fuck, I shouldn't have done that' I told myself that Ibsen would take good care of her. He must love her, in his own warped way. Anyway it was too late, now the main thing was to get some medicine and to be healthy again.

This was new ground for me, this was, not getting what the body needed. I'd always got what I wanted, I realised that now. And if that wasn't the way it was going to be in the future I would rather have dropped dead on the spot. Died young and beautiful, with my teeth more or less intact. Ibsen wasn't coming. I knew that now. I stood by the kitchen window looking out onto the street, but the fricking limp-dick was nowhere to be seen. Neither him nor Oleg.

I'd tried them all. There was only one left.

I'd shut out this option for a long time. I was frightened. Yes, I was. But I knew he was in town. He'd been here from the day he found out she had disappeared. Stein. My foster-brother.

I looked down the street again.

No. Sooner die than ring him.

The seconds passed. Ibsen wasn't coming.

Hell! Better to die than be so ill.

I pinched my eyes again, but insects were crawling out of the cavities, darting under my eyelids, scrabbling all over my face.

Dying had lost out.

The finale awaited.

Ring him or die?

Fuck, fuck, fuck!

Harry switched off the torch when the phone began to ring. Saw from the number that it was Hans Christian.

'Someone's coming,' his voice, hoarse with anxiety, whispered in Harry's ear. 'He parked outside the gate, and now he's heading for the house.'

'OK,' Harry said. 'Take it easy. Text me if you see anything. And clear off if—'

'Clear off?' Hans Christian sounded genuinely indignant.

'If you can see this is going down the tube, OK?'

'Why should I—'

Harry rang off, switched the torch back on and shone it at the wire. 'Irene?'

The girl blinked at the light with saucer eyes.

'Listen to me. My name's Harry. I'm a policeman and I'm here to get you out. But someone's coming. If he comes down here act as if nothing's happened, OK? I'll soon have you out of here, Irene. I promise.'

'Have you . . .?' she mumbled, but Harry didn't catch the rest.

'Have I what?'

'Have you got any . . . violin?'

Harry gritted his teeth. 'Hold out for a bit longer,' he whispered.

Harry ran to the top of the stairs and turned off the light. Pushed the door ajar and peered out. He had a clear view of the front door. He heard a shuffling gait on the shingle outside. One foot being dragged after the other. Club foot. And then the door opened.

The light came on.

And there he was. Big, round and plump.

Stig Nybakk.

The department head at the Radium Hospital. The one who remembered Harry from school. Who knew Tresko. Who had a wedding ring with a black nick. Who had a bachelor flat in which it was impossible to find anything out of the ordinary. But also a house left by his parents he hadn't sold.

He hung his coat on the stand and walked towards Harry with his hand outstretched. Stopped suddenly. Fluttered his hand in front of him. A deep furrow in his brow. Stood listening. And now Harry knew why. The thread he had felt on his face when he entered, which he had taken to be a spider's web, must have been something else. Some invisible fibre Nybakk had wound across the hall to indicate whether he had had any unwelcome visitors.

Nybakk moved with surprising speed and agility towards a cupboard. Stuck his hand in. Pulled at something and the matt metal gleamed. A shotgun.

Shit, shit, shit. Harry hated shotguns.

Nybakk took out a box of cartridges, which was already open. Removed two large, red cartridges, held them between first and middle finger.

Harry's brain whirred and whirred, but failed to come up with any good ideas, so he chose the bad one. Took his phone and began to press.

H-o-o-t a-n-d w-a-j-p

Shit! Wrong!

He heard the metallic click as Nybakk broke the gun.

Delete. Where are you? Out with 'j' and 'p' and in with 'i' and 't'.

Heard him loading the cartridges.

w-a-i-t t-i-l-l h-e i-s

Tiny bloody keys! Come on!

Heard the barrel click into place.

i-n t-h-e w-i-n-c

Wrong! Harry heard Nybakk's shuffling gait come closer. Not enough time. Would have to hope Hans Christian could use his imagination.

l-i-g-h-t-s!

He pressed 'send'.

Harry could see Nybakk had raised the shotgun to his shoulder. And it struck him that the pharmacist had noticed the cellar door was ajar.

At that moment a car horn hooted. Loud and insistent. Nybakk flinched. Looked to the sitting room, which faced the road. Hesitated. Then went into the room.

The horn hooted again, and this time it didn't stop.

Harry opened the cellar door and then followed Nybakk, didn't need to tiptoe, knew the hooting would drown his footsteps. From the door he watched Nybakk as he drew the curtains aside. The room was filled with blinding light from the powerful xenon headlamps on Hans Christian's estate car.

Harry took four long strides, and Stig Nybakk neither saw nor heard him approach. He was holding one hand in front of his face to shield it from the light as Harry reached both arms round Stig Nybakk's shoulders, grabbed the gun, pulled the barrel into his fleshy neck. Dug his knees into the back of Nybakk's legs, forcing both of them down as Nybakk desperately fought for air.

Hans Christian must have realised the hooting had done its job, because it stopped, but Harry continued to apply pressure. Until Nybakk's movements slowed, lost energy and he seemed to wilt.

Harry knew Nybakk was losing consciousness. After a few seconds without oxygen the brain would be damaged and after a few more Stig Nybakk, the kidnapper and brain behind violin, would be dead.

Harry took stock. Counted to three and allowed one hand to let go of the gun. Nybakk slid to the floor without a noise.

Harry sat on a chair panting. Gradually, as the adrenalin level in his blood sank, the pain from his chin and neck returned. It had been getting worse by the hour. He tried to ignore it, and pressed 'O' and 'K' to Hans Christian.

Nybakk began to groan softly and hunched up into the foetal position.

Harry searched him. Laid everything he found in his pockets on the coffee table. Wallet, mobile phone and bottle of prescription pills. Zestril. Harry remembered his grandfather had taken them to prevent a heart attack. Harry stuffed the pills into his jacket pocket, put the muzzle of the shotgun to Nybakk's pale brow and ordered him to get up.

Nybakk looked at Harry. Was about to say something, but changed his mind. Struggled to his feet and swayed.

'Where are we going?' he asked as Harry nudged him forward into the hall.

'Downstairs,' Harry said.

Stig Nybakk was still unsteady, and Harry supported him with one hand on his shoulder and the gun in his back as they clambered down to the cellar. They stopped by the door where he had found Irene.

'How did you know it was me?'

'The ring,' Harry said. 'Open up.'

Nybakk took a key from his pocket and twisted it in the padlock.

Inside, he switched on a light.

Irene had moved. She was cowering in the corner furthest from them, trembling, one shoulder raised, as though afraid someone might hit her. Around her ankle was a shackle attached to a chain that led up to the ceiling, where it was nailed to a beam.

Harry noticed that the chain was long enough for her to move around. Long enough for her to switch on the light.

She had preferred darkness.

'Release her,' Harry said. 'And put the shackle on.'

Nybakk coughed. Held up his palms. 'Listen, Harry—'

Harry hit him. Completely lost his head and hit him. Heard the lifeless thud of metal on flesh and saw the red weal the gun barrel had made across Nybakk's nose.

'Say my name one more time,' Harry whispered and felt himself forcing out the words, 'and I'll plaster your head against the wall with the wrong end of the gun.'

With quaking hands Nybakk unlocked the shackle on her foot while Irene stared into the distance, stiff and apathetic, as though none of this concerned her.

'Irene,' Harry said. 'Irene!'

She seemed to wake up, and looked at him.

'Get out of here,' he said.

She pinched her eyes as if it cost her every ounce of concentration to interpret the sounds he had made, to convert the words into meaning. And actions. She walked past him and into the cellar passage with a slow, fixed somnambulist gait.

Nybakk had sat down on the mattress and pulled up his trouser leg. He was trying to attach the narrow shackle over his fat white calf.

'I . . .'

'Round your wrist,' Harry said.

Nybakk obeyed, and Harry jerked the chain to check it was tight enough.

'Take off the ring and give to me.'

'Why? It's just cheap tat—'

'Because it's not yours.'

Nybakk coaxed the ring off and passed it to Harry.

'I know nothing,' he said.

'About what?' Harry asked.

'About what I know you're going to ask. About Dubai. I've met him twice, but both times I was led there blindfolded, so I don't know where I was. His two Russians came here and collected goods twice a week, but I never heard any names mentioned. Listen, if it's money you want I've—'

'Was that it?'

'Was that what?'

'Everything. Was it for money?'

Nybakk blinked a couple of times. Shrugged. Harry waited. And then a kind of weary smile flitted across Nybakk's face. 'What do you think, Harry?'

He motioned towards his foot.

Harry didn't answer. Didn't know if he wanted to hear. He might understand. That for two guys growing up in Oppsal, under the same conditions by and large, an apparent bagatelle of a congenital defect can make life dramatically different for one of them. A few bones out of line, turning the foot inwards. *Pes equinovarus*. Horse foot. Because the way someone with a club foot walks is redolent of a horse tiptoeing. A defect which gives you a *slightly* worse start in life, for which you find ways to compensate, or you don't. Which means you have to compensate a bit more to become Mr Popular, the one they want: the boy who leads out the class team, the cool dude who has cool pals and the girl in the row by the window, the one whose smile makes your heart explode, even though the smile isn't for you. Stig Nybakk had limped through life, unnoticed. So unnoticed Harry couldn't remember him. And it had gone reasonably well. He'd got himself an education, worked hard, been made head of a department, had even begun to lead the class team himself. But the essential ingredient was missing. The girl from the row by the window. She was still smiling at the others.

Rich. He had to become rich.

Because money is like cosmetics, it conceals everything, it gets you everything, including those things which it is said are not for sale: respect, admiration, love. You just had to look around; beauty marries money every time. So now it was his turn, Stig Nybakk's, Club Foot's.

He had invented violin, and the world ought to be at his feet. So why didn't she want him? Why did she turn away in barely concealed disgust even though she knew – *knew* – that he was already a rich man and would be richer with every week that passed. Was it because there was someone else she was thinking about, the one who had given her the foolish tawdry ring she wore on her finger? It was unjust, he had worked hard, tirelessly, to fulfil the criteria in order to be loved, and now she *had to* love him. So he had taken her. Snatched her from the row by the window. Shackled her here, so that she would never disappear again. And to complete the forced marriage he had taken her ring and put it on his own finger.

The cheap ring Irene had been given by Oleg, who in turn had stolen it from his mother, who in turn had been given it by Harry, who in turn had bought it at a street market, where in turn . . . it was like the Norwegian children's song: 'Take the Ring and Let It Wander'. Harry stroked the black nick in the ring's gilt surface. He had been observant and yet blind.

Observant the first time he had met Stig Nybakk and said: 'The ring. I used to have an identical one.'

And blind because he hadn't reflected on what was identical.

The nick in the copper that had gone black.

It was only when he had seen Martine's wedding ring and heard her say he was the only person in the world who would buy a tacky ring that he had linked Oleg with Nybakk.

Harry had not doubted for a moment, even though he hadn't found anything suspicious in Stig Nybakk's flat. Quite the contrary, it was so utterly devoid of compromising objects that Harry had assumed at once that Nybakk had to be keeping his bad conscience elsewhere. The parents' house that stood empty and he could not sell. The red house on the hill above Harry's family home.

'Did you kill Gusto?' Harry asked.

Stig Nybakk shook his head. Heavy eyelids. He seemed sleepy.

'Alibi?'

'No. No, I don't have one.'

'Tell me.'

'I was there.'

'Where?'

'In Hausmanns gate. I was going to see him. He had threatened to expose me. But when I got to Hausmanns gate there were police cars everywhere. Someone had already killed Gusto.'

'Already? So you planned to do the same?'

'Not the same. I don't have a pistol.'

'What have you got then?'

Nybakk shrugged. 'Chemistry studies. Gusto was suffering from withdrawal symptoms. He needed violin.'

Harry looked at Nybakk's tired smile and nodded. 'So whatever white stuff you had you knew Gusto would inject it on the spot.'

The chain rattled as Nybakk raised his hand to point to the door. 'Irene. May I say a few words to her before . . .?'

Harry watched Stig Nybakk. Saw something he recognised. A damaged person, a finished man. Someone who had rebelled against the cards fate had dealt him. And lost.

'I'll ask her,' he said.

Harry found Irene upstairs in the sitting room. She was in a chair with her feet tucked up underneath her. Harry fetched a coat from the hall cupboard, draped it over her shoulders. He spoke to her in a whisper. She answered in a tiny voice, as though afraid of the echoes from the cold sitting-room walls.

She told him Gusto and Nybakk, or Ibsen as they called him, had worked together to trap her. Payment had been half a kilo of violin. She had been locked up for four months.

Harry let her say her piece. Waited until he knew she had run out before asking the next question.

She didn't know anything about the murder of Gusto, beyond what Ibsen had told her. Or who Dubai was, or where he lived. Gusto hadn't said anything, and Irene hadn't wanted to know. All she had heard about Dubai were the same rumours about his flitting around town like some kind of phantom and that no one knew who he was or what he looked like, and that he was like the wind, impossible to catch.

Harry nodded. He had heard that image rather too often of late.

'HC will drive you to the police station. He's a solicitor and will help you to report this. Afterwards he'll take you to Oleg's mother where you can stay for the meantime.'

Irene shook her head. 'I'll ring Stein, my brother. I can stay with him. And . . .'

'Yes?'

'Do I *have* to report this?'

Harry looked at her. She was so young. So small. Like a baby bird. It was impossible to say how much damage had been done.

'It can wait until tomorrow,' Harry said.

He saw the tears well up in her eyes. And his first thought was: At last. Was about to lay a hand on her shoulder, but changed his mind in time. A strange man's hand was perhaps not what she needed. But the next instant her tears were gone.

'Is there . . . is there any alternative?' she asked.

'Such as?' Harry said.

'Such as never having to see him again.' Her eyes would not release his. 'Ever.'

Then he felt it. Her hand on top of his. 'Please.'

Harry patted the hand, then placed it back in her lap. 'Come on, I'll take you to HC.'

After Harry had watched the car go, he went back into the house and down to the cellar. He couldn't find any rope, but under the stairs hung a garden hosepipe. He took it to the storeroom and threw it at Nybakk. Looked up at the beam. High enough.

He took the bottle of Zestril tablets he had found in Nybakk's pocket. Emptied the contents into his hand. Six.

'You've got a heart condition?' Harry asked.

Nybakk nodded.

'How many tablets do you have to take a day?'

'Two.'

Harry put the tablets in Nybakk's hand and the empty bottle in his jacket pocket.

'I'll be back in two days. I don't know what your reputation means to you. The shame would certainly have been worse if your parents had been alive, but I'm sure you've heard how other prisoners treat sex offenders. If you don't exist when I return then you're forgotten, your name will never be mentioned again. If you do, we'll take you to the police station. Got that?'

Stig Nybakk's screams followed Harry all the way to the front door. The screams of someone who was totally, totally alone with his own guilt, his own ghosts, his own loneliness, his own decisions. Yes, there was something familiar about him. Harry slammed the door hard behind him.

Harry hailed a taxi on Vetlandsveien and asked the driver to go to Urtegata.

His neck ached and throbbed as if it had a pulse of its own, had become alive, a locked-up inflamed animal made of bacteria that wanted out. Harry asked if the driver had any painkillers in the car, but he shook his head.

As they turned towards Bjørvika Harry saw rockets exploding in the sky above the Opera House. Someone was celebrating something. It struck him that he ought to do some celebrating himself. He had done it. He had found Irene. And Oleg was free. He had achieved what he set out to achieve. So how come he wasn't in a celebratory mood?

'What's the occasion?' Harry asked.

'Oh, it's the opening night of some opera. I took some elegant types there earlier this evening.'

'*Don Giovanni*. I was invited.'

'Why didn't you go? It's supposed to be good.'

'Tragedies make me so sad.'

The driver sent Harry a surprised look in the mirror. Laughed. 'Tragedies make me so *sad*?'

His phone rang. It was Klaus Torkildsen.

'Thought we were never to speak again,' Harry said.

'Me too,' Torkildsen said. 'But I . . . well, I checked anyway.'

'It's not so important any more,' Harry said. 'The case is wrapped up as far as I'm concerned.'

'Fine, but it might be interesting to know that just before and after the time of the murder Bellman – or at least his phone – was down in Østfold. It would have been impossible for him to make it to the crime scene and back.'

'OK, Klaus, thanks.'

'OK. Never again?'

'Never again. I'm going now.'

Harry ended the call. Leaned back against the headrest and closed his eyes.

Now he should be happy.

Inside his eyelids he could see sparks from the fireworks.

PART FOUR

38

'I'LL JOIN YOU.'

It was over.

She was his again.

Harry moved forward with the check-in queue in the large concourse at Gardermoen. He had a sudden plan, a plan for the rest of his life. A plan anyway. And he had an intoxicating feeling he could not describe with a better word than *happy*.

The monitor above the check-in desk said 'Thai Air, Business Class'.

It had happened so fast.

He had gone straight from Nybakk's house to Martine at the Watchtower to return her phone, but had been told he could keep it because she had a new one. He had allowed himself to be persuaded to accept a coat that was hardly used, so that he looked relatively presentable. Plus three Paracet pills for the pain, but he had refused to let her examine the wound. She would only want to dress it, and there was no time. He had rung Thai Air and fixed himself up with a ticket.

Then it had happened.

He had rung Rakel, told her Irene had been found and that with Oleg's release his mission was accomplished. Now he would have to leave the country before he himself was arrested.

And that was when she had said it.

Harry closed his eyes and played back Rakel's words yet again: 'I'll join you, Harry.' I'll join you. I'll join you.

And: 'When?'

When?

Most of all he had wanted to answer 'now'. Pack a bag and come now! But he had managed to think rationally to some degree.

'Listen, Rakel, I'm a wanted man, and the police are probably keeping an eye on you, hoping you'll lead them to me, OK? I'll go alone tonight. Then you follow tomorrow on the evening flight. I'll wait in Bangkok. From there we can go on to Hong Kong.'

'Hans Christian can defend you if you're arrested. The sentence won't be that—'

'It's not the length of the sentence that worries me,' Harry said. 'As long as I'm in Oslo Dubai can find me. Are you sure Oleg's in a safe place?'

'Yes. But I want him to join us, Harry. I can't travel—'

'Of course he'll join us.'

'Do you mean that?' He could hear the relief in her voice.

'We'll be together, and in Hong Kong Dubai can't touch us. We'll wait a few days and then I'll get a couple of Herman Kluit's men to travel to Oslo and escort him.'

'I'll tell Hans Christian. And then I'll buy the plane ticket for tomorrow, darling.'

'I'll be waiting in Bangkok.'

A small silence.

'But you're wanted, Harry. How are you going to board the plane without—'

'Next.' Next?

Harry opened his eyes again and saw the woman behind the desk smiling at him.

He stepped forward and gave her his ticket and passport. Watched her type in the name on the passport.

'I can't find you here, herr Nybakk . . .'

Harry put on a reassuring smile. 'In fact I was booked on the plane to Bangkok in ten days' time, but I rang an hour and a half ago and had it changed to this evening.'

The woman pressed some more keys. Harry counted the seconds. Breathed in. Out. In.

'There it is, yes. Late bookings don't always show up right away. But here it says you're travelling with an Irene Hanssen.'

'She's travelling as previously planned,' Harry said.

'Oh, yes. Any luggage to check in?'

'No.'

More pressing of keys.

Then she frowned. Opened the passport again. Harry steeled himself. She placed the boarding card into the passport and gave it to him. 'You'd better hurry, herr Nybakk. Boarding has already started. Have a pleasant trip.'

'Thank you,' Harry said with rather more sincerity than he had anticipated and ran to security.

It was only on the other side of the X-ray machine, when he was about to pick up keys and Martine's mobile phone, that he noticed he had received a text. He was about to save it with all Martine's other messages when he saw the sender had a short name. B. Beate.

He sprinted to gate 54. Bangkok, final call.

Read it.

'Got the last list. There's one address that wasn't on the list you got from Bellman. Blindernveien 74.'

Harry stuffed the phone in his pocket. There was no queue by the counter. He opened his passport and the official checked it and the boarding card. Looked at Harry.

'The scar's newer than the photo,' Harry said.

The official studied him. 'Get a new photo, Nybakk,' he said and returned the documents. Motioned to the person behind Harry to indicate it was their turn.

Harry was free. Saved. A whole new life lay before him.

By the gate there were still five stragglers in the queue.

Harry looked at his boarding card. Business class. He had never travelled in anything but economy, even for Herman Kluit. Stig Nybakk had done well. Dubai had done well. *Were* doing well. Are doing well. Now, this evening, at this moment, the punters were standing there, their faces quivering and hungry, waiting for the guy in the Arsenal shirt to say: 'Come on.'

Two left in the queue.

Blindernveien 74.

I'll join you. Harry closed his eyes to hear Rakel's voice again. And then it was there: *Are you a policeman? Is that what you've become? A robot, a slave of the anthill and ideas other people have had?*

Was he?

It was his turn. The woman at the desk raised her eyebrows.

No, he was not a slave.

He passed her his boarding card.

He walked. Walked down the tunnel to the plane. Through the glass he could see the lights of a plane coming in to land. Coming over Tord Schultz's house.

Blindernveien 74.

Mikael Bellman's blood under Gusto's nails.

Shit, shit, shit!

Harry boarded, found his seat and sank deep into a leather seat. God, the softness of it. He pressed a button and the seat went back and back and back until he was lying in a horizontal position. He closed his eyes again, wanted to sleep. Sleep. Until one day he awoke and was changed and in a very different place. He searched for her voice. But instead found another, in Swedish:

I have a false priest's collar; you have a false sheriff's badge. How unshakeable is your faith in your gospel actually?

Bellman's blood. '. . . down in Østfold. It would have been impossible for him to . . .'

Everything fits.

Harry felt a hand on his arm and opened his eyes.

A Thai flight attendant with high cheekbones smiled down at him.

'I'm sorry, sir, but you must raise your seat into the upright position before take-off.'

Upright position.

Harry breathed in. Took out his mobile phone. Looked at the last call.

'Sir, you have to turn off—'

Harry held up his hand and pressed 'Call'.

'Thought we were never to speak again,' Klaus Torkildsen answered.

'Exactly where in Østfold?'

'Pardon?'

'Bellman. Where in Østfold was he when Gusto was killed?'

'Rygge, by Moss.'

Harry put his phone back and stood up.

'Sir, the seat belt sign—'

'Sorry,' Harry said. 'This isn't my flight.'

'I'm sure it is. We've checked passenger numbers and—'

Harry strode back down the plane. He heard the patter of feet behind him.

'Sir, we've already shut—'

'Then open it.'

A purser had joined them. 'Sir, I'm afraid the rules don't allow us to open—'

'I'm out of pills,' Harry said, fumbling in his jacket pocket. Found the empty bottle with the Zestril label and held it to the purser's face. 'I'm Mr Nybakk, see? Do you want a passenger to have a heart attack on board when we're over . . . let's say Afghanistan?'

It was past eleven o'clock, and the airport express was almost empty as it raced towards Oslo. Harry absent-mindedly read the news on the screen hanging from the ceiling. He'd had a plan, a plan for a new life. Now he had twenty minutes to come up with a new one. It was lunacy. He could have been on a plane to Bangkok. But that was the point; he *could* have been on a plane to Bangkok now. He simply didn't have the ability, it was a deficiency, an operating fault; his club foot was that he had never been able to tell himself he didn't care, to forget, to clear off. He could drink, but he sobered up. He could go to Hong Kong, but he came back. He was undoubtedly a very damaged person. And the effect of the tablets Martine had given him was wearing off; he needed more, the pain was making him dizzy.

Harry had his eyes focused on headlines about quarterly figures and sport results when it struck him: what if that was what he was doing now? Clearing off. Chickening out.

No. It was different this time. He had had the date of the flight changed to tomorrow night, the same flight as Rakel. He had even reserved a seat for her beside him in business class and paid for an upgrade. He had wondered whether to tell her about what he was doing, but he knew what she would think. He hadn't changed. There was still the same madness driving him. Nothing would change, ever. But sitting there, beside each other, with the acceleration pressing them backwards into the seat and then feeling the lift, the lightness, the inexorable, she would finally know they had left the old days behind them, beneath them, that their journey had begun.

Harry got off the airport express, crossed the bridge to the Opera House, walked over the Italian marble towards the main entrance. Through the glass he could see the elegantly dressed people making conversation, with finger food and drinks behind the ropes in the expensive foyer.

Outside the entrance stood a man wearing a suit and an earpiece, his hands in front of his crotch as if facing a free kick. Broad-shouldered, but no beef. Trained eyes that had spotted Harry long ago, and were now studying things *around* him that might have some significance. Which could only mean that he was a policeman in PST, the Norwegian security service, and that the Chief of Police or someone from the government was present. The man took two steps towards Harry as he approached.

'Sorry, private party . . .' he began, but stopped when he saw Harry's ID card.

'It's nothing to do with your Chief, pal,' Harry said. 'Just need to have a few words with someone. Official business.'

The man nodded, spoke into the microphone on his lapel and let Harry pass.

The foyer was a huge igloo which Harry could see was populated by many faces he recognised despite his long exile: the press poseurs, TV's talking heads, entertainers from sport and politics, plus culture's *éminences* more or less *grises*. And Harry saw what Isabelle Skøyen had meant when she'd said it was hard to find a tall enough date when she wore heels. She was easy to spot towering above the assembled guests.

Harry strode over the rope and ploughed a path through with a repeated 'sorry' as white wine slopped around him.

Isabelle was speaking to a man who was half a head smaller than her, but her ingratiating, enthusiastic facial expression suggested to Harry that he was several heads higher than her in power and status. Harry was three metres away when a man appeared in front of him.

'I'm the officer who's just been talking to your colleague outside,' Harry said. 'I'm going to have a word with *her*.'

'Be my guest,' said the guard, and Harry thought he could hear a certain subtext.

Harry took the last steps.

'Hi, Isabelle,' he said and saw the surprise on her face. 'Hope I'm not interrupting . . . your career?'

'Inspector Hole,' she answered with a screech of laughter as if sharing an in-joke.

The man beside her was quick on the draw with his hand and said – rather superfluously – his name. A long career on the top floor of City Hall had presumably taught him that popularity with the common man was rewarded on election day. 'Did you enjoy the performance, Inspector?'

'Yes and no,' Harry said. 'I was mostly glad it was over, and I was on my way home when I realised that there were a couple of things I hadn't got clear.'

'Like what?'

'Well, as Don Giovanni's a thief and a philanderer surely it's only right and proper that he should be punished in the final act. I think I understood who he is, the statue that comes to Don Giovanni and takes him down to hell. What I'm wondering, however, is who told him he could find Don Giovanni at that particular spot? Can you answer me that . . .?' Harry turned. 'Isabelle?'

Isabelle's smile was rigid. 'If you've got a conspiracy theory it's always interesting to hear. But perhaps another time. Right now I'm speaking to—'

'I need to have a couple of words with her,' Harry said, facing her interlocutor. 'By your leave, of course.'

Harry saw that Isabelle was about to protest, but the interlocutor was quicker. 'Of course.' He smiled, nodded and turned to an elderly couple who had been queueing for an audience.

Harry took Isabelle by the arm and led her towards the toilet signs.

'You stink,' she hissed as he placed his hands on her shoulders and pressed her up against the wall beside the entrance to the men's toilets.

'Suit's been in the skip a couple of times,' Harry said, and saw they were attracting a few looks from people around them. 'Listen, we can do this in a civilised or a brutal way. What's the basis of your cooperation with Mikael Bellman?'

'Go to hell, Hole.'

Harry kicked the door to the toilets open and dragged her in.

A man in a dinner jacket by a sink sent them an astonished look from the mirror as Harry slammed Isabelle against a cubicle door and forced his forearm against her throat.

'Bellman was at yours when Gusto was killed,' Harry wheezed. 'Gusto had Bellman's blood under his nails. Dubai's burner is Bellman's closest colleague and friend. If you don't talk now I'll ring my man at *Aftenposten* and have it in tomorrow's paper. And then I'll place everything I have on the public prosecutor's desk. So what's it going to be?'

'Excuse me.' It was the man in the dinner jacket. He maintained a respectful distance. 'Any help required?'

'Get the fuck out of here!'

The man seemed shocked, perhaps not so much at the words but the fact that it was Isabelle who had uttered them, and he shuffled out.

'We were shagging,' Isabelle said, half strangled.

Harry let her go and he could tell from her breath that she had been drinking champagne.

'You and Bellman were shagging?'

'I know he's married, and we were shagging, that's all,' she said, rubbing her neck. 'Gusto appeared out of nowhere and clawed Bellman as he was being thrown out. If you want to tell the press about it, go ahead. I assume you've *never* shagged a married woman. But you might consider what press headlines will do to Bellman's wife and children.'

'And how did you and Bellman meet? Are you trying to tell me this triangle with Gusto and you two is quite by chance?'

'How do you think people in positions of power meet, Harry? Look around you. Look at who's here for the party. Everyone knows Bellman's going to be Oslo's new Chief of Police.'

'And that you're going to get a position in City Hall?'

'We met at some opening or other, a premiere, a private view, don't remember what. That's how it is. You can ring and ask Mikael when it was. But not tonight perhaps, he's having quality time with the family. That's just . . . well, that's how it is.'

That's how it is. Harry stared at her.

'What about Truls Berntsen?'

'Who?'

'He's their burner, isn't he? Who sent him to Hotel Leon to take care of me? Was it you? Or Dubai?'

'What in heaven's name are you going on about?'

Harry could see. She really didn't have a clue who Truls Berntsen was.

Isabelle Skøyen started to laugh. 'Harry, don't look so crestfallen.'

He could have been sitting on a plane to Bangkok. To another life.

He was already on his way out.

'Wait, Harry.'

He turned. She was leaning against the cubicle door and had pulled up her skirt. So high that he could see stocking tops and garters. A lock of blonde hair fell over her brow.

'Now that we have the toilets all to ourselves . . .'

Harry met her eyes. They were misty. Not with alcohol, not with desire, there was something else. Was she crying? Tough, lonely, self-despising Isabelle Skøyen? And? She was yet another bitter person willing to ruin others' lives to get what they thought was their birthright: to be loved.

The door continued to swing both ways after Harry had left, chafed against the rubber seal, faster and faster, like an accelerating and final round of applause.

Harry walked back over the covered bridge to Oslo Central, down the steps to Plata. There was a twenty-four-hour chemist at the other end, but the queue was always so long, and he knew that over-the-counter pills did not have the muscle to kill the pain. He continued past Heroin Park. It had started raining, and the street lamps shimmered in the wet tramlines up Prinsens gate. He considered the case as he walked. Nybakk's shotgun in Oppsal was the easier option. Furthermore, a shotgun gave him more room for manoeuvre. To retrieve the rifle from behind the wardrobe in room 301 he would have to enter Hotel Leon unobserved, and he couldn't even be sure they hadn't already found it. But the rifle was more final.

The lock on the gate behind Hotel Leon was smashed. It had been broken recently. Harry presumed that was how the two suits had got in the night they came visiting.

Harry went in and, sure enough, the lock on the back door was damaged as well.

Harry climbed the narrow stairs that doubled as an emergency exit. Not a soul in the corridor on the second floor. Harry knocked on 310 to ask Cato if the police had been. Or anyone else. But there was no answer. He put his ear against the door. Silence.

No attempt had been made to repair the door to his room, so a key was, in this respect, superfluous. He pushed at the door and it opened. Noticed the blood that had seeped into the bare cement where he had removed the threshold.

Nothing had been done about the window, either.

Harry didn't switch on the light, entered regardless, fumbled behind the wardrobe and verified that they had not found the rifle. Nor the box of cartridges, which was still next to the Bible in the bedside-table drawer. And Harry realised the police had not been there, at Hotel Leon; the occupants and neighbours had not deemed it necessary to involve the law on account of a few miserable rounds from a shotgun, at least as long as there were no bodies. He opened the wardrobe. Even his clothes and suitcase were there, as though nothing had happened.

Harry caught sight of the woman in the room opposite.

She was sitting in front of a mirror with her back to him. Combing her hair, from what he could see. She was wearing a dress that looked strangely old-fashioned. Not old, just old-fashioned, like a costume from another era. Without understanding why, Harry shouted through the smashed window. A short yell. The woman didn't react.

Back on street level, Harry knew he wasn't going to cope. His neck felt as if it was on fire, and the heat was making his pores pump out sweat. He was drenched and felt the first bouts of the shivers.

The music in the bar had changed. From the open door came Van Morrison's 'And It Stoned Me'.

Pain-killing.

Harry walked into the road, heard a shrill desperate ring, and in the next instant a blue-and-white wall filled his field of vision. For four seconds he stood quite motionless in the middle of the street. Then the tram passed and the open bar door was back.

The barman gave a start as he looked up from his newspaper and caught sight of Harry.

'Jim Beam,' Harry said.

The barman blinked twice without moving. The newspaper slid to the floor.

Harry pulled euros from his wallet and laid them on the counter. 'Give me the whole bottle.'

The barman's jaw had dropped. The EAT tattoo had a roll of fat above the T.

'Now,' Harry said. 'And I'll be off.'

The barman glanced down at the notes. Looked up at Harry. Reached for the bottle of Jim Beam, keeping his eyes fixed on him.

Seeing the bottle was less than half full, Harry sighed. He slipped it into his coat pocket, looked around, tried to think of some memorable words for a parting shot, gave up, nodded and left.

Harry stopped at the corner of Prinsens and Dronningens gate. First of all he rang directory enquiries. Then he opened the bottle. The smell of bourbon made his stomach knot. But he knew he would not be able to perform what he had to do without an anaesthetic. It was three years since the last time. Perhaps things had improved. He put the bottle to his mouth. Leaned back and tipped it. Three years of sobriety. The poison hit his system like a napalm bomb. Things had not improved; they were worse than ever.

Harry bent forward, stuck out an arm and supported himself on a wall, so that he would not spatter his trousers or shoes.

He heard high heels on the tarmac behind him. 'Hey, mister. Me beautiful?'

'Sure,' Harry managed to utter before his throat was filled. The yellow jet hit the pavement with impressive power and radius, and he heard the high heels castanet into the distance. He wiped his mouth with the back of his hand and tried again. Head back. Whiskey and gall ran down. And were regurgitated.

The third time it stayed put. For the time being.

The fourth hit the mark.

The fifth was heaven.

Harry hailed a taxi and gave the driver the address.

*   *   *

Truls Berntsen hurried through the murk. Crossed the car park in front of the apartment block illuminated by lights from good, safe homes where they were bringing out the snacks and pots of coffee, and maybe even a beer, and switching on the TV now the news was over and it was more fun to watch. Truls had rung into Police HQ and said he was ill. They hadn't asked him what was wrong, they had just enquired if he was going to be away for the three days without a sick note. Truls had answered how the hell could anyone know if they were going to be ill for precisely three days? What a country of bloody shirkers, what bloody hypocritical politicians claiming that people *actually* wanted to work if they could. Norwegians voted for the Socialist Party because they made it a human right to shirk, and who the hell wouldn't vote for a party that gave you three days off without a doctor's note, gave you carte blanche to sit at home and wank or go skiing or recover from a hangover? The Socialist Party knew of course what a perk this was, but still tried to appear responsible, preened themselves with their 'trust in most people' and declared the right to malinger as some kind of social reform. The Progress Party was even more bloody infuriating as it bought itself votes with tax cuts and hardly bothered to conceal the fact.

He had been sitting and thinking about this the whole day while he went over his weapons, loading, checking, keeping an eye on the locked door, scrutinising all the vehicles that came into the car park, through the sights of the Märklin, the enormous assassination rifle from a case years ago which the officer in charge of confiscated arms probably still thought was at Police HQ. Truls had known that sooner or later he would have to go out for food, but waited until it was dark and there were not many people about. At a little before eleven o'clock, closing time at Rimi supermarket, he had taken his Steyr, sneaked out and jogged over there. Walked along the aisles with one eye on the food and the other on the customers. Bought a week's worth of Fjordland rissoles. Small, transparent bags of peeled potatoes, rissoles, creamed peas and gravy. Chuck them in a pan of boiling water for a few minutes, cut open the bags and squelch it onto the plate, and if you closed your eyes, damned if it didn't remind you of real food.

Truls Berntsen was at the entrance to the apartment block, inserting the key in the lock, when he heard hurried steps behind him in the darkness. He whirled round, frantic, and his hand was already on the pistol butt inside his jacket as he stared into the terrified face of Vigdis A.

'D-did I frighten you?' she stammered.

'No,' Truls said curtly and went in without holding the door open for her, but heard her manage to squeeze her fat through anyway before it closed.

He pressed the lift button. Frightened? Course he was bloody frightened. He had Siberian Cossacks on his tail. Was there anything about that which was *not* frightening?

Vigdis A panted behind him. She was as overweight as most of them had become. Not that he would have said no, but why didn't anyone come straight out with it? Norwegian women had got so fat they were not only going to snuff it from one of a whole sodding range of illnesses, but they would also stop the race from reproducing; they were going to depopulate the country. Because in the end no man could be arsed to wade through so much fat. Apart from their own, of course.

The lift came, they went in and the wires screamed in pain.

He had read that men were putting on at least as much weight, but that it wasn't visible in the same way. They had smaller bums, and just looked bigger and stronger. As he did. He looked a bloody sight *better* than ten kilos ago. But women got this rippling, quivering flab that made him want to kick them, see his foot disappear in all the podge. Everyone knew that fat had become the new cancer, yet they bellyached about the slimming hysteria and applauded the 'real' woman's body. As though doing no exercise and being overfed was some kind of sensible model. Be happy with the body you've got, sort of thing. Much better for hundreds to die of heart disease than one person should die of an eating disorder. And now even Martine looked the same. Right, she was pregnant, he knew that, but he couldn't get it out of his head that she had become one of *them*.

'You look cold,' Vigdis A smiled.

Truls didn't know what the A stood for, but that was what was written by her doorbell, Vigdis A. He felt like punching her, a right hook, with all his strength, he didn't need to worry about his knuckles with those bloody hamster cheeks. Or fucking her. Or both.

Truls knew why he was so angry. It was the mobile phone.

When they had finally got Telenor to track down Hole's phone they had seen it was located in the city centre, around Oslo station, to be precise. There is probably nowhere in Oslo so jam-packed with people day and night. Then a dozen police officers had trawled the crowds searching for Hole. They had kept at it for hours. Nada. In the end a fresh-faced cop had come up with the banal idea of synchronising their watches, spreading around the area and then one of them would ring his number every quarter of an hour. And if anyone heard a phone ring at that moment, or saw anyone taking out a phone, they had to pounce, it had to be here somewhere. No sooner said than done. And they had found the phone. In the pocket of a junkie sitting half asleep on the steps at Jernbanetorget. He said he had been 'given' the phone by a guy at the Watchtower.

The lift stopped. 'Goodnight,' Truls mumbled and got out.

He heard the door close behind him and the lift start again.

Rissoles and a DVD now. The first *Fast & Furious*, maybe. Shit film, of course, but it had one or two scenes. Or *Transformers*, Megan Fox and a good, long wank.

He heard her breathing. She had got out of the lift with him. Some pussy. Truls Berntsen was going to get laid tonight. He smiled and turned his head. It met something. Something hard. And cold. Truls Berntsen strained his eyeballs. A gun barrel.

'Thank you very much,' said a familiar voice. 'I'd love to come in.'

Truls Berntsen sat in the armchair staring down the muzzle of his own pistol.

He had found him. And vice versa.

'We can't keep meeting like this,' Harry Hole said. He had positioned the cigarette in the corner of his mouth so that he would not get smoke in his eyes.

Truls didn't reply.

'Do you know why I'd rather use your gun?' he said, patting the hunting rifle he had placed in his lap.

Truls continued to keep his mouth shut.

'Because I'd prefer the bullets they find in you to be traced back to *your* weapon.'

Truls shrugged.

Harry Hole leaned forward. And Truls could smell it now: the alcoholic breath. Hell, the guy was drunk. He had heard stories about what the man did in a sober state, and now he'd been boozing.

'You're a burner, Truls Berntsen. And here's the proof.'

He held up the ID card from the wallet he had taken from him along with the gun. 'Thomas Lunder? Isn't that the man who collected the dope from Gardermoen?'

'What is it you want?' Truls said, closing his eyes and settling back in the chair. Rissoles and a DVD.

'I want to know what the link is between you, Dubai, Isabelle Skøyen and Mikael Bellman.'

Truls recoiled in the chair. Mikael? What the fuck did Mikael have to do with this? And Isabelle Skøyen? Wasn't she the politician?

'I have no idea . . .'

He watched Harry cock the pistol.

'Careful, Hole! The trigger's more sensitive than you think. It's—'

The hammer of the gun rose further.

'Wait! Wait, for Christ's sake!' Truls Berntsen's tongue circled his mouth in search of lubricating saliva. 'I know nothing about Bellman or Skøyen, but Dubai—'

'Yes?'

'I can tell you about him . . .'

'What can you tell me?'

Truls Berntsen took a deep breath, held it. Then let it out with a groan. 'Everything.'

39

THREE EYES STARED BACK AT Truls Berntsen. Two with light blue, booze-rinsed irises. And a round, black one, which was the muzzle of his own Steyr. The man holding the gun was lying rather than sitting in the armchair, and his long legs stretched out on the carpet. He said in a hoarse voice: 'Tell me, Berntsen. Tell me about Dubai.'

Truls coughed twice. Bloody dry throat.

'There was a ring at the door one night. I lifted the intercom handset, and a voice said he wanted to have a few words with me. I didn't want to let him in at first, but then he mentioned a name and . . . well . . .'

Truls Berntsen held his jaw between thumb and middle finger.

The other man waited.

'There was an unfortunate business I thought no one else knew about.'

'Which was?'

'A detainee. He needed to be taught some manners. I didn't think anyone knew I was the one who had . . . taught him.'

'Any damage?'

'Parents wanted to sue, but the boy couldn't point me out in the line-up. I must have damaged his optic nerve. Blessing in disguise, eh?' Truls laughed his nervous grunted laughter, then shut up quickly. 'And now this man was standing outside my door and he knew. Said I had a certain talent for sailing under the radar, and he was willing to pay a lot for a man like me. He spoke Norwegian, but with a bit of an accent. Sounded pretty decent. I let him in.'

'You met Dubai?'

'I did. He was alone. An old man in an elegant but old-fashioned suit. Waistcoat. Hat and gloves. He told me what he wanted me to do. And what he would pay. He was a careful guy. Said we wouldn't meet face to face again, no phone calls, no emails, nothing that could be traced. And that was fine by me.'

'So how did you organise the work?'

'The jobs were written on a gravestone. He explained to me where it was.'

'Where?'

'Gamlebyen Cemetery. That was where I got the money as well.'

'Tell me about Dubai. Who is he?'

Truls Berntsen stared into the distance. Tried to get a sense of the equation's pluses and minuses. Of the consequences.

'What are you waiting for, Berntsen? You said you could tell me everything about Dubai.'

'Are you aware what I'm risking by tell—'

'Last time I saw you, two of Dubai's guys were trying to fill you with lead. So even without this gun pointing at you you're already in the doghouse, Berntsen. Spit it out. Who is he?'

Harry Hole's eyes bored into him. Saw straight *through* him, Truls thought. And now the hammer on the gun was moving and his equation was becoming simpler.

'Alright, alright,' Berntsen said, holding up his palms. 'His name's not Dubai. They call him that because his pushers wear football shirts advertising an airline that flies to the countries round there. Arabia.'

'You've got ten seconds to tell me something I haven't worked out for myself.'

'Hang on, hang on, it's coming! His name's Rudolf Asayev. He's Russian, his parents were intellectual dissidents and political refugees – at least that's what he said at the trial. He's lived in lots of countries and speaks something like seven languages. Came to Norway in the seventies and was one of the hash-trafficking pioneers, you could say. He kept a low profile, but was grassed up by one of his own people in 1980. That was when selling and importing drugs carried the same sentence as treason. So he did a long stint. After being released he moved to Sweden and switched to heroin.'

'About the same sentence as hash but a lot better mark-up.'

'Sure. He built up a network in Gothenburg, but after an undercover policeman was killed, he had to go underground. He came back to Oslo about two years ago.'

'And he told you all this?'

'No, no, I found this out on my own.'

'Oh, yes? How? I thought the man was a phantom no one knew anything about.'

Truls Berntsen looked down at his hands. Looked up again at Harry Hole. Had to smile, almost. For this was something he had often wanted to tell someone. How he had tricked Dubai himself. But there had been no one to tell. Truls licked his lips. 'He was sitting in the chair where you are now, with his arms on the rests.'

'And?'

'His shirtsleeve slipped back and a gap opened between his gloves and jacket sleeve. He had some white scars. You know, the kind you have when you remove a tattoo. And when I saw that on his wrist I thought—'

'Prison. He was wearing gloves so as not to leave fingerprints you could check against the register afterwards.'

Truls nodded. Hole was pretty quick on the uptake, had to give him that.

'Exactly. But after I'd agreed to the conditions he seemed a bit more relaxed. And when I went to shake hands on the deal he took off one glove. I lifted a couple of semi-decent prints from the back of my hand afterwards. The computer found a match.'

'Rudolf Asayev. Dubai. How has he managed to keep his identity hidden for so long?'

Truls Berntsen shrugged. 'We see it at Orgkrim all the time. There's one thing that separates the Mr Bigs that aren't caught from those that are. A small organisation. Very few links. Very few trusted aides. The dope kings who reckon they're safest with an army around them are always busted. There's always some disloyal servant, someone who wants to take over or grass to get a reduced sentence.'

'And you only saw him once, here?'

'There was one other time. The Watchtower. I think it was him. He saw me, turned in the doorway and left.'

'So, it's true then, this rumour about him flitting around town like a phantom?'

'Who knows.'

'What did you do at the Watchtower?'

'Me?'

'The police aren't allowed to operate there.'

'I knew a girl working there.'

'Mm. Martine?'

'Do you know her?'

'Did you sit there watching her?'

Truls felt the blood rushing to his head. 'I . . .'

'Relax, Berntsen. You just eliminated yourself from inquiries.'

'Wh-what?'

'You're the stalker, the guy Martine thought was an undercover officer. You were at the Watchtower when Gusto was shot, weren't you?'

'Stalker?'

'Forget it and answer.'

'Jesus, you didn't think that I . . .? Why would I have wanted to snuff out Gusto Hanssen?'

'You could have been given it as an assignment by Asayev,' Hole said. 'But you did have a solid, personal reason. Gusto had seen you kill a man in Alnabru. With a drill.'

Truls Berntsen considered what Hole had said. Considered it the way a policeman whose life was a constant lie, every day, every hour, has to try to distinguish bluff from truth.

'This murder of yours also gave you a motive for killing Oleg Fauke, who was another witness. The prisoner who tried to stab Oleg—'

'Did not work for me! You have to believe me, Hole, I had nothing to do with that. I've only burned evidence. I've never killed anyone. The Alnabru job was sheer bad luck.'

Hole tilted his head. 'And when you came to Hotel Leon, was that not with the purpose of killing me?'

Truls gulped. This Hole guy could *kill him*, he bloody could. Put a bullet through his temple, wipe the prints off the gun and leave it in his hand. No sign of a break-in. Vigdis A could say she had seen him return home alone, that he looked cold. Lonely. Had reported in sick. Depressed.

'Who were the two guys who turned up? Rudolf's men?'

Truls nodded. 'They got away, but I got a slug in one of them.'

'What happened?'

Truls shrugged. 'I suppose I know too much.' He attempted a laugh, but it sounded like a chesty cough.

They sat still, looking at each other.

'What are you planning to do?' Truls asked.

'Catch him,' Hole said.

Catch. It was a long time since Truls had heard anyone use that word.

'So, will he have people around him?'

'Three or four, tops,' Truls said. 'Maybe just those two.'

'Mm. Got any other hardware?'

'Hardware?'

'Apart from that.' Hole nodded to the coffee table where two of the pistols and the MP5 machine gun lay loaded and ready to fire. 'I'll cuff you and search the flat, so you might as well show me.'

Truls Berntsen weighed the options. Then he nodded towards the bedroom.

Hole shook his head as Truls opened the wardrobe door and switched on a neon tube that cast blue light over the contents: six pistols, two large knives, a black truncheon, knuckledusters, a gas mask and a so-called riot gun, a short dumpy weapon with a cylinder in the middle holding large tear-gas cartridges. Truls had most of the police stock from the store where they reckoned on a small amount of wastage.

'You're out of your mind, Berntsen.'

'Why's that?'

Hole pointed. Truls had hammered nails into the wall and inked outlines around the weapons. Everything had its place.

'Bullet-proof vest on a *clothes hanger*? Frightened it will crease?'

Truls Berntsen didn't answer.

'OK,' Hole said, taking the vest. 'Give me the riot gun, the gas mask and the ammo for the MP5 in the sitting room. And a rucksack.'

Hole followed while Truls filled the rucksack. They went back to the sitting room, where Harry picked up the MP5.

Afterwards they stood in the doorway.

'I know what you're thinking,' Harry said. 'But before you make any phone calls or try to stop me in any other way perhaps you should bear in mind that everything I know about you and this case is held by a solicitor. He has been instructed how to act if anything should happen to me. Understood?'

Lies, Truls thought, and nodded.

Hole chuckled. 'Think I'm lying, don't you. But you can't be one hundred per cent sure, can you?'

Truls felt a deep hatred for Hole. Hated his condescending, indifferent smile.

'And what happens if you survive, Hole?'

'Then your problems are over. I'll be gone, I'll fly to the other side of the globe. And I won't be coming back. One final thing . . .' Hole buttoned up the long coat over the bullet-proof vest. 'It was you who deleted Blindernveien 74 from the list Bellman and I received, wasn't it?'

Truls Berntsen was about to answer 'no' as an automatic response. But something – an intuition, a semi-digested thought – stopped him. The truth was he had never found out where Rudolf Asayev lived.

'Yes,' Truls Berntsen said as his brain churned, absorbing information.

Tried to analyse what it implied. *The list Bellman and I received.* Tried to draw a conclusion. But he couldn't think fast enough, it had never been his strong suit, he needed more time.

'Yes,' he repeated, hoping his surprise was not obvious. 'Of course it was me who deleted the address.'

'I'll leave this rifle,' Harry said, opening the chamber and releasing the cartridge inside. 'If I don't come back it can be delivered to a firm of solicitors, Bach & Simonsen.'

Hole slammed the door and Truls heard his long strides down the stairs. Waited until he was sure they would not be returning. And then he reacted.

Hole had not found the Märklin leaning against the wall behind the curtain beside the balcony door. Truls grabbed the heavy assassination rifle, tore open the balcony door. Rested the barrel on the railings. It was cold and drizzly, but more important, there was almost no wind.

He saw Hole coming out of the block underneath, saw his coat flapping round him as he trotted towards the waiting taxi in the car park. Spotted him through the light-sensitive sights. German optics and engineering expertise. The image was grainy, but in focus. He could take Hole from here, no problem; the bullet would pierce him from head to toe, or – even better – exit right by his reproductive equipment. After all, the weapon was originally made for hunting elephants. But if he waited until Hole was under one of the street lamps in the car park he would have an even safer shot. And that would be very practical; there weren't many people in the car park so late and it wouldn't be so far for Truls to drag the body to the car.

Instructed a solicitor? Had he bollocks. But of course he would have to assess whether he should be eliminated as well, for safety's sake. Hans Christian Simonsen.

Hole was getting closer. The neck. Or the head. The bullet-proof vest was the type that went right up. Heavy as hell. He pressed the hammer right back. A small but barely audible voice told him he shouldn't do this. It was murder. Truls Berntsen had never killed anyone before. Not deliberately. Tord Schultz, that hadn't been him, that had been Rudolf Asayev's hellhounds. And Gusto? Yes, who the fuck had nailed Gusto? Not him at any rate. Mikael Bellman. Isabelle Skøyen.

The little voice fell quiet and the cross hairs seemed to be fixed to the back of Hole's head. Kapow! He could already see the spray. Pressed the trigger. In two seconds Hole would be in the light. Shame he couldn't film this. Burn it onto a DVD. Would have beaten Megan Fox with or without Fjordland rissoles.

40

TRULS BERNTSEN BREATHED IN, DEEP and slow. His pulse had risen, but it was under control.

Harry Hole was in the light. And filled the sights.

Real shame he couldn't film . . .

Truls Berntsen hesitated.

Thinking on his feet wasn't his forte. Not that he was stupid, but now and then things just went a bit slowly.

When they were growing up this is what had always divided him and Mikael; Mikael was the thinker and talker. The point was that Truls had made it in the end as well. Like now. Like this business of the missing address on the list. And like the small voice that had told him not to shoot Harry Hole, not now. It was basic mathematics, Mikael would have said. Hole was after Rudolf Asayev and Truls – in that order fortunately. So if Hole shot Asayev he would at least have eliminated one of Truls's problems. And ditto if Asayev shot Hole. On the other hand . . .

Harry Hole was still in the light.

Truls's finger tightened on the trigger with even pressure. He had been the second-best rifle marksman at Kripos, the best pistol marksman.

He emptied his lungs. His body was utterly relaxed, there wasn't going to be an uncontrolled jerk. He breathed in again.

And lowered the rifle.

Blindernveien lay in front of Harry, illuminated. It ran like a switchback through hilly terrain surrounded by older houses, large gardens, university buildings and lawns.

He waited until he could see the lights of the taxi fade into the distance, then he began to walk.

It was four minutes to one, and there was not a soul in sight. He had told the taxi driver to stop outside number 68.

Blindernveien 74 lay behind a three-metre-high fence, about fifty metres from the road. Beside the house stood a cylindrical brick building measuring around four metres in height and diameter, like a water tower. Harry hadn't seen any such water towers in Norway before, but noticed that the neighbouring house had one as well. Sure enough, a shingle path led up to the front steps of the imposing timber house. A single lit lamp hung above a door of dark and probably solid wood.

There was light in two of the windows on the ground floor and one on the first.

Harry stood in the shadow of an oak tree on the opposite side of the road. Unhitched his rucksack and opened it. Prepared the riot gun and put the gas mask on his head so that all he had to do was bring it down over his face.

He hoped the rain would help him to get as close as he needed. He checked that the MP5 machine gun was loaded and the safety catch was off.

It was time.

But the anaesthetic was dwindling fast.

He took the bottle of Jim Beam, unscrewed the cap. There was a barely visible heel left at the bottom. He looked at the house again. Looked at the bottle. If this worked he would need a swig afterwards. He screwed the cap back on and stuffed the bottle in his inside pocket with the extra magazine for the MP5. Checked to ensure he was breathing normally, his brain and muscles were getting oxygen. Looked at his watch. One minute past one. In twenty-three hours the plane would be leaving. The plane for him and Rakel.

He took two more deep breaths. The gate was probably alarmed, but he was too heavily laden to gain entrance over the fence at speed, and he had no desire to hang there as a live target as he had been in Madserud allé.

Two and a half, Harry thought. Three.

Then he walked to the gate, pressed the handle, swung it open. Holding the riot gun in one hand, the MP5 in the other, he began to run. Not on the shingle path, but on the grass. He ran towards the living-room window. As a police officer he had been on enough lightning arrests to know what an amazing advantage the element of surprise was. Not only the advantage of shooting first, but also shock effects in the form of sound and light could reduce an opponent to total paralysis. But he knew the shelf life of the element of surprise as well. Fifteen seconds. He reckoned that was all he had. If he hadn't knocked them out in that time they would be able to collect themselves, regroup, fight back. They knew the house; he had never even seen a floor plan.

Fourteen, thirteen.

From the moment he shot two gas cartridges at the living-room window, which exploded and became an avalanche of white, it was as though time stood still and became a juddering film in which he registered that he was in motion, his body was doing what it should, his brain was capturing mere fragments.

Twelve.

He pulled down his gas mask, threw the riot gun into the living room, swept away the largest shards of glass in the window with his MP5, placed the rucksack on the sill and put his hands on it, raised a foot high and swung himself into the white smoke billowing towards him. The lead bullet-proof vest made movement more difficult, but once he was inside it was like flying into a cloud. He heard shots being fired and threw himself to the floor.

Eight.

More shots. The dry sound of the parquet floor being shredded. They had *not* been paralysed into inaction. He waited. Then he heard it. Coughing. The kind you are powerless to restrain with tear gas stinging your eyes, nose, lungs.

Five.

Harry jerked up the MP5 and shot at the sound in the grey-and-white mist. Heard short, pumping steps. Running-on-stairs-type steps.

Three.

Harry rose to his feet and sprinted.

Two.

On the first floor there was no smoke. If the fugitive got away Harry's odds would be dramatically worsened.

One, zero.

Harry could discern the outline of a staircase, then the banister with the rails below. He threaded the MP5 between the rails, wrenched it to the side and up. Pressed the trigger. The weapon shook in his hand, but he held on tight. Emptied the magazine. Pulled the machine gun back, released the magazine while his other hand searched his coat pocket for the other one. Found only the bottle. He had lost the spare magazine while lying on the floor! The others were still in the rucksack on the windowsill.

Harry knew he was dead when he heard footsteps on the stairs. On their way down. They came slowly, hesitantly. Then faster. Then they raced down. Harry saw a figure dive out of the mist. A reeling ghost in a white shirt and black suit. He hit the banister, bent in the middle and slid lifeless down to the newel post. Harry saw the frayed edges of the wounds in the back of the suit where the bullets had entered. He walked over to the body, grabbed the fringe and lifted the head. Felt sensations of asphyxiation and had to fight the impulse to pull off the gas mask.

One bullet had torn half of the nose away as it exited. Nonetheless, Harry still recognised him. The little guy from the doorway at Hotel Leon. The man who had shot at him from the car in Madserud allé.

Harry listened. There was silence except for the hiss of the tear-gas cartridges from which white smoke was still gushing forth. He retreated to the living-room window, found the rucksack, inserted a fresh magazine and stuffed one under his bullet-proof vest. Only now did he notice the sweat running down the inside.

Where was the big man? And where was Dubai? Harry listened again. The hiss of the gas. But hadn't he heard footsteps on the floor above?

Through the gas he glimpsed another room and an open door leading to the kitchen. Only one closed door. He stood beside the door, opened it and pointed the riot gun inside and fired twice. Closed the door and waited. Counted to ten. Opened and entered.

Empty. Through the smoke he identified bookshelves, a black leather armchair and a large fireplace. Above it hung a painting of a man wearing a Gestapo uniform. Was this an old Nazi house? Harry knew the Norwegian Storm Trooper boss Karl Marthinsen had been living in a confiscated house in Blindernveien when he ended his days riddled with bullets outside the Science Building.

Harry retraced his steps, went through the kitchen, through the door behind, to the typical maid's room of the time, and found what he was looking for, the back staircase.

Usually these stairs had also functioned as a fire escape, but these ones didn't stop at an external door, quite the opposite, they continued down to a cellar, and what had once been a back door had been bricked up.

Harry checked that there was still a gas cartridge left in the magazine and mounted the stairs in long, soundless strides. Fired the last cartridge into the corridor, counted to ten and followed. Pushed open the doors, with stabbing pains in his neck, but still managed to concentrate. Apart from the first door, which was locked, all the rooms were empty. Two of the bedrooms looked to be in use. The bed in one didn't have any sheets on though, and Harry could see the mattress was dark, as if drenched in blood. On the bedside table in the second bedroom there was a Bible. Harry studied it. Cyrillic letters. Russian Orthodox. Beside it a prepared *zjuk*. A red brick with six nails in. Exactly the same thickness as the Bible.

Harry walked back to the locked door. The sweat inside the mask had made the glass mist up. He leaned back against the opposite wall, lifted his foot and kicked at the lock. The door cracked at the fourth kick. Harry crouched down and fired a salvo into the room, heard the tinkle of glass. Waited until the smoke from the corridor had drifted inside. Went in. Found the light switch.

The room was bigger than the others. The four-poster bed by the long wall was unmade. A blue jewel on a ring flashed from the bedside table.

Harry put his arm under the duvet. Still warm.

He looked around. Whoever had just been lying in this bed might of course have left the room and locked it after him. Had the key not still been on the inside. Harry checked the window: closed and locked. He examined the solid wardrobe on the short wall. Opened it.

At first glance it was a standard wardrobe. He pressed the back wall. It opened.

An escape passage. German thoroughness.

Harry shoved the shirts and jackets to the side and poked his head through the false panel. A cold gust of air met him. A shaft. Harry groped. Iron rungs had been hammered into the wall. Looked as if there were more rungs further down; they had to lead to the cellar. An image fluttered through his brain, a detached fragment of a dream. He repressed the image, removed his gas mask and forced his way through the false wall. His feet found the rungs, and when he carefully made his way down and his face was level with the wardrobe floor, he saw something lying there. It was U-shaped, stiffened cotton material. Harry put it in his coat pocket and continued down into the darkness. He counted the rungs. After twenty-two one foot touched terra firma. But as he was about to lower the other foot, the no longer quite so firma terra moved. He lost his balance, but his landing was soft.

Suspiciously soft.

Harry lay still and listened. Then he took the lighter from his trouser pocket. Flicked it, let it burn for two seconds. Let it go out. He had seen what he needed.

He was lying on top of a man.

An unusually large and unusually naked man. With skin as cold as marble and the typical blue pallor of recent corpses.

Harry detached himself from the body and stepped across the concrete floor to a bunker door he had noticed. With his lighter lit he was a target; with more light everyone was a target. He held the MP5 at the ready while flicking the switch with his left hand.

A line of bulbs came on. They stretched along a low, narrow tunnel.

Harry established that he and the naked man were alone. He looked down at the body. It lay on a rug on the ground and had a bloodstained bandage round its stomach. From the chest a tattoo of the Virgin Mary stared up at him. Which, as Harry knew, symbolised that the bearer had been a criminal since his childhood years. As there were no other visible signs of injury Harry assumed it was the wound under the bandage that had killed him, in all probability caused by a bullet from Truls Berntsen's Steyr.

Harry pressed his fingers against the bunker door. Locked. The tunnel ended at a metal plate cut into the wall. Rudolf Asayev had had, in other words, only one way out. The tunnel. And Harry knew why he tried all the other exits first. The dream.

He stared down the narrow tunnel.

Claustrophobia is counterproductive, it gives false signals of danger, it is something that has to be fought. He checked that the magazine was slotted into his MP5 properly. Sod it. Ghosts exist only if you let them exist.

Then he set off walking.

The tunnel was even narrower than he had imagined. He ducked, but he still banged his head and shoulders on the moss-covered ceiling and walls. He tried to keep his brain active so as not to give claustrophobia room to grow. And thought this must have been an escape passage the Germans had used; it all fitted with the bricked-up back door. Force of habit ensured he kept his bearings, and unless he was mistaken he was heading for the neighbouring house with an identical water tower. The tunnel had been built with meticulous care; there were even a number of drains in the floor. Strange that the Autobahn-constructing Germans should have built such a narrow tunnel. As he formulated the word 'narrow', claustrophobia took a stranglehold on him. He concentrated on counting his paces, tried to visualise where he could be in relation to what was beyond the hill. Beyond the hill, outside, free, breathing air. Count, count for Christ's sake. When he reached 110 he saw a white line on the ground beneath him. He could see the lights stopped some way ahead and when he turned he realised the line had to be marking the middle of the tunnel. From the small steps he had been forced to take he estimated the distance he had walked to be between sixty and seventy metres. Soon there. He attempted to quicken his pace, shuffling his feet beneath him like an old man. Heard a click and looked down. It came from one of the drains. The bars moved until they overlapped, like air vents in a car. And at that moment he heard a different noise, a deep rumble behind him. He turned.

He could see the light glint on the metal. It was the metal plate that had been cut into the end of the corridor, it moved. Slid down to the floor, that was what had made the noise. Harry stopped and held his machine gun at the ready. He couldn't see what was behind the plate, it was too dark. But then something glittered, like the sunlight reflecting on Oslo fjord one beautiful autumn afternoon. There was a moment of total silence. Harry's heart was racing wildly. Beret Man had been lying in the middle of the tunnel and had drowned. The water towers. The undersized tunnel. The moss on the ceiling that was not moss but algae. Then he saw the wall coming. Greenish black with white edges. He turned to run. And saw a matching wall coming towards him from the other end.

41

IT WAS LIKE STANDING BETWEEN two oncoming trains. The wall of water in front hit him first. Threw him backwards, and he felt his head strike the ground. Then he was picked up and whirled onwards. He flailed desperately, his fingers and knees scraping against the wall, trying to catch hold of something, but he had no chance against the forces around him. Then, as quickly as it had started it stopped. He could feel the currents as the two cascades of water neutralised each other. And saw something by his back. Two white arms with a shimmer of green embraced Harry from behind, pale fingers reached up to his face. Harry kicked, twisted round and saw the body with the bandage round its stomach revolving in the dark water like a weightless, naked astronaut. Open mouth, slowly flapping hair and beard. Harry put his feet on the floor and stretched up to the ceiling. There was water to the very top. He crouched down, glimpsed the MP5 and the white line on the floor beneath him as he took his first swimming strokes. He had lost his bearings until the body told him which way he had to go to get back to where he had come from. Harry swam with his body at a diagonal to the walls, so that he had maximum arm span, shoved off, forcing himself not to think the other thought. Buoyancy wasn't a problem, quite the contrary, the bullet-proof vest was dragging him down too far. Harry considered whether to spend time removing his coat; it kept drifting up above him and creating greater resistance. He tried to concentrate on what he had to do, swim back to the shaft, not count seconds, not count metres. But he could already feel the pressure in his head, as though it was going to explode. And then the thought came after all. Summer, fifty-metre outdoor pool. Early morning, almost no one around, sunshine, Rakel in a yellow bikini. Oleg and Harry were to settle who could swim furthest underwater. Oleg was on form after the ice-skating season, but Harry had a better swimming technique. Rakel cheered and laughed her wonderful laugh as they warmed up. They both strutted about for her – she was the queen of Frogner Lido and Oleg and Harry her subjects seeking the favour of her gaze. Then they started. And it was a dead heat. After forty metres they both broke the surface, panting and certain they had won. Forty metres. Ten metres to the end. With the pool wall to kick off from and unrestricted arm movement. Bit more than half the distance to the end of the shaft. He didn't have a hope. He would die here. He would die now, soon. His eyeballs felt as if they were being squeezed out of his head. The plane left at midnight. Yellow bikini. Ten metres to the end. He took another stroke. Would manage one more. But then, then he would die.

It was half past three in the morning. Truls Berntsen was driving round the streets of Oslo in drizzle that whispered and murmured against the windscreen. He had been doing it for two hours. Not because he was searching for something, but because it brought him calm. Calm to think and calm not to think.

Someone had deleted an address from the list Harry Hole had been given. And it had not been him.

Perhaps not everything was as cut and dried as he had believed after all.

He replayed the night of the murder one more time.

Gusto had stopped by, so desperate for a fix that he was shaking, and threatened to grass him up unless Truls gave him some money for violin. For some reason there had been no violin for weeks, there had been panic in Needle Park, and a quarter cost three thousand, at least. Truls had said they would drive to an ATM, he'd just have to fetch his car keys. He had taken his Steyr pistol along; there was no doubt what would have to be done. Gusto would use the same threat again and again. Dopeheads are pretty predictable like that. But when he went back to the front door the boy had hopped it. Presumably because he had smelt blood. Fair enough, Truls had thought. Gusto wouldn't do any snitching as long as he had nothing to gain by it, and after all he'd been in on the burglary as well. It was Saturday, and Truls was on what was known as reserve duty, which meant he was on call, so he had gone to the Watchtower, read a bit, watched Martine Eckhoff and drunk coffee. Then he had heard the sirens and a few seconds later his mobile had rung. It was the Ops Room. Someone had called in to say there was shooting at Hausmanns gate 92, and they had no one from Crime Squad on duty. Truls had run there, it was only a few hundred metres from the Watchtower. All his police instincts were on alert, he had observed the people he passed on the way, in the full knowledge that his observations could be important. One person he saw was a young man with a woollen hat, leaning against a house. The youngster's attention was caught by the police car parked by the gate of the crime scene address. Truls had noticed the boy because he didn't like the way his hands were buried in the pockets of his North Face jacket. It was too big and too thick for the time of year, and the pockets could have concealed all manner of things. The boy'd had a serious expression on his face, but didn't look like a dope seller. When the police had accompanied Oleg Fauke from the river and into the patrol car the boy had turned his back and gone down Hausmanns gate.

Now Truls could probably have come up with another ten people he had observed around the crime scene and tied theories to them. The reason he remembered this one was that he had seen him again. In the family photo Harry Hole had shown him at Hotel Leon.

Hole had asked if he recognised Irene Hanssen, and he had answered – truthfully – no. But he hadn't told Hole whom he *had* recognised in the photo. Gusto of course. But there had been someone else. The other boy. Gusto's foster-brother. It was the same serious expression. He was the boy he had seen by the crime scene.

Truls stopped the car in Prinsens gate, just down from Hotel Leon.

He had the police radio on, and at last came the message to the Ops Room he had been waiting for.

'Zero One. We checked the report about the noise in Blindernveien. Looks like there's been a battle here. Tear gas and signs of one helluva lot of shooting. Automatic weapon, no question about that. One man shot dead. We went down to the cellar, but it's full of water. Think we'd better call Delta to check the first floor.'

'Can you clarify whether there is *still* anyone alive?'

'Come and clarify it yourself! Didn't you hear what I said? Gas and an automatic weapon!'

'OK, OK. What do you want?'

'Four patrol cars to secure the area. Delta, SOC group and . . . a plumber perhaps.'

Truls Berntsen turned down the volume. Heard a car screech to a halt, saw a tall man cross the street in front of the car. The driver, furious, sounded his horn, but the man didn't notice, just strode in the direction of Hotel Leon.

Truls Berntsen squinted.

Could that really be him? Harry Hole?

The man had his head hunched down between the shoulders of a shabby coat. It was only when he twisted his head and the face was illuminated by the street lamp that Truls saw he had been wrong. There was something familiar about him, but it wasn't Hole.

Truls leaned back in the seat. He knew now. Who had won. He looked out over his town. For this was his now. The rain mumbled on the car roof that Harry Hole was dead, and cried in torrents down the windscreen.

Most people had generally shagged themselves out by two and gone home, and afterwards Hotel Leon was quieter. The boy in reception barely lifted his head as the pastor came in. The rain ran off his coat and hair. He used to ask Cato what he had been doing to arrive in such a state, in the middle of the night, after an absence of several days. But the answers he received were always so exhaustingly long, intense and detailed about the misery of others that he had stopped. But tonight Cato seemed more tired than normal.

'Hard night?' he asked, hoping for a 'yes' or a 'no'.

'Oh, you know,' the old man said with a pale smile. 'Humanity. Humanity. I was almost killed just now.'

'Oh?' said the boy and regretted asking. A long explanation was sure to be on its way.

'A car almost ran me over,' Cato said, continuing up the stairs.

The boy breathed out with relief and concentrated on *The Phantom* again.

The old man put the key in his door and turned. But to his surprise discovered it was already open.

He went in. Switched on the light, but the ceiling lamp didn't come on. Saw the bedside lamp was lit. The man sitting on the bed was tall, stooped and wearing a long coat, like himself. Water dripped from the coat-tails onto the floor. They were so different, yet it struck the old man now for the first time: it was like staring at your reflection.

'What are you doing?' he whispered.

'I broke in of course,' the other man said. 'To see if you had anything of value.'

'Did you find anything?'

'Of value? No. But I found this.'

The old man caught what was thrown over. Held it between his fingers. Nodded slowly. It was made of stiffened cotton, formed into a U-shape. Not as white as it should be.

'So you found this in my room?' the old man asked.

'Yes, in your bedroom. In the wardrobe. Put it on.'

'Why?'

'Because I want to confess my sins. And because you look naked without it.'

Cato looked at the man sitting on the bed, hunched over. Water was running from his hair, down the scar on his jaw to his chin. From there it dripped onto the floor. He had placed the sole chair in the middle of the room. The confessional chair. On the table lay an unopened pack of Camel and beside it a lighter and a sodden broken cigarette.

'As you like, Harry.'

He sat unbuttoning his coat and pushed the U-shaped priest's collar into the slits in the priest's shirt. The other man flinched when he put his hand in his jacket pocket.

'Cigarettes,' the old man said. 'For us. Yours look like they've drowned.'

The policeman nodded and the old man took out his hand and held up an opened pack.

'You speak good Norwegian.'

'Tiny bit better than I speak Swedish. But as a Norwegian you can't hear the accent when I speak Swedish.'

Harry took one of the black cigarettes. Studied it.

'The Russian accent, you mean?'

'Sobranie Black Russian,' the old man said. 'The only decent cigarettes to be found in Russia. Produced in Ukraine now. I usually steal them from Andrey. Speaking of Andrey, how is he?'

'Bad,' the policeman said, allowing the old man to light his cigarette for him.

'I'm sorry to hear that. Speaking of bad, you should be dead, Harry. I know you were in the tunnel when I opened the sluices.'

'I was.'

'The sluices opened at the same time and the water towers were full. You should have been washed into the middle.'

'I was.'

'Then I don't understand. Most suffer from shock and drown in the middle.'

The policeman exhaled the smoke from a corner of his mouth. 'Like the Resistance fighters who went after the Gestapo boss?'

'I don't know if they ever tested his trap in a real retreat.'

'But you did. With the undercover officer.'

'He was just like you, Harry. Men who think they have a calling are

393

dangerous. Both to themselves and their environment. You should have drowned like him.'

'But as you see, I'm still here.'

'I still don't understand how that's possible. Are you claiming that having been battered by the water you still had enough air in your lungs to swim eighty metres in ice-cold water through a narrow tunnel, fully clothed?'

'No.'

'No?' The old man smiled. He seemed genuinely curious.

'No, I had too little air in my lungs. But I had enough for forty metres.'

'And then?'

'Then I was saved.'

'Saved? By whom?'

'By the man you said was good, deep down.' Harry held up the empty whiskey bottle. 'Jim Beam.'

'You were saved by whiskey?'

'A bottle of whiskey.'

'An *empty* bottle of whiskey?'

'On the contrary, a full bottle.'

Harry put the cigarette in the corner of his mouth, unscrewed the cap, held the bottle over his head.

'Full of air.'

The old man gave a look of disbelief. 'You . . .?'

'The biggest problem after emptying my lungs of air in the water was to put my mouth to the bottle, tilt it so the neck was pointing upwards, and I could inhale. It's like diving for the first time. Your body protests. Because your body has a limited knowledge of physics and thinks it will suck in water and drown. Did you know that the lungs can take four litres of air? Well, a whole bottle of air and a bit of determination were enough to swim another forty metres.' The policeman put down the bottle, removed his cigarette and looked at it sceptically. 'The Germans should have made a slightly longer tunnel.'

Harry watched the old man. Saw the furrowed old face split. Heard him laugh. It sounded like the chug-chug of a boat.

'I *knew* you were different, Harry. They told me you would come back to Oslo when you heard about Oleg. So I made enquiries. And I know now the rumours did not exaggerate.'

'Well,' Harry said, keeping an eye on the priest's folded hands. Sat on the edge of the bed with both feet on the floor, ready as it were, with so much weight on his toes that he could feel the thin nylon cord beneath his shoe. 'What about you, Rudolf? Do the rumours exaggerate in your case?'

'Which ones?'

'Well, for example, the ones saying you ran a heroin network in Gothenburg and killed a policeman there.'

'Sounds like it's me who has to confess and not you, eh?'

'Thought it would be good to unburden your sins onto Jesus before you die.'

More chug-chug laughter. 'Good one, Harry! Good one! Yes, we had to eliminate him. He was our burner, and I had a feeling he was not reliable. And I couldn't go back to prison. There's a stale dampness that eats away at your soul, the way mould eats walls. Every day takes another chunk. Your human side is consumed, Harry. It's something I would only wish on my worst enemy.' He looked at Harry. 'An enemy I hate above all else.'

'You know why I came back to Oslo. What was your reason? I thought Sweden was as good a market as Norway.'

'Same as you, Harry.'

'Same?'

Rudolf Asayev took a drag of the black cigarette before answering. 'Forget it. The police were on my heels after the murder. And it's strange how far away you are from Sweden in Norway, despite the proximity.'

'And when you came back you became the mysterious Dubai. The man no one had seen. But who was thought to haunt the town at night. The ghost of Kvadraturen.'

'I had to stay under cover. Not only because of the businesses, but because the name Rudolf Asayev would bring back bad memories for the police.'

'In the seventies and eighties,' Harry said, 'heroin addicts died like flies. But perhaps you included them in your prayers, Pastor?'

The old man shrugged. 'One doesn't judge people who make sports cars, base-jumping parachutes, handguns or other goods people buy for fun and yet send them to their deaths. I deliver something people want, of quality and at a price that makes me competitive. What customers do with the goods is up to them. You are aware, are you, that there are fully functioning citizens who take opiates?'

'Yes, I was one of them. The difference between you and a sports car manufacturer is that what you do is forbidden by law.'

'One should be careful mixing law and morality, Harry.'

'So you think your god will exonerate you, do you?'

The old man rested his chin on his hand. Harry could sense his exhaustion, but he knew it could be faked, and watched his movements carefully.

'I heard you were a zealous policeman and a moralist, Harry. Oleg spoke about you to Gusto. Did you know that? Oleg loved you like a father would wish a son to love him. Zealous moralists and love-hungry fathers like us have enormous dynamism. Our weakness is that we are predictable. It was just a question of time before you came. We have a connection at Gardermoen who sees the passenger lists. We knew you were on your way even before you sat down on the plane in Hong Kong.'

'Mm. Was that the burner, Truls Berntsen?'

The old man smiled by way of answer.

'And what about Isabelle Skøyen on the City Council? Did you work with her too?'

The old man heaved a heavy sigh. 'You know I'll take the answers with me to the grave. I'm happy to die like a dog, but not like an informer.'

'Well,' Harry said, 'what happened next?'

'Andrey followed you from the airport to Hotel Leon. I stay at a variety of similar hotels when I'm in circulation as Cato, and Leon is a place I've stayed at a lot. So I checked in the day after you.'

'Why?'

'To follow what you were doing. I wanted to see if you were getting close to us.'

'As you did when Beret Man stayed here?'

The old man nodded. 'I knew you could be dangerous, Harry. But I liked you. So I tried to give you some friendly warnings.' He sighed. 'But you didn't listen. Of course you didn't. People like you and me don't, Harry. That's why we succeed. And that's also in the end why we always fail.'

'Mm. What were you afraid I would do? Persuade Oleg to grass?'

'That too. Oleg had never seen me, but I couldn't know what Gusto had told him. Gusto was, sad to say, untrustworthy, especially after he began to take violin himself.' There was something in the old man's eyes that Harry realised with a jolt was not the result of tiredness. It was pain. Sheer unadulterated pain.

'So when you thought Oleg would talk to me you tried to have him killed. And when that didn't work you offered to help me. So that I would lead you to Oleg.'

The old man nodded slowly. 'It's not personal, Harry. Those are the rules in this industry. Grasses are eliminated. But you knew that, didn't you?'

'Yes, I knew. But that doesn't mean I'm not going to kill you for following your rules.'

'So why haven't you done it already? Don't you dare? Afraid you'll burn in hell, Harry?'

Harry stubbed out his cigarette on the table. 'Because I want to know a couple of things first. Why did you kill Gusto? Were you afraid he would inform on you?'

The old man stroked back his white hair, round his Dumbo ears. 'Gusto had bad blood flowing through his veins, just like me. He was an informer by nature. He would have informed on me earlier, all that was missing was something to gain. But then he became desperate. It was the craving for violin. It's pure chemistry. The flesh is stronger than the spirit. We all weaken when the craving's there.'

'Yes,' Harry said. 'We all weaken then.'

'I . . .' The old man coughed. 'I had to let him go.'

'Go?'

'Yes. Go. Sink. Disappear. I couldn't let him take over the businesses, I realised that. He was smart enough, he had inherited that from his father. It was spine he lacked. He inherited that deficiency from his mother. I tried to give him responsibility, but he failed the test.' The old man kept stroking his hair back, harder and harder, as if it were steeped in something he was trying to clean. 'Didn't pass the test. Bad blood. So I decided it would have to be someone else. At first I thought of Andrey and Peter. Siberian Cossacks from Omsk. Cossack means "free man". Did you know that? Andrey and Peter were my regiment, my *stanitsa*. They're loyal to their *ataman*, faithful to the death. But Andrey and Peter were not businessmen, you know.' Harry noticed the old man's gesticulations, as if immersed in his own brooding thoughts. 'I couldn't leave the shop to them. So I decided it would have to be Sergey. He was young, had his future in front of him, could be moulded . . .'

'You told me you might have had a son yourself once.'

'Sergey may not have had Gusto's head for figures, but he was disciplined. Ambitious. Willing to do what was required to be an *ataman*. So I gave him the knife. There was only one remaining test. For a Cossack to become an *ataman* in the old days you had to go into the Taiga and come back with a living wolf, tied and bound. Sergey was willing, but I had to see that he could also accomplish *chto nuzhno*.'

'Pardon?'

'The necessary.'

'Was that son Gusto?'

The old man stroked his hair back so hard his eyes narrowed to two slits.

'Gusto was six months old when I was sent to prison. His mother sought solace where she could. At least for a short while. She was in no position to take care of him.'

'Heroin?'

398

'The social services took Gusto from her and provided foster-parents. They were in agreement that I, the prisoner, did not exist. She OD'd the following winter. She should have done it before.'

'You said you came back to Oslo for the same reason as me. Your son.'

'I'd been told he had moved away from his foster-family, he had strayed off the straight and narrow. I had been thinking of leaving Sweden anyway, and the competition in Oslo wasn't up to much. I found where Gusto hung out. Studied him from a distance at first. He was so good-looking. So damned good-looking. Like his mother, of course. I could just sit looking at him. Looking and looking, and thinking he's my son, my own . . .' The old man's voice choked.

Harry stared at his feet, at the nylon cord he had been given instead of a new curtain pole, pressed it into the floor with the sole of his shoe.

'And then you took him into your business. And tested him to see if he could take over.'

The old man nodded. Whispered: 'But I never said anything. When he died he didn't know I was his father.'

'Why the sudden haste?'

'Haste?'

'Why did you need to have someone take over so quickly? First Gusto, then Sergey.'

The old man mustered a weary smile. Leaned forward in his chair, into the light from the reading lamp above the bed.

'I'm ill.'

'Mm. Thought it was something like that. Cancer?'

'The doctors gave me a year. Six months ago. The sacred knife Sergey used had been lying under my mattress. Do you feel any pain in your wound? That's my suffering the knife has transmitted to you, Harry.'

Harry nodded slowly. It fitted. And it didn't fit.

'If you have only months left to live why are you so afraid of being grassed up that you want to kill your own son? His long life for your short one?'

The old man gave a muffled cough. 'Urkas and Cossacks are the regiment's simple men, Harry. We swear allegiance to a code, and we stick to it. Not blindly, but with open eyes. We're trained to discipline our feelings. That makes us masters of our own lives. Abraham said yes to sacrificing his son because—'

'—it was God's command. I have no idea what kind of code you're talking about, but does it say it's alright to let an eighteen-year-old go to prison for your crimes?'

'Harry, Harry, have you not understood? I didn't kill Gusto.'

Harry stared at the old man. 'Didn't you just say it was your code? To kill your own son if you had to?'

'Yes, I did, but I also said I was born of bad people. I love my son. I could never have taken Gusto's life. Quite the opposite. I say screw Abraham and his god.' The old man's laughter morphed into coughing. He laid his hands on his chest, bent over his knees and coughed and coughed.

Harry blinked. 'Who killed him then?'

The old man straightened up. In his right hand he was holding a revolver. It was a large, ugly object and looked even older than its owner.

'You should know better than to come to me without a weapon, Harry.'

Harry didn't answer. The MP5 was at the bottom of a water-filled cellar, the rifle was at Truls Berntsen's flat.

'Who killed Gusto?' Harry repeated.

'It could have been anyone.'

Harry seemed to hear a creak as the old man's finger curled around the trigger.

'It's not very difficult to kill, Harry. Don't you agree?'

'I do,' Harry said, lifting his foot. There was a whistle under the sole of his foot as the thin nylon cord shot up towards the curtain pole holder.

Harry saw the question marks in the old man's eyes, saw his brain working lightning-fast with the half-digested bits of information.

The light that didn't work.

The chair that was in the middle of the room.

Harry who hadn't searched him.

Harry who hadn't moved a centimetre from where he was sitting.

And perhaps now he could see the nylon cord in the semi-gloom as it ran from under Harry's shoe via the curtain pole holder to the ceiling lamp fitting right above his head. Where there was no longer a lamp but the only thing Harry had taken from Blindernveien apart from the priest's collar. Which was all he had in his mind as he lay on Rudolf Asayev's four-poster bed, soaking wet, gasping for breath as black dots jumped in and out of his vision and he was sure he was going to pass out any second, but fought to stay conscious, to stay on this side of the darkness. Then he had got up, and taken the *zjuk*, which was beside the Bible.

Rudolf Asayev hurled himself to the left, thus the steel nails embedded in the brick did not pierce his head but the skin between the collarbone and the shoulder muscle, which continued down to a juncture of nerve fibres, the cervico-brachial plexus, with the result that when, two hundredths of a second later, he pulled the trigger, the muscle in his upper arm was paralysed, causing his revolver to drop seven centimetres. The powder hissed and burned for the thousandth of a second the bullet needed to leave the barrel of the old Nagant. Three thousandths of a second later the bullet bored into the bed frame between Harry's calves.

Harry got up. Flicked the security catch to the side and pressed the release button. The shaft quivered as the blade sprang out. Harry swung his hand, low, past the hip, with a straight arm, and the long, thin knife blade entered midway between the coat lapels, down the priest's shirt. He felt the material and skin give, then the blade slid in up to the hilt without any resistance. Harry let go of the knife knowing that Rudolf Asayev was a dying man as the chair tipped back and the Russian hit the floor with a groan. He kicked the chair away, but stayed where he was, curled up like an injured but still dangerous wasp. Harry stood astride him, bent down and pulled the knife out of his body. Looked at the abnormally deep red colour of the blood. From the liver, maybe. The old man's left hand scrabbled across the floor, round the paralysed right arm, searching for the pistol. And for one wild moment Harry wished the hand would find it, give him the pretext he needed to . . .

Harry kicked the pistol away, heard it thud against the wall.

'The iron,' whispered the old man. 'Bless me with my iron, my boy. It's burning. For both of our sakes, bring this to an end.'

Harry closed his eyes for a brief instant. Could feel he had lost it. It was gone. The hatred. The wonderful, white hatred which had been the fuel that had kept him going. He had run out of it.

'No, thank you,' Harry said. Stepped over and away from the old man. Buttoned up the wet coat. 'I'm going now, Rudolf Asayev. I'll ask the boy in reception to ring for an ambulance. Then I'll call my ex-boss and tell him where they can find you.'

The old man chuckled and red bubbles formed at the corner of his mouth. 'The knife, Harry. It's not murder, I'm already dead. You won't end up in hell, I promise you. I'll tell them at the gate not to drag you in.'

'It's not hell that frightens me.' Harry put the wet Camel pack in his coat pocket. 'I'm a policeman. Our job is to bring alleged lawbreakers to justice.'

The bubbles burst when the old man coughed. 'Come on, Harry, your sheriff's badge is made of plastic. I'm ill. The only thing a judge can do is give me custody, kisses, hugs and morphine. And I committed so many murders. Rivals I hanged from bridges. Employees, like that pilot we used the brick on. The police, too. Beret Man. I sent Andrey and Peter to your room to shoot you. You and Truls Berntsen. And do you know why? To make it look like you two had shot each other. We had left the weapon as proof. Come on now, Harry.'

Harry wiped the knife blade on the bed sheet. 'Why did you want to kill Berntsen? After all, he worked for you.'

Asayev turned onto his side and he seemed to be able to breathe better. He lay like that for a couple of seconds before answering. 'He stole a stockpile of heroin from Alnabru behind my back. It wasn't my heroin, but when you discover your burner is so greedy you can't trust him and at the same time he knows enough about you to bring you down, you know the sum of the risks has become too great. And then businessmen like me eliminate the risk, Harry. We saw a perfect opportunity to kill two birds with one stone. You and Berntsen.' He chuckled. 'Like I tried to murder your boy in Botsen. Feel the hatred now, Harry? I almost murdered your boy.'

Harry stopped by the door. 'Who killed Gusto?'

'Humanity lives by the gospel of hatred. Follow the hatred, Harry.'

'Who are your contacts in the police and on the City Council?'

'If I tell you, will you help me to bring this to an end?'

Harry looked at him. Nodded quickly. Hoped the lie wasn't transparent.

'Come closer,' whispered the old man.

Harry bent down. And suddenly the old man's hand, like a stiff claw, had grabbed his lapels and pulled him close. The whetstone voice wheezed softly in his ear.

'You know I paid a man to confess to the murder of Gusto, Harry. But you thought it was because I couldn't kill Oleg as long as he was being held in a secret location. Wrong. My man in the police force has access to the witness protection programme. I could have had Oleg stabbed to death just as easily where he was. But I had changed my mind. I didn't want him to get away so . . .'

Harry tried to tear himself away, but the old man held him tight.

'I wanted him hung upside down with a plastic bag over his head,' the voice rumbled. 'His head in a clear plastic bag. Water running down his feet. Water following the body all the way down into the bag. I wanted to film it. With sound so that you could hear the screams. And afterwards I would have sent you the film. And if you let me go this is still my plan. You'll be surprised how quickly they release me for lack of evidence, Harry. And then I'll find him, Harry, I swear I will, you just keep an eye on your post for when the DVD comes.'

Harry acted instinctively, swung his hand. Felt the blade gain purchase. Go deep. He twisted it. Heard the old man gasp. Continued to twist. Closed his eyes and felt intestines and organs curling round, bursting, turning inside out. And when at last he heard the old man scream, it was Harry's own scream.

42

HARRY WAS WOKEN BY THE sun shining on one side of his face. Or was it a noise that had woken him?

He carefully opened one eye and peered around him.

Saw a living-room window and blue sky. No noise, not now at any rate.

He breathed in the smell of smoke-ingrained sofa and raised his head. Remembered where he was.

He had left the old man's room for his own, calmly packed his canvas suitcase, exited the hotel via the back stairs and taken a taxi to the only place he could be sure no one would find him: the house belonging to Nybakk's parents in Oppsal. It didn't look as if anyone had been there since he left, and the first thing he did was to ransack the drawers in the kitchen and bathroom until he had a packet of painkillers. He had taken four tablets, washed the old man's blood off his hands and gone down to the cellar to see if Stig Nybakk had made a decision.

He had.

Harry had gone back up, undressed, hung his clothes to dry in the bathroom, found a blanket and fallen asleep on the sofa before his mind could start churning.

Harry rose and went to the kitchen. Took two painkillers and washed them down with a glass of water. Opened the fridge and looked inside.

There was a lot of gourmet food; he had clearly been feeding Irene well. The nausea from the previous day returned, and he knew it would be impossible to eat. Went back to the living room. He had seen the drinks cabinet yesterday as well. Had given it a wide berth before finding somewhere to sleep.

Harry opened the cabinet door. Empty. He breathed out with relief. Fumbled in his pocket. The sham wedding ring. And at that moment heard a sound.

The same one he thought he had heard when he was waking up.

He went over to the open cellar door. Listened. Joe Zawinul? He descended and headed for the storeroom door. Peered through the wire. Stig Nybakk was twirling slowly, like an astronaut, weightless in space. Harry wondered if the mobile phone vibrating in Stig's trouser pocket could be functioning as a propeller. The ringtone – the four, or actually three, notes from 'Palladium' by Weather Report – sounded like a call signal from the beyond. And that was exactly what Harry was thinking as he took out the phone, that it was Nybakk ringing, wanting to talk to him.

Harry looked at the number on the display. And pressed the answer button. He recognised the voice of the receptionist at the Radium Hospital. 'Stig! Hello! Are you there? Can you hear me? We've been trying to reach you, Stig. Where are you? You should have been here for a meeting, several meetings. We're worried. Martin was at your house, but you weren't there either. Stig?'

Harry hung up and put the phone in his pocket. He would need it; Martine's had been ruined in the swim.

From the kitchen he fetched a chair and sat on the veranda. Sat there with the morning sun on his face. Took out his pack of smokes, stuck one of the stupid black cigarettes into his mouth and lit up. It would have to do. He dialled the number he knew so well.

'Rakel.'

'Hi. It's me.'

'Harry? I didn't recognise your number.'

'I've got a new phone.'

'Oh, I'm so glad to hear your voice. Did everything go OK?'

'Yes,' Harry said and had to smile at the happiness in her voice. 'Everything went OK.'

'Is it hot?'

'Very hot. The sun's shining, and I'm about to have breakfast.'

'Breakfast? Isn't it four o'clock or thereabouts?'

'Jet lag,' Harry said. 'Couldn't sleep on the plane. I've found us a great hotel. It's in Sukhumvit.'

'You've no idea how much I'm looking forward to seeing you again, Harry.'

'I—'

'No, wait, Harry. I mean it. I've been awake all night thinking about it. This is absolutely right. That is, we'll find out if it is. But this is what's right about it. Finding out. Oh, imagine if I'd said no, Harry.'

'Rakel—'

'I love you, Harry. *Love* you. Do you hear me? Can you hear how flat, strange and fantastic the word is? You really have to mean it to pull it off – like a bright-red dress. Love you. Is that a bit OTT?'

She laughed. Harry closed his eyes and felt the most wonderful sun in the world kiss his skin and the most wonderful laughter in the world kiss his eardrums.

'Harry? Are you there?'

'Indeed I am.'

'It's so strange. You sound so near.'

'Mm. I'll soon be very near, darling.'

'Say that again.'

'Say what?'

'Darling.'

'Darling.'

'Mmmm.'

Harry could feel he was sitting on something. Something hard in his back pocket. He took it out. The sun made the veneer on the ring shine like gold.

'Rakel,' he said, stroking the black notch with the tip of his finger. 'How would you feel about getting married?'

'Harry, don't mess about.'

'I'm not messing about. I know you could never imagine marrying a debt collector from Hong Kong.'

'No, not at all. Who should I imagine marrying then?'

'I don't know. What about a civilian, an ex-police officer, who lectures at Police College about murder investigations?'

'Doesn't sound like anyone I know.'

'Perhaps someone you might get to know. Someone who could surprise you. Stranger things have happened.'

'You're the one who's always said people don't change.'

'So if now I'm someone who says people *can* change, there's the proof that it is possible to change.'

'Glib bastard.'

'Let's say, hypothetically speaking, that I'm right. People can change. And it *is* possible to put things behind you.'

'To outstare the ghosts that haunt you?'

'Then what would you say?'

'To what?'

'To my hypothetical question of getting married.'

'Is that supposed to be a proposal? Hypothetical? On the *phone*?'

'Now you're stretching it a bit. I'm just sitting in the sun and chatting with a charming woman.'

'And I'm ringing off!'

She hung up, and Harry slumped down on the kitchen chair with closed eyes and a fat grin. Sun-warmed and pain-free. In fourteen hours he would see her. He imagined Rakel's expression when she came to the gate in Gardermoen and saw him sitting there waiting for her. Her face as Oslo shrank beneath them. Her head gliding onto his shoulder as she fell asleep.

He lay like that until the temperature plummeted. He half opened one eye. The edge of a cloud had drifted in front of the sun, nothing more.

Closed the eye again.

Follow the hatred.

When the old man had said that Harry had at first thought he meant Harry should follow his own hatred and kill him. But what about if he had meant something else? He had said it straight after Harry asked who had killed Gusto. Had that been the answer? Did he mean that if Harry followed the hatred it would lead him to the murderer? In which case there were several candidates. But who had the greatest reason to hate Gusto? Irene, of course, but she had been locked up when Gusto was killed.

The sun was switched back on, and Harry decided he was reading too much into the old man's words, the job was over, he should relax, he would soon need another tablet. And he should ring Hans Christian to say that Oleg was finally out of danger.

Another thought struck Harry. Truls Berntsen, a rogue officer at Orgkrim, could not possibly have access to the data in the witness protection programme. It had to be someone else. Someone higher up.

Hold on there, he thought. Hold on for Christ's sake. They can all go to hell. Think about the flight. The night flight. The stars over Russia.

Then he went back to the cellar, considered whether to cut down Nybakk, rejected the idea and found the jemmy he had been looking for.

The main door to Hausmanns gate 92 was open, but the door to the flat had been resealed and locked. Perhaps because of the recent confession, Harry thought, before inserting the jemmy between the door and the frame.

Inside, everything seemed untouched. The stripes of morning sunlight lay across the sitting-room floor like piano keys.

He deposited the little canvas suitcase against the wall and sat on one of the mattresses. Checked to see that he had the plane ticket in his inside pocket. Glanced at his watch. Thirteen hours to take-off.

Looked around. Closed his eyes. Tried to envisage the scene.

A man wearing a balaclava. Who didn't say a word because he knew they would recognise his voice.

A man who had visited Gusto here. Who didn't take anything from him, except his life. A man who hated.

The bullet had been a nine by eighteen millimetre Makarov, in all likelihood therefore the killer had used a Makarov gun. Or a Fort-12. At a pinch an Odessa if they were becoming standard equipment in Oslo. He had stood there. Fired. Left.

Harry listened, hoping the room would talk to him.

The seconds ticked by, became minutes.

A church bell rang.

There was nothing else to be gleaned here.

Harry got up and made to go.

Had reached the door when he heard a sound between the chiming bells. He waited until the next peal was over. There it was again, a gentle scratching. He tiptoed two paces back and gazed around the room.

It was by the threshold, with its back to Harry. A rat. Brown with a shiny, glistening tail, ears that were pink inside, the odd white speck on its coat.

Harry didn't know what was keeping him there. A rat here, that was no more than one might expect.

It was the white specks.

It was as if the rat had been wading through washing powder. Or . . .

Harry looked around the room again. The big ashtray between the mattresses. He knew he would only have one chance, so he removed his shoes, slipped across the room during the next chime of the bell, grabbed the ashtray and stood perfectly still, one and a half metres from the rat, which had still not detected his presence. Did the calculation, timed it. As the bell rang he leapt forward with his arm outstretched. The rat's reactions were too slow to avoid capture in the ceramic dish. Harry heard the hiss, felt it hurling itself backwards and forwards inside. He pushed the ashtray across the floor to the window where there was a pile of magazines, and placed them on top of the bowl. Then he began to search.

After going through various drawers and cupboards in the flat he still couldn't find any string or thread.

He snatched the rag rug from the floor and pulled out a warp; the long strand of fabric would do the job. He made a loop at the end. Then he moved the magazines and lifted the ashtray, high enough to push his hand in. Braced himself for what he knew would happen next. As he felt the rat's teeth sinking in to the soft flesh between thumb and first finger he flipped off the ashtray and grabbed the animal with his other hand. It hissed as Harry picked at the white grains stuck between hairs. Placed them on his tongue and tasted. Bitter. Overripe papaya. Violin. Someone had a stash close by.

Harry attached the loop to the rat's tail and tightened it at the base. Set the animal down on the floor and let go. The rat shot off and the fabric ran through Harry's hand. Home.

Harry followed. Into the kitchen. The rat darted in behind a greasy stove. Harry tipped the ancient heavyweight appliance onto its rear wheels and pulled it out. There was a fist-sized cavity in the wall through which the fabric disappeared.

Until it came to a stop.

Harry stuck his hand, which had already been bitten once, through the cavity. Felt the inside of the wall. Insulation batts to left and right. He felt above the cavity. Nothing. The insulation had been dug away. Harry secured the end of the fabric under one foot of the stove, went to the bathroom, unhooked the mirror, which was stained with saliva and phlegm, smashed it against the side of the basin and chose a suitably large fragment. Went into a bedroom, yanked a reading lamp from the wall and returned to the kitchen. He laid the chunk of mirror inside the cavity. Then he plugged the lamp in the socket beside the stove and shone it on the mirror. Pointed the lamp at the wall until the angle was right, and he saw it.

The stash.

It was a cloth bag, hanging from a hook half a metre above the floor.

The opening was too narrow to insert your hand and twist your arm up to reach the bag. Harry racked his brains. What tool had the owner used to reach his stash? He had been through several drawers and cupboards in the flat, so rewound through his database.

The wire.

He went back into the sitting room. That was where he had seen it the first time he and Beate were here. Protruding from under the mattress and bent at an angle of ninety degrees. Only the owner of the stiff wire would have known its purpose. Harry poked it through the cavity and used the bent end to unhook the bag.

It was heavy. As heavy as he had hoped. He would have to squeeze it out.

The bag had been hung up high so that the rats could barely reach it, yet still they had managed to nibble a hole in the bottom. Harry shook the bag and a few grains fell out. That explained the powder on the rat's coat. Then he opened the bag. Took out three small bags of violin, probably quarters. There wasn't a full junkie kit inside, only a spoon with a curved handle and a used syringe.

It lay at the bottom of the bag.

Harry used a dishcloth so as not to leave fingerprints on it as he lifted it out.

It was unmistakable. Lumpen, odd, almost comical. Foo Fighters. It was an Odessa. Harry sniffed the weapon. The smell of gunpowder can hang around for months after a pistol has been fired if it isn't cleaned and oiled in the meantime. This one had been fired not so long ago. He checked the magazine. Eighteen. Two missing. Harry was in no doubt.

This was the murder weapon.

When Harry entered the toy shop on Storgata there were still twelve hours to take-off.

The shop had two different sets of fingerprint equipment to choose from. Harry chose the more expensive one, with a magnifying glass, an LED light, a soft brush, dusting powder in three colours, sticky tape for lifting prints and an album for storing the family's fingerprints.

'For my son,' he explained as he paid.

The girl behind the cash desk put on her routine smile.

He walked back to Hausmanns gate and got down to work using the ridiculously small LED light to search for prints and sprinkling powder from one of the miniature cans. The brush was so small that he felt like a giant from *Gulliver's Travels*.

There were prints on the gun handle.

And there was one clear one, probably a thumbprint, on one side of the syringe plunger, where there were also black dots that could have been anything at all, but Harry guessed it was gunpowder residue.

As soon as he had all the fingerprints on the cling film he compared them. The same person had held the gun and the syringe. Harry had checked the walls and the floor by the mattress and had found quite a few prints, but none of them matched those on the pistol.

He opened the canvas suitcase and the pocket inside, took out the contents and placed them on the kitchen table. Switched on the LED light.

Looked at his watch. Eleven hours to go. Oceans of time.

It was two o'clock and Hans Christian Simonsen looked strangely out of place as he entered Schrøder's.

Harry was sitting in the corner by the window, his favourite table.

Hans Christian sat down.

'Good?' he asked, nodding to the pot of coffee by Harry.

Harry shook his head.

'Thanks for coming.'

'Not at all. Saturday's a free day. A free day and nothing to do. What's up?'

'Oleg can come home.'

The solicitor brightened up. 'Does that mean . . .?'

'Those who might be a danger to Oleg have gone.'

'Gone?'

'Yes. Is he far away?'

'No, twenty minutes outside town. Nittedal. What do you mean they've gone?'

Harry raised his coffee cup. 'Sure you want to know, Hans Christian?'

The solicitor eyed Harry. 'Does that mean you've solved the case as well?'

Harry didn't answer.

Hans Christian leaned forward. 'You know who killed Gusto, don't you.'

'Mm.'

'How?'

'A few matching fingerprints.'

'And who—?'

'Not important. But I'm leaving today, so it would be nice to say goodbye to Oleg.'

Hans Christian smiled. Pained, but a smile nonetheless. 'Before you and Rakel leave, you mean?'

Harry twirled his coffee cup. 'So she's told you?'

'We had lunch. I agreed to look after Oleg for a few days. I gather that some men will come from Hong Kong and collect him, some of your people. But I must have misunderstood something. You see, I thought you were in Bangkok.'

'I was delayed. There's something I want to ask you—'

'She said more. She said you had proposed.'

'Oh?'

'Yes, in your way, of course.'

'Well—'

'And she said she'd thought about it.'

Harry held up a hand. He didn't want to hear the rest.

'The conclusion of her thoughts was *no*, Harry.'

Harry breathed out. 'Good.'

'So she'd stopped thinking about it, she said. And started feeling instead.'

'Hans Christian—'

'Her answer's *yes*, Harry.'

'Listen to me, Hans Christian—'

'Didn't you hear? She wants to marry you, Harry. Lucky bastard.' Hans Christian's face beamed as if with happiness, but Harry knew it was the glow of despair. 'She said she wanted to be with you until the end of your days.' His Adam's apple bobbed up and down, and his voice alternated between falsetto and husky. 'She said she would have a terrible and nothing short of catastrophic time with you. She would have a fair-to-middling time with you. And she would have a fantastic time with you.'

Harry knew he was quoting her verbatim. And he knew why he was doing it. Because every word was seared into his heart.

'How much do you love her?' Harry asked.

'I . . .'

'Do you love her enough to take care of her and Oleg for the rest of her life?'

'What?'

'Answer me.'

'Yes, of course, but—'

'Swear.'

'Harry.'

'Swear, I said.'

'I . . . I swear. But that doesn't change anything.'

Harry smiled wryly. 'You're right. Nothing changes. Nothing can change. It can't ever change. The river flows along the same damned course.'

'This makes no sense. I don't understand.'

'You will,' Harry said. 'And she will, too.'

'But . . . you love each other. She said that straight out. You're the love of her life, Harry.'

'And she mine. Always has been. Always will be.'

Hans Christian regarded Harry with a mixture of bewilderment and something that resembled sympathy. 'And yet you don't want her?'

'There is nothing I would rather have than her. But it's not certain I'll be here for much longer. And if I'm not, you've made me a promise.'

Hans Christian snorted. 'Aren't you being a trifle melodramatic, Harry? I don't even know if she'll have me.'

'Convince her.' The pains in his neck seemed to be making it more difficult for him to breathe. 'Do you promise?'

Hans Christian nodded, and said, 'I'll try.'

Harry hesitated. Then he proffered his hand.

They shook.

'You're a good man, Hans Christian. I've got you saved under H.' He lifted his mobile phone. 'You've replaced Halvorsen.'

'Who?'

'Just a former colleague I hope to see again. I have to go now.'

'What are you going to do?'

'Meet Gusto's murderer.'

Harry rose, turned to the counter and saluted to Rita, who waved back.

Once outside and striding across the road between cars, there was an explosion behind his eyes, and his throat felt as if it would be torn apart. And in Dovregata came the gall. He stood bent double by the wall in the middle of the quiet street and brought up Rita's bacon, eggs and coffee. Then he straightened and walked on down Hausmanns gate.

In the end it had been a simple decision, despite everything.

I was sitting on a filthy mattress and felt my petrified heart throbbing as I rang. I hoped he would pick up the phone, and I hoped he wouldn't.

I was about to hang up when he answered, and there was my foster-brother's voice, lifeless and clear.

'Stein.'

I have occasionally considered how apt that name is. Stone. An impenetrable surface with a rock-hard centre. Impassive, bleak, heavy. But even rocks have a weak point, a place where a soft blow from a sledgehammer can make them split. In Stein's case it was easy.

I cleared my throat. 'It's Gusto. I know where Irene is.'

I heard light breathing. Stein's breathing was always light.

He could run and run for hours, needed almost no oxygen. Or a reason to run.

'Where?'

'That's the thing,' I said. 'I know where, but it'll cost you to find out.'

'Why?'

'Because I need it.'

It was like a wave of heat. No, of cold. I could feel his hatred. Heard him swallow.

'How mu '

'Five thousand.'

415

'Fine.'

'I mean ten.'

'You said five.'

Fuck.

'But it's urgent,' I said, even though I knew he was already on his feet.

'Fine. Where are you?'

'Hausmanns gate 92. The lock on the door's broken. Second floor.'

'I'm on my way. Don't go anywhere.'

Go anywhere? I took a couple of dog-ends from the ashtray in the sitting room and lit up in the kitchen amid the deafening afternoon silence. Shit, it was so hot in here. Something rustled. I followed the noise. The rat again, scurrying along by the wall.

It came from behind the stove. Had a nice hiding place there.

I smoked dog-end number two.

Then I jumped up.

The stove weighed a bloody ton, until I discovered it had two wheels at the back.

The rathole was bigger than it ought to have been.

Oleg, Oleg, my dear friend. You're smart, but this particular ruse you learned from me.

I fell on my knees. I was on a high even while working with the wire. My fingers shook so much I felt like biting them off. I could feel I had it, but then I lost it. It had to be violin. Had to be!

Then at long last I got a nibble, and it was a big 'un. I reeled it in. A large, heavy cloth bag. I opened it. It had to be, had to be!

A rubber tube, a spoon, a syringe. And three small transparent packages. The white powder inside was flecked with brown. My heart sang. I was reunited with the only friend and lover I have always been able to rely on.

I stuffed two of the packages in my pocket and opened the third. Now I had enough for a week if I was frugal, I just had to shoot up and vamoose before Stein or anyone else came. I sprinkled some powder onto the spoon, flicked my lighter. I usually added a few drops of lemon, the kind you buy in bottles and people put in tea. The lemon juice prevented the powder from going clumpy and you got all of it in the syringe. But I had neither the lemon nor the patience, now there was only one thing that mattered: getting the shit into my bloodstream.

I wrapped the tube round the top of my arm, put the end between my teeth and pulled. Found a big blue vein. Angled the syringe to give myself the biggest target and reduce the shaking. Because I was shaking. Shaking like hell.

I missed.

Once. Twice. Breathed in. Don't think too much now, don't be too keen, don't panic.

The needle wobbled. I took a stab at the blue worm.

Missed again.

I fought against my despair. Thought I might smoke a bit of it first, to compose myself. But it was the rush I wanted, the kick you get when the whole dose hits the blood, goes straight to the brain, the orgasm, the free fall!

The heat and the sunlight, they were blinding me. I moved to the sitting room, sat in the shadow by the wall. Shit, now I couldn't even see the sodding vein! Take it easy. I waited for my pupils to dilate. Luckily my forearms were as white as cinema screens. The vein looked like a river on a map of Greenland. Now.

Missed.

I didn't have the energy for this, felt tears coming. A shoe creaked.

I had been concentrating so hard that I hadn't heard him come in.

And when I looked up my eyes were so full of tears that shapes were distorted, like in a fricking fairground mirror.

'Hi, Thief.'

I hadn't heard anyone call me that for ages.

I blinked away the tears. And the shapes became familiar. Yes, now I recognised everything. Even the gun. It hadn't been nicked from the rehearsal room by passing burglars, as I had thought.

The weird thing was I wasn't frightened. Not at all. All of a sudden I was quite calm.

I looked down at the vein again.

'Don't do it,' said the voice.

I studied my hand. It was as steady as a pickpocket's. This was my chance.

'I'll shoot you.'

'I don't think so,' I said. 'Because then you'll never find out where Irene is.'

'Gusto!'

'I'm doing what I have to do,' I said and stabbed. Hit the vein. Raised my thumb to press the plunger. 'So you can do what you have to do.'

The church bells started chiming again.

Harry sat in the shadow by the wall. The light from the street lamp outside fell on the mattresses. He checked his watch. Nine. Three hours to the Bangkok flight. The pains in his neck had suddenly got worse. Like the heat from the sun before it disappears behind a cloud. But soon the sun would be gone; soon he would be out of pain. Harry knew how this had to end. It was as inevitable as his return to Oslo. Just as he knew that the human need for order and cohesion meant he would manipulate his mind into seeing a kind of logic to it. Because the notion that everything is no more than cold chaos, that there is no meaning, is harder to bear than even the worst, though comprehensible, tragedy.

He groped inside his jacket pocket for a pack of cigarettes and felt the knife handle against his fingertips. Had a feeling he should have got rid of it. A curse lay over it. Over him. But it wouldn't have made any difference; he had been cursed long before the knife appeared. And the curse was worse than any knife; it said that his love was a plague he carried around with him. Just as Asayev had said the knife transmitted the suffering and sickness of its owner to whoever had been stabbed by it, all those who had allowed themselves to be loved by Harry had been made to pay. Had been destroyed, taken from him. Only the ghosts were left. All of them. And soon Rakel and Oleg would be ghosts as well.

He opened the pack and looked inside.

What was it he had imagined? That he would be allowed to escape the curse? That he would be able to flee to the other side of the globe with them and live happily ever after? He was thinking this as he checked his watch again, wondering how late he could leave and still make the flight. This was his selfish, greedy heart he was listening to.

He took out the dog-eared family photo and looked at it again. At Irene. And the brother, Stein. The one with the grey look. Harry had had two hits in his memory database when he met him. One was from this photograph. The second was the night Harry came to Oslo. He had been to Kvadraturen. The close scrutiny to which Stein had subjected him made Harry think he was a policeman at first, but he was wrong. Very wrong.

Then he heard the footsteps on the stairs.

The church bells chimed. They sounded so frail and lonely.

Truls Berntsen stopped on the top step and stared at the front door. Felt his heart beating. They were going to see each other again. He looked forward to the meeting and yet dreaded it. Inhaled.

And rang.

Straightened his tie. He did not feel comfortable in a suit. But he had known there was no way out when Mikael had told him who was coming to the housewarming party. All the top brass, from the outgoing Chief of Police and unit heads to their old Crime Squad rival, Gunnar Hagen. Politicians would be there, too. The foxy council woman whose pictures he had stared at, Isabelle Skøyen. And a couple of TV celebs. Truls had no idea how Mikael had got to know them.

The door opened.

Ulla.

'You look nice, Truls,' she said. Hostess smile. Glittering eyes. But he knew at once he was too early.

He just nodded, unable to say what he should have said, that she looked very attractive herself.

She gave him a quick hug, said to come in. They would be welcoming guests with glasses of champagne but she hadn't poured them yet. She smiled, wrung her hands and cast semi-panicked glances at the staircase to the first floor. Probably hoping that Mikael would come soon and take over. But Mikael must have been changing, inspecting himself in the mirror, checking every hair was in the right place.

Ulla was speaking a bit too fast about people from their childhood in Manglerud. Did Truls know what they were doing now?

Truls didn't.

'Don't have much contact with them any more,' he answered. Even though he was fairly sure she knew he had never had any contact with them. Not one of them, not Goggen, Jimmy, Anders or Krøkke. Truls had one friend: Mikael. And he too had made sure to keep Truls at arm's length as he had risen through the ranks socially and professionally.

They had run out of things to say. She had run out. He hadn't had anything to say from the start. A pause.

'Women, Truls? Anything new there?'

'Nothing new there, nope.' He tried to say it in the same jokey tone as she had. He really could have done with the welcome drink now.

'Is there really no one who can capture your heart?'

She had tilted her head and winked one smiling eye, but he could see she was already regretting her question. Perhaps because she could see his flushed face. Or perhaps because she knew the answer. That you, you, you, Ulla, could capture my heart. He had walked three steps behind the super-couple Mikael and Ulla in Manglerud, been ever-present, ever at their service, though this was gainsaid by the sullen, indifferent I'm-bored-but-I-have-nothing-better-on-offer look. While his heart had burned for her, while from the corner of his eye he had registered her every movement or expression. He could not have her, it was an impossibility, he knew. Yet he had yearned the way people yearn to fly.

Then at last Mikael strode down the stairs, pulling down his shirtsleeves so that the cufflinks could be seen under the dinner jacket.

'Truls!'

It sounded like the somewhat exaggerated heartiness usually reserved for people you don't really know. 'Why the long face, old friend? We have a palace to celebrate!'

'I thought it was the Chief of Police job we were celebrating,' Truls said, looking round. 'I saw it on the news today.'

'A leak. It's not been formally announced yet. But it's your terrace we're going to pay tribute to today, Truls, isn't it? How's it going with the champagne, dear?'

'I'll pour it now,' Ulla said, brushing an invisible speck of dust off her husband's shoulder and departing.

'Do you know Isabelle Skøyen?' Truls asked.

'Yes,' Mikael said, still smiling. 'She's coming this evening. Why?'

'Nothing.' Truls inhaled. It had to be now, or not at all. 'There's something I've been wondering about.'

'Yes?'

'A few days ago I was sent on a job to arrest a guy at Leon, the hotel, you know?'

'I think I know it, yes.'

'But while I was in the middle of the arrest two other policemen I don't know turned up, and they wanted to arrest us both.'

'Double booking?' Mikael laughed. 'Talk to Finn. He coordinates operational matters.'

Truls slowly shook his head. 'I don't think it was a double booking.'

'No?'

'I think someone sent me there on purpose.'

'You mean it was a wind-up?'

'It was a wind-up, yes,' Truls said, searching Mikael's eyes, but found no indication that he understood what Truls was *actually* talking about. Could he have been mistaken after all? Truls swallowed.

'So I was wondering if you knew anything about it, if you might have been in on it.'

'Me?' Mikael leaned back and burst out laughing. And when Truls saw into his mouth he remembered how Mikael had always returned from the school dentist with zero cavities. Not even Karius and Bactus got the better of him.

'I wish I had been! Tell me, did they lay you out on the floor and cuff you?'

Truls eyed Mikael. Saw he had been wrong. So he laughed along with him. From relief as much as at the image of himself being sat on by two other officers, and because Mikael's infectious laughter always invited him to laugh along. No, *commanded* him to laugh along. But it had also enveloped him, warmed him, made him part of something, a member of something, a duo consisting of him and Mikael Bellman. Friends. He heard his own grunted laughter as Mikael's faded.

'Did you really think I was in on it, Truls?' Mikael asked with a pensive expression.

Truls, smiling, looked at him. Thought about how Dubai had found his way to him, thought of the boy Truls had beaten to blindness in remand. Who could have told Dubai that? Thought of the blood the SOC group had found under Gusto's nail in Hausmanns gate, the blood Truls had contaminated before it got as far as a DNA test. But some of which he had procured and kept. It was evidence such as this that could be valuable one rainy day. And since it had definitely begun to rain, he had driven to the Pathology Unit this morning with the blood. And been given the result before coming here this evening. The test suggested, so far, that it was the same blood and nail fragments as those received from Beate Lønn a few days ago. Didn't they talk to each other down there? Didn't they think they had enough to do at Forensics? Truls had apologised and rung off. And considered the answer. The blood under Gusto Hanssen's nails came from Mikael Bellman.

Mikael and Gusto.

Mikael and Rudolf Asayev.

Truls fingered the knot of his tie. It hadn't been his father who taught him how to do it; he couldn't even tie his own. It had been Mikael who had taught him when they were going to the end-of-school party. He had shown Truls how to tie a simple Windsor knot, and when Truls had asked why Mikael's knot seemed so much fatter Mikael had answered that it was because it was a double Windsor, but it was unlikely to suit Truls.

Mikael's gaze rested on him. He was still waiting for an answer to his question. Why Truls thought Mikael had been in on the stunt.

Been in on the decision to murder him and Harry Hole at Hotel Leon. The doorbell rang, but Mikael didn't move.

Truls pretended to be scratching his forehead while using his fingertips to dry the sweat.

'No,' he said and heard his own grunted laugh. 'An idea, that's all. Forget it.'

The stairs creaked under Stein Hanssen's weight. He could feel every step and predict every creak and groan. He stopped at the top. Knocked on the door.

'Come in,' he heard from inside.

Stein Hanssen entered.

The first thing he saw was the suitcase.

'Packed and ready?' he asked.

A nod.

'Did you find the passport?'

'Yes.'

'I've ordered a taxi to take you to the airport.'

'I'm coming.'

'OK.' Stein looked around. The way he had in the other rooms. Said his farewells. Told them he wouldn't be coming back. And listened to the echoes of their childhood. Father's encouraging voice. Mother's secure voice. Gusto's enthusiastic voice. Irene's happy voice. The only one he didn't hear was his own. He had been silent.

'Stein?' Irene was holding a photograph in her hand. Stein knew which one, she had pinned it over her bed the same evening Simonsen, the solicitor, had brought her here. The photograph showing her with Gusto and Oleg.

'Yes?'

'Did you ever feel a desire to kill Gusto?'

Stein didn't answer. Just thought of that evening.

The phone call from Gusto saying he knew where Irene was. Running to Hausmanns gate. And arriving: the police cars. The voices around him saying the boy inside was dead, shot. And the feeling of excitement. Yes, almost happiness. And after that, the shock. The grief. Yes, in a way he had grieved over Gusto. At the same time as nursing a hope that Irene would at last be clean. That hope had of course been extinguished as the days passed and he realised that Gusto's death meant he had missed out on the chance to find her.

She was pale. Withdrawal symptoms. It was going to be tough. But they would manage. They would manage between them.

'Shall we . . .?'

'Yes,' she said, opening the bedside-table drawer. Looking at the photograph. Pressing her lips against it and putting it in the drawer, face down.

Harry heard the door open.

He was sitting motionless in the darkness. Listened to the footsteps cross the sitting-room floor. Saw the movements by the mattresses. Glimpsed the wire as it caught the street lamp outside. The steps went into the kitchen. And the light came on. Harry heard the stove being moved.

He rose and followed.

Harry stood in the doorway watching him on his knees in front of the rathole, opening the bag with trembling hands. Placing objects beside each other. The syringe, the rubber tubing, the spoon, the lighter, the gun. The packages of violin.

The threshold creaked as Harry shifted weight, but the boy didn't notice, just carried on with his feverish activity.

Harry knew it was the craving. The brain was focused on one thing. He coughed.

The boy stiffened. The shoulders hunched, but he didn't turn. Sat without moving, his head bowed, staring down at the stash. Didn't turn.

'I thought so,' Harry said. 'That this is where you would come first. You reckoned the coast was clear now.'

The boy still hadn't moved.

'Hans Christian told you we found her for you, didn't he? Yet you had to come here first.'

The boy got up. And again it struck Harry. How tall he'd become. A man, almost.

'What do you want, Harry?'

'I've come to arrest you, Oleg.'

Oleg frowned. 'For possession of a couple of bags of violin?'

'Not for dope, Oleg. For the murder of Gusto.'

'Don't!' he repeated.

But I had the needle deep into a vein, which was trembling with expectation.

'I thought it would be Stein or Ibsen,' I said. 'Not you.'

I didn't see his fricking foot coming. It hit the needle, which sailed through the air and landed at the back of the kitchen, by the sink full of dishes.

'Fuck's sake, Oleg,' I said, looking up at him.

Oleg stared at Harry for a long time.

It was a serious, calm stare, without any real surprise. More like it was testing the lie of the land, trying to find its bearings.

And when he did speak, Oleg sounded more curious than angry or confused.

'But you believed me, Harry. When I told you it was someone else, someone with a balaclava, you believed me.'

'Yes,' Harry said. 'I did believe you. Because I so *wanted* to believe you.'

'But, Harry,' Oleg said softly, gazing down at the bag of powder he had opened, 'if you can't believe your best friend what can you believe?'

'Evidence,' Harry said, feeling his throat thicken.

'What evidence? We found explanations for the evidence, Harry. You and I, we crushed the evidence between us.'

'The other evidence. The new stuff.'

'Which new stuff?'

Harry pointed to the floor by Oleg. 'The gun there is an Odessa. It uses the same calibre as Gusto was shot with, Makarov, nine by eighteen millimetres. Whatever happens, the ballistics report will state with one hundred per cent certainty that this gun is the murder weapon, Oleg. And it has your dabs on it. Only yours. If anyone else used it and wiped their prints afterwards, yours would have been removed as well.'

Oleg touched the gun, as if to confirm it was the one they were talking about.

'And then there's the syringe,' Harry said. 'There are lots of fingerprints on it, perhaps from two people. But it is definitely your thumbprint on the plunger. The plunger you have to press when you're shooting up. And on that print there are particles of gunpowder, Oleg.'

Oleg ran a finger along the syringe. 'Why is there new evidence against me?'

'Because you said in your statement you were high when you came into the room. But the gunpowder particles prove you injected the needle *after* because you had the particles on you. It proves you shot Gusto first and injected yourself afterwards. You were not high at the moment of the act, Oleg. This was premeditated murder.'

Oleg nodded slowly. 'And you've checked my fingerprints on the gun and the syringe against the police register. So they already know that I—'

'I haven't contacted the police. I'm the only person who knows about this.'

Oleg swallowed. Harry saw the tiny movements in his throat. 'How do you know they're my prints if you didn't check with the police?'

'I had other prints I could compare them with.'

Harry took his hand from his coat pocket. Placed the Game Boy on the kitchen table.

Oleg stared at the Game Boy. Blinked and blinked as though he had something in his eye.

'What made you suspect me?' he whispered.

'The hatred,' Harry said. 'The old man, Rudolf Asayev, said I should follow the hatred.'

'Who's that?'

'He's the man you called Dubai. It took me a while to realise he was referring to his own hatred. Hatred for you. Hatred for the fact that you killed his son.'

'Son?' Oleg raised his head and looked blankly at Harry.

'Yes. Gusto was his son.'

Oleg dropped his gaze, squatted and stared at the floor. 'If . . .' He shook his head. Started afresh. 'If it's true Dubai was Gusto's father and if he hated me so much why didn't he make sure I was killed in prison straight away?'

'Because you were exactly where he wanted you. Because for him prison was worse than death. Prison eats your soul, death only liberates it. Prison was what he wished for those he hated most. You, Oleg. And he had total control over what you did there. It was only when you began to talk to me that you represented a danger, and he had to be content with killing you. But he didn't manage that.'

Oleg closed his eyes. Sat like that, still on his haunches. As though he had an important race in front of him, and now they just had to be quiet and concentrate.

The town was playing its music outside: the cars, a distant foghorn, a half-hearted siren, noise as the sum of human activity, like the anthill's perpetual, relentless rustle, monotonous, soporific, secure like a warm duvet.

Oleg slowly leaned over without taking his eyes off Harry.

Harry shook his head.

But Oleg grabbed the gun. Carefully, as though afraid it would explode in his hands.

43

TRULS HAD FLED TO BE alone on the terrace.

He had stood on the periphery of a couple of conversations, sipping champagne, eating from toothpicks and trying to look as if he belonged there. A few of these well-brought-up individuals had attempted to include him. Said hello, asked him who he was and what he did. Truls had given brief replies, and it had not occurred to him to return the favour. As though he wasn't in a position to do that. Or was frightened he ought to know who they were and what kind of bloody important jobs they had.

Ulla had been busy serving and smiling and chatting to these people, as if they were old acquaintances, and Truls had achieved eye contact with her only on a couple of occasions. And then, with a smile, she had mimed something he guessed was supposed to mean she would have liked to talk to him but a hostess's duties called. It transpired that none of the other boys who had worked on the house had been able to come, and the Chief of Police hadn't recognised Truls and neither had the unit heads. He almost felt like telling them he was the officer who had punched the lights out of the boy.

But the terrace was wonderful. Oslo lay glittering like a jewel beneath him.

The autumn chill had come with the high pressure. Night temperatures down to zero had been forecast on higher ground. He heard distant sirens.

An ambulance. And at least one police vehicle. From somewhere in the centre. Truls would have most liked to sneak away, switch on the police radio. Hear what was going on. Feel the pulse of his town. Feel that he belonged.

The terrace door opened, and Truls automatically took two steps back, into the shadows, to avoid being drawn into a conversation where he would have to shrink still further.

It was Mikael. And the politician woman. Isabelle Skøyen.

She was clearly stewed; at any rate Mikael was supporting her. Big woman, she towered above him. They stood by the railing with their backs to Truls, in front of the windowless bay, so that they were hidden from the guests in the lounge.

Mikael stood behind her, and Truls half expected to see someone produce a Zippo and light a cigarette, but that didn't happen. And when he heard the rustle of a dress and Isabelle Skøyen's low, protesting laugh it was already too late to make his presence known. He saw the flash of a white thigh before the hem was pulled down firmly. Instead she turned to him, and their heads merged into one silhouette against the town below. Truls could hear wet tongue noises. He turned towards the lounge. Saw Ulla smiling and running between people with a tray of new provisions. Truls couldn't understand it. Couldn't bloody understand it. Not that he was shocked, it wasn't the first time Mikael had been involved with another woman, but he couldn't understand how Mikael had the stomach for it. The heart for it. When you have a woman like Ulla, when you have such incredible good luck, when you've hit the jackpot, how could you want to risk everything for a shag on the side? Is it because God, or whoever the hell it is, has given you the things women want in men – good looks, ambition, a smooth tongue that knows what to say – that you feel obliged to exercise your potential, as it were? Like people measuring two metres twenty think they have to play basketball. He didn't know. All he knew was that Ulla deserved better. Someone to love her. Who loved her the way he had always loved her. And always would. The business with Martine had been a frivolous adventure, nothing serious, and it would never be repeated anyway. Every so often he had thought that in some way or other he ought to let Ulla know that if she were ever to lose Mikael, he, Truls, would be there for her. But he had never found the right words to tell her. Truls pricked up his ears. They were talking.

'I just know he's gone,' Mikael said, and Truls could hear from the slightly slurred speech that he was not totally sober, either. 'But they found the other two.'

'His Cossacks?'

'I still believe that all the stuff about them being Cossacks is bollocks. Anyway, Gunnar Hagen from Crime Squad contacted me and wondered if I could help. Tear gas and automatic weapons were used, so they have a theory it might have been the settling of an old score. He wondered if Orgkrim had any candidates. They were tapping in the dark, he said.'

'And you answered?'

'I answered that I had no idea who it could be, which is the truth. If it's a gang they've managed to sail under the radar.'

'Do you think the old boy could have escaped?'

'No.'

'No?'

'I think his body's rotting somewhere down there.' Truls saw a hand point into the starry sky. 'Maybe we'll find it very soon, maybe we'll never find it.'

'Bodies always turn up, don't they?'

No, Truls thought. He stood with his weight distributed evenly across both feet, felt them press against the cement of the terrace, and vice versa. They don't.

'Nevertheless,' Mikael said, 'someone has done it, and he's new. We'll soon see who is Oslo's new king of the dope heap.'

'And what do you think that will mean for us?'

'Nothing, my love.' Truls could see Mikael Bellman place his hand behind Isabelle Skøyen's neck. In silhouette, it looked as if he was about to strangle her. She lurched to the side. 'We've got where we wanted to be. We jump off here. In fact, it couldn't have had a better end than this. We

430

didn't need the old boy any more, and considering what he had on you and me in the course of . . . our cooperation, it's . . .'

'It's?'

'It's . . .'

'Remove your hand, Mikael.'

Alcoholic laughter, as smooth as velvet. 'If this new king hadn't done the job for us I might have had to do it myself.'

'Let Beavis do it, you mean?'

Truls started at the sound of the hated nickname. Mikael had been the first person to use it. And it had stuck. People had caught on to the underbite and the grunted laugh. Mikael had even consoled him by saying he had been thinking more about the 'anarchistic perception of reality' and the 'nonconformist morality' of the cartoon character on MTV. Had made it sound as if he had awarded Truls an honorary bloody title.

'No, I would never have let Truls know about my role in this.'

'I still think it's strange you don't trust him. Aren't you old friends? Didn't he make this terrace for you?'

'He did. In the middle of the night on his ownsome. See what I mean? We're talking about a man who's not a hundred per cent predictable. He's prone to all sorts of weird and wonderful ideas.'

'Yet you advised the old boy to recruit Beavis as a burner?'

'That's because I've known Truls since childhood, and I know he's corrupt through and through and easily bought.'

Isabelle Skøyen screeched with laughter, and Mikael shushed her.

Truls had stopped breathing. His throat tightened, and it was as if he had an animal in his stomach. A small roving animal searching for a way out. It tickled and quivered. It tried an upward route. It pressed against his chest.

'By the way, you've never told me why you chose me as your business partner,' Mikael said.

'Because you've got such a great cock, of course.'

'No, be serious. If I hadn't agreed to work with you and the old boy, I would've had to arrest you.'

'Arrest?' She snorted. 'Everything I've done has been for the good of the town. Legalising marijuana, distributing methadone, financing a room for fixes. Or clearing the way for a drug that results in fewer ODs. What's the difference? Drug policies are pragmatism, Mikael.'

'Relax, I agree, goes without saying. We've made Oslo a better place. *Skål* to that.'

She ignored his raised glass. 'You would never have arrested me anyway. Because, if you had, I would've told anyone who wanted to listen that I was fucking you behind your sweet little wife's back.' She giggled. '*Right* behind her back. Do you remember the first time we met at that premiere and I said you could fuck me? Your wife was standing right behind you, barely out of earshot, but you didn't even blink. Just asked me for fifteen minutes to send her home.'

'Shh, you're drunk,' Mikael said, placing a hand on her spine.

'That was when I knew you were a man after my own heart. So when the old boy said I should find myself an ally with the same ambitions as me, I knew exactly who to approach. *Skål*, Mikael.'

'Speaking of which, we need a top-up. Perhaps we should go back and—'

'Delete what I said about after my own heart. There are no men after my heart, they're after my . . .' Deep rumble of laughter. Hers.

'Come on, let's go.'

'Harry Hole!'

'Shh.'

'There's a man after my own heart. Bit stupid, of course, but . . . hm. Where do you think he is?'

'Having trawled the town for him for so long without success, I assume he's left the country. He got Oleg acquitted, he won't be back.'

Isabelle swayed, but Mikael caught her.

'You're a bastard, Mikael, and we bastards deserve each other.'

'Maybe, but we should go back in,' Mikael said, glancing at his watch.

'Don't look so stressed, big boy. I can handle a drink. See?'

'I see, but you go in first, then it won't look so . . .'

'Mucky?'

'Something like that.'

Truls heard her hard laughter and watched her even harder heels hitting the cement.

She was gone and Mikael was left, leaning against the railing.

Truls waited for a few seconds. Then he stepped forward.

'Hi, Mikael.'

His childhood pal turned. His eyes were glazed; his face was a little bloated. Truls presumed from the time it took him to react with a cheery smile that this was due to the booze.

'There you are, Truls. I didn't hear you come out here. Is there life inside?'

'Shit, yes.'

They looked at each other. And Truls asked himself exactly when and where they had forgotten how to talk to each other, what had happened to those carefree chats, the daydreaming they had done together, the days when it was OK to say anything and talk about everything. The days when the two of them had been as one. Like early in their careers when they had smacked around the guy who had tried it on with Ulla. Or the bloody poof who had worked in Kripos and made a move on Mikael, and whom they had taken to the boiler room in Bryn a few days later. The guy had blubbed and apologised, saying he had misinterpreted Mikael. They had avoided his face so that it wouldn't be so obvious, but the bloody crybaby had made Truls so angry he had wielded the truncheon with more force than he had intended, and Mikael had only just been able to stop him. They weren't what you might call good memories, but still, they were experiences that bound two people together.

'Well, I'm standing here and admiring the terrace,' Mikael said.

'Thanks.'

'There was something that occurred to me, though. The night you poured the cement . . .'

'Yes?'

'You said, I think, that you were restless and couldn't sleep. But it struck

433

me that was the night we arrested Odin and raided Alnabru afterwards. And he disappeared – what was his name?'

'Tutu.'

'Tutu, yes. You were supposed to have been with us that night, but you were ill, you told me. And then you mixed concrete instead?'

Truls smirked. Looked at Mikael. At last he managed to catch his eye, and to keep it.

'Do you want to hear the truth?'

Mikael seemed to hesitate before answering. 'Love to.'

'I was skiving.'

The terrace went quiet for a couple of seconds; all that could be heard was the distant rumble from the town.

'Skiving?' Mikael laughed. Sceptical, but good-natured laughter. Truls liked his laugh. Everyone did, men and women alike. It was a laugh that said you're funny and nice and probably clever and well worth a friendly chuckle.

'*You* skived? You who never skives and loves making an arrest?'

'Yes,' Truls said. 'I couldn't be bothered. I'd pulled.'

Silence again.

Then Mikael roared with laughter. He leaned back and laughed so much he was gasping for breath. Zero cavities. Bent forward again and smacked Truls on the shoulder. It was such happy, liberating laughter that for some seconds Truls simply couldn't help himself. He joined in.

'Screwing and building a terrace,' Mikael Bellman gasped. 'You're quite a man, you are, Truls. Quite a man.'

Truls could feel the praise making him grow back to his normal size. And for one moment it was almost like the old days. No, not almost, it *was* like the old days.

'You know,' he grunted, 'now and then you have to do things all on your own. That's the only way you get a decent job done.'

'True,' Mikael said, wrapping an arm round Truls's shoulders and stamping both feet on the terrace. 'But this, Truls, is a *lot* of cement for one man.'

Yes, Truls thought, feeling exultant laughter bubble up in his chest. It is a lot of cement for one man.

'I should have kept the Game Boy when you brought it,' Oleg said.

'You should,' Harry said, leaning against the door frame. 'Then you could have brushed up on your Tetris technique.'

'And you should have taken the magazine out of this gun before you left it here.'

'Maybe.' Harry tried not to look at the Odessa pointing half at the floor, half at him.

Oleg smiled wanly. 'I suppose we've made a number of mistakes, both of us. No?'

Harry nodded.

Oleg had got to his feet and was standing beside the stove. 'But I didn't only make mistakes, did I?'

'Not at all. You did a lot right as well.'

'Like what?'

Harry shrugged. 'Like claiming you threw yourself at the gun of this fictional killer. Saying he wore a balaclava and didn't say a word. He only used gestures. You left it to me to draw the obvious conclusions: that it explained the gunshot residue on your skin, and that the killer didn't speak because he was afraid you would recognise his voice, so he had some connection with the drug trade or the police. My guess is you used the balaclava because you noticed the policeman with you at Alnabru had one. In your story you located him in the neighbouring office because it was stripped bare, and it was open so everyone could come and go from there to the river. You gave me the hints so that I could build my own convincing explanation of why you *hadn't* killed Gusto. An explanation you knew my brain would manage. For our brains are always willing to let emotions make decisions. Always ready to find the consoling answers our hearts need.'

Oleg nodded slowly. 'But now you have all the other answers. The correct ones.'

'Apart from one,' Harry said. 'Why?'

Oleg didn't reply. Harry held up his right hand while slowly putting his left in his trouser pocket and pulling out a crumpled pack and lighter.

'Why, Oleg?'

'What do you think?'

'I thought for a while it was all about Irene. Jealousy. Or you knew he had sold her to someone. But if he was the only person who knew where she was, you couldn't kill him until he had told you. So it must have been about something else. Something as strong as love for a woman. Because you're no killer, are you.'

'You tell me.'

'You're a man with a classic motive that has driven men, good men, to perform terrible deeds, myself included. The investigation has gone round in circles. Getting nowhere. I'm back where we started. With a love affair. The worst kind.'

'What do you know about that?'

'Because I've been in love with the same woman. Or her sister. She's drop-dead gorgeous at night, and as ugly as sin when you wake next morning.' Harry lit the black cigarette with the gold filter and the Russian imperial eagle. 'But when night comes you've forgotten and you're in love again. And nothing can compete with this love, not even Irene. Am I wrong?'

Harry took a drag and watched Oleg.

'What do you want me to say? You know everything anyway.'

'I want to hear you say it.'

'Why?'

'Because I want you to hear yourself say it. So that you can hear how sick and meaningless it is.'

'What? That it's sick to shoot someone because they try to nick your dope? The dope you've slogged your guts out to scrape together?'

'Can't you hear how banal that sounds?'

'Says you!'

'Yes, says me. I lost the best woman in the world because I couldn't resist. And you've killed your best friend, Oleg. Say his name.'

'Why?'

'Say his name.'

'I've got the gun.'

'Say his name.'

Oleg grinned. 'Gusto. What's—'

'Once more.'

Oleg tilted his head and looked at Harry. 'Gusto.'

'Once more!' Harry yelled.

'Gusto!' Oleg yelled back.

'Once m—'

'Gusto!' Oleg took a deep breath. 'Gusto! Gusto . . .' His voice had begun to tremble. 'Gusto!' It burst at the seams. 'Gusto. Gus . . .' A sob intervened. '. . . to.' Tears fell as he squeezed his eyes and whispered: 'Gusto. Gusto Hanssen . . .'

Harry took a step forward, but Oleg raised the gun.

'You're young, Oleg. You can still change.'

'And what about you, Harry? Can't you change?'

'I wish I could, Oleg. I wish I had, then I would've taken better care of both of you. But it's too late for me. I am the person I am.'

'Which is? Alkie? Traitor?'

'Policeman.'

Oleg laughed. 'Is that it? Policeman? Not a person or anything?'

'Mostly a policeman.'

'Mostly a policeman,' Oleg repeated with a nod. 'Isn't that banal?'

'Banal and dull,' Harry said, taking the half-smoked cigarette and regarding it with disapproval, as if it wasn't working as it should. 'Because that means I have no choice, Oleg.'

'Choice?'

'I have to make sure you take your punishment.'

'You don't work for the police any more, Harry. You're unarmed. And no one else knows that you know or that you're here. Think of Mum. Think about me! For once, think about us, all three of us.' His eyes were full of tears, and there was a shrill, metallic tone of desperation in his voice. 'Why can't you just go away now, and then we'll forget everything, then we'll say this hasn't happened?'

'I wish I could,' Harry said. 'But you've got me cornered. I know what happened, and I have to stop you.'

'So why did you let me take the gun?'

Harry shrugged. 'I can't arrest you. You have to give yourself up. It's your race.'

'Give myself up? Why should I? I've just been released!'

'If I arrest you I'll lose both your mother and you. And without you I am nothing. I can't live without you. Do you understand, Oleg? I'm a rat that's been locked out and there's only one way in. And it goes through you.'

'So let me go! Let's forget the whole business and start afresh!'

Harry shook his head. 'Premeditated murder, Oleg. I can't. You're the one with the gun, you have the key now. You have to think about all three of us. If we go to Hans Christian he can sort things out and the punishment will be substantially reduced.'

'But it'll be long enough for me to lose Irene. No one would wait that long.'

'Maybe, maybe not. Maybe you've lost her already.'

'You're lying! You always lie!' Harry watched Oleg blinking the tears from his eyes. 'What will you do if I refuse to give myself up?'

'Then I'll have to arrest you now.'

A groan escaped Oleg's lips, a sound halfway between a gasp and disbelieving laughter.

'You're mad, Harry.'

'It's the way I'm made, Oleg. I do what I have to do. As you have to do what you have to do.'

'*Have to*? You make it sound like a bloody curse.'

'Maybe.'

'Bullshit!'

'Break the curse then, Oleg. Because you don't really want to kill again, do you.'

'Get out!' Oleg screamed. The gun shook in his hand. 'Go on! You're not in the police any more!'

'Correct,' Harry said. 'But I am, as I said . . .' He clenched his lips around the black cigarette and inhaled deeply. Closed his eyes, and for two seconds he stood there looking as if he was relishing it. Then he let air and smoke wheeze out from his lungs. '. . . a policeman.' He dropped the cigarette on the floor in front of him. Trod on it as he moved towards Oleg. Lifted his head. Oleg was almost as tall as he was. Harry met the boy's eyes behind the sights of the raised gun. Saw him cock the gun. Already knew the outcome. He was in the way, the boy had no choice either; they were two unknowns in an equation without a solution, two heavenly bodies on course for an inevitable collision, a game of Tetris only one of them could win. Only one of them *wanted* to win. He hoped Oleg would have the gumption to get rid of the gun afterwards, that he would catch the plane to Bangkok, that he would never breathe a word to Rakel, that he wouldn't wake up in the middle of the night screaming with the room full of ghosts from the past and that he would succeed in making himself a life worth living. For his own was not. Not any longer. He steeled himself and kept walking, felt the weight of his body, saw the black eye of the muzzle grow. One autumn day, Oleg, ten years old, his hair ruffled by the wind, Rakel, Harry, orange foliage, staring into the pocket camera, waiting for the click of the self-timer. Pictorial proof that they had made it, been there, reached the peak of happiness. Oleg's index finger, white at the knuckle as it curled tighter round the trigger. There was no way back. There had never been time to catch the plane. There had never been any plane, no Hong Kong, just a notion of a life none of them had been in a position to live. Harry felt no fear. Only sorrow. The brief salvo sounded like a single shot and made the windows vibrate. He felt the physical pressure from the bullets hitting him in the middle of the chest. The recoil made the barrel jump and the third bullet hit him in the head. He fell. Beneath him, darkness. And he plunged into it. Until it swallowed him up and swept him into a cooling, painless nothing. At last, he thought. And that was Harry Hole's final thought. That at long, long last he was free.

The mother rat listened. The screams of her young were even clearer now that the church bells had chimed ten and fallen silent and the police siren that had been approaching had faded into the distance again. Only the faint heartbeats were left. Somewhere in rat memory was stored the smell of gunpowder and another, younger human body lying here and bleeding on the same kitchen floor. But that had been in the summer, long before the young had been born. And the body had not blocked the way to the nest.

She had discovered that the man's stomach was harder to get through than she thought and she had to find another option. So she returned to where she had started.

Bit once into the leather shoe.

Licked the metal again, the salty metal that protruded between two of the fingers on the right hand.

Scrabbled up the suit jacket that smelt of sweat, blood and food, so many types of food that the linen material must have been in a rubbish tip.

And there it was again, molecules of the unusually strong smell of smoke that had not been completely washed out. And even the few molecules stung her eyes, caused them to water and made it hard to breathe.

She ran up the arm, across the shoulder, found a bloodstained bandage around the neck, which distracted her for a moment. Then she heard the squeals of her young again and scuttled up the chest. There was still a strong smell coming from the two round holes in the suit jacket. Sulphur, gunpowder. One was right by the heart; at any rate the rat could sense the barely perceptible vibrations as it beat. It was still beating. She continued up to the forehead, licked the blood running in a single thin stream from the blond hair. Went down to the lips, nostrils, eyelids. There was a scar along the cheek. The rat brain worked as rat brains do in maze experiments, with astonishing rationality and efficiency. The cheek. The inside of the mouth. The neck directly below the head. Then it would be at the back. A rat's life was hard and simple. You do what you have to do.

PART FIVE

44

THE MOONLIGHT GLISTENED ON THE River Akerselva, making the filthy little stream run through the town like a gold chain. There were not many women who chose to walk along the deserted paths by the water, but Martine did. It had been a long day at the Watchtower, and she was tired. But in a good way. It had been a good, long day. A boy approached her from the shadows, saw her face in the torch beam, mumbled a low 'hi' and retreated.

Rikard had asked, a couple of times, if she shouldn't, now that she was pregnant as well, take a different way home, but she had responded it was the shortest way to Grünerløkka. And she refused to let anyone take her town from her. Besides, she knew so many of the people who lived under the bridges that she felt safer there than in some hip bar in Oslo West. She had walked past A&E, Schous plass and was heading for Blå when she heard the tarmac resound with the short, hard smack of shoes. A tall young man came running towards her. Glided through the darkness, shining a light along the path. She caught a glimpse of his face before he passed, and heard his panting breath fade into the distance behind her. It was a familiar face, one she had seen at the Watchtower. But there were so many, and sometimes she thought she had seen people whom colleagues told her the next day had been dead for months, years even. But for some reason the face made her think of Harry again. She never spoke about him with anyone, least of all Rikard, of course, but he had created a tiny little space inside her, a small room where she could occasionally go and visit him. Could that have been Oleg? Was that what had reminded her of Harry now? She turned. Saw the back of the boy who was running. As though he had the devil on his tail, as though he were trying to run away from something. But she couldn't see anyone chasing him. He was getting smaller. And soon he was lost in the darkness.

Irene looked at her watch. Five past eleven. She leaned back in her seat and stared at the monitor above the desk. In a few minutes they would be allowing passengers to board the plane. Dad had texted that he would meet them at Frankfurt Airport. She was sweating and her body ached. It was not going to be easy. But it would be alright.

Stein squeezed her hand.

'How's it going, pumpkin?'

Irene smiled. Squeezed back.

It would be alright.

'Do we know her?' Irene whispered.

'Who?'

'The dark-haired one sitting over there on her own.'

She had been sitting there when they arrived as well, on a seat by the gate opposite them. She was reading a Lonely Planet book about Thailand. She was good-looking, the type of good looks that age never fades. And she radiated something, a kind of quiet happiness, as though she was laughing inside even if she was on her own.

'I don't. Who is she?'

'I don't know. She reminds me of someone.'

'Who?'

'I don't know.'

Stein laughed. That secure, calm older-brother laugh. Squeezed her hand again.

There was a drawn-out pling, and a metallic voice announced that the flight to Frankfurt was ready for boarding. People got up and swarmed towards the desk. Irene held on to Stein, who also wanted to get up.

'What is it, pumpkin?'

'Let's wait until the queue dies down.'

'But it—'

'I don't feel like standing in the tunnel so close . . . to people.'

'OK. Stupid of me. How's it going?'

'Still good.'

'Good.'

'She looks lonely.'

'Lonely?' Stein looked over at the woman. 'I disagree. She looks happy.'

'Yes, but lonely.'

'Happy and lonely?'

Irene laughed. 'No, I'm mistaken. Perhaps it's the boy she resembles who is lonely.'

'Irene?'

'Yes?'

'Do you remember what we agreed? Happy thoughts, OK?'

'Right. The two of us aren't lonely.'

'No, we're here for each other. For ever, right?'

'For ever.'

Irene hooked her hand under her brother's arm and rested her head on his shoulder. Thought about the policeman who had found her. Harry, he had said his name was. At first she had thought of the Harry Oleg had always gone on about. He was a policeman as well. But the way Oleg had talked she had always imagined him as taller, younger, perhaps better-looking than the somewhat ugly man who had freed her. But he had visited Stein too, and now she knew it was him. Harry Hole. And she knew she would remember him for the rest of her life. His scarred face, the wound across his chin and the big bandage around his neck. And the voice. Oleg hadn't told her he'd had such a soothing voice. And all of a sudden she was sure, there was a certainty, where from, she had no idea, it was just there:

447

It was going to be alright.

Once she had left Oslo, she would be able to put everything behind her. She wasn't to touch anything, neither alcohol nor dope, that was what Dad and the doctor she had consulted had explained to her. Violin would be there, it always would, but she would keep it at a distance. Just as the ghost of Gusto would always haunt her. The ghost of Ibsen. And all the poor souls she had sold death by powder. They would have to come when they came. And in a few years perhaps they would pale. And she would return to Oslo. The important thing was that she was going to be alright. She would manage to create a life that was worth living.

She watched the woman reading. And the woman looked up, as though she had noticed. She flashed her a brief but sparkly smile, then her nose was back in the travel guide.

'We're off,' Stein said.

'We're off,' Irene repeated.

Truls Berntsen drove through Kvadraturen. Trundled down towards Tollbugata. Up Prinsens gate. Down Rådhusgata. He had left the party early, got into his car and driven wherever the whim took him. It was cold and clear and Kvadraturen was alive tonight. Prostitutes called after him – they must have scented the testosterone. Dope pushers were undercutting one another. The bass in a parked Corvette thudded, boom, boom, boom. A couple stood kissing by a tram stop. A man ran down the street laughing with glee, his suit jacket wide open and flapping; another man in an identical suit was running after him. On the corner of Dronningens gate one solitary Arsenal shirt. No one Truls had seen before, he must have been new. His police radio crackled. And Truls could feel a strange sense of well-being: the blood was streaming through his veins, the bass, the rhythm of everything that was happening, sitting here and watching, seeing all the small cogs that knew nothing of one another, yet made the others rotate. He was the only one to see, to see the totality. And that was precisely how it should be. For this was his town now.

* * *

The priest in Gamlebyen Church unlocked the door and came out. Listened to the swish of the treetops in the cemetery. Peered up at the moon. A beautiful evening. The concert had been successful and the turnout good. Better than it would be for tomorrow's early-morning service. He sighed. The sermon he was going to deliver to the empty pews would deal with the forgiveness of sins. He walked down the steps. Proceeded through the cemetery. He had decided to use the same sermon he had used for the burial on Friday. The deceased, according to the next of kin – his ex-wife – had been involved in criminal dealings at the end and even before that had lived a life so full of sin it would be a mountain to climb for all those who made the journey. They hadn't needed to worry. The only mourners present were the ex-wife with their children, plus a colleague who had snuffled loudly throughout. The ex had confided to him that the colleague was probably the only flight attendant at the airline the deceased hadn't slept with.

The priest walked past a gravestone, saw on it the remains of something white in the moonlight, as if someone had written in chalk and then erased it. It was the gravestone of Askild Cato Rud. Also known as Askild Øregod. From time immemorial the rule had been that the lease of graves expired after a generation, unless an extension was paid for – a privilege reserved for the rich. But for reasons unknown the grave of the poverty-stricken Askild Cato Rud had been preserved. And once it was really old, it had been protected. Perhaps there had been an optimistic hope that it could become a site of special interest: a gravestone from Oslo East's poorest district where the unfortunate's relatives were able to afford only a small stone and – since the stonemason was paid per letter – only the initials before the surname and the dates, no text beneath. One authority had even insisted the correct surname was Ruud, and they had saved themselves a mite there as well. So there was this myth that Askild Øregod still walked abroad. But it had never had much wind in its sails. Askild Øregod had been forgotten and left – quite literally – to rest in peace.

As the priest went to close the cemetery gate behind him a figure slipped out of the shadows by the wall. The priest automatically stiffened.

'Have mercy,' rasped a voice. And a large, open hand was thrust forward.

The priest looked into the face beneath the hat. It was an old face with rutted landscape, a robust nose, large ears and two surprisingly clear, blue, innocent eyes. Yes, innocent. That was precisely what the priest thought after giving the poor man a twenty-krone coin and continuing on his way home. The innocent blue eyes of a newborn baby that needs no forgiveness for sins as yet. He could put that in tomorrow's sermon.

I've come to the end now, Dad.

I'm sitting here, and Oleg is standing over me. He's holding the Odessa shooter with both hands as if hanging on for dear life, a falling branch. Holding tight and shouting. He's gone totally mental. 'Where is she? Where's Irene? Tell me, or else . . . or else . . .'

'Or else what, dopehead? You aren't capable of using the gun anyway. You haven't got it in you, Oleg. You're one of the good guys. Come on, relax and we'll share the fix. OK?'

'Like hell I will. Not until you've told me where she is.'

'Will I get the whole fix then?'

'Half. It's my last.'

'Deal. Put the gun down first.'

The idiot did as I said. Very flat learning curve. Tricked as easily as the first time on the way out of the Judas concert. He bent down, put the weird gun on the floor in front of him. I saw the lever on the side was set for C, which means it fired salvos. The slightest pressure on the trigger and . . .

'So where is she?' he asked, getting up.

And now, now that I didn't have the muzzle pointing at me any longer, I could feel it coming. The fury. He had threatened me. Just like my foster-father had. And if there is one thing I can't bear, it's being threatened. So instead of peddling the nice version – she was at a secret rehab centre in Denmark, isolated, mustn't be contacted by friends, who might get her back on drugs, blah, blah, blah – I twisted the knife. I had to twist the knife. Bad blood flows through my veins, Dad, so you keep your mouth shut. What's

450

left of my blood, that is, because most of it's on the kitchen floor. But I twisted the knife round like the idiot I am.

'I sold her,' I said. 'For a few grams of violin.'

'What?'

'I sold her to a German at Oslo Central. Don't know what his name is or where he lives. Munich perhaps. Maybe he's sitting in his flat in Munich with a pal and they're both being sucked off by Irene, with her little mouth. And she's as high as a kite and doesn't know which dick is which because all she can think of is her true love. And his name is—'

Oleg stood open-mouthed, blinking and blinking. Looking as stupid as the time he gave me five hundred at the kebab shack. I spread my arms like some fricking magician.

'—violin!'

Oleg kept blinking, so shocked that he didn't react when I launched myself at the gun.

Or so I thought.

Because I'd forgotten something.

He'd followed me that time. He'd known he wasn't going to get to taste any meth. He had certain skills. He could read people's thoughts too. At any rate, a thief's.

I should have known. I should have settled for half a dose. He reached the gun before me. May have just brushed the trigger. It was set on C. I saw his shocked face before I hit the floor. Heard everything go so quiet. Heard him stoop over me. Heard a low, whining drone, like an engine idling, as if he wanted to cry but couldn't. Then he walked slowly to the end of the kitchen. A proper druggy does things in a prioritised sequence. He put the syringe next to me. Even asked if we should share. Sounded good, but I couldn't talk any more. Only listen. And I listened to his slow, heavy footsteps on the stairs as he left. And I was alone. More alone than I have ever been.

The church bells have stopped chiming.

I suppose I've told the story.

It doesn't hurt so much now.

Are you there, Dad?

Are you there, Rufus? Have you been waiting for me?

Anyway, I remember something the old boy said. Death sets the soul free. Sets the fricking soul free. Does it? Damned if I know. We'll see.

SOURCES & ACKNOWLEDGEMENTS

AUDUN BECKSTRØM AND CURT A. LIER for help with general police work. Torgeir Eira, EB Marine with diving. Are Myklebust and Orgkrim Oslo with narcotics. Pål Kolstø *Russia*. Ole Thomas Bjerknes and Ann Kristin Hoff Johansen *Investigative Methods*. Nicolai Lilin *Siberian Upbringing*. Berit Nøkleby *Karl A. Martinsen's Life and Career*. Dag Fjeldstad with Russian. Eva Stenlund with Swedish. Lars Petter Sveen with dialect. Kjell Erik Strømslag with pharmacy. Tor Honningsvåg with aviation. Jørgen Vik with cemeteries. Morten Gåskjønli with anatomy. Øystein Eikeland and Thomas Halle-Velle with medicine. Birgitta Blomen with psychology. Odd Cato Kristiansen with Oslo by night. Kristin Clemet with Oslo City Council. Kristin Gjerde with horses. Julie Simonsen with typing. Thanks to everyone at Aschehoug Publishing House and Salomonsson Agency.